ON RIVERTON ROAD

JESSE ELISON

Copyrighted Material

On Riverton Road
Copyright © 2020 by Jesse Elison. All Rights Reserved.
No part of this publication may be reproduced, stored in
a retrieval system or transmitted, in any form or by any
means—electronic, mechanical, photocopying, recording or
otherwise—without prior written permission from the publisher,
except for the inclusion of brief quotations in a review.

This book is a work of fiction, and everything in it is a product
of the author's imagination or intended in a fictitious manner.
While some proper names come from Blackfoot, none are meant
to resemble actual persons from there, except Billy and Layne.

For information about this title or to order other books
and/or electronic media, contact the publisher:
JPE Media, LLC
JPEMediallc@gmail.com

ISBNs: 978-1-7351566-0-6 (print)
978-1-7351566-1-3 (eBook)

Printed in the United States of America
Cover and Interior design: 1106 Design

"Your story is the groom and you're the bride. Stories choose the person and start wanderin[g]."
— MIKHAIL SHISHKIN, *MAIDENHAIR*

"It was never established whether it was the rhubarb or the beatin[g]s that had effect, or both of them together, but the truth was that in a few weeks Rebeca began to show signs of recovery."
— GABRIEL GARCIA MARQUEZ,
ONE HUNDRED YEARS OF SOLITUDE

For my brothers and certain others

CHAPTER 1

John said to. I asked how much. All a life is worth findin words for. He said share the trip we was on with the kid. Never woulda guessed the last one.

There's differences in time with a friend. Lots good but lots not so good. None more surer'n nother. Are last trip run a few nights. I couldn't sleep and will tell what I recollect. Carmen said some things ought to be told and others are better left out and up to me to judge. She'd help get it down. I never asked John where to start. Aint no draw at the beginnin or buzzer at the end.

Pulled the key out a Carmen's Camry and reached for the brown Rand. Pressed long the ridge and in the crease. On front a big permanent stain I tried rubbin out but rubbed more in. Others spattered round, and ones more noticeable where sun lightened felt. Held the pinches and my stubby fingers swept the brim. Faded white crests waved long the band and a strand a hair hung off back. Inhaled lots a days and thumbed the brim in place.

Opened the door and got one boot out, pattin the front pocket a my Wranglers. I reckoned on enough time to grab a bite before the first go-round. A pink tiara covered the gearshift and a purple horned unicorn with pink tail the middle console. Small red crystals stuck on the jockey box and more long the passenger door. My stubby fingers worked through bottles a lotion and different colored lip glosses till outlinin change. Six dimes, six nickels, and two pennies. Inside the cup holder full a hair barrettes, a couple still clipped and the rest all tangled, studded diamonds and bright purple and pink tight wound cloths and silver metal and black ones and at bottom seven quarters, a nickel and a dime, and six pennies.

My boots kicked up dust to the trunk. Inside a large cardboard box full a paints and brushes with rolls a paper piled on the side where my gear bag should be. At a bull ridin and not entered. My chest tightened, and the thought come again.

Pulled my phone from my front pocket and flipped it. A single hairline crack over 6:45. New texts from Carmen. "Have fun" and "Don't get on!!!" No new one from Jay since "pool at nail."

A haze a dust covered pickups just off a dealer's lot and others down from a day in the hills. Lots settled in my throat. Tried suckin the rim a my mouth and couldn't spit nothin and coughed and reached for Sam. God as my witness knowed she weren't there. A habit never would kick.

My boots kicked up more dust to orange makeshift corrals. Stepped on a rung and rested my arms on top. Fence run to the announcer's booth above chutes on the near side a the arena.

Fumes a manure mixed with dust fillin my lungs, and memories come into my head forgot havin. Lord if I couldn't feel em with bulls kickin up dust in pens. Each with a streak a Brahman, some more noticeable'n others.

In a far pen a Brindle with straight horns stamped by two others with none. On my right a dark red bull with head high sat in the middle and huge white-faced black bull behind. Bulls stood down fence in other pens. Some looked close to ones I knowed but not a one just like I did.

A muscular Charbray come over and swatted his horns. Was quick off the rung back on my heels.

"Bodacious's little brother Bud," my buddy Layne said from behind.

Met the Charbray's dark globes filled with specks a white and me eyein back. Flies hovered over his bulky shoulders. They twitched, and them flies stayed on. Reached through rungs and grabbed his horn with cracked edges scrapin my stubby fingers. He ripped back and into the fence.

"Rank pen. They're short riders if you want to come out of retirement."

"Shoulda brought my gear."

"Could find you some Bud."

Layne held a poker and climbed the fence. He slid his back leg over and jumped into an alley for a pen musta held the first go.

Left side a my neck fired up. Took off the brown Rand and stretched both ways, kneadin over my shirt collar and kept on for a minute. My boots kicked up even more dust to a hive a bull riders and young hands scamperin behind the chutes.

"Hey Dean," a young bull rider said.

"You draw good?" I asked.

"A real bucker. Gonna stick him."

"Keep yur chin tucked and chest out."

"That's Dean Stamper," a boy said. I didn't recall ever seein him or a single one gatherin round but nodded in their direction.

A fist pushed my back, and liquid soaked through my shirt. Turned to Jay smilin by Layne's brother Billy. Shook Billy's hand with my right and punched Jay in the side with my left.

"Easy Pard. I could spill my drinks," he said, still wearin his big smile and holdin plastic cups full a beer in each hand with foam runnin over the heads. "Sitting with Billy and Rita."

He motioned behind at the bleachers. They was a foot off the arena and a few dozen from the chutes. Faded boards a blue splints fashioned by all the seasons and bottom row a couple feet off the ground and each one after a foot higher and last above the brown Rand.

A man hailed Billy. They carried on like old neighbors. God as my witness the same at every show. A woman with nother who passed for her daughter chatted up Jay. Never seen em before but didn't mean nothin.

French Fries' salty oil broke through dust far as eyes could see, and my boots froze. Patted the change in my pockets and could taste it. My head went for a burger and told myself would be time enough between the first and second go.

People filled seats in the grandstand on the other side a the arena. Blackfoot always showed. Was more'n ten years I rode here but recollected the fans cheered loud as ones from Calgary to San Antone.

High above lights turned on real dim. A flash a concession booths on the backside a them stands come to me.

Smelled big tiger ears, sprinkled heavy with powdered sugar and heeled up in their direction.

The young bull rider appeared. "Dean, will you pray with us?"

A wave a feelins pierced my soul, haltin me in my tracks. "You bet."

God come first. Nothin surer. We kicked up dust behind the chutes to a large group, holdin cowboy hats and bowin their naked heads. The young bull rider and others took a knee. Joined em on my good one.

"Dean, will you do us the honor?" a boy asked.

Balanced the crown a the brown Rand in the palm a my hand. "Lord, all glory comes from you. We ask you share a fair bit with these boys tonight. They ride to worship you Lord. They ride to honor The Cross for redeemin the sinful. Please accept their rides as praise for savin us."

"Praise Jesus," one boy said.

"Glory to God," nother boy said.

"Strengthen their arms, stiffen their spines, and fuel their try Lord, jump for jump. Let no kick be too hard, corner too quick, belly roll too big or spin too welly to cover. Keep em in the middle Lord. In yur name, Jesus, we pray. Amen."

"Amen."

"Amen."

"Amen."

Boys kneelin and others standin put cowboy hats back on. Set the brown Rand and pushed up off my good knee.

"Thanks Dean," one said, and others repeated. A boy took my hand and one patted my shoulder. Others did the same, and the circle broke round me.

A hand grabbed hard and turned me before deep lines and unnatural marks I knowed all my life. A bull rider's name got written in scars said Roper, squattin in front a me behind chutes in Ringgold, Georgia, with blood runnin in my eyes from a gash on my forehead kissed by a long set a horns.

"Sure sorry about your brother," the man said, clenchin even harder.

My stomach twisted and nerves shot through my body. Plumb guilty. No denyin that.

"Tough break. He was too young."

Bowed plenty shamed callin myself Christian.

"How's your father doing?"

My head shot up. "Same I reckon."

"Tell him I said hello next time you see him."

"Tell him yur goddamned self when you do." Ripped my arm free and pressed my thumb and stubby fingers into my eyes. He went and still felt his grip.

Jay limped, favorin his right, and I wondered if my punch made a mark. Hell a sore rib coulda come fallin off his Kawasaki onto boulders trail ridin in the Rockies or more like a heel climbin out a his bed.

Rita saved spots on her sides, halfway up them bleachers. "Where are Carmen and the girls?" she asked.

"Church. First thing this mornin loaded my truck with a bunch a cedar Carmen got for a steal. Pizza party tonight."

"Her projects are so awesome. Which one is this?"

"Her chair one."

"She does so many awesome things with the youth, but my favorite is her annual banquet with adults for the stakes. I've learned more about spices from her in a couple nights than in twenty years of cooking."

"This one goes today and next weekend, then they skip and one more next month Car said."

"Please tell her I said hello."

"Will do."

"Where's Roper these days?" Billy asked.

"Phoenix. Got a couple crews goin since the rebound."

We all rode. Billy's nature wouldn't permit he didn't care for no one, Layne weren't the type to tip his hand, but Jay put Roper in his place more'n once. Roper carried on, not in his nature to stop. Knowin lots a things for sure, but only an idiot would believe half he claimed or said he done. We travelled for years and fell out just once and days after headed for the next show.

Rusted panels formed a half circle, cuttin off most a the arena. One bullfighter with knee and thigh pads and more round his ribs under his shirt talked to the chute boss. The other bullfighter with checkered handkerchiefs, wavin from his hips, sprinted and stopped sudden and jumped.

Bulls loaded in the chutes.

A request rung out over the PA for everyone to stand. People broke through sheets a dust and held cowboy hats and hands over hearts with specks vibratin round em. The national anthem crackled on, and cowboys and cowgirls mouthed words a the country's greatest song. A woman on a shiny brown Quarter Horse rode the edge a the arena with Old Glory at her side. The song ended, and the crowd erupted in applause.

"Ladies and gentlemen," the announcer said and went quiet till people simmered down. "It has been brought to my attention one of rodeo's greats and Blackfoot's very own is here tonight. If I'm not mistaken that's the most storied cowboy hat in the history of rodeo lore right in the middle of the bleachers. Please join me and welcome with a round of applause Dean Stamper."

The crowd broke out cheerin. Rose for em and raised the brown Rand. Felt good and sayin otherwise would be a lie before the Almighty. People in the stands kept cheerin and wavin in broken sheets a dust bouncin in the last bits a daylight.

Eminen burst over the PA. Roper said producers a bull ridins embracin pop music marked the sign a Jesus due to arrive soon as tomorrow. Not enough to feel like a teenager to and from work no more. They got everyone feelin like one at today's shows. He said if a song didn't inspire Led Zeppelin or were influenced by em made candy for the mind. What he called diminishment a synapses from firin. No idea what he meant and asked Doctor Stout, and he said candy itself weren't so bad for yur teeth but fed bad bacteria that did a number like that made things clearer. The pop music blared over the arena. Guys moved behind chutes and others climbed over em.

The announcer turned down the noise and introduced the first rider, Joe somethin from Jerome. A huge white splotched bull with big crooked horns reared out the gate and down come the boy stiff as a scarecrow on the side a his head.

The crowd done and gasped.

Billy adjusted his cowboy hat, and Rita looked away.

"Damned kid. He ain't getting up," Jay said.

Paramedics jogged into the arena. People hushed and silence set in all round quiet as a Catholic Church. The boy lay still with people hoverin over. Twenty minutes passed. A couple paramedics carried in a flat board and laid it next to him. A bunch a chute hands raised his side, and a couple others slipped the flat board under. The hands and paramedics raised it. They got walkin and one old boy stumbled and sucked out all the air left in the arena with everyone already holdin theirs. They got to the gate, and clappin started from top a the stands to bottom. Even those scared to breathe joined in.

The announcer said with the PA cracklin, "Folks, please have a prayer in your hearts for a speedy recovery. He heard your applause make no mistake about it. The dangers of riding are parts of the show, and we want to thank our excellent medical professionals. As soon as we get the okay from them, we'll get back to riding bulls. Until then sit tight with a prayer in your hearts."

"Jesus," Jay said. "He will have a hell of a headache when he gets around to waking up."

They started back and rides got over real quick but without nother rider knocked out. Boys bucked off soon as bulls passed the gate. They all landed hard and got up slow, holdin arms, huggin ribs, and hobblin on bum legs. The announcer called the end a the first go and dust ruffled from all the sighs a relief.

Night set in, and lights above the arena broke through what dust they could. People scattered for restrooms and concessions and the old beer garden. I aimed to make good on a burger and fries and cold one.

"Rita," a soft voice said. At the side a the bleachers two thin arms waved between cowboys and cowgirls movin back and forth. Carmen's cousin Verolinda stepped with her whole body in one motion by one boy and by nother like the silent boy, Charlie, Carmen got the girls watchin when they insisted turnin on TV.

"Rita. Hi Dean." Verolinda held her arms against her body and hands in a sliver a moon.

"Come up," Rita said.

"Not too many of us?" She sidestepped a boy, and her two friends took short steps between cowboys and cowgirls passin by.

Jay eyed those sittin near, and people shifted closer.

Verolinda wore a brown leather vest and white ruffled dress with yellow and blue streaked cowboy boots. She floated on the toe a her boot onto the first row and with no hesitatin her arm extended bout to embrace a big boy and half twirled, bendin her knees clearin his large belly in a red, white and blue collared Brushpopper, takin a seat next to a large pop and basket a French Fries drenched in ketchup, her boots cleared by two inches. He pawed over em like she'd try again. Her legs straightened and boots tapped one row and nother. She hugged me and took a seat by Rita. Jay and me parted for her friends.

"Dean," Jay said, puttin a pinch a chew under his bottom lip. He put the lid on a can a Copenhagen and give to a guy in a row above us. He nodded at one a the judges lookin are way from inside the fence and pointed to someone else I didn't recall. "Saw Sarah's younger sister at the Nail. Said she was gonna come over. Hey, Linda and Rita are speaking at you."

"Linda says Taylor Weeks is riding tonight," Rita said.

"You remember Taylor last summer?" Billy asked.

I put on schools at Billy's arena in Riverton. Billy run a side job coachin bull riders, trainin year round, breakin down tape, coverin every piece a equipment and cultivatin what he called the bull rider mindset. Roper said Billy got crossbreedin Gary Leffew with Bruce Lee and lots a boys was regular payin clients cross all the Western States. I just coached boys gettin on buckin bulls. Last summer a handful a kids all scared to death. Over Friday evenin and all day Saturday they got three or four head each. Can't teach much on so few, so stressed one thing. Same at every school. Stay in the center. Kids did best with visuals, and an invisible string straight through yur chest to the back a the bull worked for lots. For every turn and twist and roll and drop yur ridin shoulder and hips should keep you on it. Whether yur pushin up and string's short when he rears or yur pullin and string's long when he kicks. Always be movin cause you'll never just be there, and nothin marked desire truer'n tryin to get there.

"He's been riding really well this summer," Verolinda said.

The young bull rider appeared again with chaps and vest on and passed folks at the front a the bleachers. "Dean, I'm up this go. Will you pull my rope?"

My neck stiffened, steppin down them rows. The young bull rider's face tightened, and he turned on his heels to the chutes.

Boys moved back and forth warmin up. One whipped his free arm over his head, kickin a boot and bringin back quick in circles. Others stretched, and others jumped up and down. A boy bout did splits and turned and fell on his butt. A boy slapped his own face and did again. A boy with his shirt off and shoulder wrapped coached nother with his back stiff gettin his shoulder wrapped.

Behind the first chute two boys with chaps and gloves on leaned back. Helmets with facemasks set between their boots. A sticker a the Seahawks on front a one vest with the Velcro unfastened. A gold chain with large gold cross over the other's fastened. One puffed smoke, eyein the other one thumbin over his phone in one hand and holdin a burnin smoke in his other. I smelled sweet chew behind chutes all my life but never the bitter ash a cigarettes. The one said to the other, "You can't weaken if he blows right out of the gate."

Bout hurled.

"Dean, I'm on the other side." The young bull rider pointed and held his helmet with webbed facemask in his other hand.

The announcer introduced Judd somethin from Shelley. Followed up and over a fence into the catch pen and up and over a fence to the other set a chutes. The young bull rider jumped on back a the chute loaded with the Charbray and bounced side to side. Placed both hands on the step and pushed myself up onto my thighs and slung up to my knees. Pulled on rungs the rest a the way and braced my shins against em with toes in between.

The next gate over swung wide, and a bull jumped and landed and jumped off all fours with front and back legs high off the ground with the boy right there. He landed and turned right back, kickin high his back end, and the boy made it into his hand. He reared turnin and dropped on his nose with a powerful kick with the boy there. He turned a big corner and launched the boy with his legs kickin till they hit ground. The best ride so far and fans knowed it and hollered excited as they got all night. The boy picked up his bull rope and cussed himself, stormin out the arena.

The young bull rider put his helmet on and lowered on the Charbray, droppin his legs in his pockets. Held the rope tight, and his glove went hard and fast up and down. The young bull rider grabbed the handle and set the rope down the Charbray's back and asked me to pull. He took the end and wrapped his hand and dropped the tail cross hunched muscle and slid up.

"Let's go," he said, noddin.

The gate swung, and the Charbray bucked with back hooves near my face. He jumped and kicked straight. He spun, whippin round and the young bull rider right with him. He broke out and turned back the other way, pickin up speed and broke out again long the chutes and rolled and dropped the young bull rider.

Fans cheered, drownin out the buzzer.

A judge jogged over, showin his stopwatch. "Seven point eight."

"Score him," the chute boss said over all the crowd's hollerin.

The judge jogged back to the other judge. They give their scores.

"Eighty-Two points," the announcer yelled over the PA.

The crowd was pure pandemonium. The young bull rider raised his hands and pointed at dark sky. He knelt and pressed his helmet in the ground and bowed his head. He jumped on the chute into arms round him.

A charge run through the arena, forcin people on ends a seats and others up and shocked my body. Wanted on and nothin felt righter. Billy set on the first set a chutes pullin a rope. The crowd went alive. They kept cheerin, and Metallica blared over the PA. Felt the whole arena and seen all from back a the chute. More bulls filled em, and boys pushed gates behind em. Cowboys bounced shoulder to shoulder on em. Fans covered every seat in the stands. Eyed all the way to the bleachers with Rita and Verolinda and far as Jay with his arm round a woman with long curls bouncin through the rear entrance from where we come in.

The announcer started over the crowd, "Ladies and gentlemen, the next bull rider is from right here in Blackfoot. Taylor Weeks. Why don't you give him a hometown's welcome?"

People sittin got up with those still standin and cheered. Billy jumped off the chute with the kid on the back a the lanky, horned Brindle.

He jumped out wild. He landed and jumped, rollin right. He jumped, rollin left with the kid right there. He jumped big and landed and launched higher with his back legs sideways and his front legs as far off the ground. He landed with the kid on. He kicked like he'd turn and reared and belly rolled, and the kid stuck. He dropped and kicked his back end straight with his front hooves, sendin the kid over his head. The kid sprung at the fence. He turned on the kid with the bullfighters a step behind. The kid cleared over, and he run into it.

The kid crawled away and got to runnin before even standin up for the end a the arena. People in the stands welcomed him with loud cheers.

An eliminator draw most boys was happy to miss, but sure no truer testin a rider's heart'n out a line, dirty, force a nature. You might tap off on a spinner but had to work a pure bucker each jump.

The announcer said the kid made only seven. The crowd booed. Damned sure were or weren't somethin, a second or two-tenths shy a eight.

"Really good, really nice ride," Billy said, noddin his head.

We mingled with cowboys behind the chutes, chewin stories with old and new faces. How Roper always described the sociality. Sharin tales from one show to nother. Time measured by em. All come through. Bill and Walt Linderman, Freckles Brown, John and Benny Reynolds, Bob Schild, Harry Hart and his boy Wolf, Larry Kane, Dean Oliver, Harry Charters, Carl Cronquist, Garth Elison, and Val Dee Bell. Cotton Rosser contracted stock, Wick Peth fought bulls, Savior Hernandez bailed off Old Number Eight, and Trails End throwed every comer. All here. Then off to Big Timber.

Verolinda and her friends surrounded the kid half a horseshoe's throw off the chutes. They swarmed are way, and Verolinda led the kid, clenchin his jaw and shakin his head.

"Heckuva a ride," Billy said. "Bucked like Reindeer Dippin. Looked like when you rode him at Fort Smith. I regularly show it with some of your other rides."

"Shoulda covered him," the kid said, not liftin his head.

"Did the hard part keepin up but gotta stay in position. Be movin to meet his back. You was late. Move in time and don't matter how hard or high he kicks," I said.

The kid eyed me straight and nodded.

Verolinda wrapped her hands over the kid's arm. Her long neck movin with ease, and her back plumb with each step. She sent smiles the kid avoided. His face flushed, drownin out red bumps long his forehead, wide red lines coverin his temples and strawberry patches on his cheeks.

Rita worked through the crowd a boys. "Let's go. Got a child to pick up." She hugged Verolinda.

Me and Billy and Rita went for the back gate, and Jay come in with a more noticeable limp and his shirt untucked. He held the waist a the young woman with curls under her cowboy hat.

"Dean, Billy, Rita, this is Sarah's sister Cindy. She's on the rodeo team in Bozeman."

"Nice to meet you," Cindy said.

"Nice to meet you too Cindy," Rita said.

I seen her long ago hangin on Sarah's hip and been years since Sarah carried on at a show with her own flock a kids. Her family included nieces and nephews the same age as aunts and uncles, learned over the years real common for Mormons. Carmen had one brother, Jesús. Only the two seemed right non-Mormon and by two different sires downright anti-Mormon.

"Stopping in at Bali Hai," Jay said.

"Going home," Billy said.

"Headin home myself," I said.

Jay smiled wider. "Okay. But there's hell yet to be raised boys, and they added wings to their menu."

My body fired whole and lifted the brown Rand.

"We're gonna sing some Chris LeDoux. Sure Layne will join us."

CHAPTER 2

Eyed the clock and asked God when would I fall asleep. Didn't a full night in months. The show got me thinkin a ridin, a damned itch couldn't scratch free from. The same as past nights though. Weights set on my chest cause I did nothin for my brother and couldn't shake em. He asked, and when I wouldn't said, "You found Jesus, and you let me die."

The green lines changed to 1:14 and a minute later to 1:15. Rolled to my other side. Carmen lay with an arm over the white sheet on her body. She breathed with her lips apart. Rolled back over and brushed the sheet off my legs.

Carmen insisted on thick green carpet. She didn't care no one else had carpet like it other'n my grandparents in their old home on Shillin Avenue twenty years ago. Stuck my head into the girls' room. Blue walls surrounded their beds. Eloisa snug under her blanket, and Elena sprawled free a covers. Picked up a pink afghan off the floor and laid it over Elena's shoulders. She opened her eyes and closed em.

Waited seven minutes and headed for the porch Carmen transformed into a studio. She expanded the deck and enclosed each side with windows. The shades stayed up most the time and night filled in on a table with damps on the ends. A couple chisels the girls musta forgot to put away lay on top near a hand plane and dovetail saw Carmen musta used last. Only their combination squares seen more action. The table took pert near half the entire room and on the open floor was stools and easels by small tables with palettes on top. Small cupboards full a different numbered pencils and lots a types a paper set against the wall.

The porch light showed the rock trail from the back door to the shed big enough for Carmen's operation with her router and sander and specialty lathe at the back and table saw with a chop saw on top at the front with long workbench beneath tools on the wall between em. Carmen had me hang a dust collector on a rack next to the old window we coulda paid less to replace and open when she cut her many kinds a wood. The rack set over a box where the girls stored their pink and purple earmuffs and matchin bright green goggles.

The main need come down to gettin power. No mystery but never learned how to run it. I knowed a hot line in and load out and never touch more'n one conductor when live or you would be one and done, enough to leave to professionals. You gotta run a copper wire in each outlet to the box screw and connect the panel to a copper coil eight feet deep said Roper. He'd deliver it himself long with all the necessary wirin. I rented a front-end loader to move it. After hearin all was needed Carmen quizzed me bout amps, circuits, and tamper resistant outlets. She got a circuit tester and sure enough showed one light with no ground prime for a human one.

I asked Roper if it'd all be code after he got done, and he said, "Be code, be code, it will exceed code!"

The day come and Roper didn't show. I didn't wait not keen on losin time and started diggin a four by six-foot long box six feet deep, the very dimensions Roper give. More'n halfway a journeyman with full belt come walkin into the yard with Carmen and said, "Roper sent me." I stomped my boots on fresh dirt. He eyed the front-end loader at the other end a the hole. I went back to diggin, and the tools in his belt rattled to the shed. They come out thirty minutes later. Carmen surveyed over the edge how much progress I made in so short time but then said refill it and went inside.

"What bout the ground?" I asked.

The journeyman moved his full belt up his thighs and peered over the edge a good foot above my head. "Put a GFI circuit breaker on the panel like Roper said. I'll come back and trade out the old sockets. Didn't say anything about a tamping rod. Can you get out of there? Or should I grab some rope?"

He took me for a halfwit. I twisted, pointin the shovel at dirt steps I packed.

Praise the Almighty Carmen didn't ask to hang the deluxe dust collector model in the corner a the porch. She paid one thousand dollars online and said cost over twice as much in one a her wood workin magazines. I admired it just where I took off the box.

I had no love for carpentry and played the extra hand but most the time stayed out a the way. A livin for me, but Carmen plumb enjoyed makin things. And got the girls enjoyin it too. They knowed different species a wood by the smells. I just always told the girls get the right dimensions, fetchin supplies at the lumber yard with em, pulling two-by-fours off the cart onto the six-foot bed a the old Ford.

Headed for the front where most my nights passed on the soft purple couch in the livin room direct in front a the large window. Millions a stars runnin in indecipherable patterns. They lit up the large poplar and sprinkled the branches, drapin the old Ford and Carmen's Green Camry. In dark or in light you couldn't say for certain the old Ford's color. A silver brown but no more silver'n brown.

Opened the door into sky where I watched night after night. A dirty band a light run long right above I got seein more the more I looked. Lots a action up there and lots a shapes, even the same ones on different nights. So many shootin stars I got to wonderin how so many was left. Sam run round the corner a the house and climbed the steps. Crouched and scratched her smooth back to her curled tail and pulled her closer and sat on cold concrete, danglin my legs over the side.

The family on the left counted as the Christians in the neighborhood. He sold life and auto insurance, and his wife stayed home and took care a their large non-Mormon brood a eight children from ages fourteen to one. They loved the girls and wanted em over as much as Carmen would permit. Are neighbors on the right was declared atheists. The only ones I knowed in person. Carmen called em outdoor enthusiasts and said they didn't sit still long enough to put on weight. With their son roamed every square inch a Idaho and a fair bit beyond into Utah and Wyomin. Each weekend campin in this mountain or that desert. In all Shawn's tales I learned more bout Idaho'n all my years growin up here. For one bout exotic yurts, sure not a real word, but when Shawn and his wife and boy got feelin like goin fancy stayed in em. Nothin but a white man's igloo. When I declared as much Carmen said they probably originated with wanderin groups somewhere long the central plains a Asia. I had no idea where them plains was but also learned from Shawn bout an Idaho City. If it didn't beat all. A city I never knowed existed in its very own state, pert near in the middle. There was lots a adventures and Shawn always gettin new supplies for em sure as Carmen for her endless projects. Trucks regular droppin off boxes a new gear for him and new tools for her. Delivery boys from all the companies callin em by first names.

The funnest soundin excursions was rides down the forks a the Salmon. They was plannin for the middle one. Shawn got a new high-end fly fishin rod he broke down to the reel, some type a sleek, durable aluminum. I got the notion not bout perfectin his cast for hookin trout so much as passin time with his boy. He said when he got old enough would tie his own flies.

Durin the week Shawn had me over for beers and mapped out his next adventure. We drunk in his garage where he organized his stuff. The cleanest I ever seen with a smooth concrete floor couldn't pour on my best day. He talked bout everything but beer and gear most a all. He worked at the Idaho National Engineerin Laboratory, but what most a us just called the Site in the high desert near Arco, where my father and brother worked.

Carmen put the girls to bed and begun workin before she could say the girls' favorite phrase by Ms. Poppins in her studio past midnight, doin finish work to not wake the girls or draftin plans for her next project. I got back from Shawn's and into bed before her.

We drunk the finest beers from Denver to St. Louis. Shawn went on bout one from Deschutes in Bend and one from Blackfoot River in Helena. Once he said you won't believe it but this beer hails all the way from one a the fine breweries in all places the famous Sonomo Valley. He done himself a beer tour there and tried what they was callin the best beer in the world. I didn't get what set a valley above nother, and the idea a one beer better'n all the others sounded silly. There was lots a damned fine beers, and they come from all over. But every time Shawn described a Blue Ribbon beer I recollected on what Roper always said. Cause somethin could be the best the fact alone drove so much other success. And not just catchy but true. Just look at Patrick Swayze and how every actor tries to be him he said. And I recollected on an observation Jay made leavin the Green T after a night retellin tales bout are childhood and Roper philosophizin on the meanin with college pals from Idaho State. Jay said men was mostly folly, a word I never heard before nor since, and continued bore evidence for a merciful God we only witnessed others' actions and not their ideas. God let down his guard where both could have consequences.

One week the best beers come from San Diego, then Athens, Minneapolis, and St. Petersburg, and nother city got innovatin on hops and hints a fruit this season and nother hard at breakin through the next. Shawn carried on bout the history a craft beer, surmisin long ago was the days when the great brews only got made in Portland, Oregon or Maine. Sure no beer genius like Shawn and had no disputations he knowed his beer. God as my witness I drunk my share from the fridge in his garage, enough for an educated say on the so-called finest beer in the world from a highfalutin valley in California, makin me fit to testify with one hand on the Bible and the other stretchin high as mighty good. But I had my own favorites. And Shawn become proud a my memory. He said I musta been born with a photographic beer palate. No one ever paid my thinkin a compliment before. I recollected most what struck my fancy and forgot lots else, so knowin beers come right easy, much as readin words for some and addin up numbers for others. I downright loved Cold Smoke Scotch Ale from Kettle House and African Amber from Mac & Jack's, Shawn only got fillin growlers at Tommy Vaughn's near Jensen's Grove. Regular visits branded em on my tongue. One a the great shocks a my life come the evenin I learned neither beers was my favorite type.

Shawn pulled sleepin bags from a low cupboard, explainin they kept bodies warm in conditions below zero good for somewhere long the Rocky Mountains in dead a winter.

"It's a mummy, that's why it's so narrow with high tech insulation and microfiber lining. Feel it," Shawn said. "Won't tear either, no way, no how."

"Can test it," I said, pullin out my pocketknife from my front pocket.

"Whoa! Stand down! We waited until they came on sale at the Cabela's in Post Falls. Carla would murder me. Please never mind."

"Would be responsible for her committin one mighty great sin." Put the knife back in my pocket. "Want no part a that."

"I'll tell her you spared her eternal damnation. At least she'd have company, me of course, not you."

"Probably headed there myself. Worse for me a sinner cause I accepted Jesus."

"What an unfair hand. While I'm no authority on these matters, if there is a God, believing you are saved and getting nothing is simply cruel. We just don't know. And how much fun would it be if we did? Can I get you another beer?"

He always offered, followin him round his garage inspectin gear or viewin maps or examinin a new fiberglass canoe like with Carmen and the girls in the fabric store on how many yards to get started or feel this or what startlin color, just not sober.

After I converted to Jesus I did a second time in a whole other way. I converted the first time cause Jesus answered my prayers with a miracle but experienced what amounted to a double conversion when Roper explained he converted from no particular experience at all but cause a the universal need for Jesus. That truth alone done it. And what stuck, not the feelins a the first one.

Humans are plagued by sin said Roper. If humans have to remove their sin to return to God, then the life a Jesus explained the necessity for him to come to Earth and sacrifice for all mankind so all humans could, or else they couldn't. It made perfect sense. With buckets full a sin I understood Jesus's role even more'n Roper did. No more convincin reasonin. Pure incontrovertible logic said Roper. But then you had to help others like Jesus. A mighty shortcomin got me doubtin my eternal salvation.

"Try this one. Think you'll enjoy it."

Took a swig. "Lots a flavor. Like the one the other night. Damned good."

"Another sharp I.P.A. from a new brewery in Asheville. I'm not saying this is a definitive fact, but based on a fairly large sample size it is your favorite type of beer."

Had nother swig. "Aint my favorite beer though."

"Favorite type of beer. Like Mr. T is your favorite bull, but you readily admit he isn't your favorite type of bull because he doesn't spin in the gate." Shawn rolled his new high tech sleepin bag. "Make no mistake my friend, preference for I.P.A. makes you a certifiable Northwestern beer snob."

I could not rightly deny my hankerin for it. My limbs all stiffened with the beer froze against my bottom lip.

"I'm only saying you like good beer is all. Not all snobbery is the same as being full of everything from the Upper East Side. You were weaned on Bud Light, which is a good beer if there's nothing else at high noon in the Mojave Desert, but you've simply acquired a taste for the finest of brews. I'm no authority but liking the best of something can't be a sin, right?"

He grabbed my shoulder and led to the back porch, and we triggered the porch light. Sam run up, and I bent down and patted her head. Carla left bread and fancy sliced cheeses and pears on a picnic table with matchin wood benches. Only Jay liked cheeses as much as Carla. Had the habit a cuttin chunks off different kinds when we drunk Budweisers on his porch.

Roper said likin somethin too much qualified as a sin bout somethin else. I got his point. All idolatries favorin somethin ahead a the Lord is sin all over in the Bible he said. I didn't argue with Shawn. Was lots smarter'n me but knowed Roper set the record right.

Sam looked up at me saddled in memories I couldn't shed. She sensed em. Patted her, and are heads traced a shootin star cross the sky.

The last time my brother spoke I got through the slidin glass doors at the hospital and my stomach hardened in a knot, bendin me over for air. A nurse run over and grabbed my wrist.

"Are you diabetic? Let's get you to the ER," she said.

"Not here for me," I said, catchin a breath, "Just here for my brother."

His room stunk somethin awful. The nurses did their darndest to spruce things up. And Carmen always brought flowers. Even old dead ones she brought weeks before no one removed made the room look nice. He went plumb yellow from his face to his belly to his feet, even the whites a his eyes.

"You aren't a real Christian." He turned his head and went quiet. His face taut like rope. I couldn't eye him straight and stared at his Buddha belly. A plastic tube run out with a ball in the end. A nurse come in by one standin in the door and pressed the ball, and fluid come out. I stepped down the bed and banged the urinal hangin on the side. Was everything. I mean his very skin smelled somethin fierce. The worse his breath like his anus changed places with his throat. I folded my arms at the end a the bed starin at his huge feet the size a baby elephants'.

I wouldn't test to see if my liver matched, no matter how many times he asked. Carmen repeated to not worry. Didn't from fear but spite. But still knowed acceptin Jesus required more'n just believin in him. What would he do? Woulda done it, not botherin even testin, demandin they pull up a cot and get er done at the side a my brother's putrid bed. I complained bout failin my brother to Jay one night. Not long after we broke open the second twenty-four pack he said a all people he didn't need to tell the key to life is not lettin someone else spend yurs.

Seen my brother once more. The white walls seemed whiter and did not smell a disinfectant. Carmen brought more flowers and put em on the food tray. His eyes was lost in his face. She moved the oxygen mask, and somethin hung from his damned chin. She smoothed thin hair and wrapped his face in her hands and kissed his forehead. God knows how she stomached it. I swore his eyes watered but knowed as sure none ever flowed from the son of a bitch. A couple days later he died.

Sam and me went inside and sat on the soft purple couch, facin sky outside the window. The only thing Carmen didn't build. She bought it from one a her furnishin magazines for more'n I made in a week framin houses but for just a piece a what I used to make at one show. She added the softest purple cover. Got on somethin wet, and a paintin stuck to my arm. In are house wearin paints was common as clothes. And glad to have on shorts with paint drippin on em.

Even with all I knowed bout Jesus I still did nothin.

Flowers, kittens, dolphins and whales, and lots a different rainbow paintins hung on the walls. Carmen coached the girls on capturin ideas and feelins and believed makin pictures good practice and couldn't practice enough with proper instruction. Since they could ask for stuff Carmen got em makin things, and they was askin for stuff soon as they learned to talk. And they could talk nonstop. Lots a time only got a word in edgewise when they talked Spanish. Understood some and spoke a little, "arriba" and "andale," but they didn't have patience for me puttin more together and not much for em when I did.

Set the paintin on the arm a the soft purple couch and went for a towel. Come back to sit and seen my damned belly. Kept starin and grabbed it in the window's reflection with Sam lookin on. Felt no different. Stronger maybe from so much damned hammerin. When I seen the doctor, and not on my own accord, she said the gracy muscle inside my leg in a normal man were a string not a chord, and she couldn't stop bout the long band from my hip to my knee endin on a pad she called a starter muscle. But the Lord as my witness I thought on ridin every day and got myself a paunch.

Went to pacin up and down the back a the couch and grabbed the top a the soft purple cover with my stubby fingers. Got lost on lots a damned bright points scattered in a sea a dark pushin beyond all my imagination. How did the Lord cover so much space? My belief in him burned within me but couldn't figure on why he cared bout me. I believed he died for my sins. How he wiped em clean and kept feelin more and sometimes old ones over again struck as a pure mystery.

Are first week in the house I said we should knock out the big glass window and put in a bay window. Carmen asked what for. She felt different bout the floor. The realtor got halfway over and Carmen drawed attention to a dip and said the cost for a new one had to be taken out a the askin price. The seller put up a fuss, but Carmen held and got her reduction. Roper give me a couple hands to tear it up. Sure enough joists not crowned and twenty inches from the next. Half bowed down, includin ones in the walkway Carmen noticed first off. For finishin the best you gotta measure things for where they should be not where they are. Right dimensions goes for a whole house but nowhere more'n where yur boots set each day.

Soft footsteps come from behind, and Carmen's arms surrounded me. She pressed her head and breasts against my neck and back, only her nightgown separatin us.

"Come back to bed."

"Can't fall asleep."

"I'll help."

"Yur my shinin star, brighter'n em in the sky." I set my head on hers, eyein her dark eyes.

"I don't know what you mean."

"And brighter'n all them movie stars Jesús tells bout."

"Now I really don't know what you mean. These boobs are too big and hips too wide for the movies." She tightened her hug round my naked torso.

The moonlight showed her full and round cheeks coverin her square jaw. Her long black hair fell on her skin.

"Let Sam out and come to bed."

Opened the front door and caught a cool breeze.

Carmen waited in the hall. She headed for are room and dropped her nightgown over her round butt. Dropped my shorts.

"Count sheep."

"How many?"

She smiled and pulled me on her. Brushed her hair back and kissed her soft. She kissed me hard. She pushed her hands on my back, holdin my chest on hers. Matched her hips, rockin beneath mine.

"How many so far?"

"Forty-two."

"Go to a hundred. Start over."

At eighty-four she moaned and more. At ninety-two she went quiet, and we lay on are sides. She kissed my forehead and run her hands through my hair.

"Sleep."

Her lips curved up and nose wiggled. Bubbles rested on smooth skin a her shoulder and her belly and as far down the middle a her thighs with yellow and blue and green smeared cross em. Some on sheets added to older streaks. Carmen loved em and spared no expense for em with the highest thread count on earth. Are current sets surpassed the price a my last bull rope. Nothin less for are king size bed takin up half the room Carmen built with its grey oak frame and sideboards and baseboards intersectin at slits she carved out, not a space between or sharp edge on em, against a headboard with knots on each end and two in the middle. Combed her hair behind her ear and held her shoulder with her other one against my chest. Her breasts rose on each deep breath. Slipped my arm free and turned on my side.

Never got enough a the soft purple cover watchin them stars fade in daylight. Would try for some shuteye when Carmen and the girls went to their Mormon Ward. When lucky enough to fall asleep, dreamed the same thing in an open arena with my glove and chaps on. I turned this and that way eyein groomed dirt for my rope. Jay swung his cowboy hat on top a chute. I felt hooves poundin but couldn't see nothin and woke feelin one thing. Come stronger now, bearin down more'n when we buried my brother. Was for sure the Lord speakin at me. Didn't get what concerned my brother but knowed I hated him more dead'n alive if a thing were possible.

And Jesus just touched me on a call bout a show in Ogden. One a the stops on the final Bushwacker tour. They'd waive the entry fee and pay expenses for the chance to advertise an old champion. Unlike all other invitations over the last couple years didn't say no thanks. Nothin come out. And the show later in the day. I couldn't shake the thought a ridin there.

My elbows rested on my knees and my stubby fingers cupped my head, eyein a ring round a pie a gold, clearin hills on the horizon. It swirled inside and danced long the edge.

CHAPTER 3

Opened my eyes at tires crunchin gravel and Jesús drivin a new Ford F-150 with a body lift, makin the old Ford look like a lowrider. They lined up under the large poplar blockin the first rays a sunshine. An old man in the passenger's seat with a third man in the crew cab was Jesús' sidekicks in the Riverton Bishopric. Three doors opened, and Jesús jumped out. He come round the shiny front, and the two others grabbed door handles and climbed down.

Rose off the soft purple couch and opened the front door. Cleared most the porch and tripped, stubbin my damned toes. Hopped off the side and landed on wet grass and hobbled round in a conniption fit. Damned jerkin torqued my neck and lit a fire up and down the left side. Got holdin straight like a statue and massaged deep with every one a my stubby fingers.

"Holy Mackerel," Jesús said, pointin at the ground. "There's a box."

Sure enough. Sam sniffed it. Grabbed from under her and not heavy but not light neither.

"You all right?" Jesús leaned by me to see. "What'd you order?"

"Where in the hell did it come from?" I thought out loud, eyein the cardboard for an address. Shook and nothin moved and bout dropped and kicked it into Shawn's yard but seen my name.

"Here for breakfast." Jesús raised a bag a fresh tortillas. "Rosa made them yesterday. Brother Hamilton has fresh eggs, and we'll use the rest of Carmen's sausage. Sorry but Brother Barbre forgot the coffee."

"Got plenty." Held the box to my side and limped up the steps with em behind.

Jesús took off his suit coat and draped it over an upholstered chair near the dinner table with the glossy slab he helped Carmen put on. I told em to trade out the base for sturdier legs. The large circle plenty a space for Carmen and the girls' fancy sewin machines stored in the white enclosed chiffonier with sharp corners and lots a space on top for their current projects. The girls taught me the fancy piece's name till it stuck. Jesús tucked his tie into his shirt, rolled up his sleeves, and cleared the stove.

"Been a hot summer," Brother Hamilton said and clapped. "I sleep pretty light too."

Looked down at my junk. "I'll get my tie on and be back before you fry them eggs."

Pulled on a Bronco Wrestlin t-shirt Roper give me when he coached JV Wrestlin and Wrangler shorts Carmen bought last summer from the top a my clean clothes pile. Joined the Riverton Bishopric and pulled an upholstered chair round the glossy slab as Brother Hamilton explained the dry summer helped his potato crop, promisin a great yield. Brother Barbre smiled real quiet.

"Sorry we missed the last couple months, but we've been going in every different direction. Last month some higher-ups from Salt Lake visited the stake and was endless rigmarole." Brother Hamilton carried on bout one thing and nother, this authority sayin this but that authority sayin that, and sure sister so-an-so havin none a neither. I woulda asked after more but overcome with my body tinglin all over. I could barely wait with folded arms and back straight, breathin the mixins a the tortillas cookin and noddin at every one a Brother Hamilton's opinions.

Carmen entered, and Brother Hamilton and Brother Barbre stood.

"Hello Bishop Ortiz," she said, reachin for Jesús and kissin him.

"Good morning Sister Torres," Brother Hamilton said.

"Good morning Sister Torres," Brother Barbre said.

"Welcome counselors," she said, extendin her hand and takin theirs.

"Sit. Sit," Jesús said and laid out a fine tablecloth with light yellow lines, everyone helpin smooth over the glossy slab. He passed a stack a plates and handful a utensils. Brother Barbre set em round. Jesús put a pitcher a orange juice and cups in the middle. Brother Barbre poured for everyone.

"So tell me what the general authority had to say behind closed doors? I won't tell a soul," Carmen said.

"A bunch of statistics mostly." Brother Hamilton said and clapped. "Worth a hill of beans measuring our progress. The whole business mindset is way off track."

"Brother Hamilton, there's something to be said for being accountable, don't you think?" Jesús asked.

"To God! Not to man, Bishop. And if it was only about being accountable, well Bishop that'd be one thing, but it's about being some kind of proof. And that notion is a pure distraction. And wrongheaded."

Brother Barbre smiled real quiet not bout to get roped into controversy. I heard similar carryin on before waitin to eat with these three. I knowed the heart a Mormonism beated big business not cause I surmised as much from all their global success but from Brother Hamilton's orations when the bishopric stopped in for a bite. Other times he talked bout his old rodeoin days and mine.

Chorizo and onions overtook the whole house. Jesús stepped from the kitchen. Brother Hamilton and Carmen carried on bout Mormon politics. A yell a "Yes" from the girls' bedroom interrupted em. Elena run into the room toward Brother Hamilton, and he picked her up quick as I did and sat her on his lap, askin after the girls' pet rabbits. Jesús come in carryin Eloisa and stood her near the stove. He went back to cookin with her attached to his leg.

"I painted you a picture of the Nephi's birds," Elena told Brother Hamilton.

"A lot of birds followed Nephi and his family to America," Carmen informed Brother Hamilton and Brother Barbre.

Brother Hamilton set Elena down, and she run to the soft purple couch and picked up her paintin. Her lips pierced together showin her dimples, and she eyed me straight. Turned up my hands together ready for a set a cuffs. Carmen shot me a straight look. She hated the gesture. Told me I wallowed in my guilt.

Folded my arms against my chest. "Sorry Lena. Didn't see it last night till my arm rested on it."

She held the paintin near her chest walkin back. Carmen took it and turned the front for all to see. The birds and sky was smudges.

"It's wonderful," Brother Hamilton said. "Very impressionistic."

"We'll do another painting for Brother Hamilton. Lisa," Carmen said.

Eloisa let go a Jesús' leg and slid into the hall and back with a paintin and give to Brother Barbre.

"The ocean that almost sank Nephi's ship." Carmen smoothed Eloisa's hair, and she went back to Jesús' side.

"The white surf and big blue waves made for rough waters and reminds me of where I grew up, thank you," Brother Barbre said. Was roughly a spittin image a Jay with large jaw and broad shoulders and huge hands but handsome with wavy brown hair straight out a California tourist brochure. His family was immigrants like Jesús and Carmen's parents Brother Hamilton said. An athlete in his younger days with no scars to show for it, more unlike Jay. Would guess movie star but not All-American tailback at one a them California colleges.

Jesús hugged Eloisa and tried to get her to shift over some. She just turned two and Elena just a few weeks from bein born when Carmen and me tied the knot. Now seven and five they was lots different but lots alike. Didn't think on how I got so lucky, but the notion come lots. I figured the Lord blessed me with Carmen and the girls to remind me nothin come cause I deserved it. A damned fallen soul but for Jesus's grace.

"Fold your arms and bow your heads girls," Jesús said. "Heavenly Father, thank you for this beautiful morning and please bless this food to strengthen and nourish us and please bless Eloisa and Elena to grow up with strong testimonies of your Son and our Savior, Jesus Christ. In his name amen."

"Amen," everyone said, includin me.

Jesús took plates in front a Carmen and Brother Hamilton and filled em and took Brother Barbre's. I hoped he'd use Carmen's fresh green salsa instead a the older salsa. He filled the girls' plates and took my plate last and filled full, topped with old salsa. Took a bite and plumb overwhelmed chewed real fast. Eyed the girls' plates for what I reckoned would have plenty left.

"Did Bishop Ortiz tell you? I'm going to study the law and become his paralegal," Carmen said.

Eyed round the entire table but couldn't read no one's face and kept chewin and took nother bite, wonderin if Carmen already told me. If I learned one thing from seven years were to not ask her why she didn't tell me earlier, cause she probably did and would point out not just one but two different occasions.

"You'll be great," Brother Barbre said.

"The best," Brother Hamilton said.

"Don't becomin a lawyer take ages? Lots a wasted time," I said with a full mouth between chewin, wantin more explanation but keen on not stickin my nose in none a my business.

"I won't be a lawyer. I'll start as a legal assistant and eventually become a paralegal. I can study and certify online."

"Carmen will be running the office on her first day. I'm getting busy, and the time is right to take on the best staff possible. And having Carmen join me makes sense since she refers a lot of my business," Jesús said, movin a pan off the stove I clearly seen with more tortillas.

Brother Barbre asked bout carryin on her translation business for the courthouse and hospital. She knowed every lawyer and doctor in town and employed two girls full time.

She said she needed more free time and planned to sell to one a the girls. Pretty damned sure news to me but not sure I caught the whole exchange eyein round the table. Brother Hamilton got an extra tortilla.

"I have one more announcement." Carmen gathered the girls plates with plenty left. "My cousin Verolinda is coming to live with us, so next bishopric meeting we'll have another member of the family."

Eloisa and Elena lit up with questions from where she'd keep her clothes to if she'd teach em dancin. I gathered Verolinda would share their room while she settled some things. The bishopric didn't ask, and I speculated knowed already. Verolinda would start her senior year after summer. I could tell from Carmen's formal tone would do me good to save questions for when we was alone, but Jesús turned from the stove bout to speak.

Brother Barbre pulled out his vibratin phone and frowned. "Bishop, I hate to cut our meeting short, but the hospital has summoned me."

"What about your box?" Brother Hamilton asked.

"What box?" Carmen asked.

"What box?" the girls echoed.

"Has your dad limping around after it tripped him off the porch upon our arrival."

I went and forgot thinkin a Jesús' tortillas and eyed the stove if more was cookin. Brother Barbre walked at the door with Eloisa's picture a the wild waves. He didn't seem upset but set on movin the rest a the bishopric to Jesús' new F-150.

"Let's open it on our way out." Brother Hamilton stared me over, pryin me from the table. Felt sick with Jesús movin the last a the pans off the stove.

Fetched the box and cut the brown tape with my pocketknife. I could not believe my eyes and pulled out a brand spankin new bull rope. "Brazilian." Fondled the hard handle with an inch riser for a right hand and pressed and twisted the solid block with just the right give could get out over.

"Well I'll be. Starting up again are you!" Brother Hamilton clapped and swatted my back. "Well we are off. Come out to Church. For heaven's sake move out to Riverton and join us every Sunday!"

Brother Barbre just real patient at the door. Jesús picked up his suit coat. "I could hardly be more blessed to have the Lord guiding my every decision and Carmen too." He closed the door behind em.

They left quicker'n they come. My body tingled in pure sensation, starin at the Brazilian. The girls and Carmen cleaned the table. Carmen worked at not noticin me, not angry but seen her thinkin it over. She sent the girls to their room to get ready for Church.

"Linda is pregnant. Talk about a shock to the family and the ward, so Maria asked if she could stay with us while she carries the baby to term. She's starting to show, and I said of course. Such wonderful and challenging news. She's sure to lose her scholarship. Dean, we could raise the child for her if it meant her not losing it."

"Seen her last night and couldn't tell."

"She won't confirm it's Rocky's. Although it couldn't be anyone else's."

"Funny protectin someone over."

"It'll be a disgrace on his mission, and he'll get sent home from Phoenix."

"Why's she movin in with us?"

"Their ward is full of judgmental members, and Maria feels it's better overall."

"They should be. Sex is a sin before marriage."

"They should be more Christlike and not judge. At this stage the baby is about a lot more than sex, and it's a shame people don't get it."

"Judgin others is the one part Mormons get right like Christians."

"I think Christ said clear the beam in one's own eye before judging others."

"But didn't say nothin bout quittin on righteousness once you did."

"Her moving in is really about how judgmental Paul is. He's been that way since Maria married him. At least he's equally righteous to both of their children."

"Gonna say so but didn't need sayin."

Carmen leaned in and kissed me. "Don't get carried away about true Christianity this morning. The day is still early. And don't forget you'd been a Christian before we were married with one on my hip and one on the way."

"Took a while for Jesus to really get aholt a me and rid my wrong ways. That's why he give me you. Done lots wrong and cause for lots a Jesus's pain."

"You never tire of saying so. Jesus did quite enough without us piling more on him. About Jesus giving me you, yes you couldn't be more right." She held me where I stood the last ten minutes transfixed. "You judgmental? I couldn't have imagined such a thing." She shook her head as she pulled mine to hers and kissed me again. She laughed with her lips pressed against mine and sent more feelin through my body.

She leaned back and eyed are feet and back up. Her smile vanished. She tilted her neck and narrowed her eyes. Her breath covered my lips, and she let my head go.

"Caught by the Riverton Bishopric huh?" She tried eyein me, but I looked down.

Yur nine-five wider and softer tail with laces tight and straight all the way through. Caressed the braids and shrugged my shoulders. "Didn't order it."

"You talking about riding again and like that a new bull rope?" She waited for me to answer. "The one you always wished you'd tried?"

"Didn't buy it Car and didn't see it last night neither and right where Sam and me was."

"It's a miracle." She patted my cheek. "I have to get ready for Church."

I kept thinkin one since openin the box, the second a my life.

Carmen brought the girls out and got em sittin on the soft purple couch and brushed their hair. Tested the Brazilian, waitin for an openin. She sent em back for their Mormon books.

"Gonna take a drive to Ogden this mornin." My chest and legs burned, slidin the Brazilian faster through my stubby fingers. "Just see how I feel."

"There's no secret how you feel. Look at me."

Eyed her straight.

"Don't get hurt."

Hobbled over and picked her up and held tight with the Brazilian runnin down her back and kissed her. She went for the girls. Took a seat and run the Brazilian cross my lap over the soft purple couch. Eloisa in her bright yellow dress and Elena in her blue one entered the room. The very same ones they made on their fancy sewin machines.

    Hugged em, and they cleared the front door. Headed to the bedroom and pulled my boots on under a minute. Grabbed the brown Rand and beelined for the shed and knelt on my good knee for the straps on my gear bag below a shelf with hand saws.

CHAPTER 4

The old Ford crossed the edge a town for Riverton, passin old equipment and empty lots surroundin worn down buildins. A scrap yard with bent metal and twisted scaffolds and no sign a people sprawled long the left. Faded signs made in the fifties for an oil and brake shop passed on the right, where ten feet behind Jay leased a garage with enough space for half-dozen cars to restore. The Blackfoot River marked the beginnin a the Indian reservation. Railroad tracks next to power lines on one side and high grass passable for weeds danced in the wind on an irrigation ditch long the fenceline on the other side.

Beyond them tracks was hills with Mount Putnam behind em. Never did much cowboyin for real, but when I did pushed cattle in em. The old Ford come to the freeway overpass and broke for Riverton Road and winded round a big gravel pit and shot straight. Sam sat up, accustomed with each bump.

The borders a Jesús' ward, homesteaded by Mormons. Hell if half Blackfoot weren't. I didn't mind none growin up, but wore on me after findin Jesus. Then my brother took to em in some fashion. Not sure if he fully converted, though there was rumors got himself baptized toward the end. All them nice people sayin they believed in the Lord, takin him for some restored truth through Upstate New Yorkers on the Susquehanna River when they wasn't fendin off Iroquois Roper said. I rode with lots. Layne and Billy was but never woulda guessed. We rode since junior rodeo. Me and Billy made the high school national finals the same year, and me and Layne traveled for a couple summers on the Wilderness Circuit. Neither ever said a thing bout Angel Moroney.

My elbow rested on the open window, and grass and wet dirt spilled their sweet smells into the cab. The old Ford passed field after field a sprinkler pipes sprayin water on potato vines and climbed a small rise to the Mormon Church with pickups and cars in parkin spots. Later bunches more with enough miles combined to get to the moon and back would line both sides a Riverton Road.

A thirty-four year-old Mexican bishop even nonmembers knowed was a big deal. If I didn't witness it for myself, would say just nother Mormon story. Brother Hamilton bishoped the Riverton Ward twenty years ago and said God chose right most a the time he picked Church leaders and hit a bullseye with Jesús. Carmen said everyone expected Brother Barbre to be the next bishop, but God had a mind for Jesús, who went and chose Brother Barbre his first counselor and Brother Hamilton his second. Carmen got mighty proud, takin the girls and me to the service. The first I ever wore a tie Carmen bought for the occasion long with a new pair a navy blue Wranglers I wore for months after.

All Riverton showed. Even other nonmembers Carmen said but didn't see a one. After the ceremony Jesús throwed a fiesta to usher in all Riverton fiestas. Layne snuck cold beer and behind the house we poured in big red plastic cups, watchin a herd a kids chase each other on the manicured lawn.

Jesús had qualified to lead the Mormons after his missionary tour in Mexico City and marryin his high school sweetheart Rosa Martinez when he got back. They'd five kids so far, four boys and a girl, Esperanza. Carmen and the girls doted on her like the Princess a Persia. And true as the Bible's last word Jesús, likable as could be, bound to be mayor a Blackfoot one day.

The old Ford drove into the river bottoms. A deer dotted cross the road into trees, and the old Ford passed potato silos where two turkeys picked at a potato pile and turned on a skinny driveway, kickin up a tail a dust to a light gray 1980 Grand Am. Opened my door, and Sam jumped over and out and round the cab to the pasture slopin to Riverton Road.

A cow bawled down the far side. I'd guessed at us but knowed a calf got where her momma had a mind shouldn't be. Sam sprinted near, and cows picked up their heads. Them closest moved in front a their calves. One bawled at Sam, turnin her hind end. Sam bounced by her feet.

A double wide with aluminum trim divided the front pasture from a field a wheat on the back. Set just so like to regulate the wind.

Carmen packed tortillas still warm in a Ziploc bag. Grabbed em and headed for the porch where me and Jay drunk lots a Budweisers.

Wind pushed scents a fresh hay. Twenty feet off the double wide at an open shed three quarters stack with outer bales showed green. A short bar stool set by a half-assembled old BMW motorbike against a beam, and parts scattered below on an old tarp. Jay musta wanted fresh air to work out here and not his garage in town. No toolbox and not like him to leave a job undone. An old Harley with a piece a wood under the kickstand kissed the fence a the wheat field. Rested my hand on the gas tank and unbuttoned my Wranglers and went through the fence. The wind kept breakin my steady stream and sung off a post into the bales and through the field. Finished the last drops and buttoned up, lookin round for a Kawasaki 4 Stroke and saddlebags with tools and a mini cooler always with beers set to explode. Jay attested they was his holy trinity.

Smooth wood limbs nailed to two-by-fours set on a sturdy square base with two shorter pieces attached in the middle. An olympic bar rested on rectangular iron stands with plates stacked at the ends. Behind em an old wrestlin mat with duct tape on more tears'n clean spaces with other contraptions on the far edge. Jump rope and plastic bands hung on hooks on the back wall I never seen left overnight.

Put the Ziploc bag on a stack a plates and climbed the wood bars. Fine at five and kept on. At twenty-four my shoulders burned and called good at thirty-three. Skipped doin clean and jerks, the be-all and end-all workout for Jay. Didn't know how to do em right, and the only thing Jay ever corrected me on when I tried. Pushed a step box below open trusses with chalk marks like palms on the bottom one and jumped for it and moved my grip over the marks. Hung for two seconds and did one pull-up and nother. Was tight on eleven and did one more and dropped on the box. Jumped to the ground and stung my toes.

Sam run over. Patted her side and fetched the Ziploc bag. She bumped me the way to the double wide, and the stingin wore off some. A twenty-four pack filled with crushed cans wedged behind folded lawn chairs at the stairs. Opened the front door and Josey nuzzled me. Scratched his coat, and he jumped toward Sam. They rolled and sprinted to the pasture. I knowed better'n to let Sam run with Josey all day, long at unwindin wildness when I did. A cow bawled and then others did.

Sweet air covered everything. Jeans and shirts and underwear straddled cross a couch and a large bra draped long the horn and off the swell a the saddle on a stand in the corner. Jay win it are senior year for the state all-round, on top his bulldoggin title.

I thought on grabbin a beer from the fridge and pullin up a seat at the Formica table but decided to waste no time. Ten feet from the bedroom come a high and long snore. Then nother even louder. The slit in the doorway showed two bare backs. Jay's bubble butt skinnier'n last I seen it. His body half brown and half white with leg muscles taught, not inflated like normal. He coulda been trainin for a triathlon with Shawn. The woman's skin folded over and over down her back and thighs.

She stiffened and went quiet. Then she reached quick for a blanket Jay lay on and shook him. "Jay, Jay, you have a visitor. Wake up."

Jay craned his neck, tryin to open his eyes. He rolled over. His dark tan still showed clear lines down his chest and stomach.

"If I can believe my own eyes that's breakfast," he said and smiled big.

He admired his naked legs and run his hands through his thin hair. He placed his palms over his large indented nose and breathed deep, twistin off the bed. The woman grabbed the blanket and covered her breasts and moved her frazzled hair off her eyes.

Jay embraced my shoulders and turned me into the hall. Blue streaks patched his side and dark pins marked his chest. "You smell like Jesús visited."

"I promised Carmen to not eat em on the way out, just lucky to smell em before lockin the front door."

Lifted the Ziploc bag with two rolled and loaded. He took em and laid em on the Formica table and kept on passed to the fridge and pulled out a couple Coronas. Kicked out a thin plastic chair and rested my hands on top a the Formica table. Jay took the chair cross from me and popped the caps with his thumb and pushed a bottle over.

"Remember Annie Greenland?" He opened the Ziploc bag.

My back straighted, and the whole thin plastic chair squeaked. Eyed his every move. "Sounds familiar."

He lifted the Ziploc bag and breathed in and lowered and pushed cross the Formica table. "Go ahead. My stomach doesn't agree with me until midday."

Was up for the fridge before takin my next breath. "Where's the green salsa I brought out?"

"Finished. But there's ketchup." He went for a drawer and fetched a baggy and green and purple striped pipe.

Grabbed a near empty bottle and a half clean plate on the counter and hustled back. Turned over the ketchup.

He stuffed the end a the pipe and lit up. He took a pull and air got sweeter. "A few years behind us. Cheerleader. Laura is her aunt." He exhaled smoke, bobbin his head toward the bedroom. "She loves Mexican beer. Enjoy our bounty Pard."

"Used to tend bar for Norm at the Nail." Shook the ketchup upside down.

"The one. She took a full-time position at Bingham a while back."

"You was off to Bali Hai."

"We stopped in and sang some Alan Jackson and Garthuro Brooks. Layne sings a mean Hank Williams, which ain't always best when he's had a few and you want the mic back."

"Cindy go?" The lid on the ketchup stuck. My thumb pried it open and squeezed out the last bit and dipped the tip a the warm tortilla.

"Sings a mean Reba McEntire. All her nieces and nephews were singing in sacrament today, so cut out early. Me and Layne stopped for one more at The Nail. Lady luck had Laura spotting Norm."

Chewed long and took a swig to wash down and took nother bite. Jay watched like nothin else happenin on Planet Earth and smiled. He rose and grabbed a couple more beers.

Laura walked by in a blanket with hair sproutin out like electrical wires. She gathered clothes and headed back down the hall.

"You want breakfast?" Jay asked. "I can fry bacon with scrambled eggs."

She gripped the edges a the blanket and said, "No thanks."

"Goin to Ogden," I said.

Jay held the bottle below his lips. "Okay but gotta move Mr. Yukichi's pipe. When?"

"Day show."

"Okay." His big smile broke from ear to ear. I heard the phrase a bunch but never seen it truer on nother mug.

"God's callin me to ride again."

"Let's not dillydally then."

"Got somethin to show you."

He walked back down the hall with the same limp from last night. "Laura, you're welcome to whatever I've got in the fridge." He slipped on a pair a flip flops I heard followin me out the trailer. "You're limping and haven't even got on yet?"

Sam and Josey was nowhere in sight long Riverton Road. Halted at the cab. "That's what I'm bout to show you. What happend to you?"

"Pulled a rib while back and won't get back in place. Saw Laura on Friday at a checkup."

Opened the passenger door and stepped back. The Brazilian rolled like a rattler on the frayed seat. The Lord as my witness more backsides a cowboys and cowgirls rode there'n all the kings and queens a France warmed thrones combined.

Jay raised the Brazilian in both hands. "Nice."

Sam and Josey nuzzled between us and raised their noses, eyein it.

"Was on the porch last night with Sam and nothin. Then this mornin I tripped over it when Jesús showed up. A miracle Jay. Jesus is tellin me to ride." The words barely kept up they come so fast.

"Explains your sprightly disposition since first appearing in my bedroom."

Sounded like somethin Roper would say, but I knowed Jay meant it, whatever he meant. We turned for a Dodge Ram with its diesel engine roarin over everything.

Jay placed a hand over his eyes, blockin the sun. "And here comes Mr. Yukichi to move his pipe."

The pickup turned into the driveway and passed us. Mr. Yukichi jumped out. Josey and Sam bounced round him, and he tossed Josey and then Sam.

"Nice to see you Dean," Mr. Yukichi said.

"You too Mr. Yukichi."

"Matt's on his way for a visit. Due to arrive in a couple days. He's still with those fancy pants on Wall Street. Calls his mother every week, and last week told her he was bringing out his fiancé to meet us."

"Would like to offer my congratulations."

"I'll be sure and tell him. How are Carmen and the girls?"

"Busier'n bees round their honeycomb."

"I bet. Jay you'll sunburn your butt walking around this time of day. And you'll have everyone calling me. We'll have to call Walt to make peace again. Have you noticed any change?"

Mr. Yukichi pointed at an old cow. She limped over a dike like he just commanded her. Jay eyed her and shook his head. He took to the habit a walkin naked as a jaybird Sunday mornins and caused Jesús' first controversy as bishop. Brother Hamilton pointed out none a those on time complained, and not a woman who drove by said a thing, even though a few others who didn't was beside themselves with moral proclamations. Brother Hamilton worked as the Mormon ambassador to nonmembers in Blackfoot and brokered a treaty Jay musta forgot.

He handed me the Brazilian and headed to the trailer. His white cheeks risin with each step in sync with snaps a his flip flops. Near five feet six inches, just a shrimp by

Jay at over six feet with his watermelon thighs and wide, flat chest, such big muscles his wiener hardly stood out. The Lord as my witness the Mormons couldn't see it from Riverton Road. I barely could next to him.

"Let me see it," Mr. Yukichi said.

Handed it over.

His fingers pressed tight. "Riding again?"

"In Ogden."

"Always thought you quit too early." He give it back. "I have something for you."

Followed to the back a his truck. He pulled the tailgate and jumped onto the bed and rummaged through a couple buckets. He stretched and removed his Red Sox ball cap, eyein cross the blue sky and crouched and opened a tool box.

Mr. Yukichi rodeoed for years, team ropin with Roper's father. They made the NFR ten years in a row, never win first but second three different times and once less'n a hundred dollars out a the gold buckle. He moved good as Brother Hamilton. Roper's father struggled to get in and out a the cab a his pickup.

"Good luck piece." Mr. Yukichi jumped down and handed me a coin. "Nearest I can tell she's over a hundred years old. A trader must have dropped her coming from Fort Hall or had other designs. Doubt that's what he would have been trading but never know."

Was like a silver dollar with half a woman's head. Flipped it.

Jay called for Josey and cleared the front a his double wide and limped his way back.

"You hurt yourself Jay?" Mr. Yukichi asked.

Jay shook his head.

"When you get going tomorrow stop at the south field on the Rez. I need you to look over the Deere. Might have to haul her to the shop."

"Okay."

"I'll move the line this morning. Lay it on Dean." Mr. Yukichi nodded and walked long fence, eyein them cows.

Cows and calves huddled under three small trees. One calf tried to suck, and the momma either run out a milk or in no mood. She moved her hind end. Maybe the calf just ate or bothered nother calf's momma. Left to my own notion a their relations.

"Been beating me to that line every Sunday for two months. Then he lets himself in and yells if I want to join him at Martha's. Not this morning."

CHAPTER 5

The old Ford bumped over Riverton Road and climbed a hill to Ferry Butte and crossed Tilden Bridge for Pingree. I hated stoppin but had no choice. My brother took back my spurs in a drunken fury. Last I asked his widowed ex-wife after em she said are father picked up my brother's gear.

Lower'n a snake's belly and meaner'n hot piss. I expect I'd kilt him if I didn't find Jesus. I knowed needed Jesus's grace still considerin it and cause for more a Jesus's sufferin. My father and my brother always rode me, flarin like ornery bulls, declarin squandered my talent and the reason I never win the world and one gold buckle that mattered. They complained who else would ride every bucker he got on and vanish for weeks with some skirt in Amarillo or Oklahoma City, Knoxville or Albuquerque, and lots more.

My brother bought me silver tipped spurs after I win the Wilderness Circuit the first time. He stole em back the day I told him was hangin em up, spewin on bout wastin em.

He rode bareback and made the Finals. Then followed my father into engineerin. They run a company cleanin up nuclear waste at the Site. The doctors couldn't say if radiation or alcohol did more harm. Not a lick sober since sixteen, but they said heavy doses a poison kept him from bein a candidate for a liver transplant. Why he pressed me, his only brother, to give half mine.

I wouldn't test. Not cause he didn't deserve it. That had no doubt bout but knowed what Jesus expected. I asked over and over how could I believe in him and not follow him and sacrifice for my own brother? The sin a lettin my brother die bore down hard. Once on Jay's porch went on bout failin Jesus in fits a spittin my Budweiser. Was messed up said Jay. And after I finished blatherin might ponder whether Jesus's sacrifice made more sense separatin out the bad from the good, and if were no good Jesus couldn't do nothin for you. Made me feel better at the time and whenever I thought on it after but knowed weren't true. The Christian Bible taught Jesus sacrificed for bad and not good in people. Not my place to tell Jay to read it when I didn't but knowed folks who did.

The old Ford passed potato vines for hundreds a acres and turned on a dirt road into a field with a shack in the middle. Laura pursed her lips and asked a question I didn't hear good. Jay snored, leanin on the door.

The old Ford stopped on a smooth patch a dirt.

"Won't take a minute," I said and cut the engine.

Dogs barked from within. Rested my sore toes six feet from the slanted door frame no amount a shims could make plumb and tryin would jam it. I didn't need to ask the Lord. Knowed for myself would be the best thing for it, beyond truein up.

Raised my hand, and the door opened. A two-by-four come right at my head and knocked me back, and my head blacked. The brown Rand lay five feet from my hands, and I wondered after Laura screamin from the cab a the old Ford like she seen a bear. A door a the truck opened and quick footsteps covered dirt. Set back on my haunches and raised my hands to ward off nother blow. Two black labs stopped barkin with muzzles in my face and the two-by-four in midair.

"What's a goddamn woman doing at my door?" My father growled from inside the deep reveal.

A hand reached above and yanked the two-by-four, and my father tumbled through the doorway.

"Give it back goddamnit."

"You all right Dean?" Jay asked. He throwed the board, skippin on the ground and brushed the labs. "You're cut."

Tapped a warm stream a blood on my forehead. Jay lifted under my shoulder. Went dizzy. He held till my boots got under me.

"You old bastard," I said.

"What's all the babbling about?" my father yelled.

"It's me, Dean, yur son."

"Dean the anointed one has returned! I always figured you for a woman but never heard you scream like one. I bet your protecting angel is Jay himself. Is your moron twin Roper hiding in the shadows? Here I expected the home teachers but get the three stooges." He squinted so tight he gone blind.

Jay picked up the brown Rand and smoothed the dent and give over. Sam bumped my leg and stood with her ears straight. My father's labs circled her.

"Get," Jay yelled, and the labs scattered.

"You crazy old coot," I said.

"What? Speak up son! Your mighty words won't move me if I can't hear them. You're a real fool's fool son. Why are you here bothering me? Rise up and tell your old man."

"I'm standin in front a ya. Come for my spurs," I shouted and rested against the door frame.

"If that isn't the most imbecilic thing I've ever heard. Did you believe God commanded his chief angel to burry them in the back to be found by a chosen bull riding generation? They are far more likely in the biggest let down of all hall of fame. Why bother me son? Why bother me?"

"Sheila said you had em."

"With your brother's gear? I expect she's lying as she was inclined to do, but I'll look since you bothered to make the trip out."

The labs followed him inside and the back door opened and closed.

Laura moved my hand pluggin my head and said, "What's wrong with your dog? She's quiet as a silent picture show."

"Sam's from the line of the oldest and wisest dogs in the world and doesn't bark. Straight from Africa," Jay said.

"Never heard of such a thing. You got a nice cut. Could use a stitch or two. Jay, could you look for some gauze and tape and some ice too? A butterfly Band-Aid would do nicely."

Jay bent through the doorway, and Laura wrapped a torn piece a shirt on my head and where she got it I couldn't tell. She finally finished.

Put the brown Rand on.

My father come round the corner, squintin at Laura. "You don't look like the silhouette of Carmen dear. You must be with Jay, an undiscriminating man after my old burned heart." He turned like he seen me. "I didn't find them son. You've been deceived and wasted a nice drive and unnecessarily tormented your dying father. You should have called first."

"When you get a phone you old codger?" Jay asked, clearin the doorway and grippin bandages and a small bag a ice.

"No one invited you into my humble abode Jay. Your manners certainly haven't improved." My father turned one way and then the other. "By some stroke of luck I've been spared Roper's presence. Maybe God does exist." He smiled wide. "I bid you all a fine adieu." He walked bowlegged back round the shack.

Took off the brown Rand and smoothed the crown. Laura removed the torn cloth and went to fixin the new wound on my head.

I wanted no part a my father's business but set on lookin for myself. Rounded the corner where the roof slanted near three feet above ground. An object flew by my face. Then a thud hit the middle a my chest. Sharp pain spread cross to my arms and started stumblin. Jay's hand pushed me upright.

My father looked up from my brother's manure-stained red gear bag. "Watch out! Don't you announce yourself on another man's plat of land? Found them and figured you for gone and thought I'd let them lie in the weeds with the other unwanted junk."

Warm blood wet through my shirt. I couldn't say nothin, so hot my eyes watered and ears pounded. Jay picked up the spurs and handed em over black as ash. Tightened each a my fists over a rowel sure they'd tear up my palms. Pain pulsed through my chest.

"Don't waste time thanking me. Go son." My father struggled to get off his knees.

The idea come to charge and knock him down and stomp his spine into the ground.

"You old bastard."

"What are you mumbling about son? Make yourself known."

"You old bastard."

"What are you waiting for my pretty narcissus?" He pressed his hands on the bag tryin to rise up. "Did yet another pool appear and catch your attention? Be gone! For all that is merciful. Leave me."

I heard him call names before with no idea what he meant and never cared to find out. But the way he said em always burned my skin. Looked for a strong stick to strike his head and hobbled for one pokin from behind a small shed.

Jay grabbed my arm. "Have a good day Mr. Stamper."

My father looked up sudden. "The hell it is Jay. Hasn't been one for a decade. I'd consider one flirting with this side of good if I could determine when to relieve myself." He finally got off the ground and lifted my brother's gear bag and hobbled to the shed.

"I'm ridin today," I yelled, sputterin over snot and spit with blood soakin my ripped shirt and just as soon sick I said a damned thing.

My father's head poked out the shed. "My son deciding to ride? Now? Done chasing women I know, but you don't have it anymore my son. Not a bit. You'll learn that in short order, measured in seconds. Is pure fancy for you now. Is for most people all of the time, and you'll discover what that's like."

"Jesus called me to."

He squinted hard. "Absolutely pathetic." He come all the way out the shed. "Hold on there. I have something for you." He went for his shack and hesitated, turnin his head without movin his scrawny back. "I had a dream about your mother. All these years I hoped she was dead, and after I began to believe she really was, the feeling came to me she probably wasn't, so I started looking for anything reminding me of her to burn."

He disappeared inside. A minute passed, and he come out with a buckskin jacket with fringe cross the chest and down the sleeves.

"And I'm throwing away my own prized possessions after my last doctor's appointment certain my visit to the undiscovered country is fast approaching. Here's the last thing I have of your mother's. You've saved me the matches and have rights to it since you're a mirror image of her."

He threw my mother's buckskin jacket at my boots and turned for the back door.

Laura picked it up and brushed dirt off. She placed it under her arm and said, "Unbutton your shirt."

Cleared each button, and she wiped blood from a small gash in my chest. She placed real gentle gauze on and white tape over. "Button up."

Eyed my father in the back doorway fixed on me like he never seen me dress before. "You ought to see Doctor Barbre."

"What?" He looked direct at the sun and back at me. "He's an orthopedic surgeon. What's he going to do? Reset my rectum? No doubt he'd take his hacksaw and cut me open in as many places as he could charge for. While he's at it maybe even take a scalpel and slice my eyeballs to remove my goddamn cataracts." He closed the back door.

Laura pressed my mother's buckskin jacket into my hands. "Put it on."

Tight in the shoulders but got all the buttons through their holes. "Yur a fine nurse."

"I work the front desk in the emergency room and am waiting for a position in billing. You are beautiful, like everyone has always said, a real clean-shaven mountain man."

CHAPTER 6

The old Ford backed off the smooth patch a dirt. Not a damned cloud in sight. The roll a the engine passed field after field with silos scattered in em. Sam lay with her paws over the seat between Laura and me. She looked up and knowed what I felt. My stubby fingers smoothed her back and patted her head down.

Them spurs wasn't the only thing my brother give me. On my eighth birthday, my father, brother and me sat at the large wood table in the dinin room, separate from the kitchen in are old house. Big and small pieces a sharp glass sendin light in all directions hung over head. I asked to see are mother, and my father said to ask for somethin else. I didn't and quit eatin supper. We all wanted the same thing, but no one ever said it. I couldn't recall what my mother looked like or when she left. All I knowed is someone told my brother she moved to New York City, and he told me. My one memory a her with my brother at the Nuart Theater on Broadway, people come from behind fancy drapes on an old stage. Her and my brother excited and for what I could never tell. One mornin I woke to a beautiful woman in a silver frame with hearts on the corners. Under a note read, "Mom." My brother roomed at the other end a the hall. We met at the stairs headed for breakfast and he said, "Happy belated birthday little brother."

Years later my grandma showed me a picture a her and learned even more beautifuler'n the woman still on my dresser. Once Roper orated on beauty in a Mercedes next to a sorority girl drivin with her girlfriend in back with me. They picked us up after a show in Dallas. We went straight to the bar after neither hanged on for a score. Them girls on us like laser beams, declarin no one as big a bull ridin fans and insisted we see the city skyline from their place in Uptown. On the ride one said I defined beauty and the other concurred and Roper lit in on all its meanin. I rode in every state and lots a women felt the same.

Notions a somethin sure formed long before folks got to explainin what they meant. I win my first gold buckle in junior rodeo steer ridin in Cheyenne late in the year, just perfect for a day show. My father took me and Billy and Layne, plannin to drive to Casper for the Winston Tour in the evenin.

The day got cool with everybody walkin round in jackets. The Cheyenne arena run a couple football fields long with people fillin the grandstand.

Steers didn't take half a chute, and I learned to not waste time callin for mine. Didn't matter how I sat long as on my rope. Mine jumped straight in the air and kept leapin and turned back, rollin on his side. The crowd roared over the buzzer, and I rode an extra two seconds before dismountin.

Roper rode but didn't score in the top five. I didn't know him then but knowed his sister, Milly. Was twice are size. In Montpelier she stopped me walkin to the chutes and told me to win for her and said she did breakaway ropin and barrel racin. I told her sure would and did.

She stopped me lots after. Was strong, pullin me between bleachers and behind trailers, directin me where to touch and how hard. Was soft and warm too. And knowed it made her happy cause she always told me so after she finished.

After my winnin ride I walked with Billy toward a large tent for my gold buckle. Was grabbed from behind.

We weaved through trailers and over hitches till we reached her father's silver Silverado and matchin gooseneck. Milly opened the side door and pulled me in. Bridles hanged on the far side next to stacked saddles. She closed the door, and Jumper backed up behind the wall, rockin the trailer.

Fresh straw covered the floor. Milly pulled me on top a her. "It's warm down here."

Was practiced up and went to work, puttin my hands in her Wranglers.

"Warm your hands up first champ. Stand up." She pushed me off. She sat up and pulled off her boots and socks. She lifted her shirt over her head and pushed her jeans down and off her legs. She unstrapped her bra and slipped off her panties. "Now you."

I stopped slidin my hands together and did real quick and covered my privates.

She lay with her arms folded behind her head. "You are the most beautiful thing I've ever seen. Now come back down here with me."

Back on top she guided me in her slit and told me to push with her hands on my butt. I did and she said to push more. I kept goin and goin and started to breathe heavy and slacken. "Don't quit," she cried. I tried harder. "Good, now stop."

I collapsed to her side. We lay for a long time. She sung a song I never heard before, runnin fingers through my hair. "Let's go again."

I shifted over and started up. Minutes passed and she whispered in my ear, "You can smile too. I love when you smile with me." My body ached. I tried smilin but couldn't hold it. Straw got in my crack, and I kept hopin for a break to reach back and clear out.

"Good."

I collapsed again and scratched my hind end and fell soon asleep.

"We better go." Milly hugged my shoulders and pulled back a blanket I never felt over us. Light come through a white plastic window in the trailer door like no time passed. "One last go, before we do." She pushed me back on top.

I pumped and pumped and run out a breath, tremblin. I kept goin to Milly's sighs. I floated above and seen my body flowin in and out on its own accord. Somethin moved and Milly cried out. Someone held me in the air with me pumpin back and forth.

"Settle down now, settle down. Quit Dean now. Quit!"

My gyratin body slipped from huge hands and hit the floor. I opened my eyes with my head against the wall. Roper's father filled the doorway. Jumper rocked the trailer. A large thud come from the other side a the wall and all went black.

My head fogged over somethin fierce and heard Roper's father sayin get my things. Big hands put my clothes on real tight. My head rang on every word and mumbled no sense. Someone picked me up and laid me on a seat covered in dog hair. My shirt run up my back with straw stickin inside and vinyl touchin under me. A dog barked, and Milly shushed her quiet, gettin in. She picked straw and straightened out my shirt and tucked into my Wranglers and kept sayin I'd be all right.

"What happened?"

I come to at the sharp voice a my father and mumbled somethin but couldn't understand between more questions.

"He tripped over the hitch," Milly said over voices carryin on by us and scooted out the door.

"My son could ride Oscar if they ran him in, and he couldn't clear a piece of iron? He's been knocked out for the past hour?"

"He was feint, and his stomach bothered him every time he started to stand, so he's been lying until his dizziness passes."

I struggled to set up. Milly turned and climbed back in and pushed my chest down.

"Just rest there Dean," Roper's father said. I seen Billy bouncin between em and Layne in the window a the cab.

"Why the hell did you come out here?" my father demanded.

I rolled up again, and Milly pushed my chest down. "I wanted him to have my belt to go with his championship buckle."

I recollected the embroidered weaves with a barrel racer on back. I watched Milly run it through the loops a her Wranglers many times before.

"We're in a hurry. Get out and walk. I already paid for my ticket for the show in Casper. We need to get on the road now to make the first round."

"I sent Roper for ice. We'll send it with you," Roper's father said.

"No need at this point."

Roper's father blocked the door and leaned in. Milly squeezed my arm. He carried me between trucks with Layne and Billy's boots below me and Milly holdin my arm.

"You did beautiful today," she said.

I tried to tell her I did my honest best.

Roper's father placed me in back a my father's Caprice and grabbed my shoulders with his eyes goin real tense. "Stay awake until you get all the way back to Blackfoot." He backed out. "Hear me Billy and Layne? Don't either of you fall asleep on the drive home. Keep an eye on him."

Milly come in and placed a bag a ice on my head. "Hold on tight. You'll feel better." She rubbed my chest and pressed her belt between my side and the seat.

"Get in. One in back and one up front. Let's go. We wasted enough time," my father said.

Billy got in passin Milly gettin out. He pulled out Milly's belt.

"Gave you a pink belt. Unbelievable." My father eyed us through the rearview mirror.

"It's a pretty all right belt," Billy said and fitted my new gold buckle.

The Caprice glided smooth as a Cadillac with power like a Town Car. Billy talked bout buckin bulls. A few we was bout to see and on occasion askin Layne to refresh his memory.

"Describe what you see," Billy repeated till I got he spoke at me. On the drive to Cheyenne there was plains a rocks I recollected but now seen white mountains movin. Peaks held and others didn't with blue sea beyond em. Pleats spanned right above like waves in an ocean, small and endless near on top each other with dark blue lines on the crests. I moved my hand over the velour edge and stared into red long the top a the front bench with my boots on Billy's leg.

"The stands in Cheyenne were almost full," Billy said. "How many people you guess?"

The ice pack full a water pressed on the numbed side a my head.

"Thousands," Layne said, turnin from the front.

"The stands weren't half full," my father said.

Billy kept on till my father asked him to stop and did a minute and started up again. Clouds on a darker sky continued passin till we slowed and turned and turned, again and again and stopped.

My privates hurt bad but even more in my stomach. Nothin in my head but takin a whiz real bad. Billy opened the door and let in the night's cool air. I coulda burst settin up.

"Meet me in front of the main door. Don't go anywhere but there," my father said.

I crawled out, pressin my privates hard.

"I need to find a bathroom," Layne said.

"Me too," I cried.

"Good to hear you make some sense," Billy said. "You were worrying me carrying on like a seasick sailor."

I limped behind Billy and Layne. Each step couldn't hold it no longer. Billy led and Layne right behind into the main door a the indoor arena by old men takin tickets into a mob a grown-ups with cowboy hats movin in different directions. I followed Billy's boots through legs till I couldn't see em no more. His hand reached out and pulled me to an open door with men waitin in line and right by em to Layne at the stall doors. One opened and a man stepped out and Layne went in before everyone else. A big bearded man grumbled bout us cuttin, but Layne paid him no mind. Billy pulled me in behind. I peed myself tryin to get my fly open with my free hand and my other hand holdin the bag a warm water on my head. Billy took it, and I undid my Wranglers fast and couldn't find the fold in my underwear wet through. I pulled em down and sprayed all over the stall. Billy tore the bag right when Layne started peein and water sprayed all over are clothes. Nothin hurt so bad in all my life or felt so good tryin to hit the bowl.

"What's going on in the there?" some old man yelled, maybe the same one complainin before.

"Mind your own business," Layne yelled back.

We went back to the entrance to wait. The lines thinned with folks findin their seats. A long time passed, and Layne said he'd go find my father and jumped up the stairs.

We heard the announcer callin out cowboys' names and seconds later the crowd cheer. Billy found a bag a ice and told me to hold on my head while he hunted for my father too. I sat on a step and watched cowboys and cowgirls walk by. A few passed and made comments bout the ice pack. I didn't say nothin with my shoulder against a wall in my wet Wranglers. Not sure how long sat there but heard the crowd cheer over and over again.

Layne grabbed my shoulder. I started up with the bag full a water on my boots. "Billy has seats at the very end." He hopped the stairs and went down a hall into the arena and waited where thousands a people surrounded the outside walls. "Over here." Layne walked long ways to the first row at the end. Billy sat with space by a big man. We climbed steps and scooted in.

The bottom a the stands rose six feet from the arena's floor. Seats wrapped round to chutes all the way on the other end. Cowboys workin em looked far off. The announcer said Layne's name. I eyed him and followed his eyes to the other side where cowboys stood on a chute. A huge bull with the biggest set a horns I ever seen stood ready.

The gate swung. The bull jumped out and turned back right and the cowboy made it. He bucked hard and high, travelin down the arena. He turned coverin more'n twenty feet, and the cowboy stuck. He went higher and farther. Never more excited bout nothin all my life, standin to see best I could. His underbelly rose straight with my eyes. He sent the cowboy high and stacked on his head. The cowboy wobbled to his feet and stumbled off.

"That was the buckingest trip I ever saw," the big man said.

"Really nice," Billy said.

"What a ride," Layne said.

CHAPTER 7

Opened my eyes, restin on Laura's breast with the brown Rand on her belly. Jay turned the steerin wheel right. Set up to see what the hell for and patted my mother's buckskin jacket over the sore spot on my chest. My stubby fingers slid over the buttons with dull pain on each breath.

The old Ford stopped behind an old orange station wagon with its hood up and right set a tires in yellow grass. Down the barrow pit a cowboy rested on his haunches next to a tall man, sittin Indian style.

"A vintage wagon," Jay said, hoppin out the old Ford.

Looked like the kid from last night. His red marked face eyed us through the windshield.

We was below mountains surroundin Inkom, passin em all my years. Roper attested in spring from Portneuf to Tremonton deserved top a list a scenicest drives throughout the world. Green rollin hills mixed with long, open stretches and small valleys picturesque enough for somewhere in Europe. Other rides out West was as captivatin. Past Spencer long the Pioneer mountains as grand a spread on Earth, endin at Melrose where for the longest time thought Benny Reynolds come from. Till me and Roper stopped off for pie on are way to a show in Helena and learned Benny come from over the hill in

Twin Bridges. None more famous a Montanan but Evel Knievel and Evel from just a short way north in Butte.

A steep hill face marked the beginnin a the ride. Mounts rose on both sides a the road to Inkom where we stopped just beyond. This stretch led to a wide valley before the Malad Pass with glades, hills, and reservoirs. A large flat rock dressed in small trees at the foot a rollin hills marked the exit for Malad and start for a long valley. Twenty miles into Utah set two bushy trees, the taller leanin on the shorter one. Still further on opened to a plain where Tremonton faced the Wasatch Front, as impressive a spread there was. Roper would go on and on and on some more but wouldn't describe what you could see with yur own eyes. Most times passed by a brown blur ready for summer burn.

Laura passed the brown Rand. Held it with one hand and used the other to brace against the door, droppin on my good foot and dismountin in one turn, and Sam jumped out behind me. Left the door ajar in case Laura got a mind to stretch her legs.

Jay talked with the tall man, eyein the engine in the old orange station wagon, hella long, old heap a metal. Sam run down long the barrow pit.

"Hey Dean," the kid said at the end a the old orange station wagon.

"Looks like bad luck."

"Died on us."

"Surprised a vehicle this old still runs."

"Volvos are the most reliable of rides, but mine may have gone its last miles today," the tall man said and closed the hood. He walked down the side. "What a fine jacket in pristine shape. I'm Bruce, and you know my brother. We'd appreciate a ride to the next truck stop."

"Where you going?" Jay asked.

"Salt Lake."

"We can take you as far as Ogden."

"That would be great. I planned to drop my brother there. I would appreciate stopping at a truck stop to make a call for someone to pick up the Volvo."

"Welcome to use my phone."

"I know this sounds crazy, but I don't use cell phones. They make me physically ill, sick to my stomach, and I hate the idea of being immediately available. All impractical but all true."

"Probably smart. I've read they cause long-term health problems, some in the head but mostly in the groin. Happy to place a call for you."

"I've not seen those studies and might question their methods. But not a bad myth if that's what it takes to avoid them. Honestly, there's no rush."

Bruce went to the old orange station wagon and opened the door and pulled out a blue duffel bag and pair a sunglasses and put em on. He went to the back and opened the tailgate, and the kid pulled out his gear bag. They hauled their bags to the bed a the old Ford. Bruce leaned the seat forward to the king cab. He looked younger up close with a huge shiny forehead and thin hair in the middle. He slid in with long skinny legs and bent em, higher'n the seat, foldin his wiry arms over em. The kid climbed in against the other side and pulled the seat back.

Fired up the old Ford and slid the seat forward, waitin on a semi to pass. Caught up to speed and Bruce thanked us and made proper introductions. Laura said she hitched a ride to see her favorite sister in Roy. I didn't think to ask why she come with us or the women before since they was just takin their turns.

"There weren't many cars the last hour, but we saw a few eighteen wheelers. More people going to church these days than I expected. You all ride bulls too?" Bruce asked.

"We are today," Jay said.

"You up in Ogden Dean?" the kid asked.

"I am."

"Wow," the kid shouted and quieted down as quick.

"I've wanted to see Taylor ride since last summer, and my schedule finally worked to come home this weekend. I was fortunate to break down on the way back and not on the way to Blackfoot. His ride was nothing short of amazing, far more difficult than the other rides where cowboys fell right off, and his was better than the cowboy who got a score. His bull was powerful right from the beginning with huge kicks and quick, powerful twists. It exploded out of the gate and kicked so hard when it landed and pushed off again a fault must have opened all the way to Great Falls. At one point all four hooves were six feet off the ground with the back set pointing in one direction and the front set pointing in the other direction. That's the truth. I wouldn't believe a word but saw the whole ride with my own set of eyes. Simply astounding. I could never have imagined it. Eventually the bull kicked its back legs over its own head. I mean the back hooves went straight up bending over the head. That is the truth too. Only bent over itself was Taylor finally off. I'm a bull riding fan for life. No mistaking Taylor's bull bucked the hardest and his effort was the best. He was also fortunate to clear the fence and not a millisecond too soon. Many other riders certainly paid a high price for competing. The poor cowboy from Jerome won't ever be the same," Bruce said.

"I didn't make the buzzer," the kid said.

"Sounds like you made a great ride," Laura said, turnin with a smile.

The old Ford sped long, passin rock faces in the distance. Desert grass and brush covered large lava rocks between freeway headin north and south. Not close as between Blackfoot and I.F. but the same with enough rock for a thousand truck loads.

"He certainly did. Cowboys sitting near us said the guy who got the score didn't make eight seconds either. One of them was an old cowboy, who claimed he'd been to thousands of rodeos and said judges have gotten lenient over the years. I didn't expect everyone to be so young, and while Taylor showed he can ride, with the exception of a couple others, the rest seemed like they should have been playing in a Junior Jazz basketball league," Bruce said.

"Some of these boys act like champions for getting on," Jay said.

Bruce weren't shy bout sharin his opinions. The tiresome type unable to shut up but not stupid. Young bull riders was overmatched. They wasn't gettin younger but not practiced up and didn't have chances to develop. Bulls just got lots ranker. And kids only got experience longer they stayed on, and these days didn't stay on long. I didn't see such rank bulls till the high school national finals and my first pro shows. Only Tuff Hedeman coulda learned startin on bulls these days. And I'd seen rides scored a second, sometimes two, short a eight.

"The demand to catapult straight to results can be found in almost everything else these days. Whether sports or jobs or politics everyone wants to reach the end without doing anything to get there. That's why the BYU Economist Doctor Lonergan's book raised so many global feathers this past year," Bruce said.

"What study was that?" Laura asked. "Not the one about the DNA of humans' earliest inhabitants in the Americas showing their ancestors came from Siberia? Across the Bering Strait and not the Atlantic Ocean from ancient Israel?" She winked my way.

Her question confused me and seemed more like makins against the Mormon religion. I made no sense a the idea but knowed for sure the very first Mormons come from the Holy Land, and Mormons claimed was ancestors a people in the Americas.

"I've read those studies, and they've been tough medicine for claims about the origin of The Book of Mormon, no matter how circumscribed the location by Mormon first responders. They actually support the argument the BYU Professor makes. On my mission in Santiago, Chile, we converted many Chileans in large part due to the story of Mormonism being about their ancestors. God spoke to prophets in the ancient Americas. Many Chileans welcomed the idea progressive Westerners like us shared an ancient worldview with their ancestors at the center. I stepped off the plane in Santiago and was on my way to my first baptism. In all I baptized four hundred and twenty-one souls, three short of the record set by my first companion, my trainer. But when I first arrived, I didn't have a companion because the three other Elders who lived and studied with me in the Missionary Training Center, in Provo, got on different flights at our connections in Mexico City for other missions throughout South America. I sat alone as the plane descended in clouds hiding most of the Andes except jagged, snowcapped ridges. The height and the severity of the peaks, and what seemed like endless runs of them is still the most dramatic sight of my life. I remember thinking how majestic the peaks were breaking above the clouds, but in truth I was sick to my stomach with fear and not hiding it well.

A scraggly guy in the seat next to me asked, "First time in Chile?" We hadn't talked the entire eight hour flight from Mexico City. I sensed he was ignoring me intentionally, but he must have seen the dread on my face as we started our descent and was beside himself to admonish me.

I said, "Yes."

And he said, "No worries. They're professionals mate."

I didn't tell him my feelings were not due to any lack of belief in the pilots' ability to land the plane and told him, "I'm a missionary for the Church of."

And he cut me off, "I know who you are, your boys come through East London. A couple lived near our flat."

That took me by surprise meeting a Brit in the air over South America, and I asked, "You're English?"

He leaned in and said, "by recent way of Australia and Southeastern Mexico. I see you boys everywhere. No offense, you have radge ideas and are controlled by old duffers."

If I learned one thing in the M.T.C, it was to ask questions and more of them the better and asked, "What are you interested in?"

He made a pensive look and said, "The natural world and experiencing it. I'm going to Atacama desert. Vastness and sparsity, yes. I'll find a few new stars with any luck. That's where you find truth, in nature, through experience. No beliefs in the supernatural required, no out of body experience. Actual transcendence in the here and now."

I also learned in the M.T.C. that the skill of building on common interests was a key to developing trust and said, "I hope to enjoy the beautiful landscapes during my mission too. I'd love to hike through the Andes."

He smirked and said, "I intend to ride through the desert. I have a Yamaha 250 back home and intend to find a bike here with enough power to see places others never will."

I said incredulously, "You ride a dirt bike on the streets of London."

And he said, "Melbourne is home now, mate."

I said, "Another place I hope to visit one day."

"Then the airplane put down its landing gear, and we were in sight of the airport. Over the piercing braking I wished the English-Australian well. His name was Tim or Tom. I couldn't understand him terribly well but remember clearly his thin, patched facial hair and long braids smelling of ash and mold, which I'd smelled throughout the cabin before even taking my seat next to him in Mexico City and truth be told likely caused my upset stomach more than fear of being a missionary in a foreign country.

"I exited the plane bunched with others. I never drank coffee but knew its aroma filled the air. People watched and waved on the other side of a glass wall, and people stopped and waved back. So much warmth on both sides of the glass, but I didn't see one missionary and wondered if they forgot me.

"I joined a line for customs with businessmen and women and young Europeans shuffling forward a few steps with long pauses before a few more steps next to other lines, sliding forward at their own paces.

"A woman with an East Coast accent directly ahead of me asked whoever appeared to be native of Chile in our line and lines on both sides where the best museums were. A short man in a suit stood behind me and avoided making eye contact and regularly checked his watch. I saw the English-Australian a line over near the back and followed his gaze to a party of girls chatting in Spanish that didn't sound like what I learned over the past eight weeks in Provo.

The woman ahead of me reached a customs agent with her passport in hand and asked, "Tell me senor what are your thres favorite museums in Santiago? The kind you wouldn't want to have lived without seeing? Containing the works you wouldn't find anywhere else?"

The agent said, "Pardon, no English," and smiled and stamped her passport.

I stepped forward, and he asked, "First time in Chile?"

I answered, "Yes, sir," handing over my blank passport. "I'm here to serve two years for my Church to share a message about Jesus Christ."

He smiled. "I know. You tell your leaders keep sending los Mormones to Santiago. Good luck."

"I moved with people in what I hoped was the direction of people waiting for new arrivals. I followed through frosted glass doors, and greetings hit me like engines on takeoff. People blurred moving from face to face into standoffs and continuous reshuffling. I strained for glimpses of an Assistant to the President with his missionary name tag, but there were no gringos in a white shirt and tie.

A woman brushed her way through the people and said, "Hola Elder!" She stopped, and people moved around us. She grabbed my arm. "Welcome to Santiago, Elder. We are so honored you are here. You are truly God's servant where his work will never stop!"

The one thing I did not expect was to be greeted by a beautiful woman. She said, "We need to hurry Elder, or we'll miss the baptism."

"I followed her to a parking lot, and she stopped at a box truck tightly wedged between a silver BMW sedan and a dark green Volvo wagon. She heaved my luggage into the back and closed the door. I could barely squeeze by the BMW to climb in.

She said, "I'm sorry Elder. How rude of me. I'm Sister Herrera. I'm a ward missionary and the ward mission leader's wife. He would have picked you up himself, but he is conducting a baptism. The other Elders are backed up at baptisms too. We are enjoying a great harvest of saving souls here in Santiago."

"The road leaving the airport had tolls, and her box was broken, so we stopped at each tollbooth. She turned onto side streets and drove through endless rows of old brick houses with the city appearing in breaks of smog. She explained the Church in Santiago that seemed to begin with the generation of new members before she and her husband joined. She talked about the bishop and what general authority recently visited, and I felt like I was back in my home ward.

She paused and looked at me. "I like to practice my English with you greenies. Don't worry you'll have plenty of opportunities to practice your Spanish." I must have looked to be in shock because she reached over and patted my arm. "We're so honored to have you Elder."

"I remember the first day as if it was yesterday. The smells and the smog covering the city, how Sister Herrera continued to thank me for serving, how we made the baptism with no time to spare, and how doggone noisy the city was.

"As soon as we arrived Sister Herrera went inside, and I stood outside the ward building. A dog ran around the corner, wagging his tail in concert with his dangling tongue, begging for anything. I didn't even have peanuts from the plane ride. The dog followed me to the door, and I felt overwhelming guilt with nothing to give.

"I found other Elders inside, including my trainer who shook my hand and immediately directed me towards a baptismal font. I stood across from him at the other end. A man in a white suit descended stairs into the font, and an old woman followed behind him. Her gown set on the water, and she patted it below the ruffled surface. He took her hands and placed them on his right arm and raised his left arm. My trainer spoke quietly and directed him to the old woman's other side. The man shifted the old woman's hands onto his left arm and raised his right one. He prayed over her, and when he finished he looked at my trainer. My trainer said something only the man could hear. He said the prayer again and looked at my trainer who bowed in approval. The man lowered his free arm and placed it on the old woman's back. She freed one hand and plugged her nose, and the man sat her back in the water. The breaking water sounded off the walls and covered all of us. The man raised her, and she breathed for air, moving water from her eyes. The man looked at my trainer who bowed again.

"After the baptism I saw sister Herrera with two other women serving sweet cakes to new converts and members. Elders held back, and so did I but my stomach twisted from hunger.

"My trainer was stern and almost regal. He stood with his hands clasped behind his back and bowed slightly when ending a conversation. That one thing stood out, and then he'd turn away. He also would not speak in English, except once and only then on the first day.

"Members were stacking chairs after the baptism. I helped and felt a hand on my arm. I turned to my trainer holding a piece of paper. He lifted it, which I deciphered was a certificate of baptism with the name of the new member. Under her name were two witnesses, my trainer and me. He handed me a pen to sign. I did, and he pointed his finger at my name and said, "Elder Weeks, this is the Lord's work" and bowed his head and turned around.

"I followed him to a car on the adjoining street, and I noticed again the noises before entering the church. The stray dog magically appeared and followed us to the car. I got into the back seat next to my luggage with my knees crunched against the back of the passenger seat where my trainer sat. Right after the member started the car, Sister Herrera came out of the ward building, and the member rolled down the window. I heard what I thought Sister Herrera say was our food in Spanish, and she handed a bundle of something smelling of warm bread and spiced meat over the member to my trainer. She looked into the back seat at me and in English said, "The Lord Bless you Elders."

"I had not eaten for hours but it felt like days, and I thought about eating what she prepared the whole ride. We drove through more dilapidated houses and stopped in front of one. The member asked something about the correct pension, the only Spanish I was confident about the entire day, and my trainer confirmed it was the place. The member drove the car up on the ground on what would have been a sidewalk. Getting out of the car my legs shook and tremors ran up and through my chest while my stomach hardened. I had never been so hungry. We knocked on the nondescript door a few feet from the parked car. A young girl answered, and my trainer handed over the bundle of food Sister Herrera gave us, and I about died. I could have eaten a doorframe, if there'd been one, bending to enter the small house.

"We entered a room with children gathered around a TV and a small couch and two old folding chairs. The young girl who answered the door walked to the TV and turned it off. A loud and unified protest came from the children as they moved around the room for a place to sit, and a man with a long face entered with his fingers through empty crates and handed them to his children. He asked us to sit on the old folding chairs. My trainer gave a chair to the member and the other one to me, and he sat on a crate. Later I learned the father used the crates to move vegetables early each morning to markets with his oldest daughter who answered the door. The father left and came back distributing more crates. His wife entered and sat on the small couch next to one of the younger children. The father wore slippers and the wife and children sat with bare feet, and I moved my new shiny dress shoes to the sides of my chair.

"The young girl reentered the room and handed full glasses to the member and my trainer. She left and returned again with glasses for me and her father. I took mine and looked at the dirty water. I was aware rejecting it could be rude, so I looked at my trainer who was saying something about drinking to the girl who smiled big and said in English, "No Tea." She took the glasses back, and the member looked disappointed. She brought out a plate of sliced pieces of fruit, and my trainer took the smallest piece and passed the plate to the member, who took a piece, and I leaned to take one, and he passed the plate to the closest child, and I about fell off my chair.

"My trainer encouraged me to begin teaching. I had memorized the lesson in the M.T.C. and proceeded to struggle to explain part of God's plan for his only begotten son Jesus Christ who came to Earth and sacrificed himself on behalf of the sins of every human, so we could all live with God again if we accepted Jesus's atonement. The family listened patiently and at times the children giggled at my poor pronunciation. My trainer encouraged them to ask questions and provided counsel I didn't understand. He repeatedly gestured for me to continue. At some point my humiliation turned into excitement as I watched the family become more interested. I don't remember when, but I remember recognizing the difference in their faces. The lesson progressed, and I felt as light as I ever remembered feeling with the children and parents listening closely, and at the end I invited them as a family to be baptized into Christ's true Church. They said yes, and I about cried overcome with joy.

"For the next two months I saw Sister Herrera every week, and she would sneak in English each time, sometimes the only communication I understood for a couple of days and always out of earshot of my trainer. She was as respectful of him as everyone else. The last I heard he is the youngest bishop in the history of the First Salt Lake City Ward. Sister Herrera was always helping the missionaries even though she and her husband were busy with their four young children. She worked as a clerk at night and made deliveries during the day, and her husband worked as a pipefitter when the union called him. They met when he was working at the mines as a young man. I came to believe watching her support all the missionaries that she didn't need the opportunities to practice her English as much as she wanted me to feel comfortable during what was otherwise a raging river of confusion in those first weeks.

"Over the next two years I came to know other members like Sister Herrera. Sister Perez, and Brother and Sister Vasquez, and Brother Vargas and Sister Vargas, and Sister Fernandez, and Brother and Sister Fuentes and many others. Out of the four hundred and twenty-one converts I remember only a few of their names and only a few more faces.

"I never thought about this, and I mean I never did, until I saw an old companion at BYU and we started talking about Santiago. He told me he'd recently visited our mission and found Sister Herrera. My heart about burst hearing her name. He said she called his name out as soon as he walked through the door like she'd seen him yesterday. She gave him all kinds of news and mentioned members as if they were her own family. She talked enthusiastically about coming to visit Utah one day. Then he said he didn't find one of our converts. We'd taught every day and knew most of our investigators for only a few weeks. But not many of them kept coming to church for more than a couple weeks after we baptized them. We did not see a problem on our missions. Frankly we never had time to see one. I've since heard the missionaries in some areas of my old mission focus only on reactivating our old converts."

"There's Arimo," the kid said.

I thought to pull off earlier at McCammon for a breather from Bruce but passed right on by. Where I met Carmen. Not for the first time she said. I went to rehabilitate an elbow injury before gettin back on the Tour. Her first rodeo ever with her friend before they headed to Lava Hot Springs down the highway. Just divorced from her returned missionary no more'n a month and full a reckless passion, confessin one night born barren. I knowed explained things beyond me and her. The one time ever heard Carmen complain. The Lord sure had different designs. No more'n nother month and learned the truth.

"You are saying joining the Mormon Church was too easy for your converts to stick around," Laura said.

"Exactly right," Bruce said, pushin up his sunglasses.

He sure as hell coulda got to sayin so lots sooner.

"And to think I know a lot of inactive Mormons in Idaho and Utah. Sounds like they rival the inactive members in Chile."

"Over half of the membership most likely. In the hundreds of thousands in the whole country and throughout Latin America."

"It's probably best the blond haired, blue eyed missionaries there are not rushing everyone into the one true

Church. But at least the inactive Chileans have their saving ordinances done." Laura smiled and patted my Wranglers.

"I believe you're right, but at the same time I don't have an answer for what good we did them for their current lives here on Earth, especially since we didn't require any effort to obtain God's promises. That brings us back to the BYU Economist Doctor Lonergan's point about people having much more at the cost of being much less.

"He wrote an axis altering book, arguing the cumulative wellbeing of humankind has increased at a faster rate than cumulative human worth. To quantify wellbeing, he used access to food and housing, healthcare and education, and civic services, etcetera, that have outpaced development of dignity and virtue, and altruism and liberty, etcetera. The first classifications measured against the second across representative groups in their respective societies. He took as foundational humans are a social species with successes and failures and accounted for their own reported experiences. He brilliantly identified a combination of key variables forming a replicable model.

"He didn't rely upon evidence in mere historical trends like the decrease in violence to support wellbeing or the deluge of popular manifestations for the decrease in worth. Not that both don't provide ample case studies leading to the same conclusions. Instead, he mined good data from extensive health reports and social and economic records across countries and various layers of populations. His analysis has been confirmed as painstakingly accurate. Among his proofs were genetic histories, and many reviewers described them as game changers.

"His method tracked increases of capital from advances in technology. My favorite example was the domestication of the horse from the Eurasian Steppe to Comancheria. He meticulously showed how the technologies overlay with biological histories, spurring one leading commentator to describe his approach as the truest of interdisciplinary bonanzas. Another well known commentator declared no analysis has been more complete to base conclusions ever.

"His model in one word is awesome, in two, awe inspiring and despite constant attacks has remained unfailing. His supporters and critics alike point out the veracity stands and falls on his accounting for massive amounts of data in various phases, what he called scales, analogizing civilizations to symphonies and their cultures to movements, noting all are within an identifiable range, showing both disparate and composite forces for the resulting increases in wellbeing and decreases in worth. His model has been attacked on about every front, but its reproducibility has proved unwavering. Some experts have said it should earn him a Noble Prize.

"Many attacks focused on his method and many more denounced his conclusions. One in particular has made a life of its own in the media. Professor Lonergan argued as complacency increases, and he gave many examples, such as increased access to what populations want and more importantly need, in shortened time and space, like treatment of infectious disease, and I might add he always provides positive examples and never straw ones easily picked from the pear tree, it not only outpaces the spread of human dignity but, and here's the ticker, adversely impacts the development of it.

"The easier we have at getting the things we desire, across peoples' respective ranges of things wanted and needed, the less we have of the virtues making up defining characteristics of what being fully human means, for all people, the visceral and sensual and perceiving human, feeling and driving our reflecting and striving for meaning."

"What does he recommend?" Jay asked. "We throw away our phones?"

"Or tell our doctors no thanks a MRI would prove too helpful?" Laura asked, chucklin before even finishin.

"He is clear he would not trade his triple bypass or wish his BYU colleagues had gone without their coronary angioplasty procedures and various lifesaving cardiac surgeries for a more primitive state. In fact, he obliterates any notion of a fanciful pure state of nature. What he conjectures is the burden to be better human beings has never been greater during recorded history, and there's never been a more available and appealing alternative to essentially become a pseudo robot."

"So what's his point?" Jay asked.

"The unintended consequence of removing poverty, disease, conflict, and pain, or, in other words reaching maximal efficiency, that he conceded is worth pursuing, is dehumanization."

"Sounds like he earned whatever criticism people were foolish enough to waste their time heaping on his book!" Laura said.

"Instead of making everything real easy, what'd he say people should do?" Jay asked.

"Among his recommendations, he encourages everyone to be patient. Every single day. If you aren't doing something that challenges you to be patient, do something that does to prevent becoming absolutely superficial. Without patience humans won't develop their fullest potential. He provides one startling example of the ability to relate to others, including compassion for others they don't know and certainly for those they do, which he points out the data, while counterintuitive, shows is far less than one would likely assume. People might miss the seemingly innocuous endnote in this section where he tries to slay the sacred cow of empathy, pointing his readers to a fair bit of current research showing how unvirtuous the effects tend to be. This issue is one of a few points where the Professor may go too far, and yet right or wrong sheds a light on a topic deserving of its own discourse. Imagining what other people feel seems to me a key to connecting and relating to and ultimately valuing them. And human behavior at the most fundamental has the desire to understand others for good and bad ends. My guess is empathy is less about dehumanizing effects than it can be directed for ill ones.

"Most importantly Professor Lonergan argues humans will lose the capacity and following that loss the ability to imagine, not to be confused with fantasy or propensity to daydream both with their own value tied to our perennial egos, but creative vision, the neural substrata for development, including forming habits to overcome individual and social challenges and to reach personal and collective change and to maintain the range of emotions needed to successfully interact with a modicum of respect for others, a separate topic with its own endnote that he exhausts at some length. He probably gives the most precise definition of imagination, and the consensus, including his staunchest opponents, is it has universal application, by locating imagination between perceptions and what we see can be. And in those rare cases try to make. An immeasurable difference with infinite risks and finite rewards. However subservient to our unconscious brain, imagination's preeminence is indisputable for all bipeds with a shred of awareness. The space of our imagination is one of life's fine measures to be refined and expanded for our purposes."

"Professor Lonergun is pretty all right," Jay said.

"He is saying anything worth having required effort to have it," Laura said.

"You've summed up an important part of his argument," Bruce said.

"I wouldn't give up vaccinations no matter how easy they are to get."

"I didn't appreciate antibiotics less the second or third times," Jay said, placin his arm round Laura's shoulders and squeezin.

Bruce said, "Don't misunderstand Professor Lonergan's argument. He welcomes and encourages advancements that improve wellbeing. The benefits have the greater consensus of being worth the cost, and he's not a heretic. The difference between humans and robots is awareness and humans are closing the gap, not robots. He argues for bringing about wide scale innovation to improve all humans' circumstances but stresses even more effort is needed to keep our humanity."

"Sounds like he missed the boat, if he thinks being more like a robot is worse off than being truly human for whatever that means. If being like a robot means less pain in the world, then slap on the tin and oil me up," Laura said with her chest convulsin.

"And among other things, less imagination. You're right, again, there are tradeoffs, and they are the reasons why he argues for patience to retain our humanity and to strive to maintain it as long as possible, which becomes

Olympic for the individual if it's unrecognizable on a population as a whole."

"Let's take the Downey exit," Jay said. We all turned to the road veerin off the freeway.

Hit the brakes, and Sam sat up. The old Ford swung to the hazard lane and come to a stop. Turned my upper body, and so did everyone else. A car swerved into the far lane with the old Ford backin up. Drove fast and come to nother hard stop, then veered onto the off-ramp.

"About missed it," the kid said.

Bruce could talk. Roper would call him loquacious. I couldn't recollect hearin no one like him. I heard Donny Gay speak at award shows over the years like he couldn't stop neither, but even Donny didn't hold a candle to Bruce.

Got to the gas station and Bruce jumped out.

"He sure can talk, can't he?" Laura said at the kid.

"Yes mam he can," the kid said.

"I'm sorry, but I didn't catch your name."

"It's Taylor mam."

"You have lovely manners Taylor, but I'm nobody's mammy. Please call me Laura like everyone else. Your brother is quite the intellectual."

"Dang straight he is. Anyone need a beer?" Jay asked.

"No thanks," Laura said.

"Dean?"

"Need to focus," I said.

"Taylor?"

"No thank you," the kid said, smilin and leanin over the seat.

"Okay," Jay said and headed for the gas station.

"He does know a lot. What in God's name does he do?" Laura asked.

"He's done a lot of things. Now he runs a business selling healthy juices and natural oils. A few of my sisters, two of aunts on my Mom's side, and a bunch of cousins work for him out of their homes."

"I have to hand it to Bruce. Most people who carry on like him are compensating for something or just full of bull or both, but he is genuinely into ideas."

"Yes mam. Sorry, yes, Laura he is."

Bruce climbed back in the king cab carryin on with Jay with a twelve pack a Budweisers under his arm. Got on are way and like Bruce never shut up.

The old Ford climbed the Malad Pass and passed a glade with houses scattered in small rollin hills. On a trip long ago Roper said the village nestled in them hills only needed thatched cottages with cellars full a brewskis and wiener schnitzels to be mistakable for Bavaria, the heart a Europe he said and never even went.

"There's something wrong about the idea that removing problems makes you less human when every good human is trying to get rid of them, and the few really good ones are trying to help others rid themselves of them too," Laura said.

"Professor Lonergan does not avoid philosophical questions like the one you pose, Laura, but some of his readers miss his attention to them because he relegates them to endnotes. I can tell you would not be a weak reader. The professor admits theoretical discourses are not priorities for his argument but appreciates how enticing they are, so he doesn't avoid them when they arise. They're just in the back of the book," Bruce said.

"How long is it?" Jay asked.

"Including the tables and graphs and index and endnotes, over fifteen hundred pages. The project was quite a risk for the University of Chicago Press, but their gamble should pay off one day, albeit in the distant future, passing in sales Harvard Press's book by the other economist who stirred up so much global handwringing about the effects of capital on humans' wellbeing.

"One of the last endnotes addresses the dilemma you've identified Laura and clarifies while development entails the presence of varying struggle that is a fact aside from any judgment of value and not the same as a correlation in the form of an argument. That is an abstraction and by its nature not the fact it describes. His opponents latch on to the argument you implied and cry he's advocating for misery, claiming the position is in the same family as saying to be happy you have to experience disappointment and if you don't experience disappointment you won't know happiness. The criticism suggests a necessary pessimism would have to be true if his position is true logically."

"Is that how the book ends?" Jay said, slappin his hands on top a the dashboard and got Sam up with her ears straight. Laura patted her head down.

"Heavens no!"

Most a what Bruce said I had no notion what he meant but felt one idea like a kick all the way up my gut.

"Professor Lonergan concisely explained while logic included the characteristic of necessity, that often amounts to a persuasive distraction and inevitable faux end and his study and subsequent argument, and this was crucial, in fact, did not depend upon logic. Keep in mind logic is a constructive system, a type of language, based on connections, one thing and not another thing, excluding a middle thing. However tentative those connections, we comprehend them in the abstract. The language can be a sophisticated system that even circumscribes the necessary connections as not sufficient causes. That exercise is separate from the empirical, or factual, study the Professor is doing. Another way of saying this is logic depends upon coherence of ideas, but the Professor's study corresponds to experiences, actual facts, which are often not coherent. And also importantly not dependent upon our ideas of them.

"He is not saying there isn't inherent rationality in nature, because there is and he discusses it at length. And he is also not out to diminish the value of abstractions. He provides a cursory perusal of the best rational arguments, classical and contemporary, devoting a concise endnote to them. There's immense communicative value in abstractions, including the explanation and transmission of difficult truths. Don't be misled by the limited use of abstraction to define lines and colors or irrational markings worth millions of dollars in modern art museums. And don't hastily surmise he focuses solely on theoretical explanations for our brains' means of cognition. The Professor attends to the role of images and the linchpin of much of our understanding, the emotions, in their own endnotes, and explores the range of cognitive planning through metaphor in another one. He covers the foundational role of impressions and association of ideas and function of comparison for the underlying process much of our comprehension results from. While all of these may be more prominent, all of them become more accessible through abstraction.

"The Professor uses abstractions not only as levels of theoretical understanding but more as something to mean conceptual that builds on, interacts with, and overlaps into other concepts to form new ones. From a pencil to a spacecraft with their malleable essences and temporal boundaries and possible dimensions. Each has particulars dependent upon something else from accepted conventions to the records of them, and those from memories are a topic he grants an endnote indistinguishable from a chapter. Think about an abstraction's function as a generalization. In short, an abstraction names a value or expression, with varying levels or degrees of concreteness, with use in multiple places, and this method of sharing happens across peoples not bound by language or culture. In fact, and I use the term deliberately, abstractions have been among humans' most useful tools to develop and transfer knowledge. There's no greater evidence than symbols, the true Rosetta stones in the history of languages. Abstractions have also been among our very best means at challenging and improving knowledge. And for those committed to beauty, abstractions move us as deeply and inspire us as completely as any human invention, from poems to equations. There is no avoiding they are hierarchal and timeless and become critical parts of our fluid thinking processes and a chief component to improving them.

"But coherence of abstract explanation, especially the enchanting logical form, however useful, is not the thing itself, despite the chief characteristic of necessariness that sirens highest understanding for those of nostalgic positivistic tendencies. Not anymore than the poem is the thing it explains or the equation the quantity it defines. Yet the Professor emphatically champions abstractions for their power to unlocking imaginations beyond known empirical evidence for the yet to be discovered, sometimes still centuries away. In short, abstractions not only unlock understanding but aid in moving beyond ours.

"Despite their power, he draws attention to their limitations by reminding his readers abstractions' highest order of proofs demonstrates a portion of the actual truths in the natural world as sure as a fraction of them can be measured. The natural world is full of energy, bundled things that do the work, its various forms and conversions, pressured and spread across immense regions with fecundity and richness. The things we experience that affect and shape, harm and heal, degrade and support, and shackle and liberate us, and our reductions of them the best signs of our most thoughtful attempts, always approximations and often ephemeral.

"Make no mistake he gives abstraction ample credit. He highlights its vast usefulness in contemporary societies in the text itself, not in the philosophical pieces in the endnotes. He describes the role of abstraction in the languages of programming. Their universal application drives significant improvements, from tracking and eradicating disease to establishing global networks. In short, programming underlies our modern lives. They are expressions of logic, applied in formats of functions, or instructions that establish a framework to process quantities of information, and they are enormous accomplishments. And so why is this all important?"

Was like Bruce awoke and thought we was all dozin but not me, eyein the road ahead and catchin some a his words and not lots a others.

"Not a clue," Laura said.

"Bet he didn't quit there," Jay said.

"I'd venture you'd make a solid guess Laura, and he did not Jay. The Professor never shorts his readers. The key is that programming depends upon a sequence of connections, potentially extensive ones given a system's memory and processors, advancing awesome computational power. So to his point Laura. The crux of programming that ensures its very utility and expanding ubiquity for establishing proofs, executing computations, or organizing data, is code of definite prescription and certain meaning. The logic does not permit arriving at mutually contradictory statements. This rule isn't violated when machines learn to generalize through improved sorting schemes but is exemplified when they do. Every algorithm depends upon and ensures its set parameters. But how much of this logic is part of the fabric of reality? Nature tends towards variety, and is often an accident, or random. Albeit with many redundant runs, nature is a panoply of arbitrary and integrated contingencies with endless surfaces and edges, in actual space and time, both compressed and expanded over fair amounts of both.

"You've probably been thinking he's fixed himself between a major rock and hard place of a proverbial paradox. Earlier I said he puts forth a model that basically is an abstract equation showing how a combination of variables brings about a specific outcome. Fortunately, he doesn't have to rely upon definitions of terms or arbitrary thought experiments to get out of this fix. Instead he appeals to the natural world, to evidence, at its most dynamic and complete, and in its roughest and at its most unpredictable. When certain conditions are met there may be a predictive outcome. And looking back at things in their particular situations and order we can see how effects ended up the way they did. The process of identifying their direction substantiates the idea of determinism. Yet in many cases where we can actually identify one force acted on a separate force, the preceding actions were totally arbitrary, and I mean complete as in absolute. In short, when factors in proximity bundle in distinct and ordered processes, they may produce an event we can share. The instance of the interaction, that we often seek to unveil so that we can understand and recreate, is what we generally use the term of cause to describe. Physical laws reveal their values, and we rightfully extend great efforts harnessing as many as we can. The quests to replicate and control them have delivered on most of civilizations' consequential projects. Look no further than our cities and the ways of connecting people between them. Exploiting causes have been the key motivators for advancement through all time. There's little surprise we spend most of our time within their influences, reproducing and foretelling their inevitabilities. But events depend upon agents in a particular space that are, or are not, motivated by a range of preparation, the most cogent evidence of intention.

"Life is immaculate design separate from our best explanations where rationality encounters arbitrariness of relations where things bump up and are pulled apart from each other. Our abstractions can be useful explaining what is real even as far as they are from it but unhelpful when mistaken for it. Natural orders are textured by forces and their environment and full of variation in when and where things interact and, importantly, how they do. Understanding and revealing those details answer the whys of life."

"You succeeded in losing me," Jay said.

"He loses many primed for leftover fanciful spandrels. You don't appreciate your advantage. Regardless of one's predilections, all great minds require effort to understand them and don't presume their audience outsources responsibility to think to them.

"In short, the process is the thing, or ordering of various things in varying settings under intentional and arbitrary forces acting at small and large scales."

"I might be reading way too much into this, but you're saying a BYU Professor is saying there's not one true or necessary meaning, pretty much the same as saying there is no God, which is pretty rich coming from the Lord's university," Laura said.

"He doesn't believe they are equivalents, but your inference jumps us to a new topic where astute readers like you drew the same conclusion. The Professor points out, likely to preempt your very contention, in an engrossing endnote, the Old Testament is an example of the facts. Israel certainly attests to necessary promises, all measuring the strength of their effusive imaginations. But when you break down what happened you have experiences of agents and their relations in particular places. The evidence is of the design of life, the struggles and corresponding consequences that are often not Israel's best-laid plans but rather unpredictable and often unsatisfying events. No question they have definite effects but if the Old Testament clearly evinces one thing, not necessary ones. Apologists saying things must have happened how they did are the equivalent to secular doctrinaires with their set designs and fixed terms making indistinguishable game theory from providence. Members of team satisfied who have given up for lack of curiosity, investments they can't unwind, or beholden to fashionable ignorance masked by smug arrogance. While driven by clear purposes Israel has no final end yet they continuously strive for one, with a few drips of jest, and a whole lot of, even endless, patience. The Old Testament reveals a God of relation, and to your point Laura is not the leading consensus of the concept of God, but certainly a textual one and, irregardless of theological discursions, he cheekily invects, has contributed as mightily as anything has to the development and maintenance of our humanity. In a related compelling endnote, he explains the patterns we can discover in the Bible are as majestic as are divine the declarations surrounding them.

"I haven't mentioned his chapter on patterns and the corresponding endnotes on proteins and molecules and cells because some things should be experienced for themselves. After reading them you'll never see how things develop, or fold, the same again. His explications of emergence and organization and purpose are equal parts thorough and illuminating. No three realities are more significant or are as interconnected or face a greater threat. One commentator noted he created as complete a picture of the development of life in that chapter and endnotes as ever has been."

Was payin close attention and not cause I started understandin Bruce. Couldn't make heads nor tails bout a goddamned thing he said but didn't miss he believed folks built requirements into real life. What seemed to make perfect sense before Bruce's oration didn't seem right more I listened. I was damned sure didn't get it and would ask Roper when I seen him.

"Our realities, all humans in all cultures in all times have been an accumulation of processes, both in linear time, one birthday to the next, and as significantly in real synchronic time, a fancy way of saying not bound by chronology, when our minds produce them as they happen and reproduce them on reflection. The time we internalize has malleable orders. But with effort we capture objective time in the external natural world by accessing mechanisms in the past and forecasting them in the future. While unique in our manifestations, we're all essentially the same chemical components, experiencing the same real world in different cultures that don't solely form our unique expressions any more than they wholly reduce us to them, unless we give up on gaining access to them and beyond. All this doesn't mean there hasn't been firsts or what the ancients called efficient causes. There certainly has and more importantly are.

"While there's a stark absence of explanation for the philosophical context about logic's role in the digital world we now live in in the endnotes, the chapter on our current situation is one of the most foreboding, showing humans' success at programing has severe consequences. Programing first and foremost means specific inputs for specific outputs where instructions are carried out by processors that get more powerful each year with the evolution of gaming. The best instructions are algorithms that reduce many steps into a single rule with repeated application that can fix our conceptions at the risk of stunting development for each next generation. Their ubiquitous presence increases the density of current understanding, making expansion more improbable. Of course their applications presume good faith for the advancement of wellbeing, but human behavior and incentives driving them have always shown facts to the contrary. That unequivocal truth is sufficient to warrant a blinking red alert on their effects and deserves a tome on human nature about developing and maintaining a matured morality from the Professor or his peer."

"Be open to possibility then." Jay said.

"Yes, and we also must be vigilant and always committed to updating our best ideas and take affirmative and often unpopular steps to ensure the possible remains open when developing the systems governing our lives. We must be cautious when interpreting and translating and delivering information into our best abstract thinking that creates our realities, both psychological and physical. How abstractions function will forever demand our focus. Whether we meet such demand will depend upon our best efforts, but in the first instance we ought to consider whether we even can, the diminishing ability being the focus of the Professor's concern.

"One of my favorite examples of responsible stewardship that the Professor gives is many scientists design their own programs to ensure models will construct their conception of ideas and trace actual data, while accounting for all of what they don't know to encourage efforts to eventually discover it. They know no matter how precise and persuasive formulas and their applications, they are only as good as the best technology and available valid data and therefore have a temporal feature to their accuracy, a holding function for which is a defining feature shared by each great contribution.

"Scientific triumphs have been effectual and show even more the need to continue to explore. No groups appreciate how much we don't know in light of what we do more than quantum physicists and astrophysicists investigating mesons and quasars. Tracking the process, pinpointing a source, and memorializing facts capture a fraction of the heights we can build to. One ought to remain cautious not to find endless patterns because we can in data not based on evidence, elevate limitless expressions on our universal platforms for something more than the popular they are, and mistake complexity for potentiality or the inertia to superficiality could be irreversible.

"Many great minds strive to emulate reality. Beyond the voluminous programs fulfilling our contemporary purpose for twenty-four-hour entertainment, critical projects, none more than the tedium of neural and genome mapping, advance beyond our wildest dreams explaining our selves and as a consequence our world with promise to improve both. But even the best of those efforts has practical and commercial ceilings that the evidence indisputably shows lower as wellbeing increases, one of the Professor's most uncontroversial points."

"Then we have a new real," Jay said.

"Yes, precisely and as long as we're clear it is something other than the depths of what we call humanity has been swimming in and appreciate at what cost, which becomes impossible left with no ability to appreciate what's lost."

Bruce carried on and on and on some more. He talked bout how immediate networks was becomin and positive changes he called innovations. He said sensors trackin the external world and our internal nervous systems could advance human exploration and declared medical technologies could save the modern economy. He sounded like a TV man bout better health we'd all enjoy at far less cost if we'd order right now.

"The goal of real time symmetry is noble in understanding the world and our selves, universes themselves yet to be discovered. What isn't far off, in fact, tomorrow, is the shackling from what we could learn. Advancements to understand nature is a worthy goal, but to change that same nature a likely end to it. Take an outfielder fielding a fly ball. No enhancements to react in real time will improve the internal system running a ball down. And intending for a technology to make something possible for an internal system otherwise incapable or more dangerous replacing the development of a system that can will create new beings, not better ones. Please take the next exit."

The old Ford turned off the freeway and slowed on the off-ramp and headed for a Maverick gas station.

Bruce offered a round a thanks climbin out a the king cab.

Caught out a my eye Jay grabbin the kid. "Damn I like Bruce." He turned back. "We good on time?"

CHAPTER 8

Light come through glass doors into the hall and bounced off blue walls and white linoleum squares. Moldin set in places on the floor but bare in most others with none on door frames.

An old timer eyed us over. He wore a red sweater and green corduroy pants crumpled over blue frayin loafers and shuffled away, bumpin against the wall. His walker's aluminum legs clacked and rose and clacked. They slid a couple inches and clacked forward, and the old timer bout said somethin.

"Good morning," Laura said.

He squinted tighter and set his head back and clacked on.

A hoist blocked the way beyond. Thin cables swayed back and forth by two old timers in wheelchairs. Their heads bowed low toward each other. An empty chair with an oxygen tank on back butted into the hallway.

A wave a human flesh washed over us. I never knowed whether old folks didn't use deodorants or they just wasn't strong enough. I also never knowed if formaldehyde covered up or smelled like em. We couldn't mistaken we was some place else. My father talked bout death comin like French Fries with supper. But the thought didn't seem no righter makin are way down the hall. Sayin you expected somethin aint sayin you wanted it. No drive-through on yur way to the late movie. Was eleven fifty-nine. Time that counted Roper would say.

A door opened and nother old man, older lookin'n the first one, tapped his feet, makin sure a ground still under him. Laura paused and all halted for room enough to pass.

"Can't be late for sacrament. The deacons are coming. The deacons are coming," he said.

He hopped between taps up to the old timers sittin real quiet in their wheelchairs and patted one's head.

Jay come on a door with a large wreath pinned in middle. Vines twisted round each other and white flowers sprouted out. He knocked.

"Please come in," a soft voice said, you only heard if you was lookin for.

Jay entered with Laura and me a foot behind.

"Oh Jay, what a lovely surprise," Grammie said. "And you brought a friend. My dear, Dean too."

She melted in a small padded chair. Her neck crooked, seein with her left eye. Jay bent and outstretched his arms in the gentlest a bear hugs. Grammie's thin arms reached for his sides. They fell and reached again, shakin with patches a dried bloodstains from her wrist to her bicep below a loose blue nightgown.

She weathered lots a livin under her pointed collar bones. I broke mine twice in two different places and felt for both spots under my mother's buckskin jacket.

Grammie waved me over. Knelt on my good knee. She hugged my neck and pulled me and kissed my cheek. If light as a feather had true meanin did right then. She released me, her eyes glowin. Jay didn't move from her side, and she grabbed his hand, not lettin go for nothin.

"So much like your mother." She reached the sleeve a my mother's buckskin jacket and squeezed. "How is your father?"

"He's the same as always Grammie."

"There wasn't anything anyone could do for your dear brother." She eyed me straight. "What is this?" Her hand shook and middle finger pointed inches from my forehead. "Not a horn I hope."

"Wrong door." Pulled off the bandage.

"Oh Dean." She patted my mother's buckskin jacket.

I knowed not right and failed my no-good brother after half my liver. But my gut didn't twist for doin nothin hearin Grammie. She gone and asked plenty after my father before and cared only to answer her. The first time she mentioned my mother and not sure heard right she did. I never thought to ask after her. But if someone knowed a her, Grammie did.

"Come in, come in," Grammie said.

The kid froze in the doorframe.

Shuffled over for the wall and rested the whole side a my mother's buckskin jacket against it.

"Come in young man. My such a crowd. There are cold Cokes in the refrigerator. Please help yourselves." Her whole body motioned behind Jay. "Oh, what a wonderful surprise. I couldn't ask for anything more." She held Jay's hand with both a hers. "You need to eat more. What have you been doing?"

"Don't worry yourself Grammie. I'm okay." Jay freed an arm and wrapped Grammie's shoulders.

"Your mother told me you were getting too thin. I didn't believe her. Now how can't I? Take care of yourself, please."

Hell if he didn't get skinnier each time someone noticed. He might fit in my mother's buckskin jacket, pressin against my sore chest. Lowered my shoulder on the wall so wouldn't bother so much.

"You should find someone. We weren't meant to go at this life alone."

"I have lots of friends."

"You know what I mean. Go to Church, and you'll find her there."

"Okay."

My stubby fingers reached an older couple I knowed was Grammie's parents, seventy-six years a marriage, probably not the record in Bingham County but maybe near the top ten. They married as kids out a high school and was together into their nineties. Grammie married for half a century, probably not even in the top thousand in Bingham.

Right by her parents was old black and white photos with young people they mighta been. There was more with family in national and recreational parks and others next to RVs.

Grammie pointed herself out before. The little girl with curly blond hair by a taller girl with long blond hair next to a girl the middle a their heights. All in white Sunday dresses, lined by three boys in suits and ties before a rickety fence with a porch in back over dirt with six steps and no railins between two support beams and an empty rockin chair on the end.

The walls covered in photographs in different frames with pictures organized in rows upon rows and others in circles. One had no borders with pictures on top a each other. Lots a single pictures and classic glamour shots a Grammie's many daughters and sons and a plethora a grandchildren and great-grandchildren beneath em. Roper always keen on describin the results a Mormons engineerin a children in such a way. My eyes blurred takin em in and halted on a swaddled baby in white in a cherry wood crate. The picture just revealed fine trim long the top and bottom and a gold angel with outstretched wings on the end. Coulda been my own.

I wondered then and there if God called me to ride for forgiveness a my sins. Was all his glory I knowed covered in Grammie's memories, more'n one could count.

"I know your family," Grammie said to Laura. Grammie tested for names with no give on her passin. She met everyone who lived in Blackfoot, past and present. Made perfect sense bout my mother.

"Your mother was in our stake when she married. Such a lovely woman." Grammie patted Laura's hand. "And you young man. Come in and tell me who you are."

The kid inched in with cherry patches white as snowflakes and hands shakin bout to drop his cowboy hat.

Jay and me visited Grammie lots, and a couple years ago she moved to Ogden with daughters in Roy and more granddaughters long the Wasatch Front. Some moved from Blackfoot but Jay's mother stayed. She remarried so many times she bout matched her siblins' weddins combined.

"Oh my," Grammie proclaimed and waved her hand with the other still glued on Jay's arm.

A black woman and little girl come right in.

"Sister Tanning. Look who has visitors. Isn't this exciting," the black woman said.

Grammie's shoulders heaved with delight, and she just caught her breath. "This is my great-grandson, Jay, and these are his friends. Come over here Nateijie." Grammie took the little girl's hands in hers. "They're from Blackfoot."

Nateijie hugged Grammie.

"That's awesome." The black woman smiled, eyein round the whole room. "Say hi Nateijie."

"Hi," the little girl said.

The black woman bent low and put her arm round Grammie. "I only got Sister McDaniel's text thirty minutes ago. I'm sorry I didn't see it earlier. She has a couple of sick children this morning. We'll get you ready in a hurry." She turned on the rest a us. "Are all of you joining Sister Tanning for sacrament in the recreational center? She would love your company."

We traced the real old man's steps by the corner into a reception area with two large leather couches and a dozen chairs. Wood legs with swirlin engravins supported each one. A violet and purple and red and orange and two pink with straight backs and solid cushions. They was circled by white plastered walls and below a high ceilin a circular skylight. In the middle set a shiny black piano with a young boy. He chopped keys, and notes blurted in bundles a what I knowed was Mormon songs.

Carmen threatened a piano and woulda pulled the trigger but nowhere for one. The only thing Eloisa and Elena didn't do. My father's sister come from Bountiful to play at my brother's funeral, smack dab in the middle. She stared long before beginnin. And by time she started covered in silence. She sucked in every bit a attention and finished before everyone realized it with her starin straight like she begun. A long name printed in italics on the program, and someone said my brother's favorite. Differentest one ever seen, no desire for beets always potatoes and a number bout a high king a sorts. No one in person could dispute how mighty amazin.

Carmen sent me for my aunt, but she'd went straight back to the promised land. They announced a prepared meal in the cultural hall, a gym with foldin tables. Every time I went for funeral potatoes someone said nother nice thing bout my brother. If not so excited for each helpin woulda called em out. Not one nice thing to say, and every single one knowed it. After nother helpin the bishop come by. He said my aunt's playin stroked the heart strings and rattled the soul. I burst out laughin with potatoes goin everywhere. I rose in a fit, chokin and went for nother helpin before finishin the one I had.

Old people waddled to the front doors with wood frames and double pane glass. Yellow stoppers wedged beneath.

Crawled my stubby fingers long the pure princess pink cloth, restin my head back with my chest calm and the brown Rand on my lap.

A woman took up with Laura. They greeted old people headed out. Some pushed walkers and others was rolled in wheelchairs. A few held poles with an oxygen tank on a platform with wheels. Middle-aged people sided up with em. And everyone in their Sunday best.

A gray suit hung loose on a tall old man, takin short steps next to an even older man in a serious crouch with his white shirt tucked tight round his pear waist. The tall old man held two sets a Mormon books, one in each hand, and his sleeves bunched over em, one black and the other brown. Green leather covered Carmen's.

The tall old man leaned over the older man and said, "We can't have it both ways, and he knew it. He was impudent but most assuredly correct."

"Yes, yes, yes, yes," the older man said.

"And now we bear the collective shame of trying to erase his name." The tall old man looked mad.

"Yes, yes, yes, yes."

Jay pushed a wheelchair with Grammie in a white flowered dress next to the black woman and the little girl, holdin Grammie's hand.

Grammie beamed.

Scooted off the big chair. Rattlin carryin on got me eyein down the hall at an area with round tables and chairs. The old timer in his red sweater and green corduroy pants leaned on his walker toward a closed aluminum curtain and yelled, "Thanksgiving!"

Stems a flowers just out in a row a dirt lined the base a the wall. Beds a flowers flanked the entrance and squares a sod with brown sides and sprinkler tubes sproutin set neat to the sidewalk.

I mistook the buildin cross the street as an indoor arena drivin passed earlier. Aluminum panels at steep pitches bounced the warm sun. Now knowed the old people's recreational center with more old folks'n I ever seen headin there like a river in winter. Some old timers tiptoed and others shuffled. Most held supportin arms, and a few struggled alone. A real old man used a fancy stick with a tripod base conversin with just as old a man with a classic curved wood handle on a stick with single rubber bottom. You couldn't get no older, and they got long on their own accord. A man in a baggy shirt with yellow collars and pit stains and frayed cuffs, coverin

Mormon books in one hand and a single loaf a packaged white bread in the other, took big steps by the real oldest men and all the others.

The buildin opened like an indoor arena but instead a chutes at the end a stage had a podium with foldin chairs and below rows upon rows a white and shiny heads.

A tall thin older woman waved and said, "Sister Tanning." She ushered us into a row with Mormon green song books and papers on are seats. She hugged Grammie and the black woman and the little girl, and she turned for the middle a them rows. Grammie set in the aisle like others in wheelchairs every other row, and then Jay, the black woman and the little girl, the woman friend a Laura's and Laura, me, and last the kid. He put his cowboy hat under his chair. Fit the brown Rand under mine.

An old woman in a dark blue floral gown like Carmen made rose on the stage with an open book in her hand. Her other one shot up and come down real sudden, and a piano hidden from plain view started up.

The old folks sung, "*The spirit of God like a fire is burning, the latter-day glory begins to come forth; the visions and blessings of old are returning.*"

Thumbed through the green song book. The kid handed me his book open to the song they was singin.

The old folks was an army a voices cryin out, "*How blessed the day when the lamb and the lion shall lie down together without any ire.*"

Was Jesus Christ. Not sure most Mormons knowed real Christian meanins. Only God could make such a thing happen and only in heaven. You'd no sooner lay eyes on a bull rider nappin by a bull in a pen behind chutes here on Earth.

My phone buzzed in my front pocket. Nother old woman on the stage went for the podium.

A text come in from Carmen. "The girls are asking if you rode!?!"

The old woman begun prayin, "Thank you Heavenly Father for all thy many blessings, and please bless us and our extended families with thy holy spirit, and please bestow thy spirit on all of the missionaries wherever they might be."

I texted Carmen. "At a Mormon service with Grammie."

Never got to a show early and a few late. I showed before my ride or didn't. They run me in the best just the same, and more'n a few run one they thought would throw me for arrivin when I did.

The woman finished up a skin for the Lord to bless the livin Mormon Prophet and took her seat. A middle-aged bald man took her place. He thanked her, pushin the microphone up. He said somethin I missed, but the kid laughed with the old folks round us.

"Wednesday night we'll continue the decorations for Pioneer Day with the mutual of the seventh and eighth stakes. Even if you haven't been able to attend yet, please join us right here at seven because we have plenty to do and only a few weeks left to do it." The middle-aged bald man raised his hands up and down with each a his words.

I win them rodeos a few times. They was big shows in Ogden and downtown Salt Lake. Bar none the biggest Mormon celebration a the year.

My phone buzzed, and Carmen's text come in. "Tell Grammie hi!"

Up come the first old woman in a dark blue floral gown with a book open in one hand and her free hand high and come down fast, and the piano started right up. The kid offered me his song book.

Waved him off and opened my own to a paper with a list a news. On back a pretty man lay in a woman's lap no more'n his age. Her eyes closed like a face a glass. His slim side had a scar and arm and legs sprawled free. Lines in his arm and leg and the edges a the woman's ruffled dress coulda been real. How someone made em in stone just a plumb miracle.

The song stopped, and the kid bowed his head. On the side a the stage was two boys in white shirts and ties, standin and breakin bread. I knowed what was afoot and closed the song book on the paper. One boy knelt behind a table and said a prayer over the bread in honor a the body a Christ. He finished, and the crowd a old folks sat back in their chairs. A line a boys swung together before the table. They took trays and fanned out among the old folks. A second line stood at the table and got more trays and followed and then a third.

Bull riders in the South rode year-round, but bull riders in the Mountain West only rode indoors in winter. An old stock contractor in Darlinton bucked young bulls in his indoor arena just like we was sittin in but with hard dirt.

I rode more bulls there'n everywhere else, some trips a half-dozen and a few times a dozen. Without no doubt ridin my best and went to every big show, and they run the rankest under me. The one thing a bull rider knowed ride no matter where.

Kids got hurt practicin. No other way to learn ridin. One kid I didn't know real good tried every ride. One day took on a bull with curved Texas longhorns. On the second jump come down real hard and fast on the base. He hung and bounced like a rag doll. One bull rider kept rushin the bull and on his seventh try jumped his back and pulled the kid's arm loose.

Soon as the bull cleared out, boys knelt, touchin the kid with a huge knot on his forehead. Was deep in a dream payin no mind to all their questions. The old contractor pushed us aside and scooped the kid in his arms. One huge dirty hand cupped the kid's shoulder and the other his legs against the old contractor's enormous belly.

A boy appeared at are row and lifted a tray to Grammie. Her shakin hand took a piece a bread. Jay took one, and the tray passed long hands. My stubby fingers grabbed nothin but brown crust and stomach rumbled. Right then knowed was ready. I allowed for lots a things but nothin but an empty stomach. Boys would tell you all kinds a ways to prepare for ridin. Lots believed right in trainin yur reflexes. Reactin in time a must but not enough, but only those who rode lots a bulls knowed. I beat each bull to the jump and with nothin ever in my gut.

Boys cleared all the rows and lined up one after nother in the aisle. Them two at the table stood from behind, and the other boys headed over, givin up their trays. Each took what crumbs was left and backpedaled into three crooked lines. A boy knelt behind the table and prayed over the water as a symbol for the blood a Christ. Boys took trays and fanned out deliverin small paper cups I knowed most a the old folks would shoot. Then someone kicked the brown Rand from under my seat.

CHAPTER 9

Jay lifted Grammie from the wheelchair with her hands flat beside her face on his chest. Her eyes was closed with her white flowered dress flowin over his arm. He stepped by the wheelchair and laid her on the bed. He straightened, and she held his arm and said somethin so soft only he could hear.

Was still early. The kid sent Sam after a stick in the parkin lot. Laura went with her sister from Farminton Jay said. He leaned back against the old Ford with his eyes closed to blue sky.

Milled bout sure a my notions was right. "Gotta ask Grammie after my mother."

Jay shielded his face and opened an eye. "Okay."

Skipped straight back to Grammie's room and stuck my head in. She still lay in her white flowered dress and eyed me like she knowed I'd come.

"Grammie."

"Yes Dean."

Stepped through and closed the door.

"Do you know where my mother is at?"

"Last I heard she was in Phoenix."

Got my window down and fresh air on my face. Felt real good, better'n since my brother died. In my head seen my bull in a chute. The old Ford stopped at a light behind a Lexus, and the idea come I always knowed but never guessed so damned close. Through the intersection we come to the arena grounds and passed rows a trucks. A diesel engine nearby broke up chatter comin off the PA. All got quiet, and a stringy voice begun singin.

"They're playing the great." Jay sung, "*Your cheatin heart will pine some day and crave the love you threw away.*" Long ago in high school he declared it his personal anthem.

The old Ford turned into an open spot. The engine popped under the hood. Breathed in dirt and heat and pushed the door, gratin all the way open. Hobbled to the bed with poppin still comin from the front.

"*When tears come down like fallin rain, you'll toss around and call my name.*" Jay smiled wide and wrapped his arm round the kid's shoulders.

Water pooled under the collar a my mother's buckskin jacket. My neck moved easy side to side without no poppin. Dropped the tailgate and pushed myself up and fetched the brown lined gear bag with sun stained cover and drug to the edge and slid down. Got the handles over my arms onto my shoulders.

We passed between vehicles and stepped with folks headed for a gate.

"Excuse me," a man said on a stool behind folks movin between us in both directions.

"We're up today old Pard," Jay said.

"Didn't recognize you at first Dean. Who'd you draw?"

"We're about to find out."

No smells was more familiar'n dirt and perspirin bulls. Roper said dirt weren't just dirt but varied in nutrients, makin Bingham unique and some other county its own. And no bulls' scents was the same with differences far beyond a regular man's power. Where he got his notions I couldn't tell but one a kind perspirin sounded so damned outlandish I couldn't forget. Closed my eyes and breathed in hides we coulda been walkin by. Bits a conversations passed and boys stopped, sayin hello, and old hands tipped their cowboy hats.

Fans packed in the place, fillin the grandstand on the far side a the arena and bleachers above chutes with boys standin and riders bouncin on every patch a dirt. People jammed in behind riders and everywhere else.

Gear bags packed long the fence and bull ropes the top rail. Dropped my gear bag and brushed water from my hands and on my mother's buckskin jacket. Knelt and worked the industrial zipper but caught halfway. Jimmied up and down for half a minute. Reached in and pulled out the Brazilian. My stubby fingers glided long braided weaves and gripped and stretched em.

No open slit between ropes and tied the tail over two others and crossed over itself and under the rail and back through. Adjusted the handle up and let the new wear strip hang and took the body and stepped back into a pack a boys stumblin into each other. Grabbed and brought the end over my holt and tied a knot. Laid the end over the knot and pulled strands down for the loop. No need straightin with plenty room for a solid bull and flat like nothin more natural. Knelt on both knees and untied my old bell and groped for rosin.

"Dean Stamper," someone said.

Boots gathered round, so many there weren't no space.

"Who'd you draw?" someone else asked.

"Didn't know you had," someone else said.

"Well all be," one I knowed said, shufflin through the others.

If I disliked someone more I never met him in person. Roper called him my nemesis, whatever in God's name that meant. A three-time world champ from St. George. Was sticky but never knowed someone to ride as many spinners in the gate. The luckiest draw ever. I never seen him ride a rank bull or knowed someone with more excuses every time he didn't.

"What do you know. The arrogunest son of a bitch you'll ever see," he said.

"Hah! It ain't if you can do it," someone said.

"That there is the ridingest son of a bitch of all," someone else said. "Present company included!"

Voices jarred back and forth over top me. Water run down my back and sides. Pocketed my glove and pushed by a couple boys to the Brazilian. More bodies surrounded me and more repeatin my name with more questions and declarations. Boys bore witness to my rides they seen and those I'm sure they didn't.

"Make way," Jay said.

He pushed through boys with the kid and a line a starched cowboy hats on their heels.

"They have a proposition for you." Jay smiled and moved aside for a small pretty older woman in a red velvet cowboy hat. The crowd balled up, and fans hung over bleachers for a look-see.

"Dean, I'm Gina Anderson. I'm producing today's show. It's very nice to finally meet you," she said, extendin her hand.

Took her little hand and eyed her small face with freckles under each eye.

"When Jennifer told me she called you, she was convinced you intended to show but said the line cut off before you said you would, and then she couldn't reach you again. And when your friends came to the office and announced you were here, well, my heart about burst. I couldn't believe it. And I still can't with you right in front of me. But we couldn't be more excited to have you, and you know."

"Ladies and Gentleman," a voice come over the PA. An unmistakable deep voice every rodeo fan knowed like his own father's. None more famous. The woman and whole group turned toward the booth, a strong rock's throw above the chutes. "We've been as curious about the activity behind the chutes the past few minutes as you have," Bob Tallman said.

"You said it," a voice I recalled said. Steady as Tallman's but faster, a few beats shy an auctioneer's. Couldn't see him but sure Bob Feist rode somewhere on the far side a the arena, his horse walkin back and forth long the stands, dense with fans wide as the Hoover Dam.

"Ogden, we're on the edge of our seats. We learned one of the greatest bull riders we've ever seen showed up this afternoon. Ladies and Gentlemen I didn't believe the reports when I first heard them, but now I'm seeing with my own eyes Dean Stamper has arrived," Tallman said.

People in the stands stood and broke out with applause and carried on like I just win the world.

"Now Bob," Feist said between all the hollerin. "Every bull riding and rodeo fan thinks one thing at hearing the name Stamper. Let's run in the rankest in the pen."

The crowd broke out in louder cheers.

Got the Brazilian tight.

Tallman said, "Are you thinking what I'm thinking Bob? Because the rankest bull ever is in today's pen."

The crowd drowned out what else they said.

The small pretty older woman in a red velvet cowboy hat stood on the toes a her boots and yelled over the commotion, "Dean, I was saying, you know we did this event to showcase Bushwacker before he retired, and until you arrived we could get only one very reluctant taker. I can't imagine anyone more excited than me about you coming out of retirement today but expect he is. Naturally we want to give you Bushwacker. We'll call it a battle of champions."

Nodded and turned back to the Brazilian. Put my glove on and crushed rosin in the tail. Stroked the strip hot and flexed my hand till my stubby fingers peeled themselves free. Got more in my palm and twisted over and under the handle a dozen times.

The Brazilian fell against the fence, hangin in the sun. Rolled my glove, breathin deep and not feelin my muscles. Water dripped from the sleeves a my mother's buckskin jacket.

Cowboys in all colors a shirts made way. Someone told me to stick it on and echoed on others.

Heat bore down on the brown Rand, and light smelled comin off. Climbed a panel where pens spread with bulls in em.

A hand pushed three into a pen and jogged and grabbed the gate and swung behind em. He headed for a bucket a water and poured through the fence into a small trough. Cowboys climbed fence on my sides, and the hand looked are way and pointed at the far end.

"See him bellied next to the fence?" the kid asked.
Jay pushed a couple boys aside and climbed up.
"He's fat," Jay said.
"He can still buck."
"He better."

The hand climbed up on the other side and said, "Keep up with him to his second jump where you know he breaks as quick and strong as any bull. He could go away from your hand or as easy into it. Wouldn't hurt to lead him that way. No matter which way, his first turn will be a big one." He looked down the line a boys and back. "Ride him." He dropped off the fence.

He stole shade from a trailer with no care in all the world. His eyes set straight with white patches over em and down the side a his left one, payin no mind to all them boys lookin on.

I couldn't recollect not ridin a bull into my hand but buckin off a few away and most a my famous rides was away when my biggest moves covered em, same ones other times set me off.

The Bobs had lots in common beyond them voices, witnessin lots a bull ridin. They discussed their memories a my rides they seen or heard tell, claimin everyone surely knowed I rode Jim Jam at Denver and Little Yellow Jacket the first time at Houston and the second time at Kansas City. Yellow Jacket spun so fast people reported all a blur. They gone on even regular citizens probably seen me ride Dillinger at Oklahoma City durin his second run as bull a the year and Mosey Oak Mudslinger at Greensboro and Bones at Nashville before they was. One old timer told me after ridin Dillinger made no sense limitin a ride to a hundred, havin witnessed it with his own eyes. Talk steered to dominance a bulls. None more unrideable'n Bushwacker.

"Bob, some of rodeo's best fans live here in Utah, and the show here later this month is one of the biggest in the business and has been for years. It's only right the great bull riding fans of this great state would see Bushwacker on his final tour. Let me tell you getting him here took moving heaven and earth," Tallman said.

"Probably would have been easier to lift Ogden over the Wasatch Front," Feist said.

"Couldn't have said it any truer myself. Today is the first of its kind any of us in the business know of, Bob. Today is Utah's first show on Sunday."

The crowd broke out in applause.

"You certainly would not know by looking around the arena where there is not an empty seat, but there was a lot of concern people would turn out. The single most important point the organizers stressed since the idea took hold over a year ago and the organizers continued to emphasize until opening the gates today, is this show was to honor bull riding fans and in no way disrespect the Mormon religion. Ladies and Gentlemen, they took a lot of risks to bring you today's show. For one single but monumental reason being to get Bushwacker here, the Michael Jordan and Tom Brady of bull riding, and this Sunday was literally the only day that worked. Let the show's organizers know how much you appreciate their efforts."

Fans stood and cheered with poundin applause Grammie coulda heard cross town.

"And then who shows up? If a matchup bull riding fans have dreamed of for years, this is the one. Stamper versus Bushwacker."

Fans broke out hollerin and whistlin even louder'n before. A madness overtook em, and there didn't seem to be no stoppin.

"Couldn't have written it any better."

Jay dropped to the ground and said, "They asked us if they should run you in the beginning, middle, or end. I told them didn't matter when, you'd ride him. They picked middle, and there's plenty a time for a drink."

He declared left Budweisers in the old Ford. Folks was full a smiles at the office, and one a the girls offered me a cold bottle a water. Passed by peoples' rides back to the old Ford, and Jay pulled the tailgate. Backed up and hopped on. Sam jumped between us. Poured water in my palm, and Sam lapped up.

Ogden resembled rodeo's version a old-time religion with Patsy Cline and Loretta Lynn between rides. Jay explained the real Gene Autry to the kid.

A couple trucks down and one over a saddled blue Roan had reins tied to a trailer. She whinnied and expected Feist would trade out his ride for her. Hell if she could push bulls. She looked roughly Arabian. Roper's father owned a strawberry Roan the girls rode on most second Saturdays when Carmen took the girls to his place. Eloisa rode the past two years and Elena started in the spring. Roper's father loved havin em out. He moved healthier when they was. I reckon he seen himself as nother grandfather. He had a couple Quarter Horses I rode round his property. My father favored Quarter Horses at are spread growin up. No exotic history but bred to work he always said. We spent entire Saturdays catchin horses, ridin em, and dressin em down, and Carmen insisted are next property would include a barn and a few acres for the girls to care for horses all their own. She started lookin in Riverton. I suggested a place in Wapello.

My brother and me rode since my memories a bein alive. We started ridin bareback and never stopped till we moved to Riverside with only a backyard and my father sold are horses and give away a couple he couldn't. I didn't mind a bit not havin to feed every day. My brother did. The topic drewed a storm over the place. One a the wrongs he never forgive are father. He kept a Palomino mare at Hamilton's ranch in Riverton till he got a place a his own. And Roper's father went and got a Palomino mare a his own. She shared the same spirit as my brother. If I didn't know no better, like he become her. True as a day went long felt no guilt ridin with no mixed feelins bout her. The girls loved seein me grab mane and swing myself up, sprintin in Roper's father's three hundred and twenty acres with forty in hay direct off the corrals.

Tallman announced the break between sections. Hank Williams come over the speakers again. Not an ache nowhere in me and jumped off the tailgate.

Pushed back through one person and nother and got to my gear bag. Crouched and felt through my stuff till pullin my old shirt and ridin pants and boots.

Took off my mother's buckskin jacket and folded the arms with fringe tucked in and rolled against my stomach from the top down and set on my gear bag. A cool breeze passed through my shirt on my wet skin and dark patches stuck.

Kicked off my boots and dropped my Wranglers and balled em up and into my bag. Pulled on my ridin pants real tight and took off my shirt and them crumpled bandages dropped on dirt and buttoned up my old shirt.

Tucked the ends and sucked in my stomach and got the top button in and let out my belly pushin over the waist and smelled Whiskey Creek from my last ride.

Got on old Justin boots and run strips a an old roll a tape round the middle a one boot and tore off and did the other. Put the roll in my pocket. Took my brother's spurs out a pockets a my mother's buckskin jacket. Run the rowels over my thighs, just set enough to grab aholt with. Latched one on my heel and pulled up and did the other with em bent in.

Held before me the old vest with patches a sponsors. A Dubois whiskey folded not long after gettin started and rental car every rider wanted back in the day. Covered my costs for my last five years. Grabbed the collar and slung over my shoulders. Velcro didn't hold and hung open. Sucked in my gut and Velcro stuck. Exhaled and come undone.

The kid spun on his heels into a bunch a boys. Cowboys stared like at a statue in a museum. Everyone shoulder to shoulder, waitin for bulls and watched like I made British royalty. Patted my belly and rested my hands and thought bout noddin round to all em. People hanged over bleachers, anglin for a look. Sucked in again and tried the Velcro. Didn't stick again.

Dropped the vest and grabbed the belt a my faded-white chaps with dark blue trim long the edges with white fringes worn in places and torn in others. At bottom was red patches a potatoes with Idaho Potatoes spelled over em in fancy script. The farmer's state association proved my loyalist sponsor.

"Here," the kid said, breakin through boys still fixed, starin in place. He handed me a thin white vest with no patches. Slung over my shoulders and Velcro stuck.

A buzzin come from the gear bag. Set aside my mother's buckskin jacket and pulled my phone from my Wranglers. A text from Carmen. "Lena asked for a picture of your bull!" Then nother text appeared. "Lisa wants one of all the people." Put the phone in my front pocket.

A bull run down the chutes and others followed. Riders went to find theirs. More a rodeo's old-time religion played over speakers, and the Bobs broke in.

The kid's face glowed with news a my chute. Untied the Brazilian and rolled in a couple big loops with the bell in one hand. No seein the ground on the heels a the kid, passin through cowboys. He stopped sudden. Bulled over him with my free arm. Boys fell into each other round us. A black bull with all white face reared in a chute with a rider. Cowboys jumped off the chute onto people. The rider bailed off the other side. The bull hung his front hooves over the chute and flung his head back, sprayin snot over everyone a us. One boy still on the panel shuffled nearer and lifted his leg over the rung and pushed against his hump. He swatted his horn back, snappin the boy's leg and knockin him down. He took nother look and sprayed the rest a his snot over us and slid his hooves off the rung. A cowboy throwed a rope over his head and one tied through the top rung. Me and the kid pushed through the crowd, holdin up the felled boy, wailin to be set down.

The kid found my chute with a couple boys in are way. Pushed em aside. His patched eyes watched through the bars. Got over top and set my boots in the rails and dropped the Brazilian to his side. Set my knees on him, and his back bulged like concrete and fixed my eyes on the crest between his shoulders and let down my legs, leanin cocked with my hand and arm on a rail. Was warm and didn't shiver. The kid hooked the Brazilian and worked his hands between rungs. Grabbed and run through the loop and dropped it. Got back up the rails and leaned down and set the handle and in the rosin a the tail and tied on.

Ready to call for him. Wantin nothin else. Go where he wanted to go. No one rode where he started. You gotta move. What people said I did so good nothin come more natural. Got up the bull and when needed against him. What looked easy was keepin my head and body in line. Not somethin I thought on. Just did. My problems come the same as other riders overcommittin or gettin caught behind from a break in concentration. Just lots rarer.

Got over the top rail. The kid stood below. Pointed right next to me and pushed a boy off. The kid jumped right up and gazed at Bushwacker and back at me and back to Bushwacker.

Every inch a me got to hoopin and hollerin.

Took out my phone and flipped the cover. Quit bobbin and held over Bushwacker and hit the button and checked and sure enough got him chute and all. Pointed cross the arena at stands packed a fans and took nother and checked and flipped the cover back. Handed over to the kid. Pulled my glove from my pocket and put on. Run the old roll a tape tight round and tossed it empty.

Rides started and didn't see a one. Only seen him ready as me. Thoughts run through kickin straight and turnin back left and jumpin high and breakin right. And every jump right there over the Brazilian. Didn't think nother thing and climbed back over the top rung before the chute boss told me.

Let my legs down his sides and pulled my chaps up. Felt him breathe and tighten. Pushed my legs and leaned on a rail and untied the tail. Looked up for the kid, and he still stood starin. Waved him over to the other side. A voice said get out the way and Jay climbed up and grabbed the back a the vest. Stroked the handle back and forth quick. The kid held the Brazilian tight. Reached cross my body and stroked fast and hard till hot. Set in the handle and nodded for the kid to pull. Nodded again. Jay's arm reached cross and grabbed low on the Brazilian. Took the tail tight and laid on and wrapped round my hand and pushed the end cross his back. Slid up on my hand and nodded quick.

The gate swung and he went and pushed over. He dropped and kicked and pulled up before his hooves hit dirt. He exploded off all fours and got over. He hit and bounced and rolled away from his head and reached where we was. He kissed dirt and kicked and pulled and he reared and pushed up. He dropped and broke right and my leg and shoulder followed and pulled to meet his back. And he reared and rolled right. Shouts and screams blasted through my spine into his. He kicked and broke away from my hand and rolled ahead and hit and bounced and lost my holts. He kicked and my boots walked on sky with the buzzer drowned out by roars a the crowd. Dirt come on with his hoof passin.

CHAPTER 10

A clod with one ridge below nother and mini ones between set in front a my eye. Tried breathin. My nose cracked and dirt scratched my eye. Spit a damned rock. Sucked for air and tasted dirt. Got my tongue clearin some off my teeth. Sipped in more, and the clod stuck.

Noises from far off come toward me. They got round me, and all went quiet.

Hands set my neck on fire.

And nothin.

A shadow covered up the clod.

"Dean," a voice said.

"Dean," nother said. Reached and wiped my eye and neck burned.

"Be still! Just be still!" a voice yelled.

They kept sayin somethin.

Pushed away and sipped more air.

"Just lay still," someone said.

My arms and legs come under me and shock swallowed me whole. Hands grabbed under my arms. Rested on my hams and things went quiet.

Noise irrupted like ash from Mount Saint Helens. Ms. Dakota showed us a picture in second grade at Stalker Elementary, handin round large glossy photographs when we settled on are seats after recess playin kickball. Got on every bit a my body from my stubby fingers to my toes. Things went bright and spots faded and the damned noise increased.

A guy on my arm shouted, "Sturdy now. You're doing great." My boots set on dirt and neck burned more and all down my back. Dark specks a light covered everything.

"Keep your eyes open," a woman said.

The man and woman continued sayin see straight and passed through a gate into a posse yellin at us. Got through em to a bright yellow wall with red bands. The woman on my arm spun me round, and my head bumped off a sturdy latch. Was like a stick a wood and wondered after the brown Rand. Turned to find out and my neck set on fire and knuckled a plastic brace. And nothin below my nose.

"Keep your eyes open. Stay here please," the woman said and squeezed my arm. My forehead pounded and fire run from the back a my head through my left shoulder.

"You shouldn't have gotten up." The woman knelt at my boots. "You should have waited like we asked. Not a wise decision."

"Great ride Dean," someone said.

"Amazing ride Dean," someone else said.

Others shouted congratulations from a large group a cowboy hats. I swore a pimple-face kid in front held the brown Rand and had a mind a gettin his attention soon as this woman shoved off.

"Dean," a small pretty older woman in a red velvet cowboy hat said. She looked like the older version a one girl I went with in Texas and one in Mississippi even longer ago. "Dean," she said again like I didn't hear the first time but with a smile cross her face. "Absolutely fantastic ride! My are we all relieved you are okay."

"Great," a man shouted, squattin at my boots. "You can hear now?"

"Expect everyone can," I said funny with a flat buzz, tastin dirt and tryin to say more and stopped.

"Frickin awesome!" someone said from behind the man, risin in my face.

"I'll be damned if it wasn't the best ride ever!" someone else said.

"Please quiet down for the last time," the man said at them boys and bent in my face with his hands on his knees. "Concentrate on me. You look good, much better. Keep your eyes on me. Can you do that? That's a nice shiner on your head. Now listen real close. This is very important. You are going to need to keep your eyes open for a long time, at least for the next forty-eight hours. Can you do that? No falling asleep."

"Can you grab my Wranglers?"

"What?" He turned to the small pretty older woman in a red velvet cowboy hat and back at me. "Now listen closely to me. At a minimum you've suffered a serious concussion. Fortunately you didn't appear to be knocked out very long."

"Got my bell rung."

People laughed behind him.

"Probably ain't his first time," someone said and more laughed.

Untied the belt a my chaps and undid the top button a my ridin pants. One hundred times better.

"You are staying with us now. You were in and out. We had no idea you were going to move, and then you got to your knees. You didn't look like you'd move an inch further for some time and fortunately we could stablize your neck." The man shook his head. "And then you suddenly stood. Absolutely crazy decision."

"What?"

"You were in and out of consciousness. Acknowledging us one second and not the next. We're not out of the woods." The man reset his hands on his knees. "We're going to transport you to the hospital to run tests."

"No." Reached to undo the straps a my chaps, and the woman stopped my hand.

"We have to take you to the hospital as a precaution."

"No."

"You've suffered a serious fall on your head, you have a huge bruise forming, and your nose appears to be broken. It was absurd to get to your feet. You've very possibly sustained more than a concussion. You could have fractured your cervical spine. Or there could be internal bleeding on your brain."

He shifted, and his mouth vanished but still shouted his commands. He sounded awful perturbed with water pourin down his plump neck.

"It's necessary to run x-rays to confirm you didn't though." He rose up. "You have to go the hospital."

"Please Dean," the small pretty older woman in a red velvet cowboy hat said. She foldded her arms at the man's side.

"This isn't negotiable," the man said.

"Now yur right," I said.

"You could be a slight movement from severing your spinal cord and never walking again. We have a professional obligation to get you the care you need."

"And we'd be failing you not getting you the help you need. If cost is the concern, we'll cover every last cent. I promise," the small pretty older woman in a red velvet cowboy hat said.

Tried smilin but couldn't stretch my cheeks. "Grab my Wranglers. And kindly get me a bag a ice."

The same pimple-face kid holdin the brown Rand stepped by the boss man. Reached for the brown Rand, and he handed me my phone.

"She tried earlier, but I couldn't hear the ring," he said.

Flipped the lid. "Hello."

"Wow! I haven't seen it, but I'm getting nonstop texts and calls telling me you made the ride of the century. And then landed on your head. Are you all right now?" Carmen asked.

"Sure."

"Will they take you to the hospital?"

"No need."

"If I may," the man said and grabbed for the phone.

Knocked his head with the phone and fell to the ground.

The man stood straight with his arms crossed. "That's assault. And everyone here are witnesses."

The woman kneelin still at my side picked up the phone and handed it over.

"Pretty crowded."

"Go slow. There isn't a need to rush. Take your time."

"Aimin to."

"Call me soon, and let me know where you are."

"I will."

"Here are the girls."

"Did you get the bull Dad?" Elena asked.

"Sounds like it."

"Okay Dad. Send it to mom."

"Sure will."

"Hi Dad."

"Hi Lisa."

"Good job."

"Don't know yet."

"See you soon."

"Sure will." Closed the phone in one hand. "Would appreciate that bag a ice."

Someone broke through the people, and they all turned to see. Tried myself but couldn't and neck flared up. My stubby fingers run over the plastic brace.

"Whoa." Jay said from somewhere behind the legs a folks.

Sam darted passed everyone into my lap. Batted her high ears and cupped her head to me.

Jay sat Indian style through all them Wranglers. His arms raised high. One man knelt, bracin him.

"Careful there, I'm all right, nothing spilled," Jay said.

A woman moved through folks, and Jay reached for his cowboy hat.

"You okay?" she asked.

"Got weak in the knees when I saw you but didn't lose a drop."

One man put a phone in my face. "How do you feel after conquering the best bull ever?" he asked.

"There aint no conquerin involved, the Lord willin. But I don't rightly recall."

"Granting Jesus his due and all, but that aside, how were you able to do the impossible?"

"That's just it, there aint no separatin God's grace and what happens. That there is yur answer."

A college boy with a note pad brushed by the others. "People are calling it the battle of the old, great champions, and you won. How do you feel?" he asked.

"Better if I landed on my feet."

Folks crowdin round laughed.

"Yes, of course. You must feel something? Like you're on the top of the world?"

"Sore in the chest mostly."

"So you don't feel anything differently? Some might say invincible."

"Someone will always have somethin to say. Write that down in stone kid."

"I mean like you did the unbelievable."

"Can't recollect one way or nother but would just be doin my job."

"Everyone knows Bushwacker. And even with your history we all learned today, I can't expect anyone would have bet on a great bull rider coming out of retirement to ride him. What makes you different than other bull riders?"

"Wanted to."

The college boy took a deep breath. "Of all the legendary bulls talked about today, how did riding Bushwacker compare?"

"Kid, they all bucked in their own way."

"Please give him some room," the small pretty older woman in a red velvet cowboy hat said. I didn't notice her go but come back from thin air steppin by them reporters, peltin me with questions. "Dean, if you won't listen to reason, you really need to take every precaution to seek medical care at your earliest opportunity, so preferably before you go home but most certainly when you get there. If there's one thing you must not do over the next forty-eight hours is fall asleep. Promise me you'll stay awake."

"Sure."

"Excuse me," Jay said, pushin by. "Mam." He smiled, tippin a missin hat to the small pretty older woman in a red velvet cowboy hat. She smiled and turned back into the people. Jay held an orange Gatorade in one hand and Budweisers in his other and handed me one. Tilted my chest back and stopped when my neck lit up and took a sip, washin dirt down. Jay turned and retrieved his cowboy hat from the woman with wide hips and strong thighs who found him on the ground. Jay sat with his knees raised near his chest and clanked his Budweiser against mine. "Pretty a'right ride."

The college boy started back at me. "Isn't she an African Basenji?" he asked.

"English," I said.

"Yes, but she's originally from Africa via some kennel in Britain."

"Good for riling cows mostly. And she yodels," Jay said.

"My uncle owns a couple Basenjis for bird hunting along the mouth of the Snake River on the Oregon and Idaho border."

I knowed nothin bout such things but Sam could fly and expected if I hunted would with me.

The small pretty older woman in a red velvet cowboy hat reappeared again. "As Dean's friend, please promise me you'll look after him."

"He'll be all right in the morning."

"Please."

"Okay."

"Thank you. Dean, if you are up for coming back into the arena, we can present this to you and would mean so much to the fans." She raised a smooth cherry wood box holdin a gold buckle engraved with the head a Bushwacker and a large green stone set on top. "We planned to give it to Julio, but he insisted we give it to you. He said it was the most lustrous buckle he ever lay his eyes on. We'll make another one exactly like it for him."

"That's one highfalutin hitch to belt your pants Pard." Jay reached and took the smooth cherry wood box.

"We'll present it to you whenever you feel up to it, now or after the short go."

Rose and knees went wobbly. The woman still at my side squeezed my arm. She got my chaps off and offered to help through the door to change but all the effort made no sense. She cut tape off my boots and pulled em off. Got my buttons started, and she pulled one leg over my foot and the other leg quicker'n a hunted fox. Then sat in my skivvies, enjoyin the cool seat on my butt.

The pimple-face kid with the brown Rand brought my gear bag, and the woman told me to stand and helped get my Wranglers and boots on. Then she went and put a buckskin jacket on. Jay took the brown Rand from the pimple-face kid and set in its place.

A boy holdin a bag a ice finally showed. Tapped the plastic brace, and the woman sighed. Coulda sworn cussed me an ass under her breath. Her fingers pressed tight and released the plastic brace. She stepped up into the door and returned with a couple bags. She knelt and filled em with ice and placed the larger one on my neck against the buckskin jacket and pulled a roll a turquois medical tape from her back pocket and wrapped under my arm and round my neck and tore clean. She took off the brown Rand without askin and held the smaller bag against my forehead and wrapped the turquois medical tape like a damned crown.

Scratched Sam's ears.

The small pretty older woman in a red velvet cowboy hat walked me back into the arena. The announcers carried on and fans cheered. The small pretty older woman in a red velvet cowboy hat give me the smooth cherry wood box with the gold buckle. Fans hollered with no end in sight. Raised the brown Rand, and water run down my neck and long my spine against the buckskin jacket.

CHAPTER 11

Jay drove the old Ford behind trucks and sedans full a cowboys and cowgirls, and the feelin come a bein here before with Jay at the wheel and Sam at my side like a bee sting on my head and prickly all the way down.

The old Ford passed signs for fast food restaurants and new housin developments and turned into blue condos three stories high with green grass and trimmed bushes long clean walkways. Jay parked near a sign with a sun over waves. Me and Sam followed Jay up steps, and he turned a key into the place.

A huge TV perched on the wall just like in the back a Walmart surrounded by smaller huge TVs. A dog barked from behind a door, and Jay went in. He come out with a pink leash in one hand and one a them mini dogs with a mane a lion's hair in the other.

"Gonna take Elton for a walk and pick up some drinks from the strip mall down the street. Sit on the antique chair there."

Eyed where he pointed, and sure enough an old chair in the corner. A frayed cushion covered the seat. Dropped the brown Rand on the side and sat and shifted over some and the whole thing creaked. Sam settled at the legs. An empty pink cage balanced on the edge a the bed through the door Jay left open.

The apartment set at a cool temp. I didn't need to go all day but did now. My head pulsed stronger but cleared after a couple steps. The hall on the right led to a kitchen. Opened a door full a clothes, bright colors a slacks and blouses. Sam moved through the door Jay left open like she knowed I'd follow.

Horses covered the walls. Three painted, a couple drawn, and lots a photographs and no space between em, posin in corrals, gallopin in pastures, and lots circlin barrels. Carved wood horses covered a dresser with a gold horse in a trot in the middle. Picked it up and felt my neck pull and let go quick and come down hard. I reckoned real. From the old chair in the other room no way to see now what you couldn't miss over the head a the bed. A massive picture cut off. Front legs diggin round a barrel with dirt kicked to top. Lines in muscle run down legs straightenin, and air between a booted stirrup and horse's belly.

Sam waited by an open door into a bathroom with a pink toilet. Not just the lid but the whole damned bowl. Above a mirror set in pink wood. My nose didn't look so good. Pinched soft and hurt. Pushed my Wranglers down and shifted to hit clean the pink bowl and noticed the packs a ice melted. Pulled my Wranglers back up enough to grab my phone and flipped open and couldn't see how close but adjusted till my stream hit water.

"Yep," Jay said.
"Ice melted."
"Okay."

Closed the phone in one hand and slipped out and clanked against the pink bowl. Then a dunk in the water. I seen in my head the cracked screen sink to bottom. Bent down and my stream veered off and steadied and didn't move a feather finishin. Reached for the sidewall but too far off and slid by the pink bowl and braced on the back wall. Knelt with my neck stiff and eyed straight and fished in, coverin the sleeve a the buckskin jacket to my elbow and grabbed aholt.

Rose to my feet and leaned on the wall and started pullin my Wranglers. A pain shot through my whole body and bout fell but bumped up against the wall and held real still, breathin slow with a dull pain in my chest. Stowed my wet phone in the front pocket and pulled my Wranglers the rest a the way. My stubby fingers felt round for the pink handle and flushed with a light bit a water swirlin.

Baby steps got me all the way back to the old chair where Sam rose with the remote in her mouth. Clicked on without the secret order a buttons impossible to recollect at Jesús' house always startin on sports channels. Guys huntin alligators in Louisiana bayous stopped me. Real swamp men whose speech translated on screen for city folks. Men and one woman with extra tags they couldn't fill, and all gunnin for a money prize for hookin the biggest gator. They knowed every marsh and byway. Their motorboats went deeper into tall grass for checkin baits they set sometime before. One after nother fought a tight line, pullin in the boat. The camera slowed just as the gator come up and their partners shot through its head. Some guys carried forty-fives, others had some ought-six, and even a couple with ARs. They celebrated as if them gators was playin long.

The front door opened, and in come the stocky woman who helped Jay get off his butt at the bull ridin. The last team bagged a gator. The woman patted Sam's head and looked at the TV. "Today's producers make some interesting choices."

Jay entered the apartment, holdin the mini lion-dog in one hand against his chest with the pink leash hangin down his waist and a paper bag a groceries in his other hand. His foot shut the door, and the mini lion-dog yapped. The woman took the mini lion-dog from Jay and shushed it quiet.

She turned back with the mini lion-dog eyein me and Sam. "Had us all real worried Dean. Nice to see you flush again."

She moved like a person with somewhere to be. Her strong features fit her steps cross carpet into the bedroom. Jay sat on a couch and set the paper bag at his feet. He pulled a small sack off top and handed it over. He pulled out a bag a ice and twenty-four pack a Budweiser and peeled the cardboard back.

Lifted the small sack to my nose and couldn't smell nothin. Hot food at convenient stores a rare treat. When lucky to have some, Carmen pointed out my unshakeable trail and asked if fast food paradise were worth the enjoyment for everyone else. The only thing she rode me for. I loved taquitos in all their fast food varieties and spent the next hours hustlin through the porch into the backyard to relieve all the gas stealthy as a young brave to avoid the girls' teasin. Carmen fed me and the girls health foods, lots you'd only expect communes in California knowed existed, and some worked my innards and had me beatin the same path out back. I reckoned we'd be long gone from this woman's apartment before I couldn't help myself.

Three crisp sticks. Offered one to Jay, and he shook his head. Took a bite and a shred a beef hung out. Chewed and my throat refused to swallow so chewed more but still couldn't. Kept on chewin and started chokin and spit on my palm and took a small piece back and tried over. Got some down and picked small bits off my hand. My throat closed more and hurt but got nother piece down.

The woman opened her bedroom door in pink sweatpants and a black t-shirt, cradlin the mini lion-dog.

Passed the remote to Jay, and he handed a can over.

He give the remote to the woman, and she stopped surfin on a slim boy in a t-shirt with slender hips surrounded by women at a funny car race in a desert. The scene flashed to more women loungin at a pool and to a girl dancin inside a mansion. The guy said some words bout summer to synthesizer noise Roper always said made him hurl. They flashed back to the race and women in cutoff jeans, helpin a woman into a long car. Lookers, every single one.

"Such unabashed excess. Not even a hint of irony," the woman said. "Over and over these performances are about how real all the success is. While the legislature does everything they can continually struggling to address the actual reality people live in. I stress the actual from fanciful realities almost every day at the capitol. Everyone must be watching the same thing."

Jay scooted over and grabbed nother can. He turned and offered. Lifted the one he give me a few minutes before.

"Not a hint. And when something is ironic these days it is the unexpected, and not only because of the greatest of rockers but people won't do better. Or something is ironic because someone simply ad hoc attests it is."

She hopped off the couch with big black letters spellin pink cross her bottom and went for the kitchen. She come back with bowls a water and dog food. A bag stuffed behind the seat in the old Ford had plenty if hers weren't enough. Sam lapped up water and sniffed and nibbled at the dry, red mini dog bones.

The woman undid the medical tape on the water bags. "These won't do. Do you want to leave your jacket on? I can't count how many times I've seen you in that Rocky Mountain sombrero, and I feel like I'm seeing you for the first time with the buckskin jacket on." She went for the kitchen again.

"Fits don't it," Jay said.

I tried my memory for her but come up short. She hussled back with a handful a freezer bags. She knelt and doubled up and filled em with ice. She tucked two in the buckskin jacket on my neck and put one on my head. "Tape?"

"Some in his gear bag." Jay begun climbin off the couch.

"Don't get up." The woman pushed Jay's shoulder on her way to the bedroom. She come back with pink athletic tape and run under my shoulder on top a them bags. "I'm not going to run this around your head Dean. It's not the fancy hybrid pretape she used at the arena. This is the real thing, and you'll feel it peeling off. Don't move and let the bag sit." She left the role a pink tape on a stand with a pink vase. She took the mini lion-dog from Jay and slid next to him.

Nother video come on with a real fit guy lyin in bed. He sung and danced on an empty stage and got back into bed with nother beautiful woman. Yur classic pop song like Michael Jackson sung. The guy did sit-ups hangin in the doorway and the beautiful woman took a bath.

The bag slipped off my head onto the brown Rand. Kicked it to the side.

The woman went to surfin channels. "Years ago I read this memoir about a young man whose parents died, and he moved to California with his little brother. The climax was the young man going back to his hometown and having sex with a girl he liked in high school. He connected such gruity to his grief, justifying his indifference to her with the modern banal trope of meaninglessness. My partner's daughter was back from college interning at our office this past session, and she recently read the book and raved on about how it spoke to her generation. She had a paperback in her backpack, and I read the introduction that set up the book as ironic. And since then I've seen it referred to as a novel, which is a whole other issue. He must have realized the exaggerated title wasn't enough, but irony is not testimonial. It's part of the subject or not, whether it's limited to language or not. Nothing in this young man's story suggested he was anything other than self-absorbed. If he had done one other-centered act, that would have been ironic. Missing an expectation is a measure of distance, and calling it the opposite a pitiable and disingenuous excuse. Just how much of one depends upon how far. Even scant attention for the young man's brother was merely a reflection of him.

"And God when people do irony it's awful. It's either simplistic sarcasm, cheap, effortless, ready poison in our instant opinion and gossip age, which is so distressing there's no truer mark of the really clever than those who are simply condescending. Or the irony is so heavy-handed it's patently obvious even to the dumbest politician. There are no more satires where the shift or inversion is so startling or subtle to make unavoidable an immediate insight or begin to gestate a new point of view. I wish for more than the witty putdown or grotesque farce not when I hear and see them but every time one of these modern artists claim what is real."

"Maybe they're just having fun," Jay said.

"Sure these hunks are, Jay. But they are selling with no checks and balances to the masses, who most will never have even a glimmer of such fun, wasting their lives wishing for it. And those who wake up will have missed their opportunities. These entertainers have no shame."

I didn't catch the bur under her saddle. Jay sounded like he did. Roper woulda argued with her from the getgo. Not cause he knowed better really but loved to argue.

"I worked with Congressmen and women every day last session who were constantly considering how their constituents would interpret their votes. They have too much shame where ironies are kryptonite! And when they emerge they are devastating. But consequences are the nature of real life. Things turn in different directions from what are expected and can be great teaching moments, which invites development but has been so disparaged to the point of acceptable norms effectively erasing it. So the pieces end up affectations by commentators on the sidelines high on their perches with no reservations when assigning meanings and too put out to do the heavy lifting to track how something led to something else, which tedious accountability is antithetical to the constant repackaging for their sectarian audiences.

"Honestly, my biggest fear is nothing can compete because policies are the real arteries sustaining human lives. And nothing is more effective than shame for manipulating culture to support them. Politicians who don't get it are fools. Those who do are among the few noble ones or great puppeteers, who know their greatest tool is drama and are beside themselves to exploit it."

"Not sure how good I follow," Jay said.

Got damned confused by her notions and knowed didn't catch a lick. Just sure politics and religion not only got offensive between gentle folks but even more a confounded mess. Would be lyin sayin I thought it first. Roper said so and claimed the philosophical approach were best, and he'd get round to embracin it fully when he had enough a livin life.

"They are right to focus on the dramatic because many great lessons for fashioning a shared reality come from it. I always appeal to its value through literature, which I use every other day. My most effective examples are sharing power in *King Lear* and charting shared history in *To The Lighthouse*. They are no doubt a couple of the very, very, best, which make no mistake has a direct correlation to how we can learn from them. Only in the depths do we get their lasting imprints formed during life's harsh storms and insufferable boredoms well before and long after the dramatic moments. Life has natural and unatural orders and can be disagreeable for every person subject to the self-interests of others, where there's no greater act than to reach for one's dignity. And we certainly shouldn't wait until the end of life to do so. And each of us is entangled in the influence of others, which both restrain and enable us to follow our callings. Where situations, both our own and beyond our own making, restrict our actions, and gaining awareness of the cords often only comes, for most of us, through assisted reflection. None of the lessons emerge from the perennial fountain of supposed gaps filled by feigned proclamations.

"The dramatic is intention and consequence, full stop, of rare moments of connection and more common occurrences of divergence. It moves us along the emotional tracks of experience, raging and retreating and remaining complicit with inertia beyond our own power.

"Only exhausted and tried understanding get us to face what truly is for a reckoning and in those rarest of instances transcendence. Our best efforts are needed to understand how one thing actually affects another thing in real life. And only taking the time to identify the actual source can propel us to the depths of true understanding. The essential requirements are sweat stained, forged by undying effort and imprinted by opposition, and so often picked amidst tulip patches of contradictions and never from spaces of leisure in between. There are not viable substitutes to tested principles despite the swift currents of popular trends and quick-to-order truths. And our politics reflect and engender them."

"What are you driving at?" Jay asked.

"What we must move beyond. The cancer is recognizable in attitudes implying a complete perspective and saying something someone said or did really means something else. The audacity to do a person's valuing for her. Standard fare for junior high but is also the key to today's irony, and the surest stopper of a thoughtful conversation and chance of development for the very proclaimer. Pick a recent social issue and what we really know about a person according to someone who disagrees with her view. Otherwise we can't get to where effort is required. Look at the hard, long, and exhausting never ending train of education evolving faster than we can keep up, with no more shiny buttons, and challenges far beyond our immediate perceptions in an expanding ocean of effects beyond most peoples' reach.

"Opinions worth considering, including valid ones to supersede, take slogging through information and not just holding a trump card. Judgment requires experience and is too often thwarted by the emotional gravitas of individual indignation that surfaces to the top, which is the basis for expedient gains feeding the furor of the masses. And is the reason why pundits score by exploiting them by their illusory reductions of what things really mean for someone else. Very few people explain the fluid contexts where real things exist. Instead they embrace the instinctual route to demean and demonize with definitive recitations picked from their camps given understandings. The approach is so successful crowned experts confirm nothing else is possible, and no class is more due for a call to effort. You know what is without a shred of irony, I made more money this session than I have in any other one and didn't get a single bill close to passing. In my seven years lobbying in this state, I have contributed to many bills but only had one pass."

"How do folks go about learning what they need to?" Jay asked.

"Jay knows me pretty well Dean. I'm like one of those dolls with a string on the side, and Jay's always known when to pull to wind me up. Simple to state but extraordinarily hard to do. Among the most important activities are developing sensibilities. Only through refinement of thought and action will awareness sharpen and possibly expand. They must affect belief. So easy to say but so challenging to do. That's why I repeatedly refer to Woolf and Shakespeare. They allow us to see and feel so intimately thoughts and actions and their consequences. I'd also include developing incentives and possibilities to achieve them. And training and jobs, basic civil services, and vision, which must include working to achieve long-term goals and cooperating with others."

"How much did you haul in?" I asked.

"In the six figures, and I saved enough to keep my horses boarded for two winters."

Jay eyed her and then me. "How many you got now? Any you competing on?" He opened nother can.

"Ha, I haven't run barrels in years. We didn't discuss my grand finale last time, but then we didn't talk much." She put her hand on his neck. "Did you see the doctor?"

"This past week."

"Sure you don't want something to eat?"

"Fine now but maybe in a while."

"If you're not feeling well, you can smoke in the alley. There's always a breeze so less chance my neighbors will notice, and even if they did would never suspect me. Probably since you left California. How long were you there?"

"Five years."

"The whole time with Jennifer?"

"First two, but she'd been there a spell before."

"God she was beautiful. Not many rodeo queens went on to make a career of being a swimsuit model."

"I suppose more than we hear tell."

"Maybe, but I'd be surprised. Rodeo girls have real bodies. I've only heard of her becoming one. She went to the right place to be noticed and only minutes from where I went to college. Life isn't as big as we make it out to be. Where were you?"

"The first two years in Santa Monica. The last three in San Bernardino."

"Where Roper invested in his indie movie?" I asked.

"That was San Fernando Valley on the other side of the hills from Hollywood."

"Lost him a bundle he told me but got his name at the end."

"He came over worked up a few times, telling us about the genius director from Hong Kong and amazing cast with a famous young talent playing the protagonist. He told us about every film each of them had been in. When it flopped he insisted the general audience misunderstood the phenomenal acting that was too sublime at critical infliction points for them to appreciate."

"I've only been able to take Roper in small doses. I can only imagine how the film was. So was San Bernardino the car capitol? I heard about big shows while at school but never visited," the woman said.

"San Bernardino Valley at best an hour east of Los Angeles but closer to two or more on a lot of days. Some rough patches. I was closer to Redlands with the original McDonald's. Wouldn't say capitol. Ain't no different than a lot of other cities in California. More like the whole state is a car mecca. There's a big show on the old US Route 66. Still handle deals with a couple guys I met there who show throughout the West. Am picking up a sixty-eight Cougar to test tomorrow in I.F. for one of them with a buyer in Phoenix."

"Will you drive to the owner?"

"Now that would be the way to deliver it. Tow them on my flat deck."

"Where to?"

"Cities across California and Vegas and Phoenix and a few to Missoula."

"Too bad not back to Santa Monica or a city along the coast."

"Been to a few from San Diego to San Jose and over to Sacramento."

"You should have been a race car driver in Nascar."

"Like a course more."

"You should have got yourself in the movies is what you should have done. Sports cars and car chases to your heart's content."

"One party Jen dragged me to in the Hollywood Hills a guy asked me to be in one."

"And you told him no."

"He went on about how great I'd be. Halfway through his pitch, I told him the story sounded silly. Jen wouldn't let it go. Said guys killed to get into his movies and quit taking me to those parties."

"Who was he?"

"Couldn't say if you held up a portrait of his spitting image."

"We'd see them in Malibu near campus, but like everyone else I got to know them through the tabloids. More than one politician has told me living in fantasy land changed my politics, but how I changed wasn't from where but what, so much single-mindedness everywhere."

"When you weren't playing ball or studying."

"What'd you study?" I asked.

"I double majored in economics and theater. I love the production of both disciplines and use my education to frame every piece of legislation to weigh the benefits against the costs in how people will actually experience consequences. I'm one of the lucky ones doing what I love."

Roper and Carmen argued bout what real learnin entailed. Roper said can't happen at college, and Carmen said can't happen without an education. And neither one ever even finished.

"When did you go back to Blackfoot?"

"Going on two years," Jay said.

"For the past few years I've been boarding my horses with partners and friends. Twenty-four of my beautiful children in all, four I'm breeding, three actively competing for girls at the amateur ranks in Utah and Idaho, five on long-term leases with girls running throughout the country, two of them in the PRCA, three I'll start training this fall in Warner's indoor near Plymouth, and two more I'm working with for girls I know in Arizona who aren't running as well on their own horses this summer. Between those two and the eight competing I will be able to cover costs for the others and keep my savings for slower years."

"Sounds like you need yur own place," I said.

Jay didn't say a word and grabbed the woman's leg.

"Yes, I absolutely do, especially with the two babies and five retired I need to see regularly to care for. But I wasn't on the patriarchal ladder and missed out on my father's place. Our ranch and every other one along the Wasatch Front was far more valuable to developers, and that's what my brother who inherited the land has done, cutting up and selling lots. The truth is my father didn't work the land. He enjoyed playing a cowboy more than being one and let the place go so far the investment wasn't worth making it productive again, if it ever was. I have so many memories working my horses on it. I spent so much time in the barn and small enclosed corral in the winter and the arena in the spring and summer, it seemed like every day of the year, except for those on the road competing.

"The winter of my senior year I noticed the barn and corral coming apart. So many days they seem like one with long open fields of snow surrounding the buildings. I rose before dawn to blankets of white, breaking the smooth top to the main garage, still being used unlike the others storing old, broken-down equipment. For all my years growing up we had a hand year-round. He was a genius with machines like Jay. He lived in town but spent a lot of time staying in the main garage between spats with his wife. By my last year in high school we'd stopped most of our operations, and he wasn't needed. And if a couple seemed fated for divorce, they did. But I learned at my father's funeral they didn't. There they were walking through the line to the casket. His face was clean-shaven and stern, and he dressed as sharp as I'd ever seen him with his rope tie and starched white shirt and clean pleated Wranglers. His wife wore a dark blue dress with a white collar and greeted me with a lovely unwavering smile. He wrapped his arms around me, and I could hear his heart beat. He backed up and his strong hands clasped my shoulders, and we shared everything that was gone.

"The main garage had a walled-off breakroom with kitchen that doubled as sleeping quarters with an army cot in the corner. Our hand's wife was an amazing cook, and I grabbed what was leftover while I warmed up before going back out.

"Our barn was a classic Gambrel that Scandinavians built before my grandfather bought the land after two brothers had a falling out and one moved to Idaho. It had a huge hay loft my grandparents used to host dances that coincided with the first crop of hay when I was very young. My father quit putting them on long before my grandparents died. I want my own barn more than anything. A Gable with a dozen stalls and a two bedroom apartment connected on the side. But my dream doesn't stop there. I'll have a covered arena attached to another dozen stalls, each with its own Dutch door and direct access to a hundred acres of pasture.

"I'll never forget our barn in the winter in bitter cold mornings. I freed the latch and pushed one of the breezeway doors enough to slide by, and as fast as I could closed it on the frigid air pouring in. I entered into pitch black, but I didn't need any light knowing every space and repeated the same steps each morning to the tack room.

"I opened the door and breathed in the cold leather and flipped the light switch. Rows of bridles and halters with lead ropes lined the wall. Saddles on stands in the back and blankets lay in stacks on a shelf. I grabbed a soft hairbrush and put the handle in my back pocket and pulled a bridle with a smooth bit and rubbed it between my wool gloves.

"I worked with different horses each day on a routine set on need. I jotted down who I rode and how she was doing in a spiral notebook I kept in the first cubbyhole on the way out. I put the bridle over my shoulder and checked the notebook and picked my first stall.

"She heard me before I opened the door. I grabbed her neck and scratched with my wool gloves down both sides and hugged her. I brushed her back and down her flanks. I pulled the bridle off my shoulder and stroked her nose and led her to the tack room with the familiar perfumes to dress her.

"We made a cold, short walk to an enclosed corral originally built to hold holstein cows before their turn to get milked in an adjacent building that had long been brought to the ground with only cinder blocks left above the foundation. I spent thirty minutes with each horse, most days working with three or four but many mornings half a dozen when I expected a slow day at school. Sunrays broke through the maze of cracks, and the walls and cealing went from dark to light brown with deep breaths rising into light to hooves trotting on the hard ground."

"I can't figure how you found time to do anything but care for them," Jay said.

"The winter demanded a lot of time, especially if one got sick. I'd quarantine her and missed more than one day of school. A couple contracted colic and demanded vigilance and pricey visits by the vet, and there were always a few with needs for super clean stalls."

"How about your recycling project?"

"My best grade at Box Elder High the winter I shredded enough paper for most of the stalls. You'd make a serious mistake thinking cleaning out paper was easier bedding than straw."

"Mucked a few stalls with both. And no time left for ridin. Never." I said.

"There were a lot of days I didn't, but when I did the goal was to work a barrel in the corral. We did drills for ten minutes, and I knew who got what and who didn't and how much work was ahead running a cloverleaf before we got into the arena in the spring. There isn't a day I don't think about beginning my day there."

"How's Patsy getting along?" Jay asked.

All went quiet.

Jay knowed he said the wrong thing and put his arm round the woman. "Sorry Sandra. I really am. I should've known."

She pushed his arm off her shoulder and then pulled it closer. She handed the mini lion-dog to him. "Oh Jay." Her voice gone weak. She started cryin and scooted off the couch and went for the bedroom and closed the door.

I knowed her. People said she'd beat Scamper on his tail end, but she never did like all the others. She had a dominant run in the Wilderness Circuit. I knowed this woman too. She win the barrels most years I went to the circuit finals.

Jay bent over and put a can down and leaned and pulled his flat phone from his pocket. "He's right here," he said and handed over the thing.

"Why aren't you picking up?" Carmen asked.

"Phone broke," I said.

"What timing. Over the past few hours I've been getting a lot of calls and the last one nonstop from people we know wanting to congratulate you and people we don't asking to interview you."

"Tell em all to call back."

"Very funny. How are you feeling?"

"My head is feelin number."

"Are you sitting? Stay sitting as much as you can."

"Moved round some."

"Where are you?"

"Jay's friend's. She rode Patsy in the Wilderness Circuit."

"Is Jay driving back in the morning?"

"Guess is his plan."

"Don't leave too early. Be sure and stay awake."

"Sayin it more aint gonna make it happen."

"Helps though." She paused and fumbled for somethin. "One of the callers asked to buy the rights to your pictures. His name is William H. Cannopy. He said he's a conceptual artist based in Los Angeles."

"What pictures?"

"For the girls. News clips show you taking them, and Mr. Cannopy saw the coverage and wants to buy them for twenty thousand dollars." She paused again like on purpose. "Twenty thousand."

"A fine sum."

"I'm still shocked and wasn't sure I heard him right. I asked him to repeat himself to make sure. How'd you break your phone?"

"Slipped right out my hand."

"I repeatedly drop mine, and it still works."

"Into the john. Aint joshin you Car."

"What luck. We'll try drying it out. Twenty thousand dollars would be enough to put down on a place in Riverton."

"Or Moreland."

"I'll ask Jesús to take your phone to one of his gaming friends who can figure out how to retrieve the pictures. I've been euphoric hearing people say your ride is the best ride ever over and over again. Could it really be the best ride ever?"

"Don't reckon none sayin so seen rides in contention."

"It has a lot of people talking. Be safe, and I'll call Jay's phone later. Stay awake. Love you."

Held up the flat phone and no button to turn off and didn't fold back neither. Jay traded for a new can. He surfed to a movie channel with a small weddin in the old world somewhere near England. Sandra come back to the couch as the new couple started their first day as husband and wife. She held tissues to her eyes and laid on Jay. He set his can down and put the mini lion-dog to his side and placed his right arm round her, holdin her head against his chest with his left hand. "Mr. Yukichi might have room for a couple of your older horses." The young married girl just fun lovin and the husband an upstandin country doctor. She started takin on nicer things in her new house. She wore lots a long dresses and ordered new colorful ones. A local wily shopkeeper took advantage a the young girl's desires for fancy things. She started flirtin with a young lawyer bout her age who left town real sudden, and she took up with a rich nobleman. Sandra got off Jay's lap, and he followed into her bedroom. The girl spent lots a time runnin between the nobleman's place and her place in them long dresses, muddyin em pretty good. Once the rich guy finished with her, she struck up with the young lawyer who moved to a big city. Things heated up, and she went there a fair bit. Then the shopkeeper come to the girl for payment for the long tab she run up. She offered herself, and the old bastard denied her.

Jay opened the bedroom door. "Dean you awake?"
"Yep."

"Thought I heard snoring." He walked into the kitchen and come back with beers and give me one and went back into the bedroom.

The girl got frantic bout debts and run to the nobleman for help who like rich guys do rejected her as used goods. She run to the young lawyer in the city, and he tired a her. Sandra asked if Jay felt all right. Through the slit in the doorway his Wranglers bunched at the end a the bed. "Reach down and grab my chew please. Tired is all." Sandra twisted back runnin her hands through Jay's pockets. Her arm come up and pressed against her small breasts. She found the can and turned back. The girl found some medicine she drunk walkin on the path she traveled durin all her visits. She lay on scattered leaves. The husband and others headed out at dusk after her.

Other channels didn't offer nothin near as captivatin, just movies with big explosions or heroes actin like misbehavin idiot kids. Stopped longer on a fishin channel. Sandra muffled her cries. Surfed for one hour straight. Jay stepped from the bedroom and closed the door. He wore his Wranglers and no shirt. He sat on the floor, crossin his legs and restin his palms on his knees and straightened and didn't fall to one side nor the other. Ten minutes passed with him breathin deep, and he stood and went for beers.

"Trade me the remote," he said and give a cold can and surfed through a bunch a stuff till a sports news channel. "Listen to that." And he turned it up.

"Experts are calling it the best bull ride ever," a man said, wearin a sharp suit and tie with the coat buttoned up and a napkin in the pocket, the type you only get at a fancy restaurant. Behind him on a large screen Bushwacker froze in the air with me in some white vest gettin over him. "Dean Stamper came out of retirement earlier today in Ogden, Utah, to take on arguably the greatest bucking bull of all time, the one and only, Bushwacker. We've run programs on Bushwacker's dominance over his career, but in Ogden, on what is indisputably a holy day for many citizens of the Mormon founded state, Stamper made a whole other history." The TV cut to Bushwacker and me in the chute. A kid jumped down and run long the side, and Jay behind. The gate swung and Bushwacker blew out. He landed and hit a second jump even bigger. He went fast, kicked big, and jumped high. The angle changed, and Bushwacker bounced and then kicked big. I lost my holts straight up and went down on my head.

I knowed what I seen never matched what I experienced but couldn't recollect a lick a what was seein.

"Damn Dean. Was incredible live but looks unbelievable recorded," Jay said.

The camera cut from the crowd on their feet cheerin sudden back to me lyin motionless a few seconds and back to the crowd with faces full a fear. The camera cut back to me with chute hands and paramedics. After some time got to my knees in the middle a the help and more time passed. Then got up. The camera cut back to fans hollerin like they'd never get the chance again and back to me stumblin out a the arena.

The sports man said, "Stamper gave everyone a scare, and I quote from one official, 'He up and left on his own accord,' end quote. He even came back into the arena to accept a gold buckle."

The camera showed me next to the small pretty older woman in a red velvet cowboy hat with a couple older cowboys, and whatever they said got drowned out by the crowd. The shot held for ten seconds a pure hollerin.

The sports man said, "No mixing of the sound ladies and gentlemen. That was real applause. The kind maybe only greats like Ruth and Payton received. We've confirmed Stamper refused medical care and was completely mobile leaving the facility. Our efforts have been unsuccessful in tracking Stamper down. We've been told by various sources no one has been able to reach Stamper. The Ogden show's organizer is on the line now to discuss this monumental event."

Was struck dumb and said, "Jay rewind this. Jesús always can."

The sports man interviewed a woman on the phone sayin how delighted they was I showed, but no one stopped to think I would actually ride Bushwacker. They had no idea a my wherebouts but confirmed offerin medical care and my stable condition before I left.

Jay pointed the remote, and the screen rewinded. Back on Bushwacker in the chute. Jay let er go, and we watched again. The sports man on the screen again talked to the woman sure a my physical condition.

I seen right. "If that clock run on time, off round seven eight and clean off at seven nine. Rewind it again."

Jay did, and we watched again.

"It's not the official clock," Jay said.

"You reckon the official one is faster?" And turned eyein him straight.

Jay reached for his pocket and pulled out his flat phone and handed it over.

Stood dizzy.

"Are you staying awake?"

"I am."

"The girls said hi before I put them to bed."

"What'd they up to?"

"They prepared to teach Espee how to draw a tree. We are taking their paintings out to Jesús' for home evening. What are you doing?"

"Watchin lots a TV."

"What's on?"

"A movie bout a young woman who got herself in so much debt she kilt herself."

"That's terrible."

"She got finagled into buyin finer things, long colorful dresses mostly her husband couldn't afford. Her damned lovers stood her up when she needed em most. Shoulda got a cleanin job and paid for em herself."

"That doesn't sound very contemporary. Women of a certain class probably didn't work during the time period."

"Gathered she lived in older times near England."

"Sounds like a BBC production of a classic Italian tale."

"No subtitles."

"Were there ornate apartments with balconies and boats in port?"

"Old cottages, dirt roads and forests. Just this young girl wantin more out a life, emptyin her husband's wallet goin bout it and gettin her colorful dresses muddied up in the process."

"You watched the whole movie?"

"Just bout. Better'n I'm tellin."

"There has to be something more entertaining on."

"Not a thing. Didn't ride Bushwacker Car."

"What do you mean?"

"Short a eight."

"You must have. They scored you ninety-two points, and everyone is talking about you making the best ride ever."

"Just seen it for the third time and off before the buzzer each time. Seven point nine at most."

"There must have been a separate timer the officials went by."

"Jay said the same thing but don't expect one clock is faster'n nother. Do you?"

"You made an amazing ride. Everyone is saying it was."

"Don't make it so."

"Stay awake for now. We can talk about it when you get home."

"Won't change it none."

"Stay awake."

"I am."

Turned to hand Jay's flat phone back now wide awake not able to think bout nothin else, wantin Jay to run it back one more time. He left off the couch. The fridge opened, and Sam got through the doorway.

Jay's bruised dark back blocked most a the fridge. Mighty full on the edges. Sam and me tried eyein round him. Food containers stacked so tight and neat they belonged in a commercial.

"There's homemade pasta and fresh marinara sauce," Jay said.

He lifted a glass container a pasta and smaller bowl a sauce. Grabbed em and went for the microwave above the oven and removed the lids and hit the popcorn button like always.

"Fresh peppers from Sandra's sister's Mormon garden." Jay handed me a slice a yellow pepper.

Had my fill a Mormon gardens and never enough. Carmen said she wanted enough land for one in Riverton. She let up this summer but insisted on one every day in the spring. Once I told Shawn a Carmen's intentions. If someone shared Carmen's desire for fresh healthy food more'n Shawn and Carla, I never met em in person. Shawn said he envied lots a things bout the Mormons and nothin more'n their gardens. But even then he said they was short a perfection cause not a one had hops. Or coffee beans Carla said. The only time I seen her laugh, and she couldn't stop.

Chomped the pepper and couldn't taste nothin but darn crisp.

Jay sat a couple paper plates and silverware on the small table up against the wall. Claimed the closest chair and Jay pulled the glass container and small bowl from the microwave and set em on the small table. Stuck my fork in one square with pleated edges and chewed but couldn't taste the middle. Stuck more onto my paper plate. Jay poured sauce on his and mine.

The kitchen light showed a huge broccoli head tattooed on Jay's heart, dark enough his tan couldn't hide next to a bowl a fresh peppers in all colors and cans three high in three rows. He handed a piece a yellow pepper below the table to Sam. He picked a large green pepper and cut down the middle, gutted the seeds, and handed me half. He sliced a piece off and popped in his mouth.

"Didn't ride him." Swallowed a couple bites. "I recollected my rookie year at a show in Fort Worth eyein them unopened beers." And pointed at his stack. "Outside the office to collect my check and Sharp passed by and let himself right in. The door hung open and heard him say, if were for somethin other'n eight would be written but aint. Sure enough they zeroed him out. When I asked for my check, they tore it up and wrote me nother for more money. And to beat all still years before I even found Jesus swore then to a God I didn't believe really existed he made the best ride I ever seen. In a local cantina later the same night took a seat cross from him at a long table where one fan after nother brought him a beer till a castle between us we barely seen each other over. He kept pushin em my way but they come faster'n we could drink em."

"Who's to say he didn't really ride?"

"Him. People told him all kinds a reasons, even they was late on the stopwatch."

"Maybe they were and again today."

"Aint it."

Jay took a red pepper out the bowl and cut in half. He cleared the seeds and passed a piece. Took it and stuck a square with pleated edges and one more and contemplated more between bites. Jay sat upright and didn't move. He smiled and shook his head. Was feelin real good and sipped my beer with the pasta and fresh sauce settlin in my stomach sure a room for more. Eyed the container with plenty left.

"Let's go." Them words come with no warnin, surprisin even myself.

"Okay." Jay gutted one more red pepper. He cleaned up and handed me a few cans. He halted at the bedroom door and went in. The flashin TV showed dirt bikes jumpin dirt mounds and speedin over deep ruts.

Jay come out and closed the door behind him and wrapped his arm round my shoulders. He smiled watchin the screen with riders jumpin, wishin he could beam himself in the race. He fetched the remote and turned the TV off and cleared the room with me and Sam on his heels. Grabbed the brown Rand for the front door. The cool night pressed on us, and Sam scooted down the front stairs.

Jay come round the cab and grabbed my belt loop. "Get up." He lifted and them bags a water swooshed against the buckskin jacket. Pulled out my pocketknife and tried cuttin the pink tape under my arm and got a piece off the buckskin jacket. Jay reached over Sam and tore off more tape. "Give it here." Handed over my knife. He cut and the bag went and broke and sprayed on the buckskin jacket and over the back seat. He kept at freein the tape off my neck and drained the rest out the cab.

The old Ford headed for Idaho lit by stars and hummed long the freeway like the Snake windin through high desert. Outlines a mountains faint but there. All the rest in my head from all the times before. Down the mountain Jay wanted to stop. The old Ford rolled over one gravel road on nother to a large farmhouse with a porch wrappin round in the middle a fields. Jay said we'd get somethin for the pain into an old kitchen with a single chair and baggies coverin counters. Voices come down a hall and boys filed in. One guy went on bout bein on TV and asked for my gold buckle. He leaned down with hair puffed up and sides shaved, wearin a joker smile when he did. All the others went on watchin. He had to see for himself he said. If my neck felt right, he wouldn't finished askin the first time. A boy told Jay to follow him in back for the real good stuff, but Jay ignored him and filled a lunch sack with baggies. A big boy moved inside the doorway. The guy poked the buckskin jacket and got in my face and demanded I take off my Indian coat while indoors. Roper said humans was insatiable and cause for lots a their ruin. And if not for that, he said lackin in sense come in real close second. The guy grabbed the buckskin jacket, and I punched him. He yanked, and I fell. Jay got there, and the guy turned. They throwed and landed at the same time. A crack stunned the whole lot. The guy went down without a whimper against a cupboard. The big boy swung for Jay, and Jay exploded into his chest knockin him on his heels. Jay unloaded one crack and then nother, and the big boy dropped to his knees and covered his head. Jay pulled a punch and nodded my way. My stubby fingers squeezed the knob on a cupboard next to the fallen guy. Jay lifted under my shoulder and tilted me on a clear counter. He grabbed his lunch sack and wrapped his arm round me and lifted over the guy, a dent over his eye with blood drippin from his nose onto his shirt collar. None a the boys moved, and we cleared the back door with Sam on are heels soon as we cleared off the porch.

Jay rattled on at full tilt. My head broke long a line on my neck on each bump. Jay seen my dire pain and said was messed up and carried on faster. I wouldn't go to the hospital, just no need with feelins in my legs comin back. He went for his favorite topic he brought up in some way or nother every time he could. Silence stuck together the universe. Everything in it. He went quiet and eyed me, set on gettin my thoughts onto somethin big. The notion bout God toleratin sufferin fueled him. I coulda yelled at each bump but bit my lip sure if I did he'd go mad and run the old Ford off the freeway for a road to the nearest town. More'n release from all the noise combatin are souls. Was real space for new stars or starts. He talked so fast over the old Ford I didn't ask which but asked how it bound the universe, what I knowed so important from before so he quit eyein me. Pure openness with the pull a patterns and interactions a more patterns. Even when they occurred before was new again and interferin with em just wrong, nothin wronger. Was participatin life. God got so big you couldn't make one description and so close you didn't notice. You could touch though. Not beholden to no one thing and accessible to each and every solitary soul. Quit yappin and reach. I knowed if the bailiff sweared me in on the Good Book in a court a law, would tell straight not attackin me but goin at Jay assured his reckonin.

The old Ford pulled off the freeway onto the old highway, passed the rock pit, and up and over bumps long Riverton Road. Mornin faded in specks a light fillin the cab and bouncin off Jay's swollen hands turnin the steerin wheel.

CHAPTER 12

Fence posts bordered the field a wheat still for now. Pushed the door, and Sam jumped out. My muscles melted and reckoned coma would set in if my eyes closed. Slid my butt off the seat and my legs wobbled soon as my boots hit ground. Kicked dirt, wakin my toes. Sam and Josey sprinted through pasture to Riverton Road.

Jay's forehead set on the wheel. Nothin surer'n we could crash on gravel beds.

Wind swept round the grill a the old Ford.

"You a'right?" Stopped kickin in the dirt.

Jay turned his head on the side. "Meditating Pard. Can you walk?"

He shuffled out and are doors shut, creakin at the same time to ahalt. Jay's boots hit gravel and mine echoed behind and not a rustle a wind round us. He got through the door and turned before headin down the hall. "There's pizza in the fridge."

Pretty much nothin else in there. Reached for the box and pain shot through my neck. Dropped on my knees and breathed real slow, holdin the box and lifted one leg at a time not foolish to hurry myself and grabbed the Ranch. My boots slid slow for the Formica table, and my left toe caught a back leg a the closest thin plastic chair. Dropped the box, and slices bounced.

Flipped the lid and eyed what there was, and all my muscles hardened. The crack opened long the base a my head, and pain shot wild in my neck and shoulder down my legs.

Not bout to turn left nor right and didn't look down none neither. Learned my lesson but glanced sausage and pepperoni. Eyed only the dirty white wall facin me and felt for a slice and got one and took a bite and felt like a mix. Chewed real slow without my neck fussin.

My stubby fingers found the ranch and twisted off the cap. Run em long the cardboard for clear space and turned the bottle.

"See a ghost?"

My whole body shifted toward Jay, wearin a white towel. Got the bottle upright and screwed the lid on.

"My head bout rolled off but held tight."

Jay headed back down the hall.

I wondered how many more slices and dipped round where I guessed the Ranch poured and took a bite. My stubby fingers passed over two other slices but sure a one more.

Jay come in with a tan foam neck brace with horsehair matted on. Took and fumbled the thing. Jay picked it off the floor and wiped against his towel. He leaned his black and blue chest in my face and collared my neck. My chin set and shoulders give.

"Keep it as long as you need Pard."

"Won't be long."

A roar a diesel engine come through the front door not one a us closed. Josey barked runnin long the fence, and he carried on while tires rolled over gravel. Reached for a slice and swallowed real tight against Jay's brace.

Jay's flip flops smacked to the door and down the front steps. Chewed and swallowed slower. My stomach rumbled and stubby fingers covered the box and scanned through the mound a Ranch. Licked em clean and slid the thin plastic chair back and pushed up on the Formica table. Kicked my heels to wake my feet and went for the front door. Feelin real good stretchin in the doorway and admired the start a day. Cross Riverton Road trees hid the Snake River. Off the side rose the sun and no missin the blue sky, even without bein able to look up. Cleared the front steps, and Sam run up, bumpin my leg. My stubby fingers smoothed the top a her head.

"Has to be more than the battery. Fuel injection maybe," Mr. Yukichi said.

"Old enough a few things could've gone wrong," Jay said.

My boots crunched rock to em, and Mr. Yukichi turned, lookin mighty surprised.

"So the great return came at a price."

"Landed on my head is all."

"Looks like your whole face. Nice bump on your forehead too. More like you were in a street fight than bull riding if I had to guess. I know how the dismount went. How did the ride go?"

"Scored him ninety-two points on Bushwacker!" Jay said, slappin the tailgate.

Mr. Yukichi jumped like a shotgun gone off. "Dean. Congratulations. That's history. Never would have guessed limping like you are."

"Outrode the younger generation. Not a one wanted any part of Bushwacker, and Dean didn't want anyone else."

"Didn't cover him Mr. Yukichi."

Their carryin on dropped off a cliff.

"Says who?" Mr. Yukichi asked.

"Rules are rules no matter what someone says."

Mr. Yukichi lifted his Red Sox ball cap and run his other hand through his gray hair. "If they scored you, there's no undoing it."

"And they gave him a gold buckle with a shiny gemstone," Jay said.

"Let's see."

Jay opened the passenger door and pulled down the jockey box and run his hand through. He pulled pieces a paper out and put em back. He bent for a look under the seat and swept his arm over the floor and backed out and went round to the other side. Mr. Yukichi looked under the seat and pulled out the cherry wood box and popped the gold lid.

"Got it," Jay said, openin the driver's door and closin it. He rounded back the front a the old Ford.

Mr. Yukichi lifted the gold buckle. "That is an emerald if I ever saw one." He turned and showed me. "Richest buckle I've seen."

"Didn't expect him to get rode." Jay shifted in for a closer look, wearin his big smile.

"Would have spared some expense if they had I'm sure." Mr. Yukichi polished the green stone with the cuff a his shirt. "It's official Dean. You rode the greatest bull ever, and there's his face to remind you." He put the gold buckle back in the cherry wood box and handed it over.

"Gonna give it back." Set the cherry wood box on my gut.

"What good would that do? Probably in the papers already and on TV. The whole world will know you rode today."

"Already all over the TV," Jay said. "We already saw it."

"There you go. Can't change a thing."

"Wouldn't care if I did."

"They wouldn't have given you the buckle if you didn't ride him."

"What they believe don't change it."

"Thousands of fans seen it in Ogden and thousands upon thousands more seen it since," Jay said.

"There, it's been told." Mr. Yukichi lifted his Red Sox ball cap and set back again.

"Don't make it so."

A pickup winded on Riverton Road long the pasture up Jay's driveway. The engine flipped off, and Brother Hamilton jumped out and clapped.

"Well you were certainly called to fame and fortune!" He yelled in gators folded below his knees and cleared the bed a Mr. Yukichi's truck. "Yesterday I was in meetings all afternoon and constantly getting text messages from family and friends telling me to get to a TV as fast as I could. Saw your truck pull in and couldn't get to my gates quick enough. Good to see you with a towel Jay, especially with news vans likely to be out before long. They're already canvassing downtown. Biggest thing to happen since the Teton Dam broke. Fred, good morning."

"Good morning, Walt. Dean took home more than glory yesterday."

"Why yes he did. What an incredible shiner and your nose looks busted. Break your neck too? My Gosh. You couldn't make this out on TV, and honestly I wouldn't have imagined so much damage could be from falling on your head. I'm not suggesting it didn't look bad because it most certainly did, and I felt sick to my stomach watching, and we watched it over and over. But for heaven's sake there's a lot of different points of impact. He must have caught you with his hoof on the way down. I swore he did and sent a text message to the Bishop. I've been waiting to say this since I first saw it. Now you don't look it, but you're the same Dean I broke bread with yesterday morning. Don't you go confusing your efforts with a miracle of the Lord. You rode and you alone. And it was as amazing a feat as I've ever seen in my seventy-three years of mortal existence."

Brother Hamilton talked like Jesús' oldest boy carryin on bout his favorite baseball player I recollected cause no catch like hookin Idaho Trout and even better'n someone named after a chewy candy bar. Like when Brother Hamilton retold as a kid at his first Finals in Oklahoma and seen Freckles Brown cover Tornado. His face moved in lines and tensed all at once and repeated.

"I haven't seen as much action as you Fred, but wouldn't you agree, it was the greatest ride you've ever heard of?"

"I would and just did."

All us turned to piercin noise, and a black space car dropped down the hill on Riverton Road. Like a jet acceleratin neared the corner and slowed and the thing stopped. Then backed up. Somethin straight from Mars and none a us said nothin. It pulled in the driveway and went quiet behind Brother Hamilton's pickup with headlights stayin on.

The driver's door went straight up like in a movie, and Matt climbed out. "What are the chances when we chose to take Riverton Road we'd get to see this esteemed group?" He asked.

The passenger door went straight up, and a tall blond woman slid out.

"Ahead of schedule a day or two. You'll surprise your mother as I expect is the point," Mr. Yukichi said.

"Yes sir, but we wanted to give her a chance to get ready first, so we decided the scenic route through Riverton would buy us time." Matt grabbed for the hand a the woman. "But we didn't expect to get so lucky. Angie, meet my father Akira like your favorite film director but Fred to his friends."

"My pleasure, Mr. Yukichi," the woman said, extendin her hands.

Mr. Yukichi took both a hers in his. "And mine young lady. Please call me Akira, or if you wish Fred. Matt's mother has a proper welcome planned."

"This is Walt Hamilton, the unofficial chief of Riverton. And these are a couple of my old friends, Jay in the half toga and the now famous Dean with the beat-up face," Matt said.

"Greatness isn't a respecter of mugs," Brother Hamilton said.

"We heard the news about the ride on satellite radio when we arrived in Cheyenne and on every news channel crossing Wyoming. Everyone said the ride was the greatest he ever saw."

"It must have been extraordinary. We still have not seen it," the woman said.

"Tried many times on my phone, but service has been too spotty."

"You'll agree when you do. Dean made history," Brother Hamilton said.

"And put Blackfoot on the map. They all pointed out." Tilted up the brown Rand to correct em all at once.

"A P1," Jay said. "A true beauty, but ain't no F1."

We all eyed the black space car Jay hovered by.

"The original owner would agree. He passed on this one, and I didn't hesistate." Matt went backwards sudden like an unseen force got aholt a him.

"So few made but bet Leno has both."

My stomach growled, and everyone went quiet.

"Angie, let's find you a drink." Matt turned half round. "I'll leave you in the best of hands while Jay and I take a ride."

"Fine," she said and went red in the face.

"Will be our great pleasure," Brother Hamilton said.

"Don't get too excited Walt," Mr. Yukichi said.

"It's not like when Brigitte Bardot got left. You'll be fine," Matt said.

"She was not left. He let her go," the woman said, starin Matt down.

"Exactly, this isn't even the same thing, and you're in great hands." Matt eyed us all over. "Angie has been schooling me on foreign films, and I've been learning a ton."

"It is not necessary to mock me, and for the record we have seen some without Brigitte Bardot. Art is about the experience and not how much information you gain, don't you agree?"

I knowed enough to not say nothin.

Jay coulda been caressin the black space car and jolted at her question. "Absolutely has to be about the experience because I don't understand any of it," he said, wearin his mighty big smile.

Matt laughed, and Brother Hamilton begin to but went quiet just as quick.

The woman faced Jay. "Thank you Jay, but I do not believe understanding and experiencing art are exclusive of each other, but you are certainly in the right company."

She went for the trailer. Mr. Yukichi give his arm, and she took it. Mr. Yukichi and Brother Hamilton with the woman between em reached the front door wide open.

"Let's take our drinks here on the porch," Brother Hamilton said.

Mr. Yukichi and the woman paused for a couple seconds on the steps eyein the lawn chairs against the trailer.

"He most likely has Gatorades in the refrigerator or there's cold water from the facet," Mr. Yukichi said.

"Orange if there's one, please," Brother Hamilton said.

"Dean?"

"Plenty a Coronas."

Jay leaned over the open trunk a the black space car, pointin at somethin. Josey and Sam rustled round his feet. Matt pointed from the other side. Wind covered their conversin, and Matt tossed Jay the keys. They slid in and the doors come right down. The black space car backed out with Josey and Sam kissin the tires.

Brother Hamilton stared too. He turned and clapped. "Very nice jacket Dean."

The woman cleared the front steps with an orange Gatorade in one hand and a tall glass a water in the other.

She reached the Gatorade to Brother Hamilton, and wind ruffled her summer dress.

The black space car zoomed down Riverton Road.

"I still have not gotten use to that," the woman said.

Mr. Yukichi come down the steps and handed over a Corona.

Brother Hamilton wiped down the cleanest lawn chair in the bunch before the woman. He stepped aside, and she sat and leaned forward. He handed a chair to Mr. Yukichi and unpacked one for himself.

Grabbed a foldin chair stacked against the trailer and none sooner flattened the seat and tiredness covered me head to toe. Jerked and spilled. Worried my neck didn't take so good. The dull pain on my chest spread like a spiderweb.

"Would you have guessed you'd welcome the day with old cowboys?" Brother Hamliton asked.

"Our visit was fated after my first meeting Matt, but I would not have expected such wonderful company so early this morning," the woman said.

"We were discussing fate's indifference to one's preferences the other day, and Walt said mother fate kept people falling despite their most earnest of intentions to stay upright. Isn't that right?" Mr. Yukichi asked.

"Nearly verbatim. The notion makes about as much sense as anything else I've said, Fred, and no one knows that better." Brother Hamilton turned on his seat direct at the woman. "So tell us Ms. Angie, how did you and Matt meet? He's the crown jewel of Blackfoot you know."

"We were in Connecticut at a party of mutual friends, and they stabled horses in a large beautiful barn next to a long pasture. Since Matt and I rode we naturally gravitated to the horses, and I learned right away that Mr. Yukichi was a rodeo champion and Matt grew up a cowboy." She sat half in the sun, and wind blowed her hair one way and she reached up runnin her fingers through the other way. Short hairs on her shoulder glowed round the loose strap a her dress.

Sun heated me up between fits a wind. Battled shivers for the past couple hours but warmed now undid the top buttons on the buckskin jacket.

"Fred made the NFR as many times as Bill Russell reached the NBA finals." Brother Hamilton clapped his hands.

"Almost but unlike Russell we didn't win a title." Mr. Yukichi shook his head.

"Matt inherited the family talent with a rope."

"Had a first love in football."

"So you were smitten with an Idaho cowboy." Brother Hamilton clapped again.

"Matt's captivating energy drew me in, like he does most people, but we spent our first meeting arguing about whether rodeo was inhumane. I had always associated the tradition with animal cruelty, and here was this confident Idahoan telling me I had bought into propaganda that could not be further from the truth. My education on rodeo has been long and steady since then, but my resistance to the treatment of the animals in rodeos has not faded. And I have not been persuaded."

"No question we abuse animals, but for most of those we do have an envious life over those we don't," Brother Hamilton said.

"And the glamorous life of the rodeo bull has always been Matt's ready example." The woman sat up straight.

"In the course of my education I saw old film of you, Mr. Yukichi, and some of Dean and Jay with Matt and had a new emotion I did not expect."

"And what was that?" Brother Hamilton asked.

"A glimpse of madness I expect," Mr. Yukichi said.

Took nother sip. My stomach tightened up and had a mind a gettin a slice still on the table.

"Pity," she said. "For the cowboy who seemed to get hurt every other ride. After an incredible ride Dean explained the directions the bull had taken before landing on his back. You jumped right up and when the interviewer asked you about the fall you said you were focused on the ride and not the getoff. You were so young, and Matt noticed my shock seeing your face and reminded me last night I was mesmerized. I could not help but comment multiple times after seeing you. Like many things Matt and I were not making the same connection. What I could not believe was someone who looked like you would do such a brutal thing."

I didn't recollect no fallin on my back and no interview neither but callin her a liar bordered on impolite.

"What a fine contradiction," Brother Hamilton said. "He should have posed for his bust, or better yet in fashionable clothes for photographs taken in New York City. You know Matt won the tie-down roping title."

"I had not thought of him as a model but yes, you are right, but many things could be more suitable than climbing on the back of an angry animal intending to hurt you. And I did learn Matt won his second calf roping title that same year, which is an event I simply cannot watch."

"That is a curious observation," Mr. Yukichi said.

"And here's Matt's vindication. I am facing the cowboy everyone is talking about." She eyed me straight up. "And you are true to form, and fate would have Matt leave to do what he loves above everything else."

"Jay kept Matt's Camaro running through high school. There's a lot of history there."

"You couldn't make a bigger mistake than to stand in Matt's way. If you did, he'd certainly teach you a lesson on why you shouldn't. I'll tell you the instant for me was keeping him late on a summer night to help unload gear after a week in the Sawtooths with high adventure Boy Scouts from all the local troops, and I later learned he missed a race with a favorite date. When we went camping next the gear was mysteriously organized, nothing missing mind you but lids not where you'd expect and tighter knots than were necessary. Most young adults I did things over and over for things to set in, but with Matt, never more than once, and sometimes, if I was wise to him, I avoided even one time," Brother Hamilton said.

"She must have been some girl he missed," the woman said.

"It was the race," Mr. Yukichi said.

"Both I'm sure," Brother Hamilton said. "Speaking of missing. Ms. Angie, will you please do me a favor and take a selfie of me with the missing and now found Dean?" He pulled out a shiny black phone.

"Lisa says don't matter if yur in the picture to be a selfie you gotta take the photo yurself," I said.

They all eyed me like I gone deaf but sure proved em all wrong.

"That is how I understand it too. Who is Lisa?" the woman asked.

"One of Dean's beautiful daughters," Mr. Yukichi said.

"No doubt she's correct but sounds impossible," Brother Hamilton said. "Can you take it Ms. Angie?"

"I believe I can," the woman said.

"But you better be in the shot for me to report I've taken a real selfie."

"It'll be her selfie though," Mr. Yukichi said.

"Only technically," the woman said.

"As long as it's a real one. Everyone be sure and smile now," Brother Hamilton said.

The woman knelt beside Mr. Yukichi and nodded at Brother Hamilton. "Stand behind Dean and Mr. Yukichi." My chair slanted at Mr. Yukich, lucky cause wouldn't shift none. The woman held still the shiny black phone.

We was all quiet for a few seconds. The woman lowered the shiny black phone with her fingers glidin long the screen and give it back to Brother Hamilton. My stomach popped and patted the buckskin jacket and took nother sip.

"Going to send this one to the Bishop." Brother Hamilton pushed on the shiny black phone. We all watched like he might not. "Let him know I saw the legend himself the day after." He put the shiny black phone in his pocket and stretched like gettin out a bed. "Last night I dreamed I was there in Odgen but didn't know how everything would go." He flopped on the side a his chair and clapped. "I was next to you, could hear Bushwacker breathing each jump, and felt the ground move each time he landed. No dream was ever so real." He mumbled somethin to himself. "Ms. Angie, I never made the observation myself, but isn't your notion something of Dean looking like porcelain? Not now but regularly, and he went and rode the greatest force on Planet Earth? Curious to be sure." He slapped his knees.

"Didn't," I said.

No one could miss my stomach rumblin right then over a new gust a wind.

"Didn't what?"

"Cover him."

Brother Hamilton stretched on his chair and shook his head. His eyes went real wide. "Now that is curious. I saw it with my own eyes. Many times now and your face sure says you were the one on Bushwacker."

"Not for eight."

He straightened against his wobbly chair and just bout fell off. "Where would you get such a notion anyhow?" He started and didn't stop shakin his head.

"Clock on the TV. Off under eight and clean off at it."

"I think you're wrong and am sure the clock the officials used ran to eight seconds."

"Did or didn't. How can one clock be faster'n nother?"

Brother Hamilton paused, and his face tightened. "The officials scored you and millions of people have seen the ride." His words was slower'n every other one so far.

"No one has one thing to do with it."

Wind passed round us, and none a them blinked, waitin like words was due long the next gust or one after.

"Maybe you did," Mr. Yukichi said.

"Now wait a second Dean. You're saying I witnessed the greatest event in rodeo history but didn't really. You're talking madness!" Brother Hamilton spitted his words. "And since hearing it reported, I've carried the biggest badge of pride I've ever known, and now you're saying it was wrong. You're bound to make me go berserk if I think about it. Not to mention a single soul hasn't doubted it but you." Brother Hamilton pointed at me like I missed who he spoke at. He could drop a sermon out a church quicker'n everyone I knowed in person.

"What are you going to do?" the woman asked, sittin up with all the blood gone from her face.

All went quiet, even the wind.

Brother Hamilton clenched his whole mouth.

"For beginners, aim to give the gold buckle back."

"Is it in the box?" The woman pointed at the cherry wood box against the buckskin jacket.

Handed it over and she opened the lid. Brother Hamilton reached and took it. The sun bounced off onto his face.

"Dean, what is done is done. There's no undoing it now," Mr. Yukichi said.

Brother Hamilton bit his lips blue. He shook like he'd drop the cherry wood box and slammed the lid and clasped tight against his lap.

"If you feel strongly, maybe you should start by finding a journalist to tell your side," the woman said.

What a thought jottin in a diary but quick come the notion someone writin down might be the thing to do.

"And when he finds this journalist, then what?" Brother Hamilton asked, not at all pleasant. "Petition Congress to pass an act derecognizing the ride?"

"I am not under the impression an official act is what Dean seeks." The woman went stone-cold sober.

"Forgive me Ms. Angie but absurd talk tends to rile me." Brother Hamilton's shiny black phone buzzed, and he pulled it from his pocket. "Yes Sister Torres, he's right here." He rose and handed over his shiny black phone, still embracin the cherry wood box with his other hand.

"Dean!" Carmen's voice said before I got my ear close. "Why did Jay quit answering his phone? Why didn't you call me? I've been thinking of every bad possibility and then Jesús forwards me a selfie of you with Brother Hamilton and Mr. Yukichi and a beautiful woman."

"Don't worry none."

"You know things don't work that way. And you look like someone ran you over."

"Feel like it."

"Don't avoid my questions. Why haven't you called?"

"Jay lost his phone, and when we got to his place everyone just showed up."

"How did he lose his phone? Didn't drop it in a lake somewhere?"

"He dropped it I reckon. Don't worry yurself where."

"That doesn't make me worry less but makes me worry more. You look so much worse than I imagined. How do you feel?"

"A'right when not movin none."

"Tell me you didn't lose your phone too?"

"In my pocket."

"The girls are getting ready, and we'll be out to get you."

"Could use some shuteye."

"I'm sure you could, but you have a long ways to go still. I'll see you in a few minutes. Stay awake."

"There aint nothin I want more."

"See you soon. Stay awake."

Held up the shiny black phone, smooth as a rock on the bed a the Snake River and wondered how she'd skip.

The woman didn't look startled no more. She raised her hand against the sun and pinched her eyes openin her mouth. The words she aimed for didn't come.

"Well I feel duty-bound to say stay awake Dean. I expect you got a serious concussion knocked out like you were and being tired probably explain your state of mind. Go through the day, stay on your feet, and when you feel better rethink this crazy notion of yours," Brother Hamilton said, calmer'n before.

"And drink a lot. Nothing works better than a full bladder to stay awake," Mr. Yukichi said.

Rested the Corona on Jay's brace for nother sip.

CHAPTER 13

"Does it hurt bad?" Elena asked, again.

"Not when I sit still."

"You have to move. You can't hold still all day."

"And will hurt when I do Lena." Stern as I could muster, her questionin wearin me thin.

Carmen drove slow over Riverton Road and avoided parts washed away on the reservation after last winter. Mighty grateful with my innards touchy as my neck.

Elena carried on with more questions, and Carmen answered em.

After Brother Hamilton introduced everyone all round, Carmen asked bout the buckskin jacket, pullin pieces a pink tape off. She said it made me smell like worn leather. I asked to bring Sam, but she said we was goin to work and promised to come later or send one a her girls for her. Elena shouted I was bleedin, and all went quiet. Everyone spoke at once bout my shirt soaked through with blood, and a large spot dried on the inside a the buckskin jacket. The tall blond woman bout fainted and Mr.Yukichi went for nother glass a water. Brother Hamilton said he knowed he saw right and a hoof brushed my chest durin the fall on my head. Eloisa hates blood but missed the whole affair cause she never got out the Camry. She slept in back and still did crossin the Blackfoot River to shot after shot after shot a water from the spout a the pivot with row after row a vines passin by.

"But you can't ride the Palomino mare now. You can't get on her Dad," Elena said.

"Can too."

"You will fall right on your head when she sprints off. Her turn is on Saturday."

"She can miss a turn," Carmen said.

"Will ride her," I said. "Don't worry none."

"You hardly walk good Dad," Elena said.

"Don't mean I can't ride good."

Eloisa groaned for Elena to quiet down, but she didn't.

"People are trying to find you Dad."

"A lot of vans came by the house wanting to visit with Dad to go on TV, and we thanked them didn't we." Carmen looked in the mirror.

"They don't know you look like you Dad. They might be scared seeing you."

"They will be if they aim to bother me," I said.

"Linda texted earlier there were a lot of satellite vans in the Walmart parking lot. They'll be at our place by the time we get home."

"Then I'll put the word out for who give me the gold buckle can have it back."

"Why Dad? I'll have the gold buckle," Elena said.

"You're still thinking you didn't ride? I've watched online and doesn't look half a second short."

"Did you time it?"

"No and promise we will before you go making a renouncement to the world."

"What's the world gotta do with it?"

"What do you mean Mom?" Elena asked.

"First, your Dad and I will time the ride together before he tells anyone it wasn't a qualified ride. Second, for some reason your Dad is fixated on rejecting it being valid."

"Aint rejectin somethin aint so."

"Don't declare it into the first camera someone puts in front of you until we time it."

"Me too," Elena said.

"We will together and Lisa too."

I learned long ago Carmen knowed best but nothin would change the clock run short. Out the sides a my eyes more potato fields passed, and Carmen's dark hair covered her neck. She wore a bright yellow silk shirt with business suit tight over her chest.

"We'll make the camera trucks wait. Sally is going early to BYU Idaho. She was fantastic this summer. I'm taking her appointment with a lawyer from Boise, and then I'm in court the rest of the morning. Did you have breakfast?"

Eloisa woke and tried protestin everyone carryin on. Carmen talked to her and Elena bout when Verolinda would pick em up after she finished her mornin shift. We pulled into a parkin lot I knowed real good.

The girls got out, and Eloisa opened my door with her head restin on it and said, "You have raccoon eyes."

"The bull's hoof clipped his nose. And brother Hamilton said somehow kicked his chest," Carmen said.

"And the bump," Eloisa said, touchin my forehead. She grabbed the sleeve a the buckskin jacket. "Your collar smells like a horse."

My stomach pushed down each step and had a mind a findin the first empty stall quicker'n a mongoose.

Carmen held her large leather bag and opened the glass door and Elena braced her back against it. Carmen stepped round us toward metal detectors for the county jail.

A police officer eyed the lot a us and said, "Good morning, Ms. Torres. You brought help today. How are you girls doing this morning?"

"Good Officer Weaver," Elena said.

"Anything in your pockets?"

"I don't have any." Elena patted her dress.

Carmen put her large leather bag on the belt through the x-ray machine. Pushed Eloisa ahead and tensed up waitin my turn, squezzin my cheeks.

"You made an impressive ride yesterday," the officer said.

"You seen them camera trucks round?" I asked.

"I've heard they have gathered downtown. Guys have come in grumbling they lost their day off on account of them. Be around before long I'm sure."

"If you see em say we'll be home before long."

"I'll sure do if anyone asks. Spoke with Tyler yesterday night, and he told me about the ride. He said all the main news channels were showing it and you looked like you years ago. I found it online during the call and couldn't argue with him, but we did about the Raiders' playoff chances this year with training camps right around the corner."

The alarm went off. Stopped on the other side set to explode. I knowed no place to lose it and squeezed harder while lookin round cool as Steve McQueen, the man Roper esteemed above all other men.

"He wanted me to tell you hello if I saw you and what are the chances I would." The officer set the alarm off passin through the metal detector. "Obviously I didn't expect to this morning but hello from him. Anything in your pockets?"

My stomach popped pullin out change and my dead phone. Carmen took it. The officer waved me on with only one thing on my mind.

"Wait. You must show under your cowboy hat?"

Didn't stop, backpedalin and takin off the brown Rand and sure enough showed nothin there.

"What a shiner. You're free to go."

Jail made me nervouser'n on top a chute but not then and didn't expect nothin could right then. An officer called Carmen and just a blur. My stomach exploded, pushin the door into a restroom.

An officer raised his billy club to my chest and said, "How did you get passed the guard?"

Pushed the club down and beelined for the nearest stall. Someone come through the door.

"Holy shit, Mr. Stamper. There's a dangerous inmate in here. You have to leave," the man behind us said.

"I am crappin in one a them stalls or in my shorts," I said, my stomach rumblin over my words.

The officer looked passed me and shook his head. "Here." He opened the nearest stall and yelled, "Nothing smart Chad."

My boots slid fast and undid my Wranglers in one move. Couldn't see the lid and dropped my shorts off my cheeks just before I felt go and squeezed pacin myself with blasts a air shootin through the room.

"That you Dean?" a voice said on the other side a the stall wall.

"No talking Chad," the officer said.

A boom mightier'n the first round shot from under me, and more come in short bursts.

The voice on the other side a the stall wall started coughin. "Sorry Officer Moysh but if I'd known I was going to share my privileges with Dean Stamper, I'd never asked for them." He heaved between short breaths.

I never knowed a person more fit for fun and couldn't recollect a kegger in high school not organized by Chad and a few after.

Tried pacin the last blasts but give up and let em rip.

"It's me."

"Sure is." Chad got caughin up a storm.

"I'm done asking Chad! I'll rip you off the toilet if you don't shut up! Mr. Stamper, please don't talk to the inmate," the officer said.

"Oh my God. You dying buddy?" Was like to have throwed up in his sleeve.

"Unbelievable," the officer said, and the other one went out, coughin. "Mr. Stamper." The officer took a short breath. "Mr. Stamper that was an amazing ride yesterday. You've made us all proud." He gulped a couple times like something wanted out his throat. He cried, "Chad, hurry up! If you don't finish up right now I'm coming in after you!"

"I'm trying, I'm trying. What's this about a ride?" he said quick between short breaths.

The officer opened the door a Chad's stall, and Chad fumbled over the paper roll. "Peace man." The officer didn't move, and Chad fumbled the roll more.

"That's enough." The officer's feet hit cement.

"I haven't finished wiping man."

"Get up for the love of God!"

Chad shuffled his feet and rose up in a coughin fit. I couldn't tell if his or the officer's or a chorus a both with one fininshin and the other beginnin again.

"Pull up your jumpsuit and turn around," the officer cried between more coughin.

Chad's suit rustled and cuffs clinked. The orange jumpsuit shuffled by. "Good catching up with you Dean."

"Shut your face," the officer barked.

The force a water fillin the bowl in Chad's stall rose like had no quit and gurgled full and went quiet. My back to my feet lined stiff. I coulda been a statue in front a the courthouse settin so still. The buckskin jacket rested cool on my backside. My boots started up tappin the cement floor. My whole body gone calm and pushed my Wranglers down for more room.

Limped down the hall free as one soul could be. Officers scattered blinded by a gold buckle not even wearin. Eloisa and Elena sat on a bench below a glass window full a tables with Carmen glued to her phone next to her large leather bag.

"Sit here Dad," Elena said.

An officer nodded and walked off. Elena slid over and pulled the fringe on the sleeve a the buckskin jacket. "You have the same coat as the Palomino mare Dad. It's old Dad, but you never wore it before."

A little man in a big suit halted in all the officer traffic and said, "You can't be here near all the criminals. By gosh it's closed to all good citizens. How in the dickens did you get in here?"

"The police man let us in," Elena said.

The man eyed us and shook his head. "Don't dwaddle here a second more and go."

"We're waiting."

"Sir, I insist you take these girls forthwith!"

"We cannot move until Uncle Jesús comes."

"You have survived a fruckus sir, no doubt. With valid business here to rectify. Appeal to your best judgment though and go."

My eyes shifted direct on Elena to set the man straight again, but her eyes was on dark blue suits surroundin an enormous Mexican. A chain clung round his waist tyin his hands. He shuffled with his heels an inch apart. Two officers backed up with pistols on their hips inches from are faces. One faced the door and buzzed it open. Tattoos spotted on the Mexican's chin down his neck and covered his arms. Was hard enough to test Jay. He halted at the door, and the officers did, not a one touchin him.

He turned and said, "Hola Elena."

Elena pulled on my sleeve and said, "This is my Dad. He has a new coat like the Palomino mare."

"Bueno. Hola Eloisa."

Eloisa waved.

He shuffled through the door with all them police officers behind.

The little man in a big suit holstered a pistol and said, "It will go down in my report be sure. You have encountered evil here today. The purest kind you ever should have seen, and with good fortune ever have to see. He proves unnamed cartels long influence. The feds decided they want custody, but marshals were nowhere escorting him. You clearly saw with your own sets of eyes."

"He draws funny pictures," Elena said.

"For all the marbles dears, skedaddle now!"

A skinny tall man with hair parted down the middle said, "Good morning Lieutenant Gardner."

"Hi counselor, you'll find your client there." The little man in a big suit pointed through the glass.

"I see." The skinny tall man turned to the girls. "Good morning Eloisa. Good morning Elena." He cleared by the little man in a big suit. He knelt and shook Eloisa's hand and then Elena's. "Dean Stamper." He rose and give his hand, and my stubby fingers took it.

"I am Larry Goldberg. I drove over from Boise this morning because your wife would be here. She has helped me on many cases. She's always the smartest person in the building and not only in the jail where it isn't a big deal but every time she's in the courtroom where it most certainly is. I must be getting in as the clock is ticking."

"I bet it has since knotting your smart tie," the little man in a big suit said.

Elena pulled at the buckskin jacket down the hall from where we come and passed the metal detector. A pinstriped lawyer holdin a cup a coffee and a briefcase moved his hand and dropped the briefcase with a loud thud. Everyone turned and a boy coulda got himself through unawares. I wondered where he got coffee, never havin a stronger hankerin for nothin more right then all my life.

"We'll find Uncle Jesús here. He works here Dad," Elena said.

Didn't tell how I already knowed, pretty sure she'd never be old enough to hear everything. We climbed stairs and at top folks gathered round someone on the floor whose heels showed like the mean lady's in the show with a lion, tinman, and scarecrow Carmen and the girls liked so much. A couple medics worked into the crowd and lowered a stretcher nestled by the man.

"He's sick Dad," Elena said.

"Maybe he slipped and felled," I said.

"He's sick, so all the people are helping him get better Dad." Elena pulled forward on the buckskin jacket.

A woman peeled off the crowd right at us and said, "Blackfoot's very own Dean Stamper in the flesh. I'm a very dear friend of Carmen's, and I'm one of the lucky members of Bishop Ortiz's flock in Riverton."

"Where's Uncle Jesús?" Elena asked.

"Oh Elena, I don't know, but it's so nice to see you. And Eloisa you are getting so tall."

"But where's Uncle Jesús Dad?" Elena asked again.

"There," Eloisa said, pointin at a set a sinkin stairs in the middle a the hall.

He wore a navy blue suit, descendin them steps covered in thin brown carpet, same as in the hall. He waved, and the girls pulled me toward him. He moved his brief case to his other hand and hugged Elena and pulled Eloisa round Elena's shoulders for a hug. He let em go and eyed me over and squinted, liftin and shakin his head high.

"Have you seen a doctor?" he asked and eyed me whole over again. "Did they have you sign a waiver yesterday?"

"Can't recollect yesterday," I said.

"I'm sure you cannot."

He went for them folks gathered round the medics. One had a long black braided ponytail. The girls watched the crowd do nothin but talk in hushed whispers.

An older woman wearin big glasses saddled up next to Jesús and said, "I saw everything counselor. An officer asked Dewayne to take his protests at the assessor's office outside and had the audacity to order Dewayne to write a letter and quit coming in and Dewayne wouldn't, and the officer went to push him, and poor Dewayne took evasive steps and slipped and hit his head on the wall and the floor. He must have been really hurt because his eyes closed right away. The officer didn't even stay to help but walked away." She pointed. "The floor is much harder under the carpet there."

"Thank you Sister Yancey," Jesús said and raised his voice. "It takes courage to speak up."

One officer down the hall a fair bit watchin the group shook his head. Nother next to him covered his mouth like he started coughin.

"Let's have you lie down on the stretcher. We'll take you to the hospital," the medic with the long black braided ponytail said.

"I can probably walk," the man said, gettin up to his elbows.

"Too risky. You might have suffered a concussion. We'll give you a ride, a necessary precaution."

"Come see me Dewayne," Jesús said.

"When I feel up to it Bishop, I certainly will," the man said.

The medics helped the man sit on the stretcher. He lay back, and they raised up. The medic with the long black braided ponytail slid round, haltin like in fresh cement with wide eyes. "Dean."

Tommy just the same as I seen him last with them straight cheeks.

He paused. Then flashed the patented grin a his. "I missed Dyani's call last night on my first shift. She only moved to Philadelphia a few weeks ago. Big new healthcare consulting firm and was sure she was calling to brag on all the perks. But now I think she must have wanted something to do with your pearly blue eyes." He went straight serious and took steps closer. "We got called out to your father's place last night. He was in rough shape. We admitted him to the hospital."

Last news I got Dyani lived in Arlington, Virginia, somewhere Roper said had a great ancient river full a beautiful swans, but I guessed how he carried on right puny next to the mighty Snake. "Last seen him plumb sicker'n a dog. Probably do him some good strapped to some bed."

"Not that hospital."

"What happened?" Jesús asked.

"The Whirlpool washer didn't fall on him counselor. I can't divulge. You know that. He was real sick."

"He will get better," Elena said. "He always gets better Dad."

"So far, but his luck will run out," I said.

"Let's go see him." Eloisa said, and Elena pulled on the buckskin jacket.

Tommy eyed em and said, "We'll give you a ride."

The other medic pulled the stretcher. Tommy pushed with Jesús and me and the girls bringin up the rear. The crowd decided all the excitement ended and went back to their reasons for bein at the courthouse in the first place. The wheels rolled uneven on the brown carpet, and the lead medic opened the door with all a us on Tommy's heels for the ambulance.

"There he is," someone shouted.

People with cameras and spotlights gathered at the front doors a good spell down the sidewalk. They all turned are way, and a large bellied man in a windbreaker, carryin a camera, sprinted out ahead a the rest. He reached us and swung the camera onto his shoulder.

Jesús said, "Now, please," raisin his hands as the crowd caught up to the man with the enormous gut hangin over his pants.

A woman and a man and others put microphones in my face, and Jesús moved his arms toward em. "Now, please, please."

"What's happened? Why did they bring you to the courthouse? Was there a warrant out for your arrest?" a woman asked.

"My God, you look like you've survived a train wreck," one said.

"Mr. Stamper, where did you disappear to? Have you been in jail the whole time?" one asked.

"You're pale as a ghost," one said.

"Can we get a few words on how you rode Bushwacker?" a woman asked, movin her microphone round Jesús' shoulder.

"We're going to the hospital, please," Jesús said.

"You've been on the television and the internet nonstop since yesterday afternoon. The whole world knows you rode Bushwacker and rose from the dust to tell about it. What do you want to say to your fans?" the same woman asked with her microphone behind Jesús' back.

"Somethin for sure," I said.

Stunned em with their lights and equipment fixed. Not a one said nother word. Elena pulled the buckskin jacket like would eventually stretch. The woman who slipped by Jesús wore as much makeup as a rodeo queen. Water pooled round her eyes. She'd be perfect with a boy holdin a camera right behind her shoulder. Would be no need to write down after.

"Ladies and gentlemen Dean is bound for the hospital, so please give us space. We'll address his situation in the near future," Jesús said.

"What are your injuries? Have you broken your neck?" a man asked.

"Here's my card. We can do an exclusive," the woman caked in makeup said.

Tried noddin my appreciation.

"Dean, your chariot is leaving," Tommy called. He held open the back doors a the ambulance. Men dropped cameras and turned down lights, but the large bellied man kept his camera aimed level.

We got situated inside, and Tommy sat cross from me and the girls and said, "Go Andy."

The man on the stretcher lay with hands folded over his chest. Eloisa held onto her seat, and Elena bounced excited off hers. The ambulance rolled out the courthouse parkin lot onto the street and off the street through the hospital parkin lot up the ramp to the emergency entrance.

"Was our honor," Tommy said, openin the doors.

"When will the sirens go?" Elena asked.

"They are only for serious cases." Tommy stepped out the back and offered his hand. Eloisa went first and Elena went next. Tommy took my arms tight gettin down the bumper step.

"Dean," the man inside the ambulance said. He sat up on his elbows. "Why are the cameras chasing you?"

"Got it all wrong."

"What did you do?"

"Not what they think."

"Must have been big. Might want to let them go on thinking that way." He rested back, foldin his hands over his chest.

The slidin glass doors opened, and the nurse at the front desk come round with her large puffy perm a couple months from the last appointment.

"Oh, I'll get the doctor," she said.

"Not me. The guy in the ambulance."

"We'll attend to him too."

"Only here for the girls to see their grandpa. You got an idea where they penned him?"

"I'll check. We've all seen the video of you falling on your head, and it was terrifying. If you could see yourself, you'd say you need to see a doctor."

Quieted so the girls wouldn't hear so good and said slow, "Here for the old bastard against my better judgment is all."

She got behind a computer real quick.

The slidin glass doors opened, and Tommy and the other medic wheeled in the man with his arms folded on his chest. The nurse come round the desk with lollypops in her hand and give em to the girls. "He's in 304."

The girls' soft, warm hands held my stubby fingers. An older woman carryin a vase a flowers got on the elevator. She couldn't stop starin and didn't hold the door open neither. The butterflies between them walls was worse'n behind bars. The white got me fuzzier in the head one step after nother surrounded by all them hurt people.

The door 304 opened to a near empty room but a taut blanket outlinin a small body up to his neck. A metal poll with a clear bag hooked to an IV, runnin under the blanket. Eloisa led in and put her hands on top near the old head sideways on a pillow. She reached to his shoulder, and he opened his eyes.

"Good morning Eloisa," he said.

"Good morning grandpa. We came to see you."

"That is kind of you."

"You're sick," Elena said.

"You both look lovely. It's so nice to see you."

"You'll get better soon."

"Thank you Elena. I'm not as sick as I am uncomfortable. That's what happens when you don't stay young."

"Don't worry grandpa. You'll get better."

"I'm getting better now."

"Dad got a jacket like the Palomino mare."

"I know dear."

"It smells like her."

"I know that too."

"But we'll miss her this week because Dad is sick like you."

"Am not Lena. What happened?" I shouted.

"What happened to you?"

My necked flared up and hurt chest pounded and bit my tongue and said slow between clenched teeth, "Tommy said he picked you up. What the hell for?"

"He did, and I thought I was seeing a ghost." He eyed me hard and turned and smiled at the girls. "Of all the chances the home teachers came by with a piece of banana cream pie. My favorite. And they found me on the floor. I'd given up an upset belly ache was my undoing, but they called an ambulance and left the piece of pie for when I return home." He eyed me straight again. "What happened to you my son?"

"Don't recollect none."

"Dad rode a bull and at the end fell on his head," Elena said.

"By gah, I don't believe it," he said.

"He hurt his neck and his chest too," Eloisa said.

A nurse in matchin pink top and bottoms with an American Flag pinned to her chest walked right in, pushin a machine on wheels and said, "Mr. Stamper you have visitors. How very nice. Oh, I should have made the connection. What a coincidence. Hold on a second."

She left the machine and picked up a remote from a stand next to the head a the bed and pushed buttons till the TV turned on, mounted near the door. She flipped through two channels to one with large letters LIVE at bottom, and a woman with a microphone outside the courthouse.

A man's voice come from off screen, "Let's go back to the shots of Dean Stamper getting into the ambulance. He clearly manages with some difficulty."

The TV cut to me gettin into the back a the ambulance and couldn't climb in. Tommy pushed and Jesús come up and braced my side.

The TV went back to the woman. "I spoke with Stamper's attorney minutes ago."

She held the microphone in front a Jesús. "At this time everything is preliminary. No one is saying the organizing body of the Bushwacker tour, the city of Ogden, or any other responsible party failed to take the necessary steps to ensure Dean's medical care. We really are too early to draw conclusions they failed in their duties of care, but we've all seen what condition he's in. He couldn't move without assistance and is in severe and constant pain. There's no doubt he's suffering, so we'll take a hard look at what they should have done."

Then the TV cut to the woman. "This story has taken an unexpected twist from Stamper doing the impossible of riding what experts have said was rodeo's greatest bucking bull of all time and after a terrible wreck miraculously getting to his feet and disappearing soon after to the breaking news we are bringing you now on the doorsteps of the Bingham County Courthouse about whether Stamper has suffered permanent injuries because the officials at yesterday's rodeo should have done more to help after he fell on his head. We're going to stay on this and bring you the news in real time." She squeezed her cheeks. "Back to you Bill."

The nurse muted the TV. "Now isn't that something Mr. Stamper. We have our own town celebrity. Your son is on all the news channels, and everyone is talking about him this morning." She moved the machine closer to my father.

Coulda swore shook his restin head. "I've never heard of anything so preposterous in all my life."

The nurse walked round the bed. "Now all of you must leave the room for a few minutes. I need to check Mr. Stamper's vitals. I'm sure they are in order, but the tests need to be done. You can come back in a few minutes."

Plumb elated at kickin us out and backed up in a hurry before she changed her mind. The shoulder a the buckskin jacket bumped into the wall and a damned alarm set off from the hall.

"Oh no!" The nurse looked up from hookin my father to the machine. "You've started a code blue." She hustled over and shoved the sleeve a the buckskin jacket and closed a plastic cover on a blue button and headed for the door with more nurses crowdin in.

"Girls," my father said.

"Yes Grandpa," Elena said.

"Yes Grandpa," Eloisa said.

"Thank you for stopping to visit. Seeing you is such a pleasure."

CHAPTER 14

"They won't know where to go," Elena said.

"They'll figure somethin out," I said.

A person in a medical coat walked down the hall and turned round and others followed in the same turn. An old timer pushed a walker to the end a the hall and into nother, and a crack opened down the back a his gown.

Eloisa lay on the couch hidden in a magazine she picked from a stack on an end table. Elena leaned off a big red chair cross the lobby. "Some can sit in the front room and the others can sit on the front lawn. After their turn the next ones can come in the front room. Then the next ones."

My sore chest bobbed in agreement, while my neck held real good in place with Jay's brace. An idea come sudden. "What bout the ones we don't want in?"

"Which ones Dad?"

"Noisy ones for one."

"And the mean ones Dad."

"Them for sure."

A tall woman in purple scrubs entered the waitin area and asked quick, "Have you seen an older gentleman?"

"Yes." Elena hopped off the big red chair. "He went this way." She run toward the hall he shimmied by us into.

"Thank you, young lady." The tall woman in purple scrubs went after him.

Two men in white outfits acted like they wasn't watchin us, and Shawn walked passed em with a backpack.

Begun risin and he said, "Sit, sit. I overheard nurses you were here. They were saying you were the reason for the gobs of media in town. Congratulations on whatever you've got yourself into my friend. I can't wait to hear you tell your side. You certainly appear to have paid for whatever happened. Are those your doctors? What did they say is broken?"

"No need for doctors. Visitin their grandpa is all. Suppose he's just shy a meetin his maker but too damned stubborn yet. Never asked no doctor for sure when they expect him to."

"I'm glad to hear he's hanging in there."

"Long past due. Who you visitin?"

"Forgot Joe's backpack and came back for it. Our vacation was cut short after getting started at Craters of the Moon yesterday. We've stopped so many times and didn't think anything when Joe ran off or when he returned. We were down the road when he said he fell and hurt his arm. One look and we knew was broken, so we stabilized it and turned around for home."

"Sorry yur trip got ruined."

"Is he okay?" Eloisa asked, sittin up on her elbow.

"He's fine, thank you Eloisa. He wanted to go back out today, but we're going to stick closer to home and catch up on projects we've been neglecting."

"Tell him we'll be home with Linda, and he can come over." Eloisa straightened higher.

"Up to Linda," I said.

"She'll say okay," Elena said, hoppin off the big red chair.

"I'm sure he'll want to come over, if Linda says it's okay," Shawn said.

"Does he have a cast?" Eloisa asked.

"He does. It's plaster white."

"We'll color it for him."

"He'll be excited about that."

"Not if he don't want to," I said.

"I'm sure he will." Shawn turned closer. "Did you get your box?"

"What box?"

"I signed for it and forgot to bring it over until we left early yesterday morning."

"I'll hunt for it."

Shawn got serious and quieter. "You were sitting in the window with your head in your hands and elbows on your knees, glowin with lines literally around your shoulders and down your legs. You worried me how still you were. Then suddenly looked straight ahead and I felt caught and without thinking waved." He continued in pert near a whisper. "And as quickly felt bad disturbing you like that."

"Don't worry none. Can't recall a thing."

"Great. Come over for drinks tonight if you are free."

"I am. When?"

"Anytime. We'll be around."

The slidin glass doors opened and in come Verolinda in a light brown vest with B Bar B branded on and passed Shawn goin out. Elena hugged her hips, and Verolinda knelt and hugged her. She bent and kissed Eloisa on her forehead.

"I hope Taylor sees you. I try to tell him he'll end up like this. I hope you are all right though," Verolinda said.

"Want a coffee somethin fierce."

"We're meeting Carmen for lunch, but I have an errand to run before then. She said we can do anything but let you sleep or talk to the press. The news people are everywhere."

"His head hurts. Look," Elena said, pointin at my face.

"His neck hurts," Eloisa said, tossin the magazine and sittin all the way up. "He fell on his head after his ride and hurt his head, nose, and neck."

"And got blood all over his chest." Elena grabbed the buckskin jacket.

"Girls, listen to me but don't tell no one till yur mother says so," I said.

"What Dad?"

Eloisa put her hands on the shoulder a the buckskin jacket.

"He bucked me off." Eyed Elena straight and turned my sore chest to Eloisa.

"It's okay." Eloisa said.

"You should have jumped way away, so he didn't hurt you Dad," Elena said.

"The ride is on every TV in Walmart. And Taylor said he's never seen anything like it," Verolinda said.

"Don't tell one soul. Not one. Not yet. But I didn't cover him."

Verolinda shook her head with her mouth open and looked cross at all the people gatherin in the hall. "That doesn't make sense. Anyway, I need to drive out to Groveland before we meet Carmen. We better go."

"Can we stop to see the horses?" Eloisa asked.

"Yes Dad!" Elena shouted.

The crowd in the hall turned are way, and we all up and left.

Verolinda's Corolla putted over the Snake River, and we come on Nonpareil's stacks pushin out smoke I knowed smelled like sour socks. A car passin by slowed, and teenagers hung out the windows with their phones.

"This is getting scary," Verolinda said.

"Go fast," Elena said.

"This car doesn't go fast Lena. That's why Paul lets me drive it."

Them teenagers yelled like they spotted the King a England.

The Corolla turned right and drove straight, passin machinery parked inside a tall chain link fence. Some properties had driveways and those without sat off the road like the one the Corolla slowed and stopped in front.

An old woman with short spiky hair opened a screen door before the Corolla shut off. She wore yellow bellbottoms high above her waste with a baby blue puffy shirt. She waved and waved and waved.

Verolinda said, "I need your help carrying the food inside. Ms. Wren will have treats, and your mom said don't eat more than one." She held up one finger.

Verolinda got out and the girls followed. She pulled clear plastic bags a tamales from the trunk and handed em to the girls. She lifted sheets a taquitos wrapped in plastic and pushed the top down with her elbow. My heart stopped, and I wondered if had a hole or how noticeable one would be if I made one.

The old woman held the screen door. Got through after the rest, and the old woman took the brown Rand and set on a bureau just inside the doorway. She led Verolinda and the girls through a family room with shelves a books wall to wall, long, skinny and short, fat ones and colors from bright to dark blues to every shade a green and plenty a orange. If we jumped into a jellybean jar woulda been no different steppin into a pure blue kitchen.

"Place them on the counter there," the old woman said and opened the freezer door.

"They'll hold better in the refrigerator," Verolinda said.

"Yes of course." The old woman closed the freezer door and opened the fridge and moved food for space. Verolinda put the sheets on a table and took the bags from the girls.

The old woman took them bags, and Verolinda grabbed the sheets and give em over. The old woman set em inside and closed the fridge. I couldn't believe just how much and wondered if could join her function to eat em. She saddled up to an island counter and reached for her purse. She fetched out folded cash and give to Verolinda.

"They'll be a hit again this year Verolinda. Thank you." She slid round the counter where the girls was. "I am Jane Wren. It's been a while since I last saw you with your mother."

"I am Elena Torres-Stamper," Elena said, holdin her hand out.

"I am Eloisa," Eloisa said.

The old woman shook their hands and turned to me. "Will be sometime before you need an introduction."

"I'm Dean."

"What a pleasure to have you and your girls in my home. I know your family well. Please give Carmen my regards and your father when you see him." She up and paused. "I've very sorry about the loss of your brother."

"We just saw grandpa at the hospital," Eloisa said.

"My dear. Please let's sit and do tell me about your visit." We followed the old woman to a set a stairs down to a sunroom. Outside the glass doors a cement pad with a picnic table and lawn chairs and beyond a tidy yard fenced in with a long open pasture beyond. We took chairs round a table, and the old woman eyed Eloisa. "How is he?"

"Tired. He didn't move."

"I would imagine he was exhausted. Hospitals do that to you."

"He's fought bouts a sick stomach before. Got him again last night," I said.

"I am sorry to hear of it."

"Aint no need to be."

"Oh, the last time I saw your father was after he sold his business, which doesn't seem so long ago." She paused, again, and bowed her head. "I was sorry to miss your brother's funeral, but I was not in town and could only send flowers."

"There were so many beautiful flowers," Eloisa said.

"Carmen let us pick our favorites, didn't she?" Verolinda said, placin her hand on the old woman's.

"More'n expected," I said.

"I picked tulips," Eloisa said.

"And we planted them in the backyard to remember him," Verolinda said.

The old woman caught her breath. "When one of our loved ones die, flowers often do best to show the beautiful life we want to remember."

"Then was way too many," I said.

"Why Dad?" asked Elena.

"Oh, I'm sorry," the old woman said. "I'm very sorry for bringing up your brother. He was kind to me. I worked in the office of Stewart's Earth Works who subcontracted jobs on projects with your father and brother's company. He was always so thoughtful. And now I've forgotten myself." She pushed off the table. "I'll be back with some refreshments."

"Are you still sad about your brother Dad?"

"I feel bad sometimes Lena. Never sad. Aint the same."

"Sometimes you are sad."

"Feelins come, and I can't stop em. But only bad ones for him."

"It's okay to be sad when people die Mom said."

"For some people she's right."

The old woman stepped slow down the stairs, holdin a plate a brownies in one hand and a plate a chocolate chip cookies in the other. She set the plate a chocolate chip cookies nearest me. "Now what can I get you to drink? Milk? Lemonade?"

"Milk please," Eloisa said.

"Milk please," Verolinda said.

"Lemonade please," Elena said.

"I'll take coffee if you got some," I said.

"Will be a few minutes," she said and stepped back up them stairs to the kitchen. She halted halfway up em. "Do you take cream?"

"Black."

"When people die they go to Heavenly Father Dad," Elena said.

"The good ones."

"The bad ones too Dad. They need him too."

"More. But most don't have no call on him."

"What do you mean?"

"Lena, a person has to believe in God to get back to God. If you don't believe there's no way back."

The old woman brought a tray with drinks and set by the brownies. She lifted cups a milk and a tall glass a lemonade and handed em to the girls with Verolinda reachin for em. The chocolate chip cookie had just the right moist and hard inside.

"I've known your families very far back. I coached Verolinda's father on the swim team. And everyone in town knew your parents Dean." The old woman hesitated and right off knowed got on slippery ground.

"How?" Reached for nother chocolate chip cookie in case she took the plate.

"They were the pride of the town. Your father was brilliant and your mother a gifted singer and performer."

"First I heard a either."

"What a shame. Your father passed on M.I.T. to attend Stanford, so he could continue rodeoing throughout the West. By the time your mother graduated from high school she had been the lead in seven plays, three community and four school productions."

"Wow, that's so many. Ms. Wren is helping with our school play," Verolinda said.

"I'm only assisting Coach Taylor who is directing, and he's doing a fantastic job. And we are looking for young girls to play some important roles in the bigger scenes. You would be great for the parts, and I'm sure you'd be wonderful like your grandmother. We're rehearsing every

Tuesday and Thursday evening from six to nine, and you are welcome to join us."

"I'll ask Carmen. They had so many more plays back then," Verolinda said.

"How do you know how many?" Just got the words out between bites a the new chocolate chip cookie.

"I directed each one," the old woman said.

"You were so busy," Verolinda said.

"People were busy in a different way than they are now. And we knew each other better." She turned to me. "Your mother had a captivating stage presence. A true star."

"That there is more breakin news," I said.

"So surprising to me and certainly is a shame if you'll permit me to repeat myself. I'm not saying anything anyone else who saw her wouldn't."

"You talk like everyone seen her then."

"Everyone did. And worshiped her."

"Everyone's forgot."

"Now that would be shameful. Not so long ago the news wasn't pushed aside soon after hearing it. Now we are buried in it and can't hold on to any of it."

"I wish I could have seen her," Eloisa said.

"Me too," Elena said.

"I'll show you," the old woman said, pushin up on the table.

"What made her so good?" I asked.

The old woman paused to find the right answer. "She understood early on you'll never do better than what it is you are able to do. The key is finding and developing that thing as best you can. Come along. Bring your drinks."

Elena reached for nother brownie and Verolinda waved her hand off. Elena pulled back and frowned, and Eloisa put a chocolate chip cookie down. Picked it up and followed the girls out the sunroom.

"Sit," the old woman said like a colonel, aimin for debriefin us on all the colored books. She turned and went back the way we come. The girls took a green couch, and my tired backside hit an orange rockin chair. We waited a spell, and the old woman come back and give me a cup a coffee and little plate. "It's very hot, so blow."

Put my chocolate chip cookie on the plate and rested on the buckskin jacket. My fat thumb and index finger squeezed the handle. Sipped and scalded my tongue. Then took nother.

The old woman stepped to the west wall and pulled down a large yellow book. She held the pages open and thumbed through.

"Here we are." She stepped to Elena in the middle a Verolinda and Eloisa. The old woman bent and showed the girls a large page full a newspaper clippins. "There she is as Laurey in Oklahoma."

Eloisa eyed me and back at the picture, and Verolinda did. Rocked back and took a sip and broke a piece a chocolate chip cookie and dipped in my coffee.

"What was the color of her dress?" Elena asked.

"Yellow."

"How was the play?" Verolinda asked.

"Spectacular." The old woman lifted the large book and turned pages with more newspaper clippins. "Her performance got attention as far as the San Francisco Chronicle and wasn't her only one to get noticed." She heaved the book to her face. "A new talent emerges among the world's greatest potatoes in a brilliant performance of the romantic country life. The inspired local production could be mistaken as on Broadway for one talent alone who must be big city bound." The old woman set the large book in Elena's lap. "Many critics came to Blackfoot over those years. One came all the way from New York to see her in a roadshow. He crossed his dates and missed the performance in Blackfoot and stayed an extra week to see her in Preston."

The old woman turned back to the west wall and pulled a darker yellow book. "And here is the other half." She lifted the page close to her face again. "Nuclear engineer returns home to lead research at Navy division. Stamper believes sustainable energy is the key to the advancement of all civilization, and he stated nowhere are steps being taken with more importance than in our own backyard. He continued the future of our nation and allied countries will depend upon our efforts." The old woman placed the book open to the page she read on top a the other book. "There are many more. I'll get one of my favorites." Back at the west wall she pulled a bright yellow book. Real thin and she found the page real quick and placed on top a the other two books.

Elana said, "She looks like you Dad."

Took a sip and rocked more.

"With your regular eyes and nose," Eloisa said.

Got me settin down the plate on the floor, and a piece a chocolate chip cookie I thought I ate bounced off the buckskin jacket. Felt my puffy nose and eyes, tenderer'n even last night. The girls said what my father and brother said. I never expected em to tell the truth with plenty a reasons to suspect they didn't but never had no ground to doubt the girls.

The Corolla putted long like had nowhere else to be. Elena pulled the buckskin jacket lookin through the middle a the front seats with her eyes wide and road passin under us. In my head I still seen the old woman placin one book after nother till the stack pert near reached the girls' heads. Elena placed her empty glass on top, and Verolinda took it before the old woman returned with a nother open book. She filled my cup twice and brought a chocolate chip cookie perfect as the ones before. She picked up the piece I dropped and give to me and didn't hound me none for askin. Reached to give to Sam before realizin she weren't there and ate it myself. I never felt fuller rockin with my cup restin on the plate on top the buckskin jacket.

The old woman got me on thoughts I never had before all tingly and clear headed at the very same time. She had a peculiar view a my brother but didn't hold no turnip to all the ones bout my folks. I wondered if she didn't tell my brother my mother moved to New York City. If I speculated further she told bout a different world but knowed the real one with the girls excitable and no other way and still be Carmen's. They even raised a notch over the old woman's tales, and I bout spilled my cup twice. The first time when she said my father trained Jimmy Carter, who even I knowed as the famousest farmer to ever live, and the second time when she said they was on a submarine when he did. In a damned desert I started sayin but got to chokin on a mouthful a chocolate chip cookie. Sure if true someone shoulda went and sunk it.

Elena put her finger on the crux a the thing. Where would bad people go? If right, God would bring everyone home safe. Aint so though. Pure innocence talkin.

Not everyone would come back home sure as they didn't knowed they had one. You had to know the thing. Was the thing. Death sets the table a all the pieces a when you was alive with how they fit a right mystery a what you knowed in life.

The Corolla turned down a gravel road with poplars on both sides and light scatterin through branches. The girls pointed toward the horses. We crossed a ditch to open country with a high and long stack a hay on the left and drove by a shorter stack the size a the last house I built on the right. We passed Roper's father's place and a bit beyond a rundown three-story farmhouse full a wild kids on the other side a the road. The Corolla slowed and turned onto a dusty patch leadin to corrals and a barn.

Closed the door and the girls was already at the fence. Eloisa slipped between rungs a the corral. Elena tried followin, but Verolinda grabbed aholt a her. Got to em and climbed up restin my arms over top. The bay stood in the middle. The Palomino mare skittered long the fence, and the strawberry Roan worked up by her side. Eloisa walked down the strawberry Roan, and the Palomino mare run between em. Eloisa froze. The Palomino mare whinnied like she seen a mountain lion and dashed back and forth.

Climbed the rest a the fence and slid over and slipped my boots in rungs and worked down em. The Palomino mare reared and stomped. Elena screamed through the fence on my face. Her lungs mightier'n I knowed possible with air pressin me. Just turned and the Palomino mare run long the fence toward the far side. The Bay nudged Eloisa on the ground, and she didn't move. Limped quick to where she lay. Her hands stretched long her sides. Knelt on my good knee and lifted her in my arms. We passed by the Bay's neck and carried her to the gate and Verolinda opened it. Braced Eloisa on the fence. Verolinda knelt and patted her head and rested her hands on her cheeks. Eloisa opened her eyes. Her color come back and eyes filled, and she lifted her palms wipin em.

"You'll be a'right," I said.

The Palomino mare dashed quick long the back fence. Went straight at her and she darted back. Waited, starin her over with a mind to ride her down into the night with my head flarin every square inch on the very thought. Elena called through the fence, pointin at the strawberry Roan. Walked to her and put my arms round her neck and patted her down.

Led the Bay and strawberry Roan to the gate and left em with the girls and headed for the barn. Lifted the latch and no rustlin, not a stick a straw for mice to hide on the popcorn asphalt and not even a spot a dirt. Halters with lead ropes hung where we left em in the tack room. The door to the concrete washroom set open. Closed it on my way out and heeled up quick to the corral and handed a halter to Eloisa and one to Verolinda and carried mine direct for the end.

The Palomino mare skittered back and forth. Hopped left and then right, and she took a step and waited to dart the way I didn't. Swung the end a the lead rope in a circle and got two feet from her and struck her hip. She darted to the fence and turned. Skipped right and swung the lead rope and got her walkin straight back and she turned. Jumped her neck. Her nostrils opened wide and lined up, breathin heavy. Slipped the halter over and pulled down. She backed up to the fence and swung her hind end and pushed me in the fence and yanked up. Held and worked my elbow up the rungs and got my boots under me and pushed her head on the fence with the shoulder a the buckskin jacket. She hunched waitin. Slid the halter up, tyin and pullin on her. She pulled back and come quick. Pulled her neck and yanked the lead rope down the fence. My neck screamed with a burnin hole in my chest and water flowed under the buckskin jacket.

The girls brushed down the Bay and strawberry Roan at the front a the barn. Eloisa hid behind the Bay. Got the Palomino mare round her. The Bay lifted her head, and the Palomino mare angled to the side. Pulled on her from the bottom a the halter. She breathed deep and held her eyes high.

"Pat her down."

Elena went for feed I knowed we'd have to clean up after we was done. She hurried back with a half filled gallon a oats she could drop in a second. Verolinda helped lift the bucket to the strawberry Roan who lapped a few helpins. The Palomino mare whinnied and stamped in place. Pointed for the Bay's turn, and she lapped up a few mouthfuls. Waved for the bucket and pulled the Palomino mare's head. She hesitated a couple seconds. Released the halter and she dipped inside and nuzzled the bottom for a couple licks. Dropped the bucket and backed her to the gate and long the fence. Tied her on.

Beyond the corral nother real rundown with worn fence, long enough for ropin, but Roper's father didn't for years. Couldn't get him in the saddle if the devil prodded with his pitch fork. At the far side set a single chute with boards broke, and pieces hung loose with no gate.

The girls led the Bay and strawberry Roan into the barn. Went for the tack room and grabbed a couple blankets off the wall rack and bridles organized in a tall open wood cupboard, and Elena followed me in. Handed her a bridle she carried on my hip. Got to Eloisa and handed her the other one and Verolinda a blanket she put right on. Her and Eloisa removed the halter and strapped the bridle down. Courtin trouble liftin Elena to bridle the strawberry Roan, what I did lots since the stall doors had no space to step. Put on her blanket and led her down the alley to a bench Elena knowed to climb up, and she reached for the halter. Helped take it off, and she pulled the bridle from her shoulder. We put it on and fit the straps, and Elena held the reins. Went for the saddles and fetched the Bay's. Got it on her back and the fault line on my neck opened. Back in the tack room rested all my stubby fingers on the strawberry Roan's and breathed slow. My head bound to roll somewhere I weren't, but Jay's brace held tight. Eloisa and Verolinda worked on cinchin the Bay. Passed by em down the alley and set the strawberry Roan's saddle on the bench. Elena asked to help put it on. Got it up and over in one swing. We pulled the cinch and run round and through the ring.

We led the horses out the barn. An old Cadillac sat on the path to the road. The horses whinnied their hellos. The engine shut off, and Chris lumbered out and said, "Please stop in for lunch. Am cooking extra for the holiday."

"Much obliged Chris. We sure will," I said.

She climbed back in the old Cadillac and backed up for home sure to finish up preparations.

"But Mom wants to meet for lunch Dad," Elena said.

"Not like this one Lena, not like this one." Was just beside myself with are luck.

Eloisa sat tall on the Bay. Elena held the horn with Verolinda behind her on the strawberry Roan. Eloisa held the reins low, and the Bay walked into the middle and to the edge a the road. Elena held the reins tight with Verolinda's hands on top. Patted the strawberry Roan's neck. The saddle creaked so soft you coulda missed with hooves clackin on the gravel road. Eloisa sat relaxed, and the Bay trotted ahead. Elena still squeezed the horn, and Verolinda moved her hands on the back a the saddle.

"Soften yur hands Lena. Go ahead and rest em on the horn," I said.

"It's hard Dad. She wants to run," Elena said.

"Just let her have rein. Rest yur hands."

The strawberry Roan turned, openin her gray round eyes. Patted her down and eyed her knobbin front hocks and thought to ask Chris for a salve the girls could rub her down with.

The rundown three-story farmhouse off the road did not have one wild kid in sight. Paint peeled off more'n stuck on. The front window looked to have tape runnin down the middle. I couldn't tell if there was hinges for a door where a hole left none a the summer out. A swing tied by balin twine hovered with one side near touchin at the end a the porch. Smack dab in the middle a the lawn rose an oak tree the size a Texas with two sets a rope ladders hangin from branches. Boards run over branches and plywood lay cross others.

The Bay trotted, and Eloisa sat deep in the saddle like she didn't know no different.

"Let yur hands down Lena," I said. The strawberry Roan trotted ahead, and Verolinda reached round and grabbed Elena's hands and let out the reins. Caught up and patted the strawberry Roan's shoulder. We turned down the driveway to Roper's folks' house, and the horses clicked and clocked over gravel in dust still settlin from Chris's Cadillac. The Palomino mare whinnied, just could barely hear, and the Bay did back.

Chris's Cadillac parked in the nearest spot under an open garage. A hitchin post set off the back door. Eloisa slipped down and wrapped the Bay's reins. Took the strawberry Roan's reins from Elena and wrapped em. Verolinda slid off, and Elena reached round Verolinda's neck and got down.

We rounded the horses' tails to the backdoor. Chris waddled ahead and ushered us into the washroom.

"We all smell like Dad's collar," Eloisa declared. She lathered up and passed soap to Verolinda, and she washed quick and tried helpin Elena. Elena insisted on washin herself and kept on like in a trance. Took the soap from Elena and got plenty on the sleeves a the buckskin jacket. Chris ushered us into the dinin room. Verolinda slipped onto the bench against the wall, and Elena and Eloisa scooted in next to her. Yellow wallpaper on drywall breached in worn spots with mud behind em.

Chris set a platter a sliced baked ham with pineapple rings in the middle a the table. I ate the finest beef cuts knowed to man from Kansas City to Reno but nothin measured up to succulent ham. Nothin I tasted in person, and I ate everything. Right then the idea come to bring Carmen a plate with plenty a extras.

Chris come back with breaded green beans in one hand and caramelized butternut squash in the other. Then she brought double baked potatoes with extra bacon and onions on top and a bowl a dark Boston baked beans. She returned one last time with a bowl a jello with fresh strawberries and homemade whipped cream. Just plumb beside myself.

Dishes and helpins passed and in short order covered are plates with no space on mine, not even a sliver. Swallowed a few bites and raised my fork for a piece a ham, and Roper's father walked in. He said hello all round and left the room and come back with Chris's father, Cordell. Was old as the hills and come to shows far back as I recollected. Never havin said more'n pleasantries between us, but I knowed he fancied chew and everyone could by his boots. When I pointed out his loyalties to Roper he said old Cordell stood in pure unadulterated solidarity with Mormon founders. Roper didn't choose then to start makin sense but later expounded old Cordell believed in concert with early Mormon prophets who shared his proclivities for fine tobaccos. Had to back in them times Roper said to keep calm tendin to all their wives. I never staked a claim for lots a smarts but knowed enough one habit them founders a the Mormon religion got inspired on. Old Cordell shuffled to the table in yellowed white slippers. Roper's father pulled a swivel out and old Cordell flopped on it.

Old Cordell's mind weren't no tack, fumblin over the girls' names and mistakin em for other children. There was neighbors a plenty to confuse em with and no tellin which ones he did.

If were Verolinda's first meetin Chris, I couldn't tell the way they carried on. Roper's father just full a questions I never expected capable a musterin, and he lent on knowed bout former plays when Verolinda explained are visit to the old woman with the colored books. He went and smiled like he really gived a damn. What I had no recollection a witnessin before. Chris and him both knowed bout the school play with Verolinda and talked like Milly played in the same one. Chris conversed bout the old woman's books with a vast depository a lots more somewhere not far away. Roper's father said years ago they attended the old woman's Fourth a July bash on her back patio with a great view a the fireworks show over the Blackfoot Reservoir for the finest day a remembrance he ever had. I never heard him talk this way and paused with my mouth full on their collective recollectance a the women's chocolate chip cookies when they said in unison no one made none better. The very same feelin set in surrounded by all them colorful books and kept the entire drive from the old woman's house. Was just sore amazed hearin em witness to what I myself experienced earlier and forked nother piece a ham.

Old Cordell slurped a spoon full a squash and got nother and kept starin. His eyes got wider and didn't say nothin with his spoon below his bottom lip and neither quivered. Eyed him and took a bite a baked potato with a fair bit a buttery skin and chewed slow ready for him to blink and swallowed even slower against Jay's brace. Moved my fork cross to cut a piece a ham but didn't look away. Raised a piece, and old Cordell flicked his spoon full a squash. A bigger spoonful'n I speculated on over my face and drippin down the buckskin jacket.

Everyone sat quiet for one second. Elena started laughin, and Verolinda and Eloisa did. Chris scolded old Cordell, and Roper's father took his spoon. Old Cordell kept on eyein me and didn't blink. Verolinda covered her mouth, and Eloisa quieted some. Not Elena who kept laughin like she didn't have no choice. Wiped off my face with the sleeve a the buckskin jacket and forked in the piece a ham. Elena in a fit pointed up and down the buckskin jacket to my face. Guessin I missed some lifted the other sleeve a the buckskin jacket and brushed my other side, chewin fast in a hurry to clear my plate before the rest finished with theirs.

Visitin Chris were like Thanksgivin on repeat. No other way to describe each and every visit and no place I looked more forward to and hearin her news before, durin, and after supper. Just kind as one could be. Angels woulda fled heaven to sit at her table if God would only permit em to. And I always left with five extra pounds ready for winter. She fed Roper's father like he ranched full time, and the Lord knowed he'd chose the life over buildin houses if cattle paid, but the herd on his spread was lucky to break even every fourth year even with the price a beef's decade-on boon. He run two hundred cows and needed to double up to cowboy for a livin. His buckin bulls ate more'n their share with just enough to put on an amateur show with bulls young kids rode. When got a string a buckers he lacked sense to sell till was too old. I could render his buckin operation into a general ledger cause the finicky gains and constant losses was the topic we ended lunch on most days. Was no foreman but Roper's father treated me like one, pullin me for coffee to discuss how behind schedule we always was and lament how fussy folks got bout added expenses.

Stretched out in the recliner in Chris's front room and all the new complaints come. The new house in Rose got two months behind with the doctor threatenin suit. The place on Von Elm not even permitted. And good luck to a home owner findin legal representation with Roper's father havin used every lawyer from I.F. to Poky and year in and year out one a the biggest donors a Kiwanis's countin among its membership most a the judges in every county we built in. The girls was off seein a new dress Chris made for a girl in her ward Verolinda's age. Roper's father went back to work and old Cordell to a TV room where he spent the better part a his days watchin the same breakin news stories over and over again.

A paintin with a fat rancher with his cowboy hat over his eyes hung on the wall. Mine lined the top where smaller figures worked in back. A large loose bundle a hay between em, strands blowin in an invisible wind.

They begun movin and blurry spots for their eyes and mouths cleared. Come closer on their conversin. One spoke, wavin his arms. The other, tall and thin, grinned. The animated man told a story they both already knowed, and I suspected he told before but didn't know how they knowed or how I did. They raked and broke, wipin off water. The tall thin man picked up a jug and took a long pull, and the other man come and took the jug and lifted for short gulps between observations and lingered on. Water pooled on their necks and drenched their collars and smelled a sun. Sam bumped my leg, and I scratched her head, and she run off through uncut alfalfa. Turned for an extra pitch fork with water runnin down my back.

"Dad, Dad, Dad," yelled a voice from above, and I stared into breakin clouds in wide blue sky. "Dad, Dad, Dad," yelled the voice again, there Elena held by Verolinda.

Eloisa's head touched up against mine. "Wake up."

"I am."

"Mom said to not sleep Dad!" Elena yelled.

"You have to stay awake," Eloisa said with her hands on the buckskin jacket.

"Just restin."

"Get up Dad!" Elena yelled.

"I am."

Chris watched from the entryway and said, "You're welcome to stay. There's plenty to keep you busy."

"We should get goin." I couldn't tell my body from the reclinin chair I knowed fit perfect from lots a naps there before.

Convened at the washroom for their shoes, and they all rushed out. My shirt soaked through. Unbuttoned the buckskin jacket for air and wiped down my tender chest. Joined Chris at the back door watchin the girls. She handed over the brown Rand. The horses nibbled grass on the side a the driveway, movin to a strip leadin to an open alfalfa field ready for the next crop. The girls walked long, talkin and pattin em down.

"They are making fine horsewomen. We enjoy having them out to ride. We'll always be here," Chris said.

"Carmen wouldn't miss it."

Chris put her hand on the buckskin jacket. "You did great yesterday. Scared the excitement right out of us with your getoff though. Are you starting up again? Or was the ride one last hurrah?"

"Don't rightly know."

"You have nothing to prove. Never have. Want you to be safe though."

"I'm a'right."

"I know you are doing better now, but from your looks one might have other ideas. We were terrified while you lay there. Then you got to your knees and we held our breath for so many minutes and suddenly you stood. Oh Dean I bawled and bawled. Lynn left the room. I watched you over and over again and cried every time you got up."

The only person I knowed cared enough to say what she did and mean it. I expect there was others out there like Chris but never met nother in person. She always looked after me and my brother and never a mean word. Just pure concern and encouragement. Nothin less I swear on the head a who'd dare contradict otherwise.

"Roper called as excited as can be. He asked us if we'd seen your ride, and, of course, he went on about it being so great. He's been so busy, not once coming home the past three years, but he says he's coming home this summer. I asked him to come for the Fourth, but he said he was too busy. He said he sent you a package for his stepson, and when I asked him why he'd do such a thing, he said the boy's mother prohibited it. Then I knew to mind my own business. He said he'll pick it up when he gets to town. I'll stop by to get it."

"Don't bother yurself. When it arrives, we'll bring it out."

The girls and horses moved down the lane for taller grass before a cattle guard. Called em and the Bay lifted her head. Eloisa pulled the reins, and the Bay took a bite, greedy for grass. The girls walked with the horses' heads followin, Eloisa in no hurry and Elena skippin just to keep up.

Held the strawberry Roan and Verolinda climbed up behind the saddle. Handed her the reins and lifted Elena up and my neck cracked like glass and set her down. Took a quick knee on my bad one and rested my hand on the ground. Verolinda slid off and lifted Elena up. Braced up against the strawberry Roan, and Chris held her. Verolinda lifted under Eloisa's shoulder, and without a hitch Eloisa got her foot in the stirrup and over the saddle a the Bay. Verloinda reached for the horn and got her foot in the stirrup and up behind Elena.

Chris patted the shoulder a the buckskin jacket and said, "Go slow and take care of yourself."

"Thank you," Eloisa said, turnin and wavin.

"See you Saturday," Chris said.

"Thank you," Verolinda said.

"See you Saturday," Elena yelled with her hands on reins pasted to the horn.

The horses got on the road, and an engine roared from behind, gettin close real fast. The Bay trotted to the other side. Pushed the strawberry Roan down the barrow pit and shuffled into weeds. Turned to yell down the mad driver and a big blue suburban full a kids stuck to windows. Gravel sprayed me head to toe. The big blue suburban continued on a hundred yards and turned down the lane to the rundown three-story farmhouse. The engine kept runnin, and kids jumped out and sprinted back up the lane, waitin on the horses. We got to the head where a half-dozen a them kids hollered for the girls. Their band surrounded the horses down the lane. A German Shepherd sat at the end. Eyed real close, pattin my front pocket. Blue heelers bounced round them unruly kids. They was no friends a Sam.

We passed more kids climbin the old massive oak tree. I counted three at the trunk and double as many rascals in them branches. A stout, clean-cut man with a buzz cut, wearin a tight shirt with a printed helmet and axe, set his hands on his hips inside the frame a the missin front door. He waved at the girls, and Eloisa waved back. Elena wouldn't have noticed if he were the Archangel Michael with his outstretched majestic white dirty wings straight off the field battlin Beelzebub. She chatted kids by the strawberry Roan. They peppered her with questions and between her answers she told em to not get no closer.

A teenager appeared out a nowhere with a glass a purple Kool-Aid, offerin a place to sit. I reckoned him to mean a broken step, but he jumped over em for the swing. Twine wove together with tight knots on both ends. Sat on the slanted end, snug on the arm rest.

Verolinda moved in the circle a kids and dogs. She picked one small kid and swung it up behind Elena. Other kids rushed Verolinda, and she grabbed hands a one and twirled round and grabbed nother. She twirled one and nother till the last kid. She waved her arms and stepped side to side, and the whole brood copied. Elena had no one to yell after, ridin the strawberry Roan on the lawn. A small one in a diper couldn't been walkin more'n a month burst out in wild cries. Verolinda picked it up and set on her hip and walin quieted. The others' arms followed after Verolinda's free one movin with wind.

The Bay and Eloisa come round the old house and went round again.

Darn right delicious. Roper and me had lots a mint juleps on tabs a more'n one southern belle who fancied are company, and he took to commentin each tasted the most refreshin a all we had in the years we rode together. Roper at his truest, always havin to experiencin somethin the best, better'n the best everyone else experienced, countin himself did before. I couldn't protest, swallowin the last drop a purple Kool-Aid. Nothin so refreshin passed my lips. Eyed the whole lawn for the teenager for nother.

The porch swing soothed all my senses, and I lost time. We coulda been there for hours, and I'd slept but squealin and barkin kept me from it. Kids danced with each other, and others broke apart matchin Verolinda on one leg. She halted and pulled out her phone and waved Eloisa and Elena over. The kids stood in line waitin her next instruction. She clapped and congratulated em, and they started up clappin too. The stout man appeared at the end a the porch, hands still on hips.

Pulled myself off the swing, eyein for the German Shepherd. All the kids dropped from the tree and broke from the dances and lined both sides a the lane. The horses passed em and back on the gravel road. The high-pitched chorus ceased like we never come.

The Bay and strawberry Roan headed by the corral straight for the barn. Got the saddles and the girls got the blankets back in their places in the tack room. Just handed out brushes and Verolinda raised her phone with a text from Carmen to meet in Riverton and not home. We groomed quick, and the girls led the Bay and strawberry Roan into the corral and took off their bridles. The Bay first and strawberry Roan not a step behind steered clear a the Palomino mare. She shifted to the side. Eyed her level from her withers to croup and equal to the ends a her shoulder and hip with a straight line between. The most beautiful thing I ever seen. Went for her and she held and run my hand long her back and patted her shoulder.

Closed my stubby fingers on her muzzle and slipped the halter off, bouncin against the rungs, and she held. Patted her neck and she darted off and galloped halfway down the corral. She halted and crow hopped and kicked back.

CHAPTER 15

A hundred yards from Jesús' place a van with a satellite on top and more vans with more satellites and lots a vehicles in between in a long line with their noses in the barrow pit like arrivn at Cape Canaveral for a Space Shuttle Launch on TV in elementary school.

The Corolla crawled up to a police car with lights twirlin. Verolinda put her window down, and an officer bent and eyed us over. "How is everyone doing?" Verolinda and the girls all answered fine at the same time. "You are the car everyone is expecting. Pull in slow there."

I knowed now would be my chance to get the record right and had to find a computer handy to time the ride before Jesús got to talkin. Wouldn't get no better'n with all them vans.

A large fence blocked the front a Jesús' yard. He contracted the buildin with no time himself and not wantin to impose on me. Glad he didn't, not fond a post hole diggers. Long boards on top imprinted with horses. Halfway a door easy to miss but for a fake pearl handle. Corrals and a new shed attached to six stalls on the back a his property all for just one show horse. I asked Jesús when he planned gettin nother with all the extra space, and he said not till he could afford the one he had.

Verolinda pulled the Corolla to the thin iron gate on the driveway. Nother police car sat at the entrance with no lights on. Sheriff Caldwell stepped from behind and waved us down. My face set straight like I didn't notice. Verolinda went and stopped. He knocked on my window, and Verolinda lowered it. Moved my eyeballs his way.

"Welcome young ladies," he said, crouchin and hangin on the door. He lowered his voice. "Nice to see you on the outside Dean. You be sure and tell Jesús I'm on to him. Looks like we have no choice but to be proud of you, but don't think he is getting all this for free. Not one penny, not from the county. I have three men on overtime, not counting myself who should be on my couch right about now relaxing my puppies in the company of my old lady, ready to eat our early TV dinners in adherence with her latest dietary regimen." He leaned in close with sober breath on my face. "Organic lasagna. She texted I'm missing organic lasagna but not without consequences I'm not. This is an emergency, which our rates will reflect in the bill I send directly to Jesús' law office as soon as I get Patricia to write it up. Emergency rates Dean. And there will be no negotiating a reduction short of a final order from a court of law." He stretched pert near his whole body against the car, his belly blockin the window forcin me over. "Not one penny." He spoke up, directin where to pull into. "You ladies have a great evening and don't stare into the lights or you'll go blind. Look right into the cameras at the blank spots, and you'll be fine." He stepped back for the Corolla to pass and patted the top. "We'll be expecting prompt payment."

Near two hundred people gathered inside the fence, and lots surrounded the Corolla before we come to a stop.

The girls didn't say no single word. Elena looked nervous like she'd be asked to give a talk. The girls participatin in somethin got me joinin em and Carmen so much at their Mormon Ward. One give a talk, the other sung, or both shared a picture in primary. Mormon Wards had lots a programs and extracurricular activities, and if Carmen weren't goin then comin for are girls and everyone else's kids as busy year round as me hittin them peak summer shows.

People massed round a set a microphones near the patio. They swallowed us up under the lights. In all the pandemonium Rosa appeared, creatin space to the back a the house. At the end a the patio Jesús admired his hallowed kamado grill and lifted the top. He could orate on the effects a heat precisely as once man could said Roper. I only knowed I had me many a fine steak off it. He wore a bright red, white and blue apron and held an empty sheet. He motioned to go right in. Right behind him a fence marked his property, and on the other side an open pasture spread a hundred acres to banks a the Blackfoot River, and on its other side a field a potatoes run on the reservation.

My heart pounded on findin a computer. Planned on sayin my piece quick and then headin down Riverton Road to get Sam now with Josey way too long.

The back door opened into the dinin room. Tinfoil on platter after platter covered the light wood table where me and Carmen and the girls sat for lots a Thanksgivins. Sure my luck could get no better even if were Christmas Day with stops at every relative's place. Women I guessed from the Riverton Relief Society scurried in and out the kitchen. Each one paused to compliment the girls. I knowed without a single breath my lungs took in Rosa's kitchen full a the sweetest a smells. One a the Relief Society members come out the kitchen and set a sheet with five baked loaves a bread covered by a long thin colored cloth. Close to em blocks a real butter uncovered on small circular dishes.

All went bright as high noon on the clearest Idaho summer day. Without knowin how or when I come to raisin a cuttin knife. The back door slammed. Brought the handle in my fist fast against the buckskin jacket.

"I have a speech," Jesús said.

Didn't hitch one bit.

"Tonight we celebrate." He eyed the uncovered loaf. "Go ahead."

My hand come free and cut real slow the end. The crust broke and warmth spread over my stubby fingers.

"We will feed the masses before we address them. Not counting that slice." He stepped close, holdin a silver spatula to his chest. "How are you feeling? Is your neck progressively getting worse? Carmen said something about an open cut on your chest. I could't see how he hit you on film but doesn't mean we won't argue the wound with everything else that certainly went untreated. It's still far too soon to determine our conclusions definitively. We won't say any party was negligent clearly failing to provide you with reasonable care until all the facts have been gathered. That's not the purpose of our press conference. First and foremost, we celebrate your great accomplishment as a favored son of Blackfoot with a speech for the occassion."

Jesús would get speakin this way, his gift a eloquence Carmen explained. Went over me like other important matters. I knowed his words was different though, not like Shawn's or Roper's, with his plump smile sayin em. Smelled the fresh bread in my head and the warmth extended over my entire body, and the idea come to get to Rosa's fridge to check for her homemade Raspberry jam. The quicker before Carmen arrived, the better my chance at nother slice.

Inside the fence all the people surrounded a row a plastic picnic tables with patterned tablecloths. Till you got up close they coulda been quilt displays in one a the last pavilions before rides at the Eastern Idaho State Fair. Walked by em with Jesús. Reporters peppered me with questions till they seen I meant to not answer, good to Jesús' words to em we'd speak only after everyone ate. Wouldn't till Carmen showed. Didn't matter if Jesús did. He wouldn't see none a these folks never again. He led us back to his kamado grill and removed the top. He grabbed pinchers for a tri-tip and set on a sheet and led back in the house to the kitchen. He grabbed a long knife and cut into thin slices. Beautifully pink. He pulled out nother sheet from the oven and tore off tinfoil on two more slabs. He cut em thin, one medium rare and the other medium. Such abundance a beef he coulda fed all Riverton, if me and his boys didn't go back for seconds.

Rosa took em outside to feed the people.

Jesús took off his bright red, white and blue apron and draped over a empty bar stool. He left and returned, wearin his suit coat and smilin, runnin his fingers through his black hair.

"I know this isn't such a big deal for you. For me it's a once in a lifetime opportunity. The Lord works in mysterious ways, and he's brought many eyes on us. I don't want to fail him by wasting the opportunity to reach as many people as possible." He put both his hands on the buckskin jacket. "There's no sugar coating the truth. I'll be using your good name, and I promise to do my best."

"Got my piece to say."

"Carmen told me about your idea. Share it with gusto. Don't hold back. Let the people know the truth. You can't emphasize your position enough. They'll call you crazy. They'll call you mad. Let them. I've always appreciated your indomitable will. I'm amazed by it. Doesn't come naturally or in any great amount to the rest of us. We approach things with far more fear and circumspection."

"Where's yur computer?"

"The big Dell monitor is in my den. My Dell laptop is in my truck. Why?"

"Need to wait. Got nothin to say unless Carmen shows."

"I understand. She gives me the same confidence. I'll do my best until she arrives."

"Sure will be plenty till she does."

"If this could only be enough. I need the floodgates of work opened to get everything Rosa wants. The new F-150 was nothing if a fulfilment of a prideful desire and stretched an already strained budget."

"Nice ride."

"There's simply no denying it. I will go to the ends of the Earth to hide her from the repo man when he eventually comes. Let's fill up the people. There's one more loaf on the table there."

Jesús went for the back door and waited.

Cut a slice and went for a spread a jam.

The crowd grew even bigger and parted for Jesús. The Relief Society members filtered by packs a people, bringin dish after dish a casseroles galore, macaroni casserole first on the end a the table, right next to green bean casserole and shepherd's pie casserole, next to chicken and broccoli casserole, one a my favorites a all time, next to linguine casserole and a reporter asked if really were one and just bout shouted help yurself and find out but got focused on more casseroles, a tuna casserole with no noodles like my grandma made next to corn casserole, then sausage casserole, hamburger and rice casserole, even spinach casserole, and porcupine meat balls casserole and finally tater tot casserole and a reporter said one could be goulash casserole if such a thing were possible, all them casseroles coverin all them patterns on top a the tables with thirty-four different colored jellos in their midst and at least seven pot roasts with twelve bowls a mashed potatoes. The greatest shindig I seen in person.

A loud voice shouted from behind the microphones and asked people to quiet down and clappin followed and continued till the crowd hushed. They was confused eyein Jesús in their midst and back at them microphones wonderin how he would give his talk from the table by all the cut slabs a beef.

Everyone turned toward the patio with Brother Hamilton before microphones and cameras with lights flankin the sides. He spoke up so loud no one could ignore a single word. "Thank you all for coming. It's our pleasure to host you, many of whom have come from all over the country to be with us today. As you know Jesús will address us with Dean, but before they do the Relief Society of Riverton Ward has prepared a great meal. Now please uncover and bow your heads with me as I offer a blessing on the food."

People was shocked at the thought a prayer like they never witnessed one before, and those with cameras shut em down and some lights popped off. Those with nothin in hand looked at each other and back again.

"Dear Heavenly Father, we are thankful for the many blessings we enjoy and the opportunity to be gathered here today. We are grateful for the safety of everyone who has travelled far and wide to come to Blackfoot and ask for thy protection over them when they return to their various homes in our blessed country. We especially thank thee for the safety of Dean Stamper, for his outstanding and qualified ninety-two point ride, and his miraculous rise to be with us to share in thy glory. Not a single one of us can certainly deny the officials who scored him and our very own eyes who saw it. We all stand as witnesses to one of the greatest rides ever, if not the greatest ride in the annals of cowboys versus bucking bulls and as further witnesses to thy power for raising Blackfoot's chosen son literally from the dust, as sure as we all stand here now. We thank thee for the blessings of thy Spirit, and ask thee to bless us with thy guidance. We seek humility and to be worthy of thy love. We know all things are possible through thy Son, the Lord Jesus Christ and stand in awe of his atonement, and ask thee bless us with the strength to share it with all of our brothers and sisters. We ask thee to bless the missionaries sharing the true message of thy only begotten to the ends of the world. We thank thee for the hands who prepared the food we are about to partake and ask thee to bless this wondrous feast to strengthen and nourish our bodies and souls, in the name of thy Son, Jesus Christ. Amen."

Amens ricocheted round the people. Folks looked surprised they spoke em, and them wearin ball caps put em on again. The brown Rand fixed in my tightenin fists. I noticed Brother Hamilton blessed everyone except the girls' pet rabbits and the livin prophet just like when visitin on Sunday mornins. Eyed the whole lot for Carmen and decided no more waitin after grabbin a quick bite. And soon as got through the line had a mind to speak at Brother Hamilton face to face. Him and everyone else was wronger'n hell and wouldn't change it.

Two long lines formed at the first table with stacks a paper plates and plastic utensils. One lady smiled and pulled on the buckskin jacket. Didn't know her from Blanche DuBois, Roper's favorite actress he pined for over and over. Jesús walked among the reporters tamed round him and no sign a Carmen. The lady pulled on the buckskin jacket again. Gonna cuss her so loud Brother Hamilton would know he'd be next.

"Dean, everyone knows these are your favorite," the lady said. She removed tinfoil from funeral potatoes with steam risin and set em on a table.

In a state a plumb amazement bout did a backflip. Elbowed round folks and cut in line for a plate and fork and right back to the golden pan.

Got fired up between bites sure Carmen wouldn't show in time and set on goin on without her. Not really crossin her when right. So if she didn't arrive soon, would tell it straight. I owed her to show us got it right together but had to before Brother Hamilton or someone else said one more goddamned thing.

Decided on givin her more time and cut back in line for nother helpin a funeral potatoes.

The people ballooned round Jesús ready for his talk under the basketball hoop I hauled out in the old Ford years ago. His boys weared down the square lines and if you wasn't the wiser thought bent the rim from dunkin so hard. Already worked in when I pulled off the bed. A Lakers' ball and a Celtics' ball for each set a boys hid in a ditch somewhere. Roper said a sure sign theirs was a house divided.

Them reporters assaulted Jesús with all kinds a questions all at once. None made a bit a sense. He patted the back a the buckskin jacket with me finishin bites a my last helpin.

"It is time," he said, wavin and smilin at his questioners. He worked through all them people to the back door.

No more loaves was on the long wood table and got me wonderin if one got tucked back in the kitchen. Paintins spread where all the food was.

Jesús reached in his suit pocket and pulled out his phone. He raised his first two fingers and went for the back room.

Carmen come in the back door with the girls and Esperanza on her hips and Rosa's four boys right behind. She herded em by and grabbed the arm a the buckskin jacket and pulled me into the kitchen.

She let go and held my cheeks, restin against Jay's brace and stepped close to my busted nose. Her eyes filled. "Jay's at the hospital. He's very sick."

"Can get Jesús' computer in the den room."

"He is asking only for you."

"Let's get to the computer. Then we can set everyone right. I'll be real quick and we can get Sam and head back to town and stop in to check on him."

"There's no time."

I thought on just how he got himself in there. "From what? Okay earlier. Right now people need to hear the truth."

"He doesn't have time, and you'll have more opportunities to set the record straight."

"Let's get to the computer now."

"If you insist there's no need to time it. Be quick and don't waste a second. But I fear you'll be too late. I'll get Sam later. For you, you need to go. He may not have long, and you'll regret not seeing him."

I reckoned right then and there she knowed somethin really out a sorts.

Jesús called.

Microphones bundled like bamboo sticks on the Blackfoot riverbed. Cameras and lights shown down like the Finals come to Riverton. Pulled the brown Rand tighter.

Jesús said, "Ladies and Gentlemen. What a pleasure it's been for Rosa and I meeting you and welcoming so many new friends. I have brief remarks, and then we'll turn the time over to Dean, followed by your questions."

Eyed Carmen with her hands raised, shieldin her eyes with the girls at her side blockin the back door. Knowed she knowed best and waved em all over.

Jesús stopped speakin, and the cameras turned their bright lights on Carmen and the girls.

"Of course." He started up again.

Carmen reached and wiped somethin sticky from the buckskin jacket, and we faced the lights.

"Need a ride," I said.

Carmen walked off the patio into the people. Elena pulled the sleeve a the buckskin jacket on my left side and Eloisa wrapped round the other one on my right.

"Jesús."

He eyed me real surprised. He half smiled not sure whether to start up again or ask me to get off the patio. A second longer and he would. Shuffled up and hesitated on which microphone to speak into before choosin the biggest one.

"Gotta run folks. You all listen up. Jesús's got somethin to say, always does. Aim to be back before he's done. If I aint, sit tight and treat yurself to seconds till I am."

Pushed Eloisa and Elena to Jesús, and his smile come back. Stepped into the people and no space in between folks, or they was struck dumb and couldn't move. The buckskin jacket brushed every dog gone one and collided into one fella and shouldered round him. Sheriff Caldwell ordered people off the driveway, while Verolinda backed the Corolla onto Riverton Road. And beat all Sheriff Caldwell opened the door to let me in.

CHAPTER 16

Not long after I heard tell a Jesús' talk. Nothin got told more in the years to follow. Born to give it said Brother Hamilton. Each time someone quoted Jesús' words I recollected Brother Hamilton's prayer lightnin my fire. The whole thing got taped somewhere on the internet.

Somethin bout developin yur potential and continued on no matter where you was or who you was, continue, continue, continue. No mistakin he said lots a continues cause people quoted them parts most. Just continue, you have to continue, continue on yur way, continue all the way to yur goal, the way between one place and the other place is continuin there, continue on and one thing and nother. You think somebody woulda asked what the hell for but never heard tell someone did.

The part I knowed for pure lack a sense begun "progress happened between two pulls, one as true as the other, and the only way to one or the other was continuing there." Carmen explained Jesús meant growin pains. Maybe did but settlin somewhere was lots better. I wanted one thing. The right opposite a bein stretched. Carmen and everyone else just convinced Jesús got every last thing in his talk right but carried on bout what I done and couldn't explain what weren't so more'n no one could.

The Corolla sped long Riverton Road and turned passed the big gravel pit to the old highway, and I wondered if in Jay's situation he had the wherewithal to bring Sam to town and if he didn't would explain how bad off he really got.

And right then recollected somewhere in Ogden went the pinch in my gut shoulda done somethin for my brother over the soft hummin a the Corolla. It rolled up to the hospital. Pushed open the door and held on with my boots out. Verolinda come round and lifted under the buckskin jacket. Set my boots closer to the curb. Verolinda watched a big yellow and purple reflection cover the sky and turned ready.

"I'm a'right," I said. My legs woke and cleared the curb and tuckered out reachin the sliden glass doors.

"You sit, and I'll find his room," Verolinda said.

A middle-aged man hunched over in the big red chair. My backside hit the couch between two teenage kids on the ends. They eyed the middle-aged man cross the room with his head in his hands, tiltin his bald spot at us. He didn't look old and wore a blue collared short sleeve pullover shirt, not fancy enough to golf in but the sort. His elbows rested on kaki pants. The two teenagers glanced round me at each other.

Verolinda come back, and the middle-aged, baldin man looked up. Pushed myself up and followed her down the hall for a set a stairs. Slow gettin there and stared hard at the first step.

"Can you make it?" Verolinda called from above.

My legs wobbled up one step and the next one. Finally reached the top and Verolinda headed for a group a nurses. They all eyed me at once. One led us to a room a glass filled with machines and a bed at the end. Wires run from Jay's arms and chest cross each other to them machines. One beeped. One pumped and pumped and pumped. Then one clicked, went quiet, and clicked again. Two nurses stood at the side a the bed with masks coverin their faces. One punched buttons on one a them machines waist high.

Jay's eyes set tight and didn't move none.

"No visitors. You can't come in here," one a them nurses said, walkin right for us.

Verolinda backed into the hall where the other nurse stood, watchin through the glass.

"He's asked," I said.

"You can't come in here. Not now." The nurse raised her arms.

Pushed by and near tripped over my own boots to the foot a the bed and lifted a chart chained to the end. None a it made a damned bit a sense.

The nurse come to my side with her hand out. "I know who you are. You can't come in here Mr. Stamper. Your friend is seriously ill."

Dropped the chart, and it banged against the frame.

Jay opened his eyes.

"What the hell happened?" Come out with more anger'n I knowed had in me.

Jay pulled tubes from his ears and small prongs from his nose. Next got off wires from his chest and arms. The nurses went for his arms, and he pushed em off.

"Get now." Gettin mad, bracin long the side a the bed.

The nurses jumped back, and one hurried out the room. Jay pulled a blood pressure cuff off his arm and a monitor off his finger. He dropped his white legs over the side a the bed and pulled the IV from his arm and blood oozed out his vein. A nurse pressed bandages on the hole and run tape round. Then she held Jay's arm with both a hers.

"Much obliged Tina. Will you take them off?" He pointed to his legs.

The nurse tore Velcro sleeves off his calves and grabbed his arm again.

"Thank you." He turned and eyed me serious. "Can I catch a ride Pard?" He give his huge smile and went quick as it come.

The machines all buzzed like a mad concert. More nurses gathered outside the glass with others runnin down the hall.

The nurse braced Jay on one side and Verolinda held his other one. He wobbled back and forth.

"You don't look real good. More like a mummy when we come in," I said.

"Meditating. Done a lot since getting here. Grab my boots in the closet there would you?"

All kinds a commotion come from the hall with people blockin the door. Verolinda hurried over and back with boots and folded Wranglers and shirt. Jay directed her to set the boots down. They got him to lift his legs and get em on.

"You drop Sam off?" The sleeves a the buckskin jacket folded nice on my sore chest.

"Stop there, now just sit back down," a voice said from the door.

"Where's Sam?" Got real loud and surprised even myself.

"Running with Josey," Jay said and looked like he laughed real quick. Got me even madder.

A man in a white coat come up and said, "Now stop and set back down."

"Runnin wild all day." Gettin louder and hot as hell.

"You can't leave this room Jay." The man in a white coat raised his open palm. Bunches a nurses eyed us over his shoulder.

"She'll be all right," Jay said.

"The hell she will. How many times I gotta say it. I'll send Carmen for her straight away." Just stammered out so mad.

The man in the white jacket held up both his open palms. "Stop and sit. I can't let you pass." Half the nurses wore masks and the other half didn't but all looked to be holdin their breaths.

Eyed the man and pushed one a his hands down to pass by.

He grabbed the buckskin jacket. "Mr. Stamper, you can't leave with the patient. You would be breaking the law. I've put a hold on him, and you'd be kidnapping him."

"What in the Sam Hell you talkin bout." Stepped right into him, and he shuffled back.

"I've called security. They'll be here any minute and escort you out." He didn't let go and grabbed aholt even firmer. "You cannot leave with him. It's against the law." He carried on like I didn't hear the first time.

Yanked my arm, and he stumbled, grabbin the buckskin jacket with both hands. Clocked him with my free palm behind his temple, and he fell to his knees. Nurses burst out screamin at the door. Shocked me straight through and stumbled backwards and Verolinda and the nurse pushed me off from fallin on Jay.

Got back off my heels and went for the blocked door, and the nurses parted. A couple sprinted to the man in the white jacket on the floor, holdin his head in his hands.

A damned soft alarm sounded in the hall. Verolinda held Jay's folded Wranglers and shirt in one hand and wrapped her other tight round his waist. He swayed, and she went with him step for step and steadied him goin straight, guidin him to the top a the stairs. Covered the rear, eyein folks for badges. Verolinda still held Jay's waist, copyin his steps down the stairs.

At bottom Jay wheezed for breath. "Sorry for the hassle."

And out a my own. "Think we busted out a Alcatraz."

Nother damned soft alarm gone off in the hall. Verolinda helped Jay to the room with the teenagers and middle-aged, baldin man. His palms covered his eyes, and he cried. Verolinda and Jay passed them teenagers, coverin up and gigglin, bitin their lips.

Cleared them slidin glass doors and went for the Corolla. Loud sirens come from the other side a the hospital.

"What landed you in here?" I asked.

"I didn't understand most of it. My tests from earlier in the week revealed she's the cute version of leukemia though," Jay said.

Tipped up the brown Rand and couldn't tell her from a snake bite, and he knowed it.

"My blood went bad a while back."

Verolinda got Jay in. He set quiet against the seat. She run round the front. Just got myself in and the Corolla pulled from the curb and got the door shut.

"Where should I go?" Verolinda asked.

Jay kept quiet a few seconds and said, "Away."

I knowed he smiled the way he did.

"Jesús'," I said.

Jay didn't say nothin, and Verolinda eyed him.

"Kessler's," Jay said.

"No need. There's a spread at Jesús'."

"Only need an orange drink."

"We need to get goin. Gotta tell everyone the truth while Jesús has their attention."

"That's the time for it."

"And there was plenty a leftovers with drinks."

We cruised on Airport Road through old neighborhoods north a downtown and reached Meridian. The best part a the city's plannin in recent years moved Cal Ranch Stores and opened new liquor and wine stores. Set foot in em more'n all the others combined. A green light flashed ahead and turned into Kessler's parkin lot.

"There." Jay lifted his hand at an open spot near Bridge where the Corolla rolled in. They sat quiet and waited for somethin. I wanted to rush Jay, but Verolinda just too plumb polite.

"I will get the orange drink, and you can get dressed," Verolinda said.

"Okay."

She got out and poked her head back in. "Do you want anything else?"

Jay turned his head. "Yes but you're not old enough to buy any."

"Can grab you a chew," I said, openin my door.

"You look like you're going to tip over every other step." Jay shifted his head like to see me.

"You look lots worse'n me. Don't he Linda?"

She near froze contemplatin the matter.

"Aint no bother." I held the door tight and pushed myself up.

Verolinda cleared the entrance and went for the cooler. Close to the nearest checkout and scanned behind and nothin.

A pudgy kid with a flattop mannin the station asked, "Can I help you with something?"

"Not me and not my friend neither." And reconnoitered other checkouts but completely out a stock.

Verolinda appeared with three drinks all different colors with an orange on top. She spoke at two different people passin on their way in. She climbed back in the Corolla and twisted off the cap and give the orange bottle to Jay.

He took a long gulp. "Thank you."

Verolinda sat calm. Just got my boots in and she turned and give me a green one. Twisted the lid and wondered if meant for Jay too and took a quick sip.

"All out," I said.

"Thanks for looking. It's messed up the trouble coming your way."

"That fellow don't have no cause. And just bout missed."

"On the spot. Thanks Pard." He raised the orange bottle and tipped my way and took a swig.

Jay hadn't moved a sliver, still wearin his white robe.

"You ready yet to head for Jesús'? He might be finishin up his talk." Scooted forward and patted his seat. "And I can get Sam after I say my piece. Now let's get goin."

Jay didn't as much blink for ten seconds. "That's where I'm going." He pointed at an old green sports car next to us. "I'll owe Sam one."

Long side panels and long hood with black hardtop sent wind fast all round. Coulda been a Mustang with fat whitewall tires but too fancy.

Jay pushed open his door and rose in one single step. Wind ruffled his robe open, showin all his dark back and blindin-white butt. He stepped to the old green sports car and hesitated, catchin his hand on top a the Corolla, and the white robe blowed open to cars passin on Bridge. Verolinda got out and walked round the front. Opened my door and pushed myself out by the handle. Verolinda held Jay up. Put my arm under his, and my side bout cracked open and let go and set against the rear marker light on the old green sports car. Felt like it cracked but didn't bother checkin and slid the buckskin jacket up the hardtop.

Verolinda patted down Jay's robe and said, "You aren't okay to drive."

"Dean can."

"I don't think he's supposed to." She held him from gettin knocked over by the wind.

"Drive what?" I yelled. "Linda can drive back to Riverton."

We was like tribal elders in council thinkin up answers on the spot but without a guidin spirit or lick a sense between us. Jay's robe kept catchin in the wind, and the string whipped cross my belly against my jewels. Cars honked drivin by.

"I can drive." Verolinda nodded, fightin the wind, holdin Jay up.

Traffic builded back on Bridge with vehicles honkin. Raised all my stubby fingers and pushed em on.

"Going to Phoenix," Jay said.

Was turnin into a side show. I wanted help contemplatin out a such nonsense. "What for?"

"Where the buyer lives."

"You can't and hell if I can. Now let's go to Jesús'."

"I know who will," Verolinda said, more excited'n I seen her all day.

Jay stepped to the old green sports car. Verolinda didn't miss a beat and grabbed his arm and lassoed his far hip with her other one. She turned him round and long the back row a lights. Grabbed the door handle and pulled a heavy door. Sturdy with puffy leather and a loose leather handle inside. Wood run long the dash from end to end. Leather and firm seats dressed the inside.

Verolinda went for Jay's clothes and locked each door a the Corolla.

Took the back seat with lots a space. My legs finally relaxed and rested the sleeves a the buckskin jacket on the edge and set the brown Rand next to me. Verolinda handed Jay his folded Wranglers and shirt and put her hands at 10 and 2 on the leather wrapped steerin wheel.

"It's automatic," Jay said. "The key is below the mat."

Verolinda fiddled the key in, and the old green sports car rumbled over wind and traffic and backed and pulled forward onto Bridge and rumbled a hundred yards to B Bar B's parkin lot with a line a pickups out front. The old green sports car fit next to the last one.

Jay got himself out and walked normal. Verolinda went for the entrance, and voices carried from the back. The floor filled with new and repaired saddles and bridles.

Could smell leather in my head like lots a times before in the very spot. They sold custom leather chaps all over the entire world. Long passed the days you walked in and bought a pair with backorders extendin for months. Verolinda skipped long the aisle ten paces ahead like on her way to help a customer with bees in his underpants.

Jay and me followed into the back where a bunch a young cowboys watched Billy point at a flat screen on pause. Layne leaned on the wall next to one a the Schild brothers. They all eyed are way.

"Great timing. We analyzed Denny Flynn. Troy Dunn is next and then you're up," Billy said.

Verolinda waved over the pimple-face kid who held all my stuff in Ogden and walked straight at the Schild brother.

Eyed them boys for a spare chair and took one next to Jay who got the idea first. He kicked off his boots and stood. He held his Wranglers and dropped the legs and bent over and stepped in one and the other and pulled em up. He grabbed the robe off his chest, and it slipped to the ground. He reached his shirt and run his arms through, buttonin over the dark blue bruises and tucked into his Wranglers with plenty space in the waist. He sat and pulled his boots on.

The boys watched and not a one knowed Jay rode at their age. But all sure to know him for famous fights round town, legendary tales told cross the generations. They stared like seein Joe Louis in person.

"You did it Dean. You covered the best," one boy said, and the others nodded.

Billy let loose a big smile and said, "Made a really nice ride."

That there halted me from gettin up to correct em. Billy knowed enough to say so. Everyone else so far with an opinion just repeated what they heard from lots a people who didn't.

"He made some pretty great rides before yesterday's," Layne said. "Add Ogden to a long list." He worked by the boys with the Schild brother and Verolinda and the pimple-face kid.

But even Billy and Layne couldn't make me doubt the truth.

"Isn't the first time people said Dean made the best bull ride they ever saw. The only difference today is eveyones seen it. Billy said it a decade ago when he rode Tressbraker in Poky. Since then I heard six dozen others witness to other rides." Layne eyed each boy, and each nodded in return. He turned on me direct. "Nice ride Bud."

"Really nice," Billy said.

Then rose to tell em.

"He's born for it boys," Jay said.

Everyone went quiet, Layne and Billy and even me, waitin on Jay.

"And his drive's what separates him." Jay bowed his head, risin with his hands on his knees. "And always will." He grabbed the shoulder a the buckskin jacket. "Even when he won't be able to any more, which ain't yet for sure. Listen up here." He straightened all the way and smiled. "These guys know their business, and you'll do yourselves real good to pay close attention."

The group echoed they all knowed was so, as if truer words never spoken and carried on with what coulda been rounds a amens from believers at Roper's Christian Church.

Verolinda held the arm a the pimple-face kid. She smiled and said, "Taylor will drive us to Phoenix."

"Okay," Jay said.

Did everything I could to not have myself a conniption fit right then and there. I knowed had to get to Jesús' to set the record right and with plenty a time for seconds before pickin up Sam. Gonna speak at Verolinda direct and she passed right out the room with the pimple-face kid in tow. The whole group left the store. Come on the facilities overcome with nature's necessities and stopped before followin em out.

One street light covered all them boys with stiff chins. The pimple-face kid hauled his gear bag to the old green sports car. If not so dark I'd guessed Billy's cheeks raised. He wiped his eyes and said somethin too soft for angels to hear. Jay said thanks. Layne opened the passenger door to his blue Chevy Silverado and come through the crowd and give Jay a can a chew. He smiled, thumpin the lid.

Jay said he'd drive the first leg, and Verolinda said fine long as he told us when he got tired and made him promise he would. Her and the pimple-face kid climbed in back. The wood dash got me sore amazed somethin so darned stately had wheels under it with a mind a tellin Roper sure he never rode in somethin like it.

Jay drove slow down Meridian to Main Street. And not a rock or dip in the road. He pulled into the old Shortstop. Went for Verolinda, and she kept a step ahead. A full pot a coffee halted me in my tracks. Got a styrofoam cup and poured full. Went to pay and they was all in the old green sports car ready. Then back on Main Street for the reservation.

Verolinda tapped the buckskin jacket and handed up her phone.

"Don't let Jay drive too much. He should rest," Carmen said.

"I won't," I said loud for Jay to hear.

"He has a very serious form of cancer."

Shifted my whole body toward him. He didn't say a thing and rested his right hand on the leather wrapped steerin wheel and seen and heard nothin but in front a him.

"Laura said they would have life flighted him to the Huntsman Cancer Institute in Salt Lake for treatments, but he refused only asking for you. And now she said the police are searching for him being a serious danger to himself."

"If that don't beat all. A bunch a fuss over a man makin his own decision. Even if aint the right one is his to make."

"The rules don't work that way in these situations."

"Should in all em."

"There are all kinds of considerations. They said there's a new treatment. The doctors said they can take his own cells to target the individual cancer cells. His own immune system will multiply the right kind of cells to destroy the cancer. The procedure is working throughout the country. He has a chance. Get him to stop in Salt Lake."

"I will." And turned at Jay so he knowed what was comin.

"Get Taylor or Verolinda to drive the rest of the way."

"I will."

"I'm proud of you."

"What in tarnation for?"

"Be safe. The girls say good night."

"Tell em good night."

"How are you feeling?"

"Jay's brace itches and my chest aches."

"Don't fall asleep yet. We'll see a doctor as soon as you get back."

"Bought a bad cup a coffee at the old Shortstop to keep me up."

"Great and get more down the road."

"You know if I make good on one thing I will."

"I love you."

"Love you, Car."

"Yes?"

"Did you get Sam?"

"She's fine. I spoke with Brother Hamilton, and he texted he's been over and put Josey and Sam in the trailer. They have water and food."

"A long spell runnin wild in Riverton. First chance get her."

"I will."

Lifted the phone and Verolinda leaned up for it. The old green sports car went under the overpass and turned onto the ramp to Interstate 15 before Riverton Road.

CHAPTER 17

Jay still didn't move none focused straight ahead.

"Pull over at the Tradin Post," I said.

"Okay," he said.

The dark night lit with stars runnin over fields in all directions long the freeway. The old green sports car passed under em till exit 80 and slowed and turned right at a huge parkin lot with the casino in the distance. We got to the Sho-Ban Hotel's entrance. The fanciest stay this side a Jackson Hole. Not long ago I done an event with Wiley Peterson and a couple other bull riders and had me one a the best Ribeyes ever, damnedest kind a tender, smothered in fresh mushrooms and gravy. Didn't finish chewin one piece and at cuttin nother. And the baked potato with sour cream and bacon and chives set my heart to explode. Wiley and one a them boys didn't drink, but the other boy and me made up for em. They all carried on bout their fitness regimes more'n buckin bulls. One day bull riders woke up to maybe Ty Murray weren't pure natural and had to work at stayin one. I supposed for lots a boys could be true. After midnight Carmen called in a spacious room with a bed big as are own. Woke with shades drawn back in bright light fraid in Texas.

My eyes welded close and swung my arms wild under the sheet, mighty relieved to not be.

At the curb an old bellhop opened my door. Everyone else stayed like Jay meant to drive off to park.

I seen the sprucest bellhops before on the sidewalk outside the Waldorf Astoria in New York City. Where Roper picked, sayin the finest hotel on Earth and the most important people slept between their sheets. Right bout the hotel bein fancy. The whole damned thing took a New York City block, bigger'n them hotels in Denver and Dallas, bigger'n the two biggest from both combined. But the room damned right puny.

After the show we headed downtown for drinks with girls Roper insisted he knowed. Wantin nothin more'n to grab a bite, they all ignored me. The first place we got drinks packed people in. The girls carried on like the coolest place to be, and Roper acted his part plenty. Since gettin to New York City we heard bout this area and that area and this park and that square and all the names jumbled together. I only cared bout Madison Square Garden. The greater authority a the two girls on knowin everything in New York City said we was the stars in the most sought after part, and I be goddamned if Roper didn't turn a corner, exceedin his own regular incorrigibility. People sure stared, and Roper chatted up pert near every one like they was fastest a friends. Bout what no one with a bit a sense could rigtly tell. A bunch a mumbo jumbo, tidbits a this and that thing and this and that person. Roper soared to new heights a bullshit. All the while people wearin clothes more fit for Paris and not tyin hogs to racks for sausage. Roper patted my back for the twelfth time full a it on my way to a cab to find some grub. He insisted we all leave together, and the girls headed to the women's stall to powder up before we did.

Roper rode. I didn't. Years since it happened. Even fuller a himself in the sleek crowd he didn't bother me none. Tireder'n if I'd been roasted over a pit in hell with one single thing a hittin the sack in my head, after gettin a bite. Bout him ridin broached on lots a trips and told him more'n he told himself, but he only believed somethin if he said it. Even then weren't sure. And all he said, and he said more'n everyone I knowed in person, he didn't speak a ridin near enough. His problem come when he did got lost in a bunch a other stuff, and ridin had to be the thing and nothin else.

Got are gear bags packed and he started carryin on bout his ride. His bull this and that like he just rode Red Rock. Then he said only he coulda rode him. What stuck in my craw. Not cause a elevatin himself. That I expected. But unlike so much other stuff he said he knowed I knowed weren't true. The showmanship accustomed to spoutin off with a damned bald faced lie on top straight in my face. Hell he made the third spot by a half a point. First and second made far ranker rides. Coverin never enough. If would be, he'd made more. He mistook eight as just one more chance to shovel himself down throats near him with mine nearest and one wanted to most. He no sooner could tell the difference between one's toleratin him from one's not acceptin his views if he become a leadman. The slightest nod got him, not able to help himself.

He said it again where we got to down the street from where we started. I never ate such a meal in all my life and got nother order a chicken with peanut sauce to go.

Better'n Chinese food if such a thing is possible, and we drunk real Chinese beers. I knowed em for a great wall people mentioned for reasons not makin no sense but not for good tastin beer. One girl said Chinese invented beer long before Christian monks. I had no cause to contradict her, but Roper did on historical records bout a barley brewed by a French trapper with Jim Bridger up the Ottawa River amidst restless Algonquins far as Timmins, claimin then and there nowhere was firs traded and sealed by ceremonial toasts more'n on the Hudson Bay. Them girls fascinated like he didn't just make it up on the spot. I knowed Bridger lived long after them monks who was sure to be drinkin soon as the damned Romans kilt Jesus. Roper said them girls staked a valid claim for origins a rice brewin and variations far back into the annals a Sino-History I knowed as great epics Roper expounded upon when the mighty wall come up. He said them rice brews was round long before Saxon craftsmanship infiltrated far Eastern Asia, and them girls jumped even more sure they was right. Roper discoursed on the origin a beer before at the Green T with all the regulars on the edge a their stools. He outstretched his arms, holdin a beer with a full head and revealed Egyptians mastered the brewin art even before Christians. Not a year later durin a game a Texas holdem smokin sweet cigars at Shayne's done revised his own revelation, declarin beer begun in Mesopotamia before paper to even record it. Checked a map and sure enough no such place existed. If them girls believed so much builders a the greatest wall win beer makins first place, weren't gonna correct Roper based on his own orations for em. The girls pulled out their phones and decided on the next bar, explainin how the later crowd would die to meet real bull riders and Roper said would include meetin the only one able to ride his bull. The girls didn't miss a beat applaudin with not a lick a sense between em.

Roper wasted no time chattin up the crowd at the next fancy establishment. His eyes on me sayin with an extra breath he'd say it again and got the idea he would on the sidewalk a the last bar, waitin for the girls to return from the ladies' stall. But he didn't say nothin, and the girls come out and hailed down a cab.

One girl claimed we was on Horatio Street. And not a single Mexican growin up in Blackfoot by the name and just sure got made up like lots else I heard tell in New York City. We turned north at a small park the girls gushed over, insistin we take the time to see Washinton Square or Central Park before we flew the coop, dead certain we'd miss the hearts a the city if we didn't. They actually said it like trees provided life-givin blood, and I chuckled, the best I felt all night. The girls pointed out spots we passed and talked bout others we didn't.

Skyscrapers in the distance come toward us high as the eye could see and wondered if my mother lived in em and just how many rides up them elevators would take to find out. For all the annoyance was through them girls I met Gabby the next summer when they brought more friends long at Roper's insistence. Shackin up with Gabby weren't the first break from ridin and not the last but none more memorable. Missed lots a shows for rounds to them parks and squares heard so damn much bout on the first trip, and them first days wondered if I'd find her and eyed every passerby. I never knowed if I ever did. With Gabby I come to be sore amazed at how one with nature folks could get retreatin to it in the city. Was only foolin myself if green spaces, what Gabby named em, didn't have real captivatin power for people movin in and out a em. The longer my stay I craved em too. Beautiful as they all said not so sure, but they had an undeniable pull in the city. Beauty just were more'n what it weren't and plumb nothin there in the city for folks to know no different. Central Park sure somethin, but all its testifyin right puny on the truth.

We stopped at a light next to Madison Square Garden, and the show earlier seemed long ago as all the others. Roper's chest puffed at compliments a the girls, starin through the window. We turned right and seen the Empire State Buildin. Passin buildin after buildin it come closer with a beam a light on top. I got a poke a regret not thinkin to make time to walk up. The concrete and steel coulda filled all the buildins a Blackfoot combined. We wasted the night, except for havin the chicken with peanut sauce, minglin with yuppies, and a few blocks from the show stood the famousest buildin in the world. We went north again on a street with a thin park runnin between lanes. Green bein to the city like water to the West, the girls leapt off their seats explainin more bushes. The road climbed before Grand Central Station into a buildin and out the bottom, on my honor, and turned and a large clock marked the time when passin through. Then by a couple buildins and stopped at the Waldorf. The girls giddy on Roper's arms at the idea a comin inside.

The box a chicken with peanut sauce set tight against my side. Roper said somethin, and the girls laughed. They sat with the door open, not a one gettin out. I thanked the bellhop with a gold band round his hat and gold linin round his collar and down his pants. He welcomed me back, assurin me are gear bags arrived and offerin apologies he missed the show. Not the same one earlier who wished us luck headed out but the same one who welcomed us back from the bars the night before. He musta smelled the chicken with peanut sauce cause he asked after are dinner.

I hesitated on a gold seal and eyed gold linin above the doors but quick shucked the idea a spendin more time with Roper and them girls and pushed the revolvin doors. Halfway up the marble stairs with gold railins Roper called from the slidin doors. One a them girls hung on his arm, and the other come in with the bellhop and kept on for where I expected to powder up in a stall next to the shoeshine me and Roper stopped to have are boots polished earlier in the afternoon. Roper tipped the man twenty bucks for his boots and mine. He come at me with his shoulders raisin and plume spreadin, sure as all the gold surroundin us, and said we should stop at the hotel bar for nightcaps to continue are celebration, seein how not every day New Yorkers gotta meet as great a bull rider as him. I did not hear what come next except heels a my boots on the gleamin floor. He raised his hands in my face, and I punched him.

He fell back, and his cowboy hat went clean off. He got right up and charged, and I backed up the marble steps and pushed him toward the rail with my free hand and dropped the box a chicken with peanut sauce. The girl screamed. The bellhop stepped between us. Roper lunged, and the bellhop bounced off to the floor. I kept backin on the marble steps keen on Roper wantin to get to the ground. I didn't wrestle but watched Roper and Jay for years. Roper scrapped. He throwed a wild punch missin by a mile and lunged again. I clocked his chin, plumb shocked he didn't drop and steppin back on flat surface hit him again. He got aholt a my arm. We stumbled over. The other girl come back and joined in the screamin, their cries bouncin from the ceilin to the walls and back. Never stepped in a more stately room, and silence dominated the girls' voices except for Roper breathin. I scooted my knees up and pushed off. He didn't let go, and I kept punchin with my free hand. Right on a circle paintin full a mystical figures half dressed I noticed each time we entered and left and couldn't place the people there or above us or on every damned elevator. They musta been from California. I hit Roper again. He tripped me, and the brown Rand dropped off. Lights a bubbles run cross the ceilin outlined by more gold. Straight lines a gold and decorative shapes a gold all between plates a gold. Even the lights with bubbles was gold. Gold trim surrounded and overlaid the main light in the middle. I slid on the paintin, but Roper worked up my arm against my head. I pounded the side a his face with a hammer fist. The girls give no sign a quittin. Their shreikin possibly the most painful thing I ever witnessed. Nother bellhop, bigger'n the first, pried Roper off me.

A couple men in suits with ear pieces joined in and guided us to opposite sides a the room. We climbed a set a stairs, and I sat on a hard bench. My arm pinched tryin to stretch. If they broke us up a minute later, Roper woulda popped my shoulder. Fortunate for me on my non-ridin arm I pointed out durin all their questions. Roper sure full a surprises takin lots a solid punches.

New York City Officers walked in some time later. Half went Roper's way and the other half come mine to take their reports. The girls stood by Roper quiet but on occasion wailin. The New York City Officers switched places and asked a bunch more questions, and I give em the same answers.

All them New York City Officers huddled with folks from the Waldorf. They brought Roper and me in the middle on the very same paintin we brawled on. One set on bein the most important said two bull riders travelin together from Idaho, and some even smiled. He repeated himself and added sharin the same room. Not the same bed Roper piped in. The New York City Officers left out the slidin doors. The hotel manager pardoned us for what he called a most regrettable scene and promised Roper his own room. Roper with his busted lip, pink cheeks, and swollen nose and eyes made one contorted smile. He forgave you and insisted no charges be filed because you've been sufferin from the deepest a disappointments not ridin earlier in the evenin, and insisted we all forgive you, said the manager. Never the grudge holdin type I said and went for the elevators with the big painted fairies sore in need a shuteye. The first bellhop grabbed my arm. Bout punched him, and he handed over the box a chicken with peanut sauce.

"Mr. Stamper, what an honor to have you with us this evening," the old bellhop said.

I knowed him from lots a visits before and tipped the brim a the brown Rand.

He eyed round for my bags and probably relieved didn't bring my cooler.

"Has been a while since we've enjoyed your company. You wouldn't know it with you on every TV screen and all the captivated oohs and ahhs on everyone's lips the past twenty-four hours."

"Lots a unnecessary fuss," I said.

"And here you are. With all the news wagons in Blackfoot, I'd be lying if I didn't say I'm surprised to see you, but you picked a great night. We have a full house."

Jay cleared the front a the old green sports car and said somethin to the valet kid. The old bellhop waved the valet off and held his hands like takin a picture a the old green sports car.

"Making a quick stop Brent," Jay said.

"Evening Jay. We'll enjoy sharing her as long as we can." The old bellhop showed us the door. "We're honored Mr. Stamper. You'll be doing every last business a favor each time you step through their doors for the next twenty years only to use their facilities."

Dyani worked the floor and teel at the Clothes Horse durin high school. So did Tommy. From the back you couldn't tell em apart, tall with long black hair. She towered over me with long slender arms wrappin all the way round and always reckoned could more'n once. The Clothes Horse simply no more'n a den with clothes piled on top a more clothes. Long torn down and nothin like the gift shop the kids led into but with lots a the same things. If I coulda told, smelled a fine leathers. Cause I couldn't didn't change I knowed what did.

Jay breathed deep into a pair a moccasins. Years ago sure handmade but no one could tell now days. And no one could deny the $300 shock on the pair I admired. Didn't take mountain men to appreciate the luxury a warm fur, and they'd give their scalps sooner'n pay such a price.

The kids gone into an aisle with fine Indian fare. Verolinda rolled a couple strings a beads round her arm, and the pimple-face kid said somethin. She put a purple set on her head and tiptoed high to a rack a colorful blouses.

Jay eyed a wall a cowboy hats and tried on a cream straw one in the mirror. "Left too fast to grab mine."

"Must have real cause to forget yur cowboy hat." Woulda shook my head in the mirror but his brace held tight. No denyin not much to look at.

"How you come to the hospital?"

"Short on essential nutrients was all. Haven't been able to keep much down and caught up with me. Once they ran the IV was fine. Spot me for this one."

"Only got credit at the bar."

"Probably owe you in royalties."

"They sold the gear out long ago."

"They'll be restocking after yesterday."

"Just while everyone is still unaware I rode they will." Eyed him even harder. "They can help you in Salt Lake. Some new treatment where they take yur own cells to kill off the bad ones. They have it workin all over the country. Did they tell you that?"

Jay set perfect the cream straw cowboy hat and backed away from the mirror. "They did."

"Let's stop off and get er started then."

"Not while I have anything left." He passed by an aisle with cowboy shirts a all the brands on world champs the past decade.

Followed no more'n half a step behind. "The damned point is to get help while you still do."

"I don't believe so."

"Dyin aint much a one."

We got to the checkout counter behind a tall man in a suit loaded up on lots a Indian wear. Beads covered his forearm, and he held a wool blanket with moccasins on top.

"Only at the end when nothing else matters. I ain't trading however long until then." He set the cream straw cowboy hat on the counter.

The man in the suit claimed his goods. Behind the register stood a young boy with a high forehead and long braided black hair, fallin behind his back. No young brave, more like a young Tony Hawk sure to skippin school for the skate park at Jenson's Grove.

He scanned the cream straw cowboy hat and said, "Sixty-Five dollars."

Dropped bills and coins on the counter and handed him a hundred. He picked up a strange coin and held to his eye. "Very old coin."

"You've got a chance to keep on livin but only there." Got plumb exasperated and pointed my stubbiest finger right at Salt Lake.

Jay pulled off the tag and set on the cream straw cowboy hat. "Thanks Pard."

Verolinda got next in line and held a small leather purse with long leather strings. The skater kid give me change.

The old green sports car set where we left it right in front a the entrance. The old bellhop frowned and wished we would stay longer. He said everyone passin in and out asked after her. He thanked us for stoppin and told us to come back. Jay got in the back seat. Verolinda climbed in to drive. And the pimple-face kid still inside. The old bellhop looked into the wide open Idaho night sky and no missin its reach.

Verolinda grabbed on the leather wrapped steerin wheel at 10 and 2. She brushed her hand over switches in the wood dash fit for a cockpit. If things wasn't fancy enough a gold cat topped the wood shift. Jay sat still with eyes closed and palms restin on his lap with no shuffle, not even a peep. I give up turnin to see him still alive and seen in my head the whole stint to the Malad Pass with familiar peaks. Long before Verolinda begun the climb, Jay begun to snore.

My whole body ached with my chest poundin and folded the sleeves a the buckskin jacket to try and stop it. Jay's breathing rolled with the car's engine, clearin the top a the pass. Couldn't tell em apart. Verolinda sped through the rise till they levelled out.

The Wasatch Front lit up past Brigham City. Bright specs increased each mile. I knowed Salt Lake promised Jay's chance and recollected when I visited one a them hospitals on the hill. Didn't know if the right one but reckoned they would. What I knowed for certain we'd pass the sacred Mormon temple grounds, nowhere as spotless on all a Planet Earth.

"Take the next exit," I said.

Verolinda eyed me clear even in the dark and said, "What for?"

"Get Jay to the hospital. Take the next one."

She looked straight ahead, and Jay snored from the back.

"He made me promise not to stop for anything." She peered into the rearview mirror. "Please wake him and make him."

Tried shiftin her way but my neck fussed. Seen a pale halo over the buckskin jacket comin from outside the windshield, wonderin when in the hell did he tell her. "When?"

"After the old Indian told us goodbye, and before he climbed in the back seat. He said, Linda, promise me you won't stop in Salt Lake for anything. Don't mind Dean. Will you wake him and make him stop?"

Tried takin off Jay's brace to throw at him but couldn't find the damned tie flap. The hell if I would make him do the right thing. Just a stubborn mule, snorin over traffic all the way to the point a the mountain. Right surprised some remained.

The old green sports car sped below the endless lights on the mountain front. I couldn't tell the difference between Orem and Provo or them other Book a Mormon cities long the stretch, but I knowed Spanish Fork like I knowed Ogden. They put on a great rodeo.

"Pull off here for a hot cup a coffee," I said.

Verolinda pulled the car into Maverick, and Jay snored not missin a beat.

"Leave him be." Climbed out into a cool breeze and buttoned the buckskin jacket.

Verolinda and the pimple-face kid studied the pump. The store door clacked and a dozen different coffee makers rose behind an island full a different kinds of chips, and right in the middle an enormous plastic box with tortilla chips filled halfway next to the classic shiny yellow cheese dispenser. I did the drill for lots a years and plumb lucky couldn't smell the fumes, or they woulda took aholt right beyond my control. I ignored em for the first coffee canister with French Vanilla in small words and checked the next one with Dark Roast. I didn't know no flavors. Like coffee gone the way a beer makin with lots a kinds, happy to take mine black and lifted a styrofoam cup off a stack between all them containers.

Verolinda and the pimple-face kid come in. Pointed em to the hot food and left money on the counter. The pimple-face kid waited on Verolinda like a professional attendant. She said somethin, and he walked down the aisle and opened a door and pulled out two cans a colored sugar caffeine drinks and pops. Verolinda grabbed a bag a dried fruit and one a roasted almonds.

Verolinda got in back a the old green sports car, and Jay quit snorin and sat with hands turned up on his lap. The pimple-face kid handed him an Orange pop and got behind the leather wrapped steerin wheel. Then on the road for where we'd turn before Parowan toward Panguitch on Highway 89 crossin the border.

Durin the day you couldn't beat rides on this stretch for all the vistas. What Carmen called em. She brought the girls before Elena turned three. The most dramatic landscapes in the West made a red rock. They filled oversized picture books on coffee tables out East. I knowed cause I seen em at Gabby's friends. Red rock designs more'n one person could count all packed on layers with more red rock no other person could neither. The first time on the way there I said the girls wouldn't recollect nothin bein so young, and Carmen said weren't the point and havin lastin impressions they couldn't shake was. I made them rides lots before meetin Carmen and didn't stop for the ragged cliffs and twirly spirals and canyons in between. One trip we seen the Colorado River below like a horseshoe, sure as everything I ever seen. Eloisa said looked like my belt, still young not accustomed to sense. And every time after I hunted for my belt under the couch or behind a chair it crunched like a stretch a the Colorado River. I couldn't say for the girls on the first or the next times or expect I ever would. I couldn't explain the feelin for myself. Bein in a state a awe would suffice said Carmen. Ready for the girls gettin old enough to go in them canyons where rivers still run. Carmen hatched plans for such expeditions and knowed would make good on em.

Sipped my coffee, hot as soup right off the stove. On early trips to Utah took whatever kind, lots barely tasted better'n a day's old piss not fit for a Boy Scout. One trip I couldn't find none and just got to a cultural festival at a large indoor arena in Provo. Come with Dyani in a caravan a vehicles real early in the mornin with lots a waitin round when we got there, so went huntin for a cup a coffee and tried every convenience store for a mile and not a cold pot in a one. More'n one attendant asked if was old enough to buy some and told the last one not with Tennessee Whiskey in it. I give up and skipped when couldn't jog no more climbin a damned hill passed big school buildins to the indoor arena in time to see Dyani dance in her headdress with new eagle feathers her mother sewed in place the week before. The arena expanded large enough to put on a big show.

Dyani didn't watch TV, and when everyone quieted down past midnight we left the hotel and walked on the wide road to an open unlit field cross the street from an enormous outdoor sports arena. The biggest I seen with enough concrete to build a bridge over the Rockies to Colorado. Dyani took off her sandals and sprinted to the middle. Pulled my boots and tucked em under my arms and after two steps wished I pulled off my socks too. We barely heard cars on the wide road long the enormous outdoor sports arena. She twirled herself round in circles, eyein the stars. She grabbed my hands and swung me. No barn dance in my soggy feet. "Come," she said and pulled me down on my knees in wet grass. "My tibo." She breathed real soft, and I never caught mine. Just started and she slipped from under and pushed me on my back. Her long black hair covered the grass. Huge slabs a concrete rose in the sky just waitin one day to put on the biggest show ever with crowds' cheers reachin far as Idaho. I would never tell the beginnin a so much pain for her. We lay there for a long time and slept.

A light pierced are eyes. Dyani grabbed my arm, and I jumped at it. A man said stop. A damned cop. He backed up, tellin me to slow down and moved the light to the side, askin who we was. His thin face didn't smile, but his eyes opened wide. I explained we come from Blackfoot for the cultural festival at the indoor arena on the hill. He asked what part we was in, and I laughed considerin if he seen a real cowboy and Indian before. I pointed to Dyani and blurted out she did the sun dance. She hushed me with her stare and took to explainin her part now this officer knowed even what the organizers didn't, the only secret I didn't ever keep. Mighty shamed and not a second after I said it, swingin my boots. He asked more questions, and Dyani carried on with answers he warmed to. He congratulated her and offered a ride to are hotel I took for a trick. His car with no flashin lights set on the road between the big field and the enormous arena. I rested on bars in the window, holdin my boots mighty pleased not walkin with wet socks in em. He drove straight to are hotel just like he said he would.

Verolinda tapped the shoulder a the buckskin jacket with her phone.

"How is Jay?" Carmen asked.

"Commanded us to not stop."

Her voice broke. "Get him somewhere safe. He needs to be safe and comfortable."

"He's got us headed somewhere for sure."

"Sheriff Caldwell has called twice now. A lot has happened since you left the hospital. He's been taking calls all night. Police forces in five states are looking for the plates on Linda's Corolla. The first time he called he said on a national watch call with federal agents one of them recommended prosecuting Linda for a federal crime of transferring fugitives across state lines. He said he yelled into the intercom and demanded the federal agent's name and said he cleared his throat and said if one more career advancing idea came from him or anyone else on the call would be his last. He asked if they all knew a real threat when they heard one. He told them he'd be in his finest law enforcement regalia at the Mayor's office first thing in the morning to complete the offical forms for Verolinda to receive a key to the city for delivering you guys wherever you were destined or if she decided to leave you on the side of the road. He asked if he had made himself sufficiently clear, and the head federal agent on the call said he had. Everyone is guessing where you are going. Some suggested

Canada, others Vegas, and someone even suggested Three Forks, Montana. Sheriff Caldwell said it was probably the most credible source but made very clear he wasn't asking me where you were going or if I had heard from you."

"Phoenix is where Jay's got us headed."

"Linda told me earlier. Sheriff Caldwell assigned himself as the exclusive contact to the families for all the agencies gathering information on your whereabouts and said he preferred not to know and he frankly didn't care as long as you stay far away.

"Doctor Thurgood called a press conference within an hour of you picking up Jay, and he demanded the police release the video of your assault on him and insisted they bring the gravest felony charges possible against you. He was emphatic about retaining the most astute legal representation first thing in the morning for expert counsel on a tortious cause of action against you. He said it's highly likely, if not a reasonable medical certainty, that he's suffered severe and permanent injuries and will seek all pecuianry, compensable and punitive damages recoverable under our legal system for his extensive pain and suffering, and even for the slightest impact on his ability to perform at the highest level of care of his specialty training and for all the unpardonable national humiliation he's endured. I've sat in his deposition and expected more flowery descriptions, but in his defense he was noticeably flustered in front of the cameras. Sheriff Caldwell said Doctor Thurgood has been hounding police stations from Great Falls to Laramie for news of you and the reason for most of the calls he's getting."

"Woulda kicked him in the head if I'd knowed he'd stir up such trouble."

"Sheriff Caldwell is not worried about the incident at the hospital. He said two nurses gave statements that Doctor Thurgood was already falling before you hit him, and they said you were kind of falling yourself. He couldn't reveal the details, but nurses gave statements on an incident a year ago at the hospital involving a certain nurse on an exchange from Mud Lake and incident of a slapping of an unnamed doctor much harder than your punch, and no formal complaint was filed by the assaulted doctor.

"Sheriff Caldwell said the bigger problem is all the news vans had their sensationalism quotas filled by Jesús ready for their great exodus out of town to the next circus, but now Dr. Thurgood has them sticking around like gluttons to see when you'll reappear next and he prays you'll be nowhere close to Blackfoot when you do.

"There might be even more news people now in town. There's a dozen on our road. It's surreal. Jesús said the main thing is you're safe. There's two dozen vans outside his office, and he's considering another speech but may wait for you to resurface first. He understands Jay's situation and says don't rush back and don't resist if law enforcement escorts you into custody but try to keep the details straight of when and where they put you."

"Same thing he used to always say."

"Let's hope it's stale advice. Sheriff Caldwell called again a few minutes ago after he was interviewed on TV by Diane Sawyer. His first comment to her was the hospital incident has been most regrettable for stirring up so many more smarmy wasps. And he was even wearing a tie. Diane Sawyer asked if Blackfoot had ever experienced anything like the city was now, and Sheriff Caldwell said he could remember some rowdy Eastern Idaho State Fairs but nothing like this and was reminded of Carnival in Sao Paulo when he was on furlough in the Navy but thank God people had more clothes on. He said there are no available hotel rooms from I.F. to Poky with people going as far as Dillon to find one, and he warned people to keep the peace or he'd gladly fill up his last few empty cells at the county jail beyond their holding capacity. That was the last thing he told Diane Sawyer."

"Damn his tiny cells. I need at least one van to stick round to tell the truth to."

"I'm certain you'll have your pick. Dean, Sheriff Caldwell called the second time because right after the interview with Diane Sawyer he took a completely unrelated call about you and Jay visiting a farmhouse early yesterday morning and now a boy is in a coma. My guess is Jay dropped his phone there too. Sheriff Caldwell said everyone is cooperating, and no one is saying Jay started the fight, but things don't look good for the boy. The local prosecutor is already saying he'll seek manslaughter charges if he doesn't pull through. He apparently comes from a well-heeled Utah family who won't go quietly into the night said Sheriff Caldwell."

"Was a big boy and reckon no one who knowed him is shocked hearin he got what was comin to him. Just got his ticket punched by Jay."

"Sheriff Caldwell said he'll stall for as long as he can given Jay's condition. He said he's concerned for Jay and the boy but really fears what the press will do when they learn you were involved. He's praying the boy holds on and you guys stay gone until the media and their gawkers get bored and leave town. He's had to call members of the police forces of American Falls and Shelley for help and hasn't had the time to ghost write a note for the mayor to request emergency funding from the governor, which he insisted the mayor deliver tomorrow or he'll drive to Boise himself no matter how crazy things get in town."

"Guess everyone has a little good in him."

"He said they'll eventually bring Jay in though to give a statement, and depending on the boy's condition they might book him."

"If it comes to it, he won't go easy if he goes at all."

"He doesn't have long."

"He knows better'n everyone."

"Sheriff Caldwell said the local department that brings him in will rue the day they did if Jay takes his last breaths at their station. We agreed that Jay's mother will bring legal Armageddon down on them. She's no stranger to the courts and not just because of her half-dozen or so divorces. She doesn't live in Rose in a big house on the Snake River on alimony alone. I know of at least two cases she was the prevailing party in business disputes. The last time I saw her she was reading the riot act to a couple of lawyers who were trembling in their suits, and I learned later they were her own with the out-of-town, white-shoe Seattle firm of Marston and Foreman L.L.P."

"Aint half a what she's capable a doin. Seen her tan an ex's hide in broad daylight. Three a his friends sat in a dually watchin till Jay told em to pick him off the ground."

"I believe it. How are you?"

"Better some stints and not so good the rest a others but can feel my legs most a the time."

"Stay awake. Stay awake as long as you can. Please let me talk to Linda."

Reached back and Verolinda took the phone. The old green sports car hummed down the highway. Everything went quiet but Jay snorin. After a bit I wondered if Verolinda didn't start up with their own duet with a mind a joinin em.

Relaxed my chin, wishin for a head rest and stretched my eyeballs under speckles a light in the sun roof, damned surprised didn't notice em before.

The pimple-face kid looked straight over the leather wrapped steerin wheel, and the old green sports car crossed over double yellow lines and back. He reached between his legs for a can a pop and took a sip.

I never felt young as he looked and couldn't help wonderin after Verolinda. "How long you been friends with Linda?"

He turned with his Stetson tilted up. "Since she moved into my ward in the second grade."

"She's Car's favorite and smarter'n everyone her age."

She could go to the college a her choice said Carmen. Had her a scholarship to dance at one a them schools out East specializin in plants, set on becomin a heart surgeon one day. Verolinda give no reason for doubts. Whenever with the girls she answered every one a their questions. I never seen nothin like it in all my life. I couldn't recall answerin more'n one and most times none.

"I know. She's going to be a doctor."

"Exactly. What in the Sam Hell she hangin round a bull rider for?"

He took his time. "I don't know." He eyed the rear-view mirror and back at the road. "We're just friends." He went quiet. After a few minutes he piped up. "I know her whole family. Her father was my teacher before he died. Nothing's more important than family to her."

Nothin surer for Mormons everywhere I knowed without some pimple-face kid tellin me. Struck me wronger each a the hundred times I heard it like lodgin nother fire brand on my stomach. Between my ornery father and missin mother and bastard brother had enough proof to contradict the whole damned religion.

"Can't be. God is more important." The answer I give lots before. Then an even more obvious one come real sudden. "When comes down to it so is air." Sure Roper wouldn't even have a comeback to.

"I mean it's one of the most important things." He paused, eyein the road and then back. "I know her family is one of the most important things to her. She's a great person. She has a great family. I'm lucky to be her friend."

"Aint no denyin lots a what's considered best bout life turns out to be plumb luck, and you do yurself real credit recognizin yurs."

"Not for you. You don't need luck. You're the best."

"Lots a people are real good at what they do. No one is the best."

"Will you keep riding?"

Lifted my coffee for a sip and the old green sports car dipped and rose and cold coffee spilled on the buckskin jacket.

"Slow down on them uneven patches will you." The lid didn't set on tight. Held it and the cup. Then took a sip.

"Sorry."

Eyed round for napkins but there was none and used the sleeve a the buckskin jacket to wipe coffee down the front. "Don't know."

"I watched your rides growing up. My buddy Raker has a DVD of all of them going back to back for a couple hours to Tool from the early ones to to more recent ones. It took him weeks to make, but he said they had to be in order. I couldn't believe I gotta see you for real. It's been playing in my mind a hundred times."

"Just nother ride."

"Really?" He eyed me quick and back at the road.

"What I seen a it."

"I never saw a bull more rank. How do you do it? How do you ride so good?"

"Aint all bout what I do, though it's important. Difference is in what I want to do."

"How do you mean?"

"That's what I want. My daughters want to play with their rabbits. My boss wants to build houses. Car wants to have a Mormon garden. I want to ride.

"A lot of people want to ride."

"How much? Most guys not enough. Even real good riders."

"So you want to ride a lot?"

"All I want is to ride."

"But."

"Before, then, and after."

He went quiet ponderin my words.

"Like when you only want one thing and want nothin else. You want something else, that there weakens yur try. Whether a guy covers him or bucks off you know how he wanted it. That's the thing. Hangin on is the rest."

"So you have to be good too?"

"Damned right. But practice up even more. Where skill comes from and most important where to build yur try."

"So it was your drive and your experience on display yesterday. Someone on TV said that and stuck with me. He said your ride was so great it's once in a lifetime we get to witness such an event."

"He said what?"

"He said."

"Heard you just fine. What a line a bullshit. People are full a it. One a the surest things in life. Truth is he bucked me off."

"What do you mean?"

"Didn't make eight."

"They scored you."

"One fact don't make nother."

"Everyone's seen you ride him."

"They mighta but don't make it so."

"How do you mean?"

"Don't matter. I'll tell em."

"When?"

"Back in Blackfoot before all them damned cameras."

"I wonder what they'll do."

"Got nothin to do with what the truth is."

He grabbed the can a pop and took a sip. He fired a string a questions like beams on reflectors up north long the road. He asked after the smallest a details. How many plaits was best for a bull rope? And after things out a one's control. Should yur free hand be in front or to the side on a bull with lots a drop? And for unheard a explanations. How did a bull get so much lift? And things no one could know. What made one bull a chute fighter and nother a spinner? Hell he even asked after things not possible. If I could choose one bull to ride who would it be? Crossin the border to the first hint a daylight he beat all.

"What do you do to get out of the well?"

My head finally climbed out a the kid's whirlwind a ideas. "What do you think you can do?"

"I've visualized one big move behind with my free arm right as the bull plants his feet for the next turn."

"You what?" Gettin more clear headed on his every word.

"I see myself getting out of the well by."

"Heard what you said. Why you spendin time visualizin?"

"In my mind I'm practicing for when the next time it happens."

"Some things you can't practice so stick to those things you can. You get yurself in the well and get to yur feet fast as you can. And stay on em."

"I mean before he bucks me off."

"There aint no before. If yur in the well you bucked off, and only thing you should be thinkin is gettin yur feet under you soon as you hit dirt. Or you might hang, or worse he tramples yur skinny spine in the ground."

Bull riders was full a lots a crazy ideas, but this one took the cake. He just as sure put on a cape to fly back on. Nice as kid and all but havin such stuff in his head. Stay out a the well. Would said it again but there was no fixin others' nonsense by repeatin yurself. Up to em to get beyond it.

We passed Page and turned and twisted down a great descent and sun rays broke over a high mountain a red rock on are left Carmen said durin are last trip rose a huge plateau's edge runnin for miles beyond Gap. The old green sports car passed over more dips with clay mounds on both sides and red mesas far off. I knowed a few tradin posts on this very stretch with lots a makeshift ones like fruit stands. One a the busiest in Cameron served up the succulentest fry bread you ever imagined. And not just tacos neither but starters and deserts too. From some seats you seen the outskirts a the Grand Canyon while eatin yur entire course a fry breads.

One trip long this way we stayed in the Anasazi Inn. My tailbone hurt so bad I didn't sit for days. Roper met a medicine man in the parkin lot, and he hailed me over and said he knowed what ailed me. Didn't bargain a dollar less a his full askin price. He chanted and when finished bent for his bag and pulled out a root and leaf. He sliced em thin and crushed em with the butt a his pocket knife in an old plastic cup he found on the ground. He sent me for hot water I fetched from are room. He mixed his medicine and said drink it hot. The dirty water scolded my throat and sat in peace the same evenin.

Scarecrow power lines towered long the road and red sand and dirt spread for miles runnin into scattered sagebrush like the desert back home with a blue blanket over the San Francisco Peaks.

My neck tightened for the first time in hours and turned my sore chest.

Jay sat opened eyed with palms on knees in last a the night. "Covered some ground."

"Headed for Flagstaff."

"Making real good time."

"Start a day."

"You caught it Pard."

Sipped nothin but air from my cup a coffee.

Got to the base a the San Francisco Peaks as far from Flagstaff like we just left Blackfoot headed for Poky, but we passed more trees into the mountain town. Jay told the pimple-face kid to pull over for gas where a sign declared what road we was on. I knowed where we was with Route 66 veerin ahead just before a hill thick a ponderosa pines with a mighty fancy telescope on top. The last rodeo Jay gone with me for my last pro show in Flagstaff and when I asked if he wanted to ride long, he answered he would if after the show we visited that hill.

I rolled my bull rope and bent down to put it in my gear bag and Jay got to kickin his boots excited as I ever recollected him. We winded up the hill in all them ponderosa pines to hidden buildins. I barely kept up to the first a the round ones and Jay talked nonstop to himself and folks there about telescopes in em. One found a planet by old fashioned picture takin on glass plates. Inside nother wood panels on the bottom half and boards crossed and fixed to the ceilin on the top half circled on trailer tires with a long fancy telescope in the middle. Found evidence are universe were still growin. And pointed at the night full a stars with Jay beamin like havin all his Christmases at the same time.

Two men set on the sidewalk with huge backpacks, one upright and other on its side. A trowel tied onto one. They musta fancied themselves modern-day Johnny Appleseeds with their faces painted in dirt and wearin flip flops. One fired up a mini stove to heat water while the other held a silver bag with Chinese food on the cover.

Jay nodded at each car drivin by.

Went in the convenient store for a new cup a coffee and back out under a minute on the sidewalk right by them two environmentalists, carryin on with Jay smilin. He asked after mountains they seen and ones they planned to summit next. They said nothin invited awe like the Canadian Rockies but somethin on Agassiz Peak trailed em down like on a holy pilgrimage they did years before in Santiago, Spain. They couldn't wait to climb Humphreys'.

Verolinda handed Jay an orange drink. He took a couple sips and nodded one more time and directed us all back in the old green sports car for Interstate 17. Ridges with pines on top passed till they thinned to bushes on both sides and give to brush in open desert for where rock mountains surrounded Phoenix.

CHAPTER 18

Verolinda turned up her phone and said take the next exit through an old neighborhood and down one street and cross nother to a busy one and into an older complex. The windows all down, and Jay sat Indian style with the cream straw cowboy hat over his eyes.

They was huntin someone. I didn't care to ask but needed to relieve myself and followed em up a flight a stairs. Verolinda knocked on apartment 334. No one answered.

"They are gone for the day," she said.

"Who?" I asked.

"The missionaries."

Why in the Sam Hell so early after missionaries was affairs I had no earthly business in, wantin over soon as humanly possible.

"Seen a couple white shirts pedalin on a side road two turns back."

Verolinda skipped down the stairs.

Jay sat in the driver seat and asked, "Where to?"

"Down the street," Verolinda said, gettin in back and leanin over the seat on the lookout.

Jay chuckled like chasin a bounty on their heads. Cars passed and one pulled up behind but no white shirts pedalin bicycles. A few miles twistin round the neighborhood come cross a main road. Pulled rank for nature's call.

"Pull into the first convenient store you see," I said.

And a couple miles on one appeared. Opened my door and got my boots on the ground before we stopped.

Beelined to a marked door on the corner and pulled the knob. Didn't budge. "Goddamnit." Pulled again and again.

Jay leaned against the wall like in a line a two. Went round him for the front door and a bell rung. Five people deep lined up. Cut to the counter. "Need yur men's key."

A tall skinny Mexican kid looked up from the lotto machine and said, "El vaquero, it's occupied."

Did bout everything I could holdin in and opened the door to the sound a the bell straight back for the marked door on the corner. Jay stayed up against the wall. Didn't feel my damned neck for the first time in hours, bobbin back and forth. The longest minutes a my life went by. The door opened to a big guy with a full beard and held a key. Grabbed it on my way by. The restroom just like others I knowed from travelin cross the country. Right filthy with modern works a art combined and overlayed on each other in all kinds a colors and shapes between bunches a writin. Settled on the warm seat with uneven edges. Nothin more pressin with nowhere else to be.

Gone out and passed Jay goin in as Verolinda run cross the parkin lot. Her chest high, threatenin to leap with each step. A couple white shirts wearin helmets halted on the side a the road, and sure enough both wore ties tucked into their shirts. They pedaled against traffic to her. Some bastard honked his horn, and the second missionary, half the size a the first, smiled and waved. They hopped their bicycles onto the sidewalk and straddled the frames. Verolinda rose straight on her toes and clasped her hands. The taller missionary didn't move a feather. A few seconds passed, and no one did with sun shinin off their helmets. The taller missionary bowed, droppin his hands.

Engines roared and tires rolled by and by.

Verolinda's eyes and cheeks touched. The smaller missionary took off his helmet. Verolinda clasped her hands over her stomach, and the taller missionary raised his head. Verolinda wrapped him in her arms. The smaller missionary shuffled and grabbed the taller missionary's bicycle. The smaller missionary pointed at the taller missionary who took off his helmet and handed it over.

Tuckered out and parched turned for Jay, but he went, talkin to a couple boys near the hood a the old green sports car. Headed back inside and the bell rung goin in. Cut to the front again. "Got some coffee?"

"It's not any good vaquero." The tall skinny Mexican kid pointed at the back wall. "But I brewed a new pot."

Picked up the first a three pots and pulled a paper cup from a stack on the counter and poured. Took a sip and filled up to the top and walked to the cooler for an orange pop.

The tall skinny Mexican kid smiled and eyed me the whole way. "Did caballo throw you?"

"He bucked a'right." Roper would say by a wild mare or filly in are younger days. He said where, dependin upon the nearest river, lots a times long the Rio Grande. Geography just the main thing to explainin life he claimed and his specialty among thousands a other things.

The bell rung goin out passed boys goin in. Handed Jay the orange pop in the midst a boys surroundin the old green sports car. Verolinda coulda been holdin up the taller missionary, and the smaller one beamed. He shook the nearest person's hand and smiled so wide he couldn't been happier. He moved to the next person and did the same.

He got to me and took my hand real firm and said, "What a pleasure to meet Verolinda's friends. I've heard many great things about her."

I'll be damned if his smile never quit between one word, and he said the same thing to the pimple-face kid and Jay like he knowed us all since elementary school. His unmistakable Mormon niceness you couldn't help suspect an imaginary lariat tied to a faucet on a baptismal font. But this boy seemed he meant it. Carmen would say without an ounce a guile.

The crowd parted for a lowrider with loud exhaust and rolled next to the old green sports car. The driver door opened, and smoke come out. A short boy with a bandana tied over his eyes got out and one from the other side like in a movie. A larger dangerous boy got out the back. Whether they seen the crowd gatherin and wondered what was the fuss or stopped for pops, sure not somethin meant to ask a one.

"Who owns this?" the dangerous boy asked.

Jay smiled.

"Nice little pony. What's in it?"

The sun rose bakin the buckskin jacket. The hot coffee took aholt, sippin and waitin for whatever.

They all eyed the old green sports car with interruptions from the smaller missionary none minded. He chatted up the dangerous boy and reached into his backpack and pulled out a blue book.

"Already have one little man." The dangerous boy patted the smaller missionary's shoulder.

My boots heated up and went for the last a the shade at the corner a the buildin. Tilted the brown Rand and leaned against the wall and rested on my haunches.

Opened my eyes and the smaller missionary smiled next to Jay who still talked to the dangerous boy under the hood a the old green sports car. They turned when a small Toyota electric car rolled up and welcomed a bald man, and all turned back at the same time under the hood a the old green sports car. The smaller missionary pointed, and Jay and the dangerous boy nodded.

Verolinda and the taller missionary sat on the curb. Her spine straight with her head level to the slouchin taller missionary. She reached and turned his face to hers, and her other arm roped his back.

The dangerous boy handed Jay a piece a paper, and Jay put it in the pocket a his shirt. Them boys climbed back into all the smoke in the lowrider.

Verolinda turned at the sound a my boots and said, "We'll follow the missionaries back to their apartment."

They pedaled with the smaller one in the lead. We got to apartment 334, and the smaller missionary welcomed everyone by name. He offered cold water from the tap, and everyone accepted to the person. He turned on the faucet and filled small yellow hard cups like ones we pulled out a dog food for my father's Golden Retrievers. The missionaries' bicycles set against the wall under the top three old livin Mormon prophets next to the Mormon Jesus with outstretched hands in a long white dress Roper always said too unbefittin a the risen Lord. He professed the attire impractical for the millennial job ahead. I reckoned a picture a the young, handsome Joe Smith hung over them missionaries' beds.

The smaller missionary said he come to Blackfoot for the Eastern Idaho State Fair with cousins from Sugar City. Three years runnin the oldest Travis win a blue ribbon for his fine poultry. I walked the north pavilions every year and never seen one single chicken. He went on bout Travis's top breeders, explainin the key to ideal body confirmation from how muscle carried, especially long the keel. Jay nodded like he knowed already. And Roper keen on sayin animals at the World's Fair from Seattle to Chicago couldn't match the majesty a the draft horses in Blackfoot every September. And this smaller missionary with not a drip a contradiction went right on to prove it.

The taller missionary stared at Jay sittin on the only plastic chair. The forearms a the buckskin jacket rested against a bare yellow counter. Verolinda left the table with her phone, and the taller missionary kept eyein Jay.

The smaller missionary carried on with his smile still goin strong. He asked Jay bout the last car he built, and Jay discoursed on no less'n three different rides in his garage in town.

Verolinda come into the room and handed over her phone.

"How are you feeling?" Carmen asked.
"Worn thin. Gonna crash soon God willin," I said.
"Have you stayed awake the whole way?"
"Most a it."
"How is your neck?"
"Got its course to run."
"I set up an appointment for next week. How is Jay doing?"

"Same."

"What's his plan?"

"Don't rightly know his intentions."

"Make sure he's safe. Please give Linda your ATM card. She's going to need it to buy tickets home for her and Rocky." Sure enough he win a scholarship to play slotback for Brigham Young.

"How's Sam?"

"She spent the night inside Jay's trailer. We plan to pick her up soon. The girls want to say good morning."

"Hi Dad," Eloisa said.

"Hi Lisa."

"How is your head?"

"Clearin up."

"It'll get better. Don't worry. Here's Lena."

"Hi Lena."

"Get Linda Dad."

Give the phone over and pulled out the card.

Verolinda lowered the phone. "Will you please write down the pin?"

"Aint no need. Year Frost win the world."

CHAPTER 19

Jay drove fast on long roads passin one huge ranch development after nother. Rock mountains with jagged ridges stretched round in every direction. Hikers paradise without a single tick, just roadrunners dartin cross paths, rattlers surpisin thirsty dogs, and hungry bobcats after sack lunches. Turnin off the longest road a my life Jay drove down one I reckoned a close rival.

"Should I have asked Linda for her phone?" the pimple-face kid hollered from back a the old green sports car.

"I know the way," Jay said on the road in contention for the longest on Earth and tapped the break turnin onto a new one like they moved the Daytona 500 to Phoenix and the only car entered. Left the last a the ranches and passed a huge house with lots a space between the next huge house and rock mountains not far behind. Jay slowed at one long driveway and skidded onto it. A large lot with three other sports cars out front a ten car garage attached to an enormous mansion. Jay broke real sudden before a wide stone path and kilt the engine and laid on the horn.

"Grab your gear bag and wait," Jay said and handed the keys to the pimple-face kid.

Swung my boots to the ground and could smell burned rubber. Got out and picked up my heels to catch up with Jay on a grand porch where two large slabs fit an impressive frame. Wood slats run the length above and on the sides, passin for a fortress. Iron handles with a bird spreadin wings on one slab and nother hidin between em on the other level with the brown Rand. I reckoned the pieces required a crane to pull off a front-end loader.

Nothin happened. "Should the kid honk again?"

"He sees us." Jay went tight lipped and his right hand balled. He'd take his last breath before throwin his last punch.

A mighty slab parted, and a black man tall as a tree stepped by the thick edge. He wore a baby blue sweater with a zipper over a white shirt stiched with just half a ping-pong with a bright pink collar and white slacks and white shoes. I wondered if the fancy getup didn't mean he win a world championship but held a golf club. Roper fancied himself the greatest and fond a sayin he'd play "any table anywhere" and repeated lots he come to his superior skills too late and coulda made the Olympics if he'd only got the proper mentorin at an early age. The tall man eyed the old green sports car with the engine still cracklin.

"You son of a bitch." The tall man stared down Jay. "She's Flip's now as far as I'm concerned. I am certain she's not in the condition I accepted."

"Okay." Jay didn't flinch.

The tall man eyed the old green sports car like he didn't have no choice and shook more. "You sore fool. Your problem is with Flip. This is the last time I'll say it. Next time will be through my lawyers."

Jay didn't say nothin.

The tall man stepped back and set the golf club inside the huge slab and back less'n a foot from Jay.

"All this time and you finally find my pony. You son of a bitch." He shook even more. Seven seconds a nothin passed. "Was there something else Jay? Right now you and your friends are free to drive her back the way you came, but you stand here much longer and you won't enjoy that luxury." He glanced my way. "I'm not doubting the sincerity of your backup, but he's clearly been through the wringer and the kid isn't holding a bag of firepower. I can smell it from here. You don't look so hot yourself old friend like someone busted you out of the ICU."

Jay backed up off the grand porch.

The tall man followed us to the edge. "Hey Dean, how did she ride?"

Focused on Jay but turned back. "Real smooth."

"I derive a great deal of pleasure hearing you say so. You're still lighting up the networks. You do the impossible and look to pay the ultimate price only to rise like a phoenix to receive a hero's reward. And you go and vanish. Everyone clamoring for your whereabouts and you appear like a conqueror at a Roman feast. Then when your lawyer has us all ready for a grand pronouncement, you leave and some doctor claims you ran him down and, poof, gone again. Could be a dime novel. And here you show up on my doorstep with Jay Dobson. Unbelievable. That son of a bitch."

Jay took the keys from the pimple-face kid, and the tall man leaned farther out over the grand porch. Jay tossed em in a row a trimmed wild bushes in the front yard a this tall man's personal desert.

"Let's go," Jay said.

The tall man started off the grand porch with both hands in pockets a his spotless white pants. He eyed the old green sports car like not seein what was really seein and halted at the hood.

"Gawd the electric shaver. Fins in the scoop, definitely a G." He raised his large hand to his chin and turned to Jay. "390?"

Jay nodded.

"The ultimate pony. Right at home with my Marauder." He shook his head. "Would have kept her for yourself if she was a GT-E with a 427." He tore his gaze off the old green sports car are way.

"Only came in automatic."

"That's right, you'd only have one of the three mythical 428s for yourself."

"They're out there."

"That's your fix Jay. How she rides is as important as the boom behind her, more important most of the time."

"Had chrome rims. Told him only steel. He got them two days ago."

"14 inches?"

"With 215 tires."

"I'll trade them out for 225 bias's."

"I figured."

The tall man circled the old green sports car and hesitated. "Cracked reflector." He brushed his hand long the continuous tail lights and smiled not able to tear his eyes from em.

Jay headed into the desert.

Different level cactuses spread in patches. Some with two heads and others three. One just a fork and others straight like Twinkies. All old as the real wild west and probably here long before. Tumble weeds rolled by to a Joshua tree full a spiky leaves I knowed enough looked planted, probably uprooted from California. Waved the pimple-face kid off. Jay eyed them branches, and his chest shuddered. He bent, puttin his hands on his knees.

"What in the hell bout bein out a ride in this heat tickles you?"

"A son of a bitching lawyer." He caught his breath. "Sicking more son of a bitching lawyers on me." He breathed a couple more times and straightened and his chest settled. "I'd give anything to be around for it." He grabbed the shoulder a the buckskin jacket. "And we ain't out a ride. I promised Taylor one."

Heat spread over my whole torso. My neck felt real good. Better'n I reckoned could. Jay looked from where we come where the tall man wandered in a patch a trimmed weeds and crooked twigs.

He passed the Joshua tree with us in the trail a his dust, and are heels kicked in silence a the desert.

"Where in the hell are we goin?" I asked.

He stopped and breathed deep. He bent restin his arms on his legs. After thirty seconds he straightened. "John's." He pointed at a huge mansion a fair bit in the distance. "Marty's younger brother." He pointed back from where we come.

Comparin one big house to nother comes down to one's fancy. Their outsides take different shapes and insides are rearranged, but they amount to the same thing in lots a extra space. None a which people will use but sure like knowin is there.

Water dripped out the bottom a the buckskin jacket. The desert come on an asphalt road, runnin hundreds a yards in opposite directions with heat jumpin off each step. Pulled the brim a the brown Rand low. A football throw ahead the pimple-face kid toted his gear bag while Jay took up the rear.

Are boots tapped quiet to a fountain in front a the massive mansion. My legs wobbled with my gut full a thirst and rested my arms on the surroundin stone wall. I knowed Carmen would say the thing most exquisite. Tall thin trees and small cactuses rose round a wide porclean bowl. A woman knelt by it, focusin straight with pinched eyes. Nowhere a sign a water.

Felt Jay eyein her. "Determined ain't she?"

Her back knee just off the ground with her bare toes foldin.

Jay braced long the top a wall to the other side sure bound for water we missed. Her other leg straightened with her heel raisin. One hand pressed to the ground with thin fingers extended. The other pressed against her side. If I jumped the wall and got through roughage for a better look, I reckoned would make out veins in her arms and hands.

"Meet Alice. See the line across her shoulders? Like she carried a stick with buckets." Jay didn't move his hands from the wall and didn't look up.

Seen no such line but a shirt stuck to her straight back with sleeves rolled up her arms and a dress torn below her knees. Long hair matted her scalp. A bucket tipped on its side less'n a yard off.

"Jay," a voice boomed.

An enormous black man stepped down marble steps a one mighty long front porch. Tall as the lawyer we ditched and twice his size.

"My God," he boomed even louder. "My God, come in, come in." His long outstretched arms closed wavin us in.

The front room circled open space. Not a thing in it. Not even a bench to rest. We passed through a hole in the other side to a room full a couches and different colored large chairs. At the far end sat a large piano with the lid up on a raised floor with a long glass wall and desert runnin behind.

"I missed a text from Martin until after my system was tripped. I had thought maybe a coyote but then saw he said you were on your way. Please sit." His large open palms ushered us to the softest lookin chairs I ever seen.

He went for a marble counter off the side a the room. He come back with glasses a lemonade. Gulped the perfect tartness down and lowered my glass. The man walked back to the marble counter. He brought back a pitcher and refilled me to the top and waited for the pimple-face kid and Jay to finish and poured em full too.

Jay dropped into a massive red chair. The man sat cross from him, and the pimple-face kid and me took are own mighty chairs close by.

"You look beat through my friend. You haven't replied to my texts. Not like you. Being here offers some relief but only confirms my fears from our exchanges last week." The man leaned forward off his chair.

Jay drunk his lemonade. He smacked his lips. "Thought I'd stop by for that drink and see Apple."

The man paused and sat back in his chair. He bowed his head on his massive chest. He lifted his head with his eyes filled full a water. "Okay, okay." His big voice fadin and him continuin noddin.

He rose and went back to the marble counter. "We finished my last bottle of Pappy when you were here last."

He run his huge hand over his face and paused. He nodded his head. "I have an Eagle Rare I have been waiting to open." He rummaged through shelves. "Actually I know just the bottle in the cellar."

His huge back passed from behind the marble counter through a hole in the wall into a rounded walkway. Pure speculative thoughts run through my head if this man associated with the auction circuit where Jay met all sorts. They was automobile enthusiasts, worshipin heightened prowess a men's mechanical achievements said Roper after Jay turned us down for goin to one a are last shows bound for one a his own. Always chasin down the classic car, where he drummed up more restoration work'n had space and time for.

Reached for the pitcher a lemonade on a small table and poured my glass full and set the pitcher down heavy.

Jay lay in his chair more'n sat.

The pimple-face kid remarked there was twelve mighty chairs and each could seat two people. Sudden feelins struck and wondered if I could get up from mine. What kind? Who made it? And the others? And how much did one cost? Lots a questions all at once. I wished for my phone to snatch a photo to show Carmen. She might build me one if I peppered her long enough. The colors from green and red to mixes I would venture no guess, and little wood tables the same as the one holdin the pitcher a lemonade scattered by each one.

The man passed through the large hole in the wall with a bottle in one hand and tumblers like thimbles in the other. He set the goods down on the marble counter and opened an ice box and dug with grips and dropped a round piece in each tumbler. His fumblin smile tried to set beneath red swollen eyes. He stepped heavy and his mighty chest heaved, settin the tumblers down next to the empty pitcher. He opened his mouth but didn't say nothin and wiped his eyes. He sat and wiped em again with his enormous forearm. "A Midwinter Nights Dram." His words barely come out.

He poured all four tumblers full and set the bottle down. He picked up one and handed over to Jay.

"Jay."

Jay opened his eyes. He took the drink and paused against his lips and breathed in. "Perfect." He lowered the tumbler on his chest.

The man give me one. He raised one to the pimple-face kid, but he waved him off and said, "No thank you."

"To my friend." The man's voice cracked and tipped back in one gulp.

Jay opened his eyes and took a sip.

The man shot the pimple-face kid's and poured himself nother.

Damned if I couldn't taste it and just burned but not like regular whiskey.

"What's it?" I asked.

"Bourbon," the man said.

"That German?"

"Kentucky Whiskey."

"Been to lots a shows there and never had this stuff. Not bad."

"This is from Utah. A wonderful new contribution to the great whiskey tradition."

"Smoothest a the stuff I ever tasted. Not what my brother or father drunk." Never takin to the burn down my gullet and gut out my asshole. No question a sure and fine way to get lit quick but never seen the hurry. This Utah Kentuckian moonshine glided down and whole body warmed up.

The man run his huge hand over his face and red eyes. "You're all welcome to stay the night. We can grill, and you're welcome to cool off in the pool and take your time, resting as long as you want. There's no hurry, so please stay. Please make yourselves comfortable."

"Want to see Apple," Jay said, openin his eyes.

"Of course. Of course."

"And give these guys a tour."

"A what?" I said, takin nother sip.

"John studies light, so everything you can imagine and a lot you can't."

"I'm a nuclear engineer by training but mostly design now," the man said.

"What's that?" I asked.

"Energy," the pimple-face kid said.

"Yes, you're right," the man said.

"My older brother's friend is one. He works at the Site out of Arco."

"What's his name? I might know him?"

"I don't remember."

"His brother's name is Bruce R. Weeks, and he knows a lot of stuff," Jay said with eyes wide open.

"Then it's no surprise he has friends at the Site. Brilliant people. A big and important facility. Been many times and stopped in Riverton to see Jay on the way. You'd be surprised how well I know Blackfoot."

"Aint much to wrap yur head round," I said.

The man eyed me straight. "By Jove you are a spitting image of one of Phoenix's great artists. Come with me."

He rose with the bottle and poured himself nother and bendin poured Jay and me where liquid rose above the lip. He fumbled the small cap on the bottle and let it lie as it lay.

The pimple-face kid didn't make long as his right arm, and I barely did his left. Jay passed for one leg, risin next to the right one.

Was plumb one with my chair, not wantin up if I could get up. Warmth spread throughout my chest and took a sip a his wonder whiskey. They all stopped and eyed me. Stood beyond my own power. My legs went light pickin up my boots into a big hole in the wall behind em.

The man led into a room and down a long hall and through nother hole into an empty room with a glass ceilin full a light but not too bright. Two sets a plain, finished wood benches sat back to back in the middle and headed for em. Got halfway and noticed my boots and nothin else. The others halted inside the hole, eyein the wall.

"This is the most recent addition to the room. It's called Waves and Vibrations."

The pimple-face kid rose on the tips a his boots, and Jay swayed back and forth. Mostly gray buildins and streets and a few brown buildins near the front and tired orange roofs on buildins in back. The lines barely showed where one begun and nother ended. A wide street parted em to the right under a brackish haze with clouds above.

"I thought a man stood on a roof for this view of the city. Then I noticed here to the right." The man pointed at an orange roof. "This edge of the building establishes a point of view, which is level with a window." There was tons a windows in the paintin he musta seen through an old one with smudges and breaks refractin light. "Now see there." The man pointed at a brown spot near the bottom. "The outline of a person waving at the viewer of the scene. His appearance is less about why he's up a poll than he sees the onlooker. He suggests the viewer is looking through a window, not to mention all the roofs are pitched with nowhere to stand."

We all eyed the thing closer. Had my own idea the person needed to clean the window or replace the damned thing.

"And this perspective from a painter concerned with expressions through masks. A remarkable departure. Or I've wondered is it?"

"Sounds like a big fan of Halloween," Jay said.

A real pagan holiday more popular'n Christmas said Roper. I never believed and expected no one but he did. Took a sip a the wonder whiskey and head got warmer.

"His masks conveyed the grotesque and possible feelings beneath them."

Not even Jay asked what the hell the man meant. Jay took a sip, admirin the grimy view.

Turned round and eyed the walls where more paintins hung. Clean patterns run over and under em I missed at first. Some etched in the wall and others raised. The darndest thing a room full a pictures like ones in New York City and not a bit shocked by the waste a space, knowin too common among some folks from when me and Gabby dressed up for her soirees, what she called weekend functions when I drunk too much but never on purpose. Drinks didn't taste a alcohol in New York City, and never noticed how much till I felt how much. One night lucked onto a bench and learned one more thing durin them soirees. Casins was as big a deal or bigger'n the muddled pictures in em. I never guessed wood swirled so many damned ways. I studied em one soiree after nother with lots a people bent in tuxedos they probably owned outright, and always with Gabby's unlikeable, sheek friends, accustomed to sayin upon greetin em. I never had the heart to tell her an Arab leader she really called em. Roper woulda but Gabby paid him no mind. The one who told me after one a the first ones he come with us, not missin a beat chattin up everyone we seen but not one word to me.

The man admired more paintins down the wall, and Jay and the pimple-face kid followed. A half step behind, and the pimple-face kid halted. Two stepped by his side in the nick a time but got a splash on the buckskin jacket and wondered if some got on the floor. Run my boot over where I reckoned spilled just in case and started on thinkin a cussin the pimple-face kid, and the man pointed again.

"On the Cliffs."

"Looks like the Oregon coast," the pimple-face kid said. "Our family used to go during the summer. My mother is from there."

"Yes, like haystack rock on Cannon Beach."

"But the water isn't so blue and looks warmer. But the rock on the beach is the same. My brother Bruce climbed on top too."

"A big rock possible to get marooned on. The bright hues on a par with the unforgettable feeling of the place but not a natural one."

"There's smudges on the bottom," Jay said.

And we all eyed the corner.

"Maybe not enough to simply capture the idea, and he didn't want us to think it was anything but a painting. Or he didn't finish."

"How many do you have in all?" the pimple-face kid asked.

"Counting my most recent acquisition, forty-two. I will get the picture." He went for the corner and lifted a tablet computer like Carmen's off a stand. He come back movin his finger on the screen and handed it over.

An old rock house under clay tile roof. The ground the same rusted gray as the background. In a sliver a shade on the nearside a woman in a red apron observed a boy facin away with his hands clasped, while nother boy with a pant leg rolled up held a stick over his shoulder on shaded steps off the front. A corner door and an old skinny door frame on the upper level in the middle with the bottom half filled with orange and yellow bricks and top half with a couple thin wood panels. Smatterin a yellow run long the wall, and part passed for a ghostly figure spillin on the ground. A window outlined in blue night with lights on top blocked by a orange cloth with a stick and somethin on the end, maybe a Goldfish in a bowl. I couldn't say, and no one did one way or the other.

Jay swayed before nother paintin.

"Riverton."

Plain wood on each side with no single crook or crack and rough long the edges outlined a field. Brown wheat stems with large full heads a kernels you could count run from the bottom to a sea a fuzzy small ones in a batch swayin near the middle with a swath at the end. Wood panels on a cream white farmhouse jutted from the outskirts. And near back two people wearin ball caps in waiters leaned against shovels on a ditch bank before an unseen stretch covered in blue sky.

"By Phoenix's finest artist, and if I was to guess she could be your older sister, minus the black eyes and broken nose." The man turned his huge self right at me. "This is my second piece by her. Her largest gallery is in Scottsdale, and I've visited many times. I had the pleasure to hear her lecture at Taliesin West as part of a fund raiser to increase adult reading programs throughout the state. My guess is she really lives most of the year in Santa Fe with other western artists, especially during the summer."

"Went to a rodeo in Santa Fe a long time ago," I said.

"Probably only a few cowboys there anymore but a lot of artists," Jay said.

"There are many there, but were even more in the eighties and nineties. Now they scatter throughout the West. Like cowboys I imagine," the man said.

"Lots live in L.A, artists not cowboys."

"Many there are doing abstract or expressionistic work, or a combination of both. I can't infer the concepts behind most contemporary work, which seems to be the point. Freedom to do whatever one wants and more arbitrary the better. The stick is unmistakable when artists rise above their peers by becoming a brand. The most effective way for living artists to compete with the great dead ones. Contemporaries emphasize their uniqueness and unite in rejecting any suggestion of the general, and I can't name a single great work that hasn't relied on it. I can only trust my intuition and hope for a positive quarter in the markets so I can buy another piece I like."

Jay took a sip with just a bit a the wonder whiskey left. "I've been to a few of their parties and never understood any of their talk and from overhearing a fair share no one else did either. But they always served fine liquor, where I drunk a lot of great cognacs, compliments of the host." He stared at the field for a few seconds and turned on his heels for a bench. And not a step behind.

Jay polished off his drink. He took a deep breath eyein the glass ceilin with his arms long the top a the bench, restin the empty tumbler on the edge. The sun didn't bare down and couldn't figure why.

"I didn't see the dog before," Jay said.

"What dog?" I asked.

"On the side of the field running at the two farmers. If I had to guess she was a blue heeler through a hole in the barbed wire fence. Didn't see any cows on the other side but made out a couple pies left behind."

"Might be the painter leavin to yur imagination."

"She's showing hers and not relying on ours. They were clear if you looked close."

"Missed em."

"Ain't the artist's job to make sure you see Pard."

"Hell if I could tell if I did see and talkin bout a dog. You talk like she's Paden's."

"The more one sees the more one can. How art works."

"What the hell you carryin on bout?"

Jay paused and eyed his empty tumbler. He looked back at the ceilin and said soft, "Running in my thoughts."

"What the hell's art?"

"Creating something true I expect."

"Aint sayin much."

"Does for those who know I'd guess."

"That there's some notion."

"No mistaking Pard." He went even softer, eyein the bright sky on the other side a the ceilin. I couldn't bend my neck back more'n half an inch and held tight, puffin my chest and breathin out again, holdin the bench with both hands to keep from wobblin off. A question come real sudden to put the whole damned thing to bed.

"So what makes art art?"

Jay didn't move his outstretched arms. "You do a thing you're able, best you can."

"Makes art?"

"Necessary beginning to it. The thing to become art."

"Somethin has to set somethin apart from somethin else or aint its own thing."

"And a few things do. Like beauty."

"Gettin nowhere real fast."

"For those who work for it it does."

"There you go again."

"Best way art was explained to me was by Marty. He says before you know what art means you have to step back to understand why it could mean it. He says you can only start with our own views, the only ones we will ever really know, which ain't a given. All other views are separate, but we catch them in our own expectoriums, which he says is our view and includes comprehending others' views. Something that breaks the boundary of our expectorium to take one beyond and can also break the boundary going inside ourselves. Art is the reveal in either direction."

"So say what it is before I go for nother drink."

"It's mainly form. Like balance. What people most often agree upon or squabble about or reject outright, the aspects of the form."

"The form? You couldn't just say so?"

"More taking the form of a thing in all its dimensions, most of them hidden but as important as the surface we see. But not just its form, because whatever the form it takes is in relation to our expectorium. Forms have their position depending on their purpose. Developing the form gets to its meaning and has corresponding power to reset one's expectorium."

"Art is beauty. Beauty is form. And form is balance." I sat back and fought closin my eyes. "What the."

"Not just the form though. And there's not one, and most times a form doesn't fit the classification folks are saying is the form that defines it Marty says. He says the great stuff is too big for an old form and takes a new one. Beauty is the effect right away for some and after a lifetime of effort for others when they see it."

"The form but more'n one and sometimes a damned new one." I set back and focused on the wall to calm me from spinnin.

"A whole lot of it is form Pard, so remembering that will serve you real good. And will be enough to settle on. But the effort depends on recognizing it is tied to you. It doesn't come from nothing and not by chance, which ain't the same as it being unexpected and many times is. With a bit of good fortune it's taken when you're able, which is true for comprehending and creating it."

"Seems like all it could apply to ugly things just the same." I said out a frustration for his espousin such notions.

Was puttin forward the opposite a thing I learned to do from Roper.

"What do you have in mind?"

"Bad things havin their own forms." I eyed nothin straight.

"Marty says bad means a situation or characteristic limiting one's ability to expand one's expectorium. How bad is measured by how limited the opportunity is to develop. Evil is straight forward intentional action or inaction stabilizing or increasing the bad form. You're onto something Pard."

"Jesus Jay. Leave some pettifoggin lawyer to come up with such a word. Yur talkin stuff I could repeat over and again and never get round to gettin. Even with all the time in the world I'd never get beauty and form and evil in the belly a my own expectorium."

"Doesn't mean it doesn't take. Things ain't measured by the thing itself."

What in the Sam Hell I thought for the umpteenth time. The man and the pimple-face kid carried on bout Blackfoot toward the hole in the wall and out the room. Jay rose after em. Got up fast bent on a drink I reckoned earned outright. My body went light and sat right back down. The idea come to turn out a the next room.

Jay turned and waited. Rose slower and heeled up to em.

"You really believe all that?" Caught up pert near out a breath at the hole in the wall.

"Sure."

"What's art really?"

He went quiet and eyed the room over one last time. "It connects an idea or feeling to us I suppose."

"But what?"

"Art makes our experience for as long as we hold it."

"Like a perfect chair."

"Sure. I was thinking my next ride."

We entered the hall and walked to the end marked by a large steel frame with heavy glass doors. Through em the largest garage I ever seen but with no cars. The man pulled one glass door open. A half-dozen glass circles divided up the ceilin with rows a tables with boxes and machines below. An enormous plastic tent cut the room off.

Jay followed the man to a fancy wood box, and the man pulled out a shelf with a square glass case long as a record sleeve. It had a bunch a pieces a different sizes a glass like a butterfly collection. The man set the case back in the box and moved down the row and by a table into the next row. He stopped at a box near a machine and pulled out a nother case. He opened it and grabbed a set a clamps with white paddin on the ends and lifted a piece a glass. The man moved to a machine and touched a button and a contraption come down. Them clamps placed the piece a glass in. The man pushed the button again, and the contraption went back up.

Jay sat at the machine and looked into a hole at the end. He put his hands on a pad at the bottom with buttons. Then come his wide smile. The man led me and the pimple-face kid to nother machine. Beat the pimple-face kid on the seat and tried the eyehole. The man pushed a button and the hole moved out and up and down but couldn't get an angle on the damned thing with Jay's brace on. Shifted on the seat but still couldn't. The frustratinest thing missin what you knowed for certain were somethin. Got up and the pimple-face kid took the seat.

The man explained he designed them machines and the lenses in em and got all em manufactured by a company in Korea. He said he owned patents on em and more'n everyone else combined. He pointed at all the machines and said all the lights and endless information got recorded in em and pointed to the tented middle a the long garage. He went on bout the machines takin lenses with more space'n one could imagine. He used different combinations a their angles for capturin variations a light, or colors and stored em. Just awful convinced the more light helped you see better and all its effects no matter yur affects he said. The most complete way to see and record the invisible world and the actual virtual images a the visible world we see. I had no hankerin for invisible things, but my head pounded wonderin what the pimple-face kid seen. The man told him and Jay to come long, and they pulled back wide eyed.

He led to the tent with a zipper door right by a box full a goggles and medical masks. He passed em out, and we dressed up. He unzipped the door open. A linin inside the tent made all it darker'n I guessed when lookin in from the outside. The man seen me eyein it and said he could adjust to pitch black and cost more'n all but a few a his machines. He zipped up the door and went for a large chair set tall as an architect's next to a high flat work bench with a large machine in front. Other tables set long the sides with stands holdin large pieces a glass. A tall steel stand held one at least ten feet cross and three feet thick, or I couldn't see straight. The man took the large seat and pushed a button on the machine. Lights went on and a screen fired up. He pressed more buttons and a long end come up, and he said the machine took time to heat up. It did and the long end extended a foot and shot a light beam at the large glass circle. A real damned beam a light traced colors beyond the humanly imaginable. The man pushed more buttons, and the light slowed and so did them colors. Sometimes he made the beam thinner and times thicker. Like a laser show in Vegas but right before are eyes.

He shut er down and then led to the other side a the tent. He unzipped a door into an even larger space, and we unloaded are goggles and masks into nother box. A set a stairs rose to a circular box on a big pole like a hoverin carousel but higher off the ground. Two sets a monster truck wheels on pillars marked both sides. The girls loved to ride the plastic horses since they was small, and a buildin close to a bull ridin in Helena filled with em and counter a ice cream just inside the entrance. We went early before the show, and the girls insisted on stayin overnight for when they opened the next day. They musta road half the horses in all. I tried half the ice cream flavors while they did.

The stairs swayed under the man all the way to the top, and he opened the door and bent near in half to get in. We followed into a small theater with rows a chairs circled on the wall. A long cannon with a hole at the end bolted down in the middle able to descend into the floor. Jay took one a the first seats. The pimple-face kid and me took the next ones. The soft seats tilted and didn't have to bend my neck. The man sat on a bench and reached the wall and turned off the lights. White dots run overhead like the night sky I knowed from all my nights watchin. The man said the constellations was current with the rotation a the Earth in are solar system and could fade out into are galaxy and neighborin ones beyond. He programmed the stars on the ceilin to move round us, far less expensive havin the universe rotate round the Earth. Jay and the pimple-face kid laughed. He said he'd raise the room and open the top and slide back the roof for a better view a where we fit in if we stayed the night. Then he didn't say nothin for minutes, but his heavin chest bounced round the walls a the room. We sat in dark with them endless formations over us. Found the big dipper with no problem.

The man breathed and held his breath and gulped for air. "Let's get something to eat." His voice broke, and he shifted off the bench and switched on the lights.

Closest to the long cannon and stepped to the eyepiece for a better look and didn't need to bend my neck.

CHAPTER 20

A single steel door opened to a real garage, long for sure but not like the football field one we just left. I counted thirty-four cars and again and all shinin and in mint condition. Jay went direct to the cheeriest colored one you ever seen parked in the middle. He walked up and down and round it. The hood level with clear lines and soft edges. Twin scoops set on the front. Even I knowed had no equal. The man rested his hands over his chest and opened a box on the wall. He pulled out a set a keys and tossed em to Jay.

Jay climbed in on the white vinyl bucket seat. The man waved us over. I seen Comet on the hood sure we was in for a ride like no other.

"They used one as the pace car in the Indy 500. One of the three cars Jay rebuilt for me." The man ushered us in.

He pushed a button on his phone, and one a the garage doors opened. Jay fired up the cherry car and put the curved shift in reverse. It rumbled quieter, backin out. He drove by the empty fountain with the woman battlin the sun. The man hopped out and lumbered up the set a marble steps. He fetched the pimple-face kid's gear bag from the large open empty room.

The cherry car glided over each mile like travelin top a cloud and each turn like beginnin nother. Jay and the man discoursed lots a things, some familiar and most not, Martin this and Flip that, and the back nine bein far more difficult'n the front nine. But goin for burgers I got, and the cherry car rolled on.

We got to a stop light, and the man turned his massive chest. "Other than from my own kitchen or off one of my own grills, and by the way I never can provide too much proof so when you are in town again please stop by, we can get three of the best hamburgers in the world, all skillet cooked, within a twenty-three mile radius. We'll stop for the best one that is on our way."

Every place I ever visited someone made the best burger on Earth. I'll be damned if time and time again they was all right in all their many different approaches and unique takes. Delighted on are fortune and on the thought in the future a makin good on his promise. Folded the arms a the buckskin jacket to hold in the feelins a joy in the comfort a the purrin back seat.

The man directed Jay over one street, and the cherry car turned to an old, small dilapidated buildin and rounded to the drive-through behind a new black Ford Super Duty with double suspension and more power'n Satan with tool boxes on each side a the bed. I swore knowed the back a the head bobbin to umistakeable blarin a Achilles Last Stand, sure accustomed to bangin invisible drums with seamless transition to rippin on his air guitar.

Jay laid on the cherry car's horn. The head froze, and the driver's door opened. Roper leaned out with his fist and raised his middle finger. Jay laid on the horn again and rolled down the window and flipped the bird back.

Roper bent for a better look and burst out, "Jay! Wowsers! Now that's a ride!" The flat menu machine next to him fired up, and Roper turned back. He leaned into his cab and drove forward.

Jay's hands glued to the shiny wood steerin wheel and turned long the curb to the flat menu machine. The man give are order for four burgers and fries, three Cokes and a homemade chocolate milkshake for Jay.

"How big are they?" I asked.

"Half of a pound," the man said.

"If I don't eat all mine, you can have the rest," Jay said.

The Super Duty idled at the takeout window, and Roper opened his door. He bent toward the clerk with a handful a bills and counted out a few. The clerk handed over four full greasy bags. Roper took em and got himself back into the cab.

He stuck his head out. "Tell Dean he made a nice ride." His head went back in and popped out again. "But they marked at least ten high on an old, fat, slow bull. He was that close to jump kicking the length of the arena like Skoal Pacific Bell." And his head popped back into the cab. The Super Duty pulled out a the lot, blastin enough exhaust to smother all human life.

We got are order, and the man passed a bag back. Grabbed first and passed a burger to the pimple-face kid and pulled out the other one. Was bitin in before Jay pulled off the lot.

Jay shouted over the cherry car's roar everyone could have a taste a his homemade chocolate milkshake. The pimple-face kid dropped a French Fry on the clean white seat. Picked it up real quick with a mind to cuss him but thought the better with no way to over the rumble a the car, so tried shakin my head but Jay's brace kept me from it.

Jay chased dark clouds for Chino Valley. A ways down the freeway he passed back his untouched burger and fries. Took a bite and the savoriest ever and next one the same till nothin left. Never caught em but got off the exit and streets splashed against the belly a the cherry car.

Got downtown and turned onto a new street and Jay said, "On old Whiskey row, one of the great roads of the West."

Now a whiskey drinker reckoned educatin me or the pimple-face kid, if he ended up one.

Water set on one street and the next and covered the road we pulled onto for the arena with Thumb Butte behind. Not half the size a the Big Butte and smaller'n the little Buttes before Craters a the Moon you could see from high stretches on Interstate 15 just passed Poky.

Lights above the concourse lit up and dusk set in. An old woman holdin a walkie talkie waved down Jay, and the cherry car slowed to a stop. He rolled down his window and pointed at us in back. The old woman talked into the walkie talkie and waved us on.

Jay pulled into an open space, and the man climbed out and put the seat down for me and the pimple-face kid. We got out on wet ground. Jay didn't move his hands from the shiny wood steerin wheel. The man watched a horse and his cowboy pass. People filled seats beneath the concourse. A cowboy's name run over the PA.

"Stick it on," Jay said.

"Thanks for the ride," the pimple-face kid said.

"I'll find a seat and catch up with you later," the man said.

"Okay," Jay said.

The man's hands shook like they just pulled from a freezer.

A bronc rider made the buzzer, and the fans cheered. One a the pickup men followed the buckin horse long the fence inside the cinder block wall.

The man didn't move, and his shakin hands wiped water from his swollen red eyes. He raised his mighty arms and massive shoulders heaved, headin for the grandstand with the concourse set on top where I knowed housed concessions.

Jay raised his tanned arm from out the window and tilted up the cream straw cowboy hat.

"Real nice ride."

Water dripped off the sleeves a the buckskin jacket. Mighty glad not a day show.

"Thanks."

More cowboys passed by, and the announcer called for the next ride.

"Could use a cold one."

Eyed round for the pimple-face kid, but he went. Stumbled on wet ground, hoppin over a mud spot, and a couple a old cowboys hailed me down. I knowed em from before. They was rodeo hands who seen lots a action between em. They said their pieces bout all the damned attention and moved on to see the show.

Two young boys got in my way. One lifted a camera with a brown canvas hoodie. The other one held a short rod with a microphone on the end covered in plastic and one a them tablet computers in his other hand. They said they was video journalists from Arizona State out makin a documentary bout the real West and overheard people talkin I am the bull rider on TV the past couple days. Nothin could be more fortuitous one kept sayin. And asked if I wouldn't be in their film. I didn't say so but buckaroos rode wild stock for fun long before someone in starched jeans and new long sleeve shirt decided to sell tickets to see em.

Asked for one a their phones to call Carmen and glimpsed the cherry car with Jay's arms wrappin round the shiny wood steerin wheel and head on the dash with the cream straw cowboy hat against glass.

One boy fretted over findin a computer with a printer.

Directed him to the office down the road where I paid entry fees so long ago couldn't rightly say when.

He handed over the phone and run off at a dead sprint.

"I'll have Jesús put together some papers to sign," Carmen said.

"No way I'll do nother day in Prescut."

"This documentary will allow you to set the record straight once and for all."

"How's Sam?"

"We picked her up. She's fine."

"Bout time. I aint waitin on these boys." And my next complaint vanished, just sure as one thought bounces out nother. I gathered my thinkin on Car's notion a gettin the truth on the record right here and now and be done with it. "When he gets back we'll get er all straightened and wrapped up."

"How's Jay?"

"Restin."

A hand clasped the buckskin jacket. Turned to knock it off, and the pimple-face kid let go. He wore chaps and taped glove, holdin a helmet. "I'm in the next go."

Handed the phone over and heeled up over wet ground and even wetter mud. Concrete holdin pens stained from heavy rain. Cut through lots a boys ready to ride, and the pimple-face kid put on his helmet and climbed a chute. Drops a water hung below each rung, and a pitch-black bull with a hump a muscle and short stubbed horns stomped. He kicked the gate and rattled all them drops and stayed on. Elbowed a cowboy at my side and reached for a rung on the chute and hopped up on my forearm, pullin up to my chest. The pimple-face kid pointed at his rope on the other side. Dropped to the ground and passed behind the chutes. A hand popped a gate into the arena. Trekked through fresh mud and climbed up. The pimple-face kid set in the pitch-black bull's pockets and give over the tail and reached cross his body and warmed up and down, hard and fast. He put the handle off the side and grabbed aholt and said pull. My whole body burst, pullin the rope. He reached cross and took it and run round his hand.

Scooted muddy boots down rungs with my hands followin em and stepped for ground and none. My whole backside went stiff as a board. Tried rollin from one side to the other and neck itched under Jay's brace. The barrel man in white painted face with a large flappy foam red cowboy hat lifted my shoulders. Mud caked the back a my Wranglers and up the sleeves a the buckskin jacket. Went to set the brown Rand and an old chute hand backed into me. Grabbed a rung and wiped my eyes with the back a my hand. Nother chute hand popped the latch and the old chute hand pulled rope, swingin the gate.

ACKNOWLEDGMENTS

Reaching the end of On Riverton Road tested my constitution, one rewrite at a time. Fortunately there were many stops at the Alexandrian stacks of my life, and I'm grateful for the conversations there.

I gained details about rodeos and arenas throughout the West with Jimmy Young, Lane Frost's ride on Mr. T on the Winston Tour with Vance and Rhonda Avery, the science of bucking bulls with Justin Gentry, the World's Oldest Rodeo with Judd Mortensen, bull ropes and rank bulls with Josh and Jeremy Elison, and from Lane Frost's "Bull Talk" and instructional videos on YouTube by Wiley Petersen. More details came from visits about cattle and Riverton with Layne Hamilton, the history of Blackfoot rodeos with Jim Elison, favorite casseroles with Gayle Elison, Santiago de Chile with Denisse Barrera, serious and loose research with Jed Elison, untangling arguments with Jeremy and Michelle Elison, fine-tuning Bruce's speech with Michael Thurgood, floors and doors with Kevin Button, woodworking with Matthew Nelson, disease and hospitals with Shawn Wren, running electricty with Pete Fitzgerald, dancing with Nathan Cottom, and horses with Brady Weaver. I couldn't have imagined better resources.

Many thanks to Ruth Ann and Wally Hardy for their continued encouragement and Michael Cannon, Anthony Palermo, Jason Baruch, Glenn Bukowski, Adam Schwartz, Dan Lonergan, and Jordan Silverboard for their thoughtful comments. And to David Lin who did exceptional work on the cover photographs.

Made in the USA
Monee, IL
10 November 2023